THE UNMENTIONABLES

THE UNMENTIONABLES

Lance Carbuncle

vicious galoot books, co
tampa, florida

The Unmentionables
© 2017 by Vicious Galoot Books, Co.

ISBN: 978-0-9822800-9-6 (paperback)
ISBN: 978-0-9987911-0-4 (ebook)

Vicious Galoot Books, Co.
412 East Madison Street, Suite 1111
Tampa, Florida 33602

Cover art and interior illustrations: Joseph Tomlinson
Interior print design and ebook formatting: B10 Mediaworx

No part of this book may be used or reproduced in any manner whatsoever without written permission except in the case of brief quotations embodied in critical articles and reviews. For information, address Vicious Galoot Books, Co., 412 East Madison Street, Suite 1111, Tampa, Florida 33602.

This book is a work of fiction. The characters, dialog, and incidents are drawn from the author's imagination (except where otherwise noted) and should never, under any circumstances whatsoever, be construed as real in this or any alternate universe. Any resemblance to persons living, dead, or undead, is entirely coincidental.

Dedicated to Angus, Ruca, Max, and Nadia.

Being your dad has made me a better person.

PROLOGUE

Findlay, Ohio

Edge of the Great Black Swamp Region

March 30, 1892

As the natural gas drill spiked the ground near the outskirts of the village, the men had no idea what they were in for. When they bored six hundred feet into the earth, the ground boomed and a dark cloud spewed forth, enveloping the workers. It seemed that they had breached the ceiling to hell as the stench fumes knocked them off their feet. The men dropped to their knees, clutching at their throats, choking and gagging on the foul emanations. And the cloud latched on to a passing gust of wind and streamed over the town as it continued to seep from the gashed earth.

Of the three men working the drill, two dragged themselves away, blinded and sucking air, and found their way back to town where they sought medical attention. The other, James Lytle, lay there in the dirt beside the wound in the ground. The gas filled his head and set him to sleeping, during which ghastly, blood-soaked images played out in his dreams. And when Lytle awoke, he struggled to his feet and staggered his way home.

Mary Lytle helped her husband into the house and into bed. James lay there, eyes wide open, twitching and moaning, sometimes waving his arms before him as if fending off an attack. His daughters, Hester and Beatrice, watched from the corner of the room, silently praying for the man who had always been a good father. They could tell something was very wrong. And when he regained consciousness in the morning, James woke his wife by parting her hair with a hatchet. His high-pitched scream shocked Beatrice and Hester awake. The girls cowered and screeched in the corner as their father tore their lives from them, piece by piece, whack by whack with the hatchet.

Then James wandered the main street of the village, covered in blood and gore, babbling and gripping the murder weapon. Only when approached by the constable did he snap out of his spell. He willingly surrendered and allowed himself to be held in the county jail. Once in his cell, James' madness disappeared as quickly and completely as it had fallen upon him. And with the realization of what he had done, James prayed to God to take his life.

There was something in the miasma released from beneath the earth that drove James to madness. That cloud fell not only on James and his coworkers. It smothered the entire village in its maleficent madness. And as if in answer to James' prayers, before the end of the day one thousand respectable citizens gathered outside of the jail with guns and clubs, pitchforks and implements of destruction. The constable locked himself in his office and refused to come out, leaving the villagers to their plans. The mob stormed the county jail and dragged James, now paralyzed with remorse, from his cell. They strung him up twice, first hanging him from a bridge over the Blanchard River and then from a telegraph pole, before finally discharging their rifles dozens of times, punching holes into his already dead body.

As James Lytle's perforated corpse dangled from a rope, slopping bodily fluids into a pool at the foot of the pole, the cloud hanging over the city lifted and dispersed to the corners of the county. And the angry mob quickly lost its fire after committing the village's first and only lynching. The villagers dropped their shovels and pitchforks and other implements of destruction and shuffled away, not talking or making eye contact with anybody else. Just as James did with his family, the angry mob had lost control with him. And just as with James, the people of the village regained their senses. Thereafter, James Lytle was seldom mentioned again amongst the villagers.

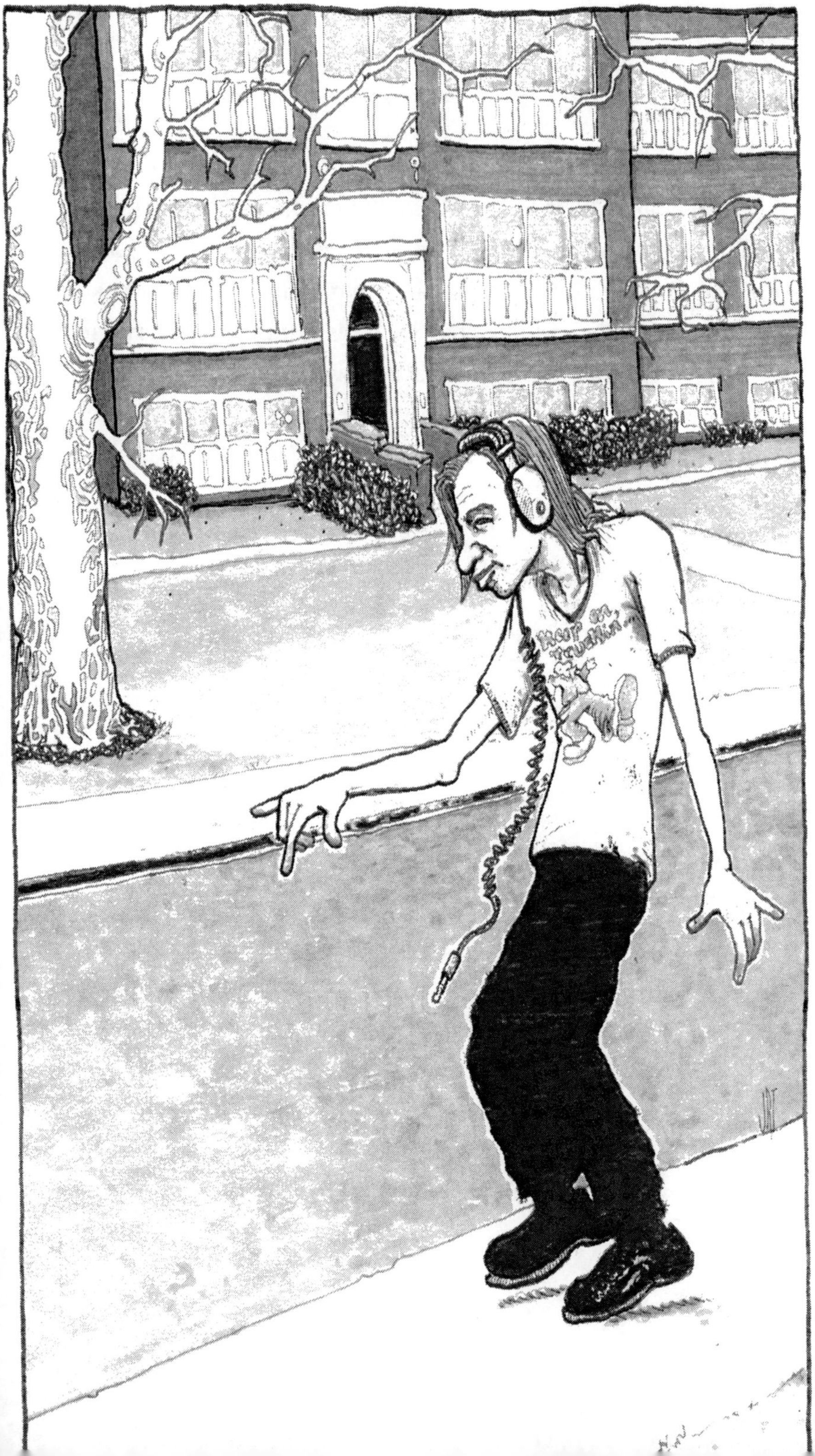

PART ONE

1

The Big Bopper bounces down Main Street, bony shoulders hunched up, head thrust forward, bobbing to some sublime groove that only he can hear. The cord to his enormous headphones swings, unconnected to any source, back and forth like a windshield wiper trying to clear the stains of sweat, dirt, and grease ground into his tattered *Keep on Truckin'* t-shirt. He snaps his fingers, squints his eyes, moves his lips, as if the headphones' cord picks up a cosmic wave beamed across the universe and aimed only at him to enjoy.

The Big Bopper, for that is the only name anybody in town knows him by, simply bops. He is an unmedicated, crazy-brained, cosmic-groovin', smooth beat loopin', bouncin' and boppin' machine. Even he doesn't remember his own name. It seems to him like it could be Walsh, but he doesn't really know. He knows how to bop, though. A wild current pulls the Big Bopper off of Main Street and drags him along, bopping and snapping his greasy fingers. He don't question it. That's life, man. Some force moves him and he is washed along with it, bopping and snapping all the way. There's no point in fighting it. Everything feels right when he goes with the cosmic flow. And the groove from his headphones is so righteous.

    The Big Bopper stops in front of the school. He knows better than to cross the street and go closer. People get nervous when they see him on school grounds. As long as he keeps his distance nobody calls the cops and nobody raises a fuss. He stays put across the street, though, because something is about to happen. He feels it. The pulsing groove in his headphones intensifies. He stands, hunched over, noggin bobbing like a drunken bobble head doll, snapping his fingers and staring at the front of the building. And then the school's buzzer goes off. Wild energy pulses from the building, nearly bowling him over, and he knows that something big is starting. He feels it, man. He really feels it. Then the current pulls him again, like a rope around his chest, and he allows himself to be washed along to whatever comes next.

2

And then the bell rings. Greg Samsa springs from his chair, knocking over nerds and jocks and nobodies, leaving papers and pencils and overturned backpacks in his wake. Greg throws the classroom door open, cuts to his right past his overstuffed locker, launching himself into the air and down the top flight of stairs, his feet peddling as if on a bicycle but touching none of the steps until making contact with the landing between the floors. Vice Principal Blight hikes up his pants and gapes as Greg jukes around him and bounds from the landing toward the second floor of Donnell Junior High School.

"Stop right there, young man," Mr. Blight warbles ineffectually, his plea falling flat and tumbling down the stairs behind Greg.

When his feet smack down on the second floor of the school, Greg cuts to his left and sprints down the hall, past the principal's office and gymnasium and Miss Demerit's classroom. The soles of his shoes leave black scuffs and a faint odor of burnt rubber trailing behind him. His longish, oily hair flags in the air. At the end of the hall, Greg slides down the handrail that divides the flight of stairs, leaping off before reaching the first floor, legs still pumping in the air, landing and sprinting for the school's rear exit. And though he dreads it, going out the rear exit means passing the shop classrooms. But the jeers and taunts he might receive from the shop class kids are nothing compared to what he fears if he fails to get away from the school.

The sounds of table saws and grinders and AC/DC blare out of the shop class doorway. The aroma of sawdust and solvents and stains floats out of the doorway. A brownish banana also flies through the doorway, striking the side of Greg's head, knocking his thick-lensed aviator glasses askew. In his peripheral vision, Greg sees the Courtney brothers, Tim and Jim, standing there smiling with their yellowed and chipped teeth, wearing the same dirty clothes that they wear every day, and laughing. Greg imagines he can see stench fumes wafting off of their unwashed bodies.

"Enjoy the fruit, you fruit," laughs Tim.

"Yeah, you alien-looking faggot," says Jim as he and Tim slap each other on the back and revel in their wit.

But the Courtneys' stench and taunts now dissipate and disperse in the air behind Greg. Tim and Jim pose no threat to Greg as he bursts through the exit doors and into the schoolyard. A clear path to the alley behind the school reveals itself. And Greg sprints past Mr. Corbin, the geriatric school custodian, for the relative safety of the town's tangle of backstreet alleys. Mr. Corbin harrumphs something gruffly, but Greg does not hear. His feet carry him away quickly, before the janitor's words can reach him. The adrenaline courses through Greg's system and his heart races as he flees the perils of Wade Busby.

Earlier in the day, between third and fourth period, Wade Busby singled out Greg. Wade, the only kid in the eighth grade with a beard and tattoos. Wade, the only kid in the eighth grade with a driver's license. Wade, the only kid in the eighth grade for the third time. All of the students, and even some of the teachers, gave Wade a wide berth in the hallways. And Greg never so much as made eye contact with Wade. But Wade noticed him anyway and accosted Greg outside of Mr. French's Spanish classroom.

Before Greg knew what was happening, Wade's pockmarked face loomed inches from his own. "You think you're bad or something, don't you?" Wade snarled. "I heard you said you can kick my ass. You think you're better than me? I heard the shit you been saying about me." Flecks of spittle sprinkled Greg's face and he could smell the tartar-stink of Wade's teeth.

"I didn't say anything about you," Greg stammered. It was absurd to even think that he would talk smack about Wade. Greg, all one-hundred-and-seven anemic pounds of him, never spoke ill of anybody in the school, and especially not about the mouth-breathing, rotten-breathed troglodyte standing there ready to rip his head off. And despite the pure terror that he felt, Greg also found himself briefly mesmerized by the sticky strand of spit at the edge of Wade's mouth that spanned the gap from the bottom lip to the top, stretching and contracting with each word that Wade said, but never breaking. And then Greg snapped back to reality and protested, saying, "This is a mistake," trying to back away. But Donnie Price pushed him from behind. And the force of the push crashed Greg into Wade, knocking him backwards for just a second.

And then Wade was on him, thick hands locked on Greg's biceps, lifting him and slamming him into the wall, the violence of the collision forcing the air out of Greg's lungs in a dry, thin puff. The feral look in Wade's eyes told Greg that he was about to get hurt very badly. A crowd gathered in close to watch the beating. Wade's sidekicks – Donnie Price and Chop – moved in just behind him to get a close-up view of the imminent bloodshed.

Greg struggled against Wade's hold but could not break his grip. As a last resort, he kicked out, planting a knee in Wade's crotch. The knee landed square where Wade's balls should have been, but something didn't feel right. There should have been a soft spot that yielded to the strike. Instead, it hurt Greg's knee.

Wade flinched but did not crumple like Greg expected. He flashed his stinking grin and said, "I've got balls of steel." But that wasn't exactly true. Wade's balls were actually very common human testicles, containing seminiferous tubes, blood vessels, ducts, epididymides, and other such anatomical niceties, all made from human cells and formed into meaty lumps that lounged in a temperature-regulated flesh hammock. And, while Wade's balls contained, perhaps, a very small amount of iron – due to his high red meat intake – they certainly were not made of steel. Wade's balls, while very common (if slightly oversized) were, instead, protected by an athletic cup. Years of bullying taught Wade that his victims, when cornered, would usually try to strike at his most vulnerable spot. That, coupled with his spot on the varsity wrestling team, accounted for Wade's constant cup wearing.

Wade removed his left hand from Greg's arm and drew it back, fist clenched tight and ready to strike, mouth grimacing. Greg closed his eyes and waited for a blow that never came.

"¿Que pasamos, mis estudiantes?" Mr. French pushed through the crowd and pulled Wade away from Greg. "¿What is going on here, boys?"

Donnie Price, smiling his shit-eating grin, interjected, "They're just horsing around, Mr. French. Samsa wanted to see if he could escape one of Wade's wrestling holds. Ain't that right, Samsa?"

Greg exhaled deeply, as if he were deflating, and nodded his head.

"Well, I'll have no horseplay here in the hall," said Mr. French. And he clapped his hands at the kids, saying, "Everybody get to class. ¡Vamanos ahora, mis estudiantes!"

The kids in the crowd dispersed and scurried for the classrooms, hoping to beat the bell. Greg slunk into Mr. French's classroom, away from Wade and his chums (who were heading to their remedial reading class). Sweating and shaking, heart thumping in his concave chest, Greg flopped into his desk and spilled his books onto the ground. He stared straight ahead and gasped for air, nearly hyperventilating, trying to control his panic and utter dread. He knew that trying to defend himself probably only made things worse.

Greg barely noticed his best and only friend, Jim Halloway, sitting down beside him and saying, "Wow, you really crapped the bed there. You know Wade's only going to want to get you worse now, don't you?"

🦅 🦅 🦅 🦅 🦅

Findlay's alleys provide the perfect cover for juvenile delinquents to congregate, to smoke and drink and fight and make out. Teenagers in the backstreets are practically invisible to the town. The police rarely patrol the alleyways. Adults avoid them. The alleys are the perfect rug to sweep the town's problems under so that its quaint façade can remain intact. And Greg knows the dangers of the back streets. He knows that he could run into any of the bastards from school who threaten to beat him up. He could encounter kids who, without violent intentions, would still tease him, kids who call him E.T. because of his slight resemblance to the alien from the movie, *E.T., the Extraterrestrial*. (And, at times when Greg is honest with himself, he has to admit that he does look somewhat like E.T., with his wide-set, bulging eyes, flared nostrils and elongated upper lip. But that still doesn't make it right, and it doesn't make the nickname hurt any less). So Greg navigates the alleyways, banking on the chances that his quick retreat from school will have him far away before any of his tormentors have even left school grounds.

Greg cuts through backyards, climbs chain link fences, and skitters through the alleys, seeking the safety of home. His house is not far, but the direct path leaves him too vulnerable, so he resorts to running down the one-laned back streets and cowering behind bushes. Once far enough from the school, his instincts tell him he can stop beside the dumpster behind

Karchers' Carryout to catch his breath. The life of a tormented runt makes for great cardio, what with the running all of the time, but still Greg gasps for oxygen to feed his overtaxed and trembling body. And when the shaking stops and his breathing returns to normal, Greg emerges from behind the dumpster and scans the area for Wade and his thugs. Home is close now, and Greg moves cautiously along the backstreets, jumping at every sound, ready to mad-dash scramble for his life. And his knee hurts from slamming it into Wade's athletic cup earlier, but the dull ache is nothing compared to the damage that Wade will inflict if he catches Greg.

Like a schitzy tomcat, Greg jumps at sudden noises. He looks toward the sky and sees an old pair of his sneakers hanging from a power line, tossed there on another occasion when Wade caught him on his way home from school. For just a brief moment Greg loses himself in the clouds above, wishing he could somehow float in them, above and away from all of the hassles down on the ground. And he envies his old shoes because nobody can touch them up there.

Without warning, a hand grabs Greg's arm and yanks him back down to earth. He knows it must be Wade grabbing him, getting ready to do something far worse than just ripping his shoes off and throwing them up and out of reach on a power line.

When Greg is flung around, it is surprisingly not Wade who faces him. It is Johnny Close, with his head cocked sideways on his crooked neck, his nervous tic twisting his already-creepy smile up into something even more horrible. Johnny is a twenty-something with a puzzle of a body that looks like it had been broken into one hundred pieces and then put back together wrong, and with some of the pieces missing. Johnny, with his crooked neck resting his head on a pointy shoulder. Posture like a ninety-year-old man. Legs bowed out and pigeon-toed. If he weren't so creepy, people would probably feel sorry for him. The kids all shout "Crooked Neck," at him when he comes around on his wobbly ten-speed bike and they chase Johnny away if their numbers are sufficient to bestow such courage. Otherwise, kids flee when they see Old Crooked Neck because he is widely known as a toucher, a fondler, a diddler.

Greg tries to pull away from Crooked Neck, but Johnny yanks him close and leans in, his swoop of black hair falling down over eyes that seem too small and too far inset. A cloud of whisky fumes envelops Greg.

"Hey, Greg," Johnny says. "It's good to see you. I've been trying to watch you through your windows, but you always have your curtains closed. You should open them up and wave hi to me sometime."

With his free hand, Johnny reaches down and pulls off the safety pin that holds the front of his pants closed. The pants fall open and slip down enough in front to reveal Johnny's erection trying to poke out of his discolored underpants. Johnny is thin like a skeleton, and his extremities are bent and frail and malformed. But he is a man and Greg is just a kid. Greg tries to pull away, but the thin hand grips his arm even tighter. And Johnny takes the open safety pin and pokes it into the meat of Greg's forearm, twisting it around a bit and saying, "I hope you've had your tetanus shots, kid."

Greg yelps like an injured dog and tries unsuccessfully to break away. But Crooked Neck's spindly arms and delicate-looking hands are deceptively powerful. Johnny keeps a tight hold and pokes the safety pin at Greg's arm several more times, a twisted grimace on his face showing his immense pleasure. A new idea crosses his mind, an idea that lights up his face. Johnny drops the pin to the ground and reaches his free hand into his tented underpants. Johnny says, "You're gonna touch it, pretty boy."

But Greg has a different thought on the matter. Ever since being deprived of his sneakers by Wade, Greg has worn work boots that lace up above the ankles to ensure that his shoes are not so easy to remove. Greg pulls back, and kicks and kicks and kicks again at Johnny's malformed legs. The steel toes of the boots are like an axe head chipping away at Crooked Neck's shinbones and shooting jolts of pain up his lower legs. Greg continues kicking until the hand releases his arm. Johnny's dinged up legs fail him and he falls back, away from Greg, his trousers now dropping to his knees, and his underpants still tenting over his hard-on.

Greg is free to flee and he turns to run the rest of the way home. But he makes it no more than five steps before realizing that Wade, Donnie, and Chop are blocking the alley.

"Get him. Fuck him up," barks Wade.

Enough is enough, thinks Greg. *It's not worth fighting this anymore.* He shuts his eyes and braces for the tackle that he knows must be coming. Time slows down. It seems to Greg as if it stops. Nothing happens. He's not thrown to the ground. No hands find a place on his throat. No fist lays a knock on the side of his head. No foot sweeps his legs out from under him. First the silence, then the sounds of violence.

Greg turns and sees Wade, Donnie, and Chop atop Crooked Neck, hitting and kicking, poking and gouging. Wade puts a headlock on Johnny and cranks his neck straight. The boys overwhelm Johnny, inflicting lumps and lacerations, cuts and contusions.

And Greg becomes a non-issue to the bullies. He leaps over their BMX bikes, resisting the urge to stomp the spokes, and sprints the rest of the way home.

Crashing through the wrought iron gates at full speed, Greg barrels toward the wide stairs at the front of his house and launches over the first three steps, knowing that the rot has progressed to a point where whoever sets foot on them might fall through. He skids to a stop once on the porch. Much like the rest of the enormous house, the porch is rotten in many places and poses a danger of collapse to one unfamiliar with its decrepitude. A sense of safety sets in. Neither Wade nor any of the other jerks from school would dare pursue Greg onto his own property, for fear of reckoning with Wally.

The front door sticks, it seems, and tries to bar Greg's entry. Like the rest of the house, the door only cooperates when it wants to. Greg twists the doorknob and throws his shoulder against it. And the door gives a little but does not open all of the way. Greg rears back and throws his shoulder at the door again. But before he makes contact, the door flies open and Greg stumbles through, falling face first into the mansion's front hall.

Laughter fills the foyer. It was not the door being difficult. It was Wally, the worst big brother ever, holding the door and waiting to yank it open at just the right moment. Wally and his friends, Lumpy and Eddie – with their jean jackets and Def Leppard shirts and cigarettes tucked behind their ears – really yukking it up at Greg's expense. They surround Greg and push him back to the ground as he struggles to stand.

Wally stands over Greg, smiling, and says, "Oops. I didn't realize that you were trying to get in."

"Yeah," says Eddie, smiling too, with his pointy little teeth and wrinkled-up weasel nose. He flips his feathered hair out of his eyes. "We're real sorry. Hope you're okay there, buddy." He puts out his hand as if to help Greg up, yanking it back and laughing again just before Greg can grab it.

Lumpy – so nicknamed because of the purplish acne conglobota nodules that cover his face and neck – tries to imitate Eddie's hair flip, but his bangs just stick to his oily forehead. "Nice try, E.T.," says Lumpy. And he puts his shoe on Greg's shoulder, pushing him down to the floor again.

"E.T.," Eddie echoes, laughing too hard, as if he hadn't already heard the nickname hundreds of times. "Good one, Lumpy."

Wally punches Eddie in the arm and says, "Shut up, you stupid knob! That little faggot's my brother."

Confusion blotches Eddie's face. Everybody was having fun at Greg's expense. But now Wally is turning on Eddie for no apparent reason. Eddie tries to process the situation. Was Wally just kidding around? Or is he seriously now taking up for his little brother? Eddie knows that Wally sometimes gets mad and confused for no real reason and has to be eased back into the moment. It usually happens when Wally is really high. And, no surprise, Wally is really high.

"Come on, Wally," says Eddie, defensively. "We was just having fun. You know, having a laugh. Even you call him E.T., right?"

A spark of thought dimly illuminates Wally's bloodshot eyes. "Oh yeah. Whatever, man," he says. "Let's go upstairs. I need a smoke."

From somewhere in the house, a woman's voice shouts, "I don't want anybody smoking in this house!"

"Just kidding, Ma," says Wally as he pops an unlit Blue Llama into his mouth and winks at Lumpy.

Greg remains seated on the floor. Wally, Eddie, and Lumpy turn away. Side by side, jostling each other with sharp elbows and slaps to the heads, arms, and necks, laughing like stoned buffoons, they ascend the grand curved staircase to the second floor.

"Oh, yeah, you little shit-turd," Wally says from the top of the staircase, "Mom wants to talk to you before you go anywhere or do anything."

🦅 🦅 🦅 🦅 🦅

Big Shirl twists her substantial body and adjusts the pillows that prop up her various parts, wriggling her 409 pounds of womanhood like a dog preparing its bed. Soft Batch cookie bags, Cheese Whiz cans, and other foodstuff packages litter the bed and the floor around it. A Gummi Bear hides in terror, clinging to the underside of her right bicep. She slurps the remainder of her Tab and drops the empty soda can to the floor amongst a littering of Diet Orange Slice cans and Zima bottles. Big Shirl's king size bed monopolizes most of the floor space in the television room. She points the remote at her big-screen TV (its enormous cabinet takes up a good deal of the remaining floor space) and hits mute. She sweeps her fiery red hair from her eyes and beams a beautiful smile at Greg.

"Oh, honey, I'm glad you're home," says Big Shirl. The strap on her housedress slips down her right shoulder, knocking off the Gummi Bear, who leaps over the side of the bed to land and cower amongst empty boxes and food wrappers, hoping to evade capture and ingestion. The slip of the housedress reveals enough freckled, flabby bits to make Greg cringe as Big Shirl negotiates herself into a sitting position. "Come give mama a hug."

Reluctantly, Greg sidles up to the bed, looking about as excited as a teenage boy can be about giving his morbidly obese mother in a housedress a hug, and leans in to let Big Shirl engulf him in her fat and flabby arms. The affection repulses him and comforts him at the same time. Big Shirl leaves evidence of her love on Greg's cheek in the form of a bright red lipstick print. He pulls back, eyes her suspiciously, and says, "What?"

Big Shirl smiles, pauses, clears her throat. Her eyes dart to the TV. "Oh, look. Phil Donahue is wearing a skirt." On screen, a grey haired, bespectacled talk show host prances about in a plaid skirt, much to the astonishment of his audience members.

"I don't give a crap about Phil Donahue, Mom. What's going on? I can tell something's wrong."

"Well," she says, "the raccoons ripped a hole in the wall of your room and most of the ceiling. Someone, probably Li'l Shirl, has been feeding them again. They're expecting us to take care of them. So they're coming around, getting into everything. You probably left food in your room and they tore everything up. There's nothing I can do about it now. You're going to have to find a new room."

Greg's eldest sibling, Li'l Shirl, looks just like her mother, with like proportions and the fiery hair, but lacks the vigor and love and good humor that Big Shirl exudes. Unlike her mother, Li'l Shirl is slow and simple and sluggish.

As they talk about her, Li'l Shirl peeks into the room. Her mouth forms a silent "oh," and she takes off at full speed when Greg makes eye contact with her. The footsteps of the retreating sister shake the floors and echo throughout the first story of the house.

"It's just as simple as that, Mom?" Greg complains, incredulous. "The raccoons tore up my room and I have to move into another one. No big deal, right? But it is a big deal, Mom. It's a big deal because this crap happens all the time. I want a room that I can stay in. I keep having to find new rooms in this crapshack of a house and I'm tired of it. And it's a big deal because Li'l Shirl has no business roaming about the house and feeding vermin. She should be kept locked down in the basement and things would be a lot easier."

Complaining about the situation does not help, though. And Greg knows that his grievances will do nothing to bring back his old room. He shakes his head at Big Shirl and starts to talk, but no words come to him. He slumps in defeat, turns and leaves, heading to the stairs to seek out a new bedroom.

It's true that Greg repeatedly has to move into new rooms. But there is no shortage of rooms in the old, three-story, gargantuan, Victorian Queen Anne. In 1890 the house was built for, and designed by, a gas and oil tycoon who spared no expense to create the opulent mansion that it once was. With six fireplaces and five bathrooms, a basement more aptly described as a dungeon, a wraparound front porch, grand stairs at the front of the house and a crisscross of narrower stairways for the helpers throughout the rest, as well as workers' quarters, the place is a twisted maze of a structure. Some of the stairways go to nowhere and terminate at the ceilings. The old house is riddled with hidden rooms and passages, chutes for garbage and laundry, dumbwaiters and hidden safes. To everyone but the long-dead owner, the place has been a constant surprise of new rooms, hidden hallways, and eccentric designs. The old house truly was a beauty in her prime, before time and flooding and neglect robbed her of her grandeur.

Now bricks crack and drop from the house's exterior, like a lizard sloughing off dead skin. Dandelions and various weeds proliferate in the clogged rain gutters. The wraparound front porch sags and collapses in parts. Plywood sheets cover broken windows. Raccoons ravage the house, both inside and out, tearing holes in the walls and ceilings, ripping the stuffing from beds and furniture, even sometimes brazenly raiding the cupboards in the kitchen. When the vermin problem gets bad enough, Wally and his friends club the coons for sport. But more always take their place. Neglect has rendered the old house a crumbling, collapsing, pitiful structure. She is old and needy, with no one to give the love and maintenance she deserves. The only thing that remains sound is the wrought iron fence that surrounds the property, with its spiked posts like spontoons and creepy metalwork creatures.

The building's decline began when Greg's grandfather, Montag Samsa, bought her from the original owner, a Mr. Smythe, for a pittance. Nobody knows exactly what prompted the transaction, or why Smythe packed up and moved out of town abruptly upon selling the house to Montag. There were thoughts and theories, conjectures and speculations, posited by the townspeople. There were whispered rumors and hushed innuendo about Montag's obtaining the house through fraud or blackmail. The stigma of the carnival hung about Montag like a cloud of flies over a fresh dog turd. And the villagers suspected extortion or chicanery. What more could they expect from carnie-folk like Montag. And Montag's appearance did nothing but fuel the speculation as to his malfeasance.

Montag Samsa exuded showmanship. His exaggerated strut rocked him back and forth, as if he were walking atop waves that no one else could see, his long, fine, black hair flowing behind him. Simple but graceful flicks of his wrists punctuated his words and hinted at something amazing about to happen. The man was a walking parlor trick, from the long fingernails that threw sparks and smoke when he clicked them together, to his ability to painlessly pierce his flesh with skewers for the entertainment of others, to his habit of plucking coins from thin air and giving them to children. He smelled of sweat and dirt and the excitement of the circus, and the smell was earthy and not altogether unpleasant. As part owner of the Coogler and Sparks Pandemonium Shadow Show, he cultivated the curious appearance of a sideshow ringmaster with his longish beard split down the center and each half of the face-pelt tapering down to points that hung over his chest and terminated around the nipples. Montag's face always clenched tight on the left side to hold the monocle that he used to examine everything and everybody. Brightly colored tattoos twisted about his body as colorful serpents that writhed and slithered with each twitch and tightening of his muscles. The tattoos covered nearly every inch of skin. Inked-in sky-blue teardrops leaked from his right eye, and hypnotic eyeballs covered his palms, looking as if they blinked when he held up his hands and flexed them. And of course there was the standard magician's top hat that he wore and occasionally plucked random objects and small animals from.

Montag was different from the villagers, no doubt. They viewed him as a curiosity, an eccentric. And while they would have reveled in the thrills of his carnival shows were he merely a showman passing through on tour, the fact that he established his residence in their village deeply disturbed most of the townspeople. And though Montag had retired and no longer toured with the carnival, his lifelong show business friends still frequented his mansion. It was one thing for the villagers to see the shows at a traveling carnival and marvel at the sights and sounds and embellishments on humanity, but it was another to have the sideshow move into town and take up residence in the nicest house in the city. On any given day, passersby could witness a pinhead and a rubber-man playing cards on the front porch, or perchance a fat lady breastfeeding a dog-faced boy on the lawn. A visiting strongman might wrestle a team of dwarves just for fun, tossing the little people high into the air and catching them just before they crashed into the earth. Mustachioed Italian men, clad in brightly colored tights, pranced and bounced on high wires strung across the front yard. On clear days, the incessant music of the calliope could be heard for miles around Montag's house. Such antics were fine and fantastic when witnessed in the context of a carnival show outside of city limits, but when they became a common sight, it was an annoyance and a nuisance. Exotic animals chained to trees, yowling in heat and spraying musky scents, were unacceptable. Strange looking people with physical deformities and tattoos and flamboyant dress were not the types that the proper people of "Flag City," Findlay, Ohio, liked to tolerate on an ongoing basis.

 A petition passed through the town and found its way to Constable Pingle, demanding that he escort Montag Samsa to the town limits and see that he never set foot in Findlay again. Pingle, his bravery bolstered by the support of the town, promptly appeared at Montag's front porch, rifle in hands. A mob armed with shovels and rakes and implements of destruction escorted Pingle to the Samsa Mansion and stood in the street, jeering and cheering Pingle on. And when the front door creaked open, Pingle stepped into the house with Montag. The mob hooted in support of the ouster and began applauding minutes later when a vacant-eyed Pingle exited the house.

Pingle stood at the edge of the wraparound porch and waved his gun nonthreateningly at the people as if trying to push them away. "Go home," he shouted. "You've no reason to molest this nice man. He has every right to be here. Go home now, I say."

As the jeers grew, the mob threw back the wrought iron fence gates and advanced on the house. But before they could reach the front porch, Pingle fired a warning shot into the air. "Go home, I say," he said blankly.

Circus freaks poured through the front door and assembled behind Pingle. Pinheads and lobster people. A giant with an Afro and mutton chops. Mr. McGreg, with a leg for an arm and an arm for a leg. A crew of human skeletons. A surly hermaphrodite. Dwarves and chicken head biters. Benders. The strong man and the fat lady. Roustabouts and creepy clowns. And the angry mob realized that Montag's people somehow outnumbered them. Something about the crew hinted at very bad results for anybody who attempted to storm the house. The townspeople turned, knowing they were licked, and their mob splintered into separate people with individual thoughts who shuffled and grumbled their way home, cursing Pingle's betrayal and the cowardice of their co-conspirators. From that day forth, Montag Samsa lived peacefully in the big house, unperturbed by angry townspeople armed with shovels and rakes and implements of destruction. And, from that day forth, the name Samsa invited scorn, distrust, and derision on its bearers in Findlay.

While the bricks and plaster and roof of the house crumbled down around Montag Samsa, he occasionally repaired parts of the building that were in imminent danger of collapse, and studied his books – often written in dead tongues – on necromancy and divination and alchemy and other esoteric dark arts. During that time, he also fathered a son, Walter, with the bearded lady. And Walter grew up in the house, surrounded by carnies, eventually impregnating the fat lady's daughter, Big Shirl, thrice in rapid succession with Li'l Shirl, Wally, and Greg. Unwilling to adapt to the responsibilities of fatherhood, Walter packed a bindle and hopped a train car on the east side of town shortly after Greg's birth. Walter rode the cargo car to parts unknown, never to return to Findlay or his family. Rumors sometimes wafted up from the southern states that Walter established residence in Gibsonton, Florida, amidst a thriving carnie community, but he was never seen again by his father or extended carnival family in Findlay. With an aching heart, Montag redrafted his will, leaving his estate to Big Shirl, and then sat himself on the back porch, flicking sparks from his fingers and mumbling to himself. The tattooed tears running down his cheeks grew fuller and turned bluer. And when the hurt weighed too heavily on his chest, he gave up the ghost. With his passing, the glue that bound his carnival family together dissolved, and little by little, the lobster people, giants, pinheads, and others drifted away, leaving just Big Shirl and her children in the decaying mansion. A single slab of marble, set flush with the ground in the mansion's back yard and six feet above Montag's remains, marks the year of both his hundredth birthday and his death. Otherwise, the tombstone reads, simply:

Montag Samsa
म सही फिर्ता हुनेछु

The old carved oak door to Greg's room hangs open, clinging to the doorjamb by one sturdy hinge, conceding defeat. Greg pulls the door off of the jamb and sets it against the wall. The magnitude of the destruction whams him in the gut. The scene is wild like a soccer riot with hooligan raccoons. Pillows gashed open and thrown across the room. Greg's favorite books and Mad magazines torn from the shelves, ripped and tattered from sharp varmint choppers. A scuffle breaks out on the floor between three coons fighting over a half empty box of Chicken in a Biscuit crackers. And they yowl and screech and scratch, sounding almost human, gnashing out at each other, until finally the largest, roundest, most pompous coon vanquishes his competition and rolls onto his back, plucking the tasty little crackers from the box and crumbling them into a mouth that looks a little too much like it is smiling.

Greg eyes the dark brown lumps and logs of raccoon scat that cover his bed and quickly decides that he will no longer be sleeping there. One particularly mellow coon squeezes out a turd atop a pillow, looking Greg in the eyes the entire time. It does this not with malice or spite. In fact, when it is done, the little animal averts his eyes and turns away slowly, sadly.

The raccoons do not shy away from Greg. They act as entitled as uninvited in-laws. They pick through Greg's belongings without a glance or fear of retaliation. A banging on the second story window scatters the pests, though.

Greg looks to the window and sees the smiling moon-face of his best and only real friend, Jim Halloway. Big Shirl always told

Greg that it is better to have just one good friend than a bunch of fair weather mates. And that wisdom was not lost on Greg. Jim was always around for Greg when things got bad. Jim didn't care what other people thought about him hanging around with Greg. Jim, who didn't call Greg E.T. Jim, who helped Greg secure ladders made from two by fours to the sides of the mansion and leading up to various windows because sometimes it really is just more fun for boys to climb up the side of a house than to take the routine entrances of first story doorways.

Jim bangs on the window again and it sends the raccoons running for cover, jumping into the hole they tore into the wall, climbing between the bedroom walls and above the ceiling. Greg mopes over and unlocks the window so that Jim can roll through it and into the room.

"Wooo-eee!" says Jim, surveying the destruction, lighting up the room with his wide, straight, gap-toothed smile. His brown hair hangs over his eyes, the unparted bangs cutting a straight line across the bridge of his full cheeks and rounded nose. He flips his head, throwing the hair back and clearing his vision to take everything in. "What the crap happened here?"

Greg drops to the floor and starts kicking debris away with his feet, clearing a space on the floor for himself. "Li'l Shirl's been feeding the coons again. They tore clear through the plaster of my wall and ransacked the room. And what a perfect way to top off the worst day ever." Greg grabs an empty Orange Slice can and bounces it off the wall in frustration.

"Yeah, Wade's on the warpath," Jim says, clearing a spot on the floor for himself to sit. He grabs the Chicken in a Biscuit box and pops a couple of crackers into his mouth. "He's saying he's gonna get you. I saw him and Donnie and Chop tearing around on their bikes after school. They were real wound up."

"Yeah, they're wound up all right. They almost caught me on the way home. But they got distracted by Crooked Neck and I got away."

Jim snorts, "Crooked Neck? I hate that guy. Once my dad caught him peeping in our windows and he beat the tar out of that weirdo. What did they do to him?" Jim shakes out the last of the cracker crumbs onto his palm and licks them up.

"They were whippin' him pretty good last I saw. I suppose he had it coming, too. He tried to make me touch his pecker right before they came along."

"Cripes," Jim starts. "You are like a freakin' magnet for abuse. You need to start standing up for yourself."

"I did. I kneed Wade in the balls and it didn't even faze him. It just made him madder."

"You need to stop being a victim. Kick one of those guys' asses. Chop is smaller than you. He's just a short little fella."

"I don't want to. I'm not a fighter."

"Well, shit. Ain't that great," says Jim, and he bulldozes more of the mess on the floor with his foot. "You're just always going to be the victim then, aren't you? How's that make you feel?"

"I don't know," says Greg. "Sometimes I don't feel much of anything anymore. It's almost like I'm dead inside. I don't sleep well. I don't dream much, but when I do, it's like all of the color is gone from my dreams. And I don't seem to have a shadow a lot of the time. That's how it makes me feel, to answer your question. I don't know, I just wish all of those assholes would disappear. I'm so tired of all these hassles. I wish Wally wasn't such a jerk. He's my big brother and he should be sticking up for me. But he's just as bad as them."

"Maybe I'll kick their asses for you. Well, maybe not Wade. But I can take Chop or Donnie. Then maybe they'd leave you alone."

"Nah," sighs Greg, "you're better than that. Don't drop down to their level." Greg lies back on the floor, his eyes tearing up. "Just let it go. It's gotta change somehow."

And they sit in the room, silent. Greg doesn't move. There is nothing more to say and no need for words. They know it sucks. And Jim knows that Greg will get over himself. Jim just sits and waits, eventually stretching out on the floor and drifting into a nap.

And once Greg has marinated in his self-pity long enough, he stands, stretches, and nudges Jim awake. "Hey, butthole," Greg says. "Let's go play some Atari."

Like many of the other hidden rooms and passages in the house, Greg discovered his lounge by accident. The old pushbutton light switch on the wall beside the bookcase in an upstairs room seemed not to control any lights or sockets. But, one day Greg was leaning against the side of the bookcase, idly pushing at the on and off buttons and wishing he had a place to hide from Wally (who had just dealt him a pummeling). When Greg mashed both buttons in at the same time, the bookcase slid sideways under his meager weight and revealed another hidden room, furnished with red velvet couches and chairs and ottomans. Little by little, without letting on to Wally about the new room, Greg furnished the lounge with a TV, his Atari system, his record player and a knee high stack of old blues records that he found in the basement.

The missiles scream toward the cities, leaving glowing, 8-bit trails streaking behind them. As their paths cross, a mid-air geometrically-expanding detonation demolishes them before impact, saving the cities below. But the onslaught swells in intensity. A barrage of missiles enters the zone and proves to be more than the defender can handle. One city is hit and explodes in an enormous mushroom cloud. Then three more cities fall in swift succession, first exploding in billowing clouds of smoke and then leaving nothing but burning heaps of rubble. Two more cities still stand defiantly against the invasion, and the defender valiantly resists. But with each rocket that the home base denies, the incursion increases in intensity and magnitude, until the attack becomes more than one base can hold off. And as the last two cities fall to the invaders, the black sky erupts in a pulsing orange, yellow, and green explosion.

"High score!" yells Jim. "Suck on that, pal." He yanks the Missile Command cartridge out of the Atari system and jams Space Invaders into the slot. "Let's play something else. And how about we turn the game's sound on and turn that old timey music down? Or even better, how about you put on some Quiet Riot or something?"

Greg pushes up his glasses and scrunches his face in distaste. "I don't want Quiet Riot playing in here. That's the kind of crap the assholes listen to. That's the crap that blares out of the woodshop. It's the soundtrack to my daily torment. How about some Def Leppard? No thanks, that's what I hear when Wally is pounding the stuffing out of me. AC/DC? Yeah, that would go great with

Wade Busby's fist upside my skull. That music is nothing but a reminder to me of all of the crap I have to put up with. It puts me on edge to hear it. When I'm in here I want to feel safe and happy, not jumpy like someone's gonna kick my ass."

"And the blues makes you feel happy?"

"Yeah. I don't know why," says Greg. "Or maybe happy's not the right word. Content. Calm. Not unhappy. Whatever you want to call it, those old blues records soothe me. I get lost in them and forget everything that happens to me outside of this room."

The stack of LP records sits patiently on the phonograph's automatic changer spindle, waiting for the current record to finish. And when the needle hits the end of the last groove, the record player's automatic arm lifts and pulls it out of the way for another record to drop. A vinyl disc plays all the way through and then the next one drops on top of the already spinning stack. The top record takes seconds to catch up to the revolutions of the other discs, incurring minor scratches and damage to its grooves in the process. And the needle picks up the scratchy sounds of black men bemoaning their plights to the accompaniment of jangly, finger-picked guitars and harmonicas and accordions, pumping the sounds through cheap speakers and filling the lounge. The heartfelt, and sometimes oh-so-sad crooning soothes the nerves of the white boys who know little about the black experience in the nineteen twenties, thirties, forties, and so on. But something in the tone and the emotion connects with Greg on a gut level. And the records that he just happened to discover one day in the basement provide him with an escape from the daily and significant hassles he endures. Lead Belly drops, and his prison recordings wipe away the day. Sun House drops and starts spinning. And his off-tempo, off-tune singing still sounds so right. Robert

Johnson...Little Walter...Lightnin' Hopkins...Clubfoot Jasper Moberly...Big Mama Thornton...the blues keep coming. And the boys play games on the Atari – Pitfall and Asteroids and Adventure – until their wrists cramp and their left thumbs ache from constantly mashing down that one red button on the joystick. At the end of the last record, the record player arm pulls up and away and rests itself in its crutch.

Silence settles over the lounge as dusk blankets the city. Jim flips the Atari's power switch off and sits back. "You feel a little bit better, dude? Did that help to take you away?"

Greg smiles, displaying big teeth in the process of being trained by braces. His eyes don't dart around looking for the next attack. His lids even droop a little. Oily hair falls down over his glasses and he swipes it out of the way. "Yeah, I always feel better in here."

"How about you make this your room, then?"

"No way," Greg says. "Wally and his little friends have never been able to find us in here. If I make it my room, it will be discovered. I need to be safe and keep them from finding out about the lounge. It doesn't matter if there are thirty other rooms in this house that could serve the exact same purpose. If Wally finds out what this room means to me, he will take it, and probably break all of my stuff in the process just to be a dick. I'll find another room. I've realized that with this house. You need to take your time and it will lead you where you need to go eventually. And I don't feel the house telling me that this is my bedroom. So let's talk about something else."

"You want to talk about what you need to do about Wade?" Jim says.

"No. Screw that noise. That's the last thing I want to think about."

"How about girls?" Jim beams a smile and raises his eyebrows.

"What about 'em?" Greg smiles back.

"I don't know. How about we talk about why you don't have a girlfriend?"

"Shut up," says Greg. "You're starting to be a dick, too."

"No I'm not. Why don't you answer me?"

Greg wrings his hands and then jams them into his pockets. "Seriously, Jim? You're gonna do this to me. Just look at me, there's your answer. No girl wants to be my girlfriend. That's why I don't have a girlfriend. I'm scrawny and everybody says I look like E.T. Who would want to be my girlfriend?"

"I would," says Jim, making Greg laugh nervously and move away from him just a little on the couch. Jim groans. "Don't get all weirded out. I mean if I was a girl. You're a good guy. You'd treat a girl right. You'd do fine with girls if you just gave it a chance. Or maybe you don't like girls."

"Shut up," says Greg again. "I like girls just fine."

"Oh yeah? What do you like about them."

"I don't know," says Greg. "They're different. I like the way that I feel nervous around them. I like the way they laugh. I like that they aren't mean to me. And they smell nice. Sometimes when a girl walks by she leaves behind the odor of her shampoo or perfume or whatever it is that makes girls smell so good. I'll just stop right in that spot, close my eyes, and breathe her in. It's nice."

"Yeah," agrees Jim, and he shrugs his shoulders. "Except for when they wear too much perfume. Then it means they got a stinky puss and they're trying to cover it up."

Greg wrinkles up his face in disgust, but Jim doesn't even acknowledge his reaction. So Greg continues, "And I like the way they look, too."

The Unmentionables

"Yeah," says Jim. "They look nice."

"Yep," agrees Greg. "I like the way a girl looks when she pulls her long hair through the back of a baseball cap. And you can see her bare neck and her ears."

"Or when a girl's purse strap crosses her chest and pushes down on her shirt, accentuating her boobage," says Jim as he uses both hands to pinch the fabric of his shirt at chest level, pulling it out into two faux-breasts, and winks at Greg.

"Yeah," Greg laughs at his friend. "Seatbelts do the same thing very nicely, too."

"Well, it sounds like you ain't queer then." Jim grins.

"Screw you," laughs Greg, "You're queer."

"Am not and you know it, Greg. I bet I'm the only kid in eighth grade who's done it with a girl." The claim is not braggadocios, but merely a statement of fact. For the previous several weeks, Jim had been going to Lori Bursitis's house immediately after school and making hurried, inept, awkward intercourse with her on the dirty couch in her parent's detached garage before Lori's mother got home from work. The couch smelled of tobacco smoke and cat urine, a fact that mattered very little to Jim at the time. But, because of the mental connection between those odors and his first sexual experiences, Jim will at some time in the future realize that the smell of cat piss always gives him a boner.

Greg says, "Yeah, but that's with Lori. It almost doesn't count because she's the sluttiest girl in the school."

"Have you slept with her?"

"Well, no," says Greg. "But everybody says she gives handjobs to high school guys during her lunch hour."

Jim leans in toward Greg and says softly, "Everybody also says you like boys. Does that make it so?"

The conversation makes Greg nervous. He knows he shouldn't have said those things about Lori, and recognizes that they were said out of jealousy. The last thing Greg wants to do is hurt his friend. He puts the palms of his hands together and presses hard, as if praying vigorously, and looks down, trying to will a change of subject. "Sorry," he says. "I'm just joking around."

"Me too," says Jim. "Seriously, though, I know you like the concept of girls. But what about the reality of girls?"

"Meaning what?"

"Meaning, who do you like?"

"I don't know," says Greg. "I kind of like Kelsey."

A chirp of a laugh escapes Jim's lips as he sprays Orange Slice from his mouth. "Creepy Kelsey Stevens? Seriously? She wears thrift shop clothes and talks to herself all the time. In fourth grade she used to run into the boys' room at school and try to look at kids' dongs. And she has those weird-ass seizures."

"Shut up," says Greg defensively. "I like her. And she actually talks to me, doesn't look at me like I'm something she would scrape off of her shoe. Once she lent me a pencil in class when I didn't have one."

"Yeah, I'm sure she's nice," Jim says, "but I hear that her parents are brother and sister. And that her brother is in an insane asylum."

"Yeah, I think we've established that just because people say something, it doesn't necessarily make it so."

"That's true," agrees Jim. "But I know that they found dead baby pigs in her locker last year. I saw them empty the locker with my own eyes. What's that all about?"

"I don't know," says Greg. "But I know that I get nervous going into algebra class, nervous that I'm going to see her. And then nervous that I might not see her."

"Yeah, but...Creepy Kelsey, you know?" Jim says, scrunching up his face. "I mean, you can do better than her."

"Who am I gonna get for my girlfriend?" asks Greg, pressing his hands together, rocking forward and back nervously. "Maybe Lori Hettler or Julie Billingsley? That's pretty likely because all of the cheerleaders want a scrawny guy that everybody picks on and calls E.T. You're right, I can pretty much take my pick."

Reality knocks and Jim answers the door. He realizes that he is trying to pump Greg full of ideas that can never really be. Greg does not have lots of options as far as girls go, and it's unfair for Jim to give him false hopes. "Well," says Jim, "I could have Lori fix you up with Beth Perkins. She's willing to fool around with anybody. She gave Tracy Robbins a handjob and twenty hickeys. And I heard she even did it with Coach Manlove once."

"And that's gross enough for me to say no thanks," says Greg, his right eye ramping up to a nervous tic, twitching like it's sending out a Morse code message for Jim to stop pressing him. "I don't like Beth. She's not nice. She laughs when people pick on me and she calls me E.T. And it's not like she's got any room to go making fun of me. That girl waddles like a penguin with her plump butt, out-turned feet, and pointy shoes. And her face always looks like she's sucking on something sour. No thanks. I prefer Kelsey."

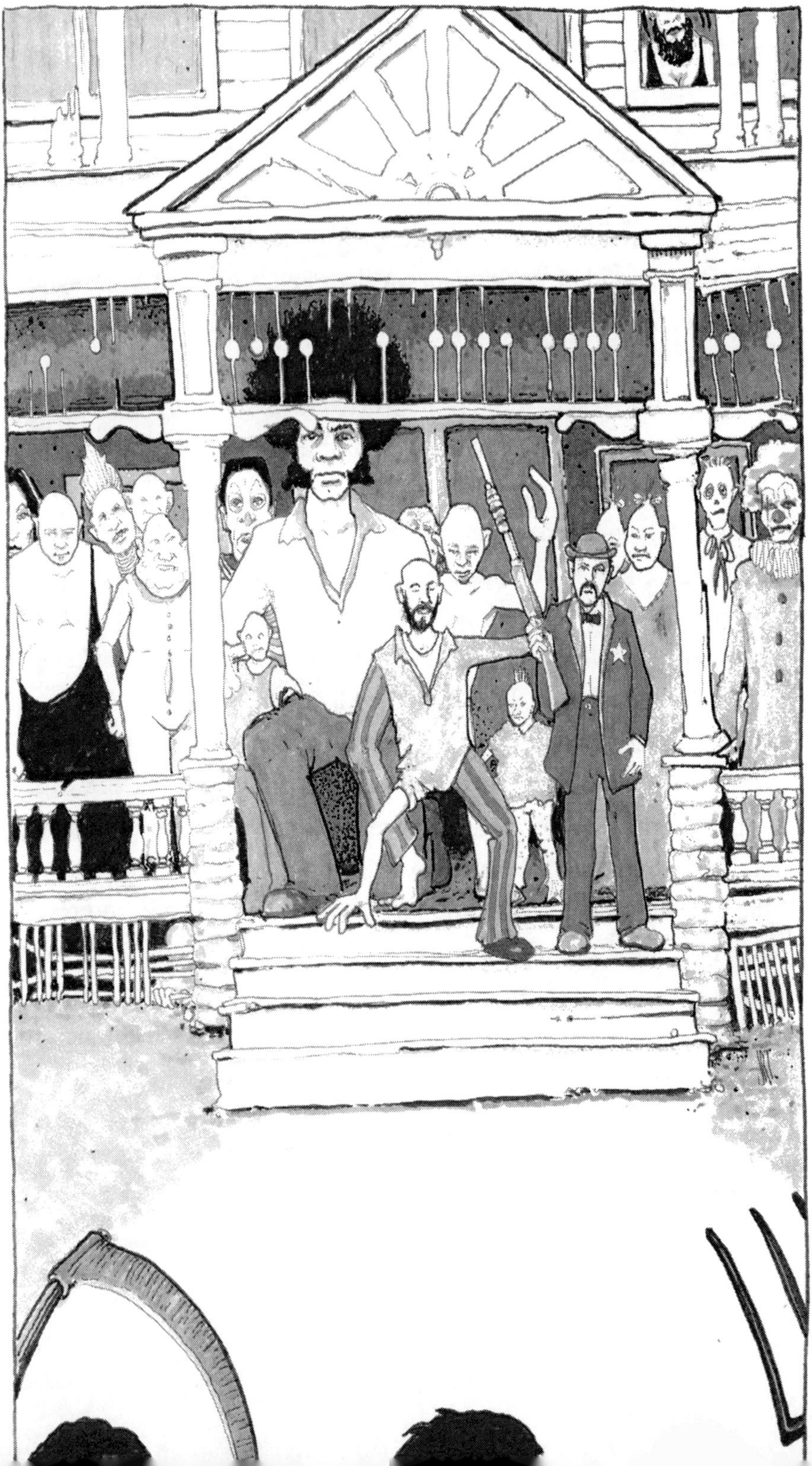

3

And in the pre-dawn darkness, he bops through Findlay to the rhythm of his own personal groove, taking a left here and a right there. Just before dawn pries open the legs of a new day, he bops onto Evergreen Terrace and past the dilapidated mansion that dominates the street. The dangling cord of the Bopper's headphones picks up the strains of a calliope, and the music merges with the beat already in his headphones into a funky melodic circus-stew, going, *dum-dah-dah-da, dum-da-dah-dah-dah-da, dum-dah-dah-da, dum-da-dah-dah-dah-da.* His pace changes ever so slightly to accommodate the tempo of the new jam. Pausing for just a moment, still moving to the music, the Big Bopper stares up toward a gabled dormer window near the top of the house and nods his head. A lone turkey vulture perched atop the house's foremost turret issues a low guttural hiss that spurs the Bopper to movement again. The Big Bopper resumes his funky strut, and the vulture follows his progress with interest. But the Bopper don't care. He just goes where the force pulls him. There's no point in trying to fight the pull. It's like trying to fight sleep – you always give in eventually. So he keeps bopping, because that's the thing to do. He's on the road again and he has a lot of territory to cover before he rests.

4

And then the bell rings. Greg waits for his homeroom to clear out before he jumps into the flowing stream of adolescents buzzing about in the halls and trying to make the most of the three minutes they have to socialize, visit their lockers, and make it to first period without being tardy. Boys playfully jostle each other and wrestle until teachers intervene and send them on their ways to class. Girls primp and preen in mirrors stuck to the inside of their locker doors, putting on lip gloss, mascara, pimple cover up, and other miscellaneous facial goo. Weaving through the throngs of his classmates, Greg stays quiet and tries to make himself invisible. Head bowed down and hands clasped together, like a Buddhist monk under a vow of silence, he makes not a noise and casts no shadow. His eyes constantly scan for Wade and the Courtney brothers and any number of other possible hassles.

Weaving in and out of the traffic on the stairs, Greg makes his way to the bottom floor of the school without incident. The pungent odor of formaldehyde rolls out of Mr. Bowderman's science class, making Greg's eyes water. He briefly glances into the classroom and sees Mr. Bowderman's girthy figure – clad in blue jeans, flannel shirt, and suspenders – leaning over and tying a fetal pig's legs out at the edges of a dissection pan. Greg hears Mr. Bowderman bragging to somebody in the classroom about how he went to Woodstock and saw Sha Na Na live. The sight of the splayed-out piglet disturbs Greg, and his mind wanders into daydream territory where he is the subject getting ready to undergo incisions and punctures and lacerations. And Greg knows how the piglet must feel. That is the way that he feels every day he has to go to school – like he's going to get pinned down and cut open for all to see his gooey and gross insides. Momentarily lost in his thoughts, Greg bumps into an open locker door, knocking something loose that falls to the ground with a moist plop.

"Hey ya big hump, watch where you're going." It's Kelsey, and she drops to her knees to scoop up a bagged fetal pig that she pilfered from the science classroom. She quickly stuffs it in her locker and clangs the metal door shut.

Before the locker closes, Greg sees that it is packed full with bagged fetal pigs, their little pink snouts and curly tails and hooves jammed in and twisted about in uncomfortable contortions. And then Greg raises his gaze and looks at Kelsey. Panic flushes her cheeks and neck. She wears her hair pulled back through the back of a Cleveland Browns baseball cap. Greg averts his eyes from her panicked face to her thrift store dress. And despite the loose, ill-fitting garment, Greg can make out evidence of Kelsey developing into a woman. He imagines that a purse strap across her front would help to emphasize the budding lumps under the dress. Despite his earlier attempt to move quietly and inconspicuously through the halls, Greg just stands and gapes at Kelsey for several awkward moments, trying to bring himself to say something.

But Greg has nothing to say. He freezes right in front of Kelsey. The flow of the other kids along the hall becomes background noise and he forgets his efforts to become invisible to the other students. The only movement he can manage is that of pumping all of the blood from the rest of his body right into his crotch. And he knows that one of his repeated bouts of turgidity has commenced. Unable to even flinch, Greg stands before Kelsey with his hands clasped together, sprouting an uncomfortable and painfully obvious erection.

Kelsey glances down at Greg's trousers, smiles, and says, "Wow. I'd like to get a look at that one." She grabs Greg's hand and yanks him into motion down the hall and away from the science room. She says under her breath, "Come on. Come with me."

Greg holds tight to Kelsey's hand and lets her lead him down the hall. He adjusts himself within his pants with his other hand. And when they reach the inset doorway for the boys' locker room, Kelsey yanks him out of the hall. Still holding Greg's hand, Kelsey whispers: "Meet me here after school. I need help liberating those little oinkers. Okay?"

But Greg is still unable to respond. His only focus is on the warmth of Kelsey's grip, and the throbbing embarrassment in his trousers.

"Okay?" she says again, squeezing Greg's hand and bringing him back to the moment.

Greg's brain cycles through all relevant factors – the need to avoid beatings after school, the chance to help the girl he crushes on, the sweet feel of her hand in his, the risks of not getting away from the school in time, the chance of being caught and branded as a fetal pig thief – and he gives the only possible answer. "Okay."

Kelsey leans in awkwardly and kisses Greg on the cheek, the brim of her hat knocking his glasses catawampus. "Thanks, Greg. I knew I could count on you."

Without further discussion or warning, Kelsey turns on her heels and runs down the hall, leaving Greg with the warm sensation of her hand in his, dissipating moisture on his cheek from the kiss, the pleasure of being addressed by his real name, and a persistent throbbing hard-on that will invite ruthless teasing and taunting in gym class.

The locker rooms odor tells the tale of an ongoing battle between caustic cleaning agents and defiant molds and mildews. Underneath that aroma, the stank of sweaty socks and gym clothes fights for superiority. The sulfuric emanations of Mr. Corbin's silent and uncontrollable flatulence also swim about in the mix, sometimes assuming dominance, and sometimes dissipating and yielding to the other aromas. Mr. Corbin stands on a ladder, humming and pooting, switching out the blinking fluorescent tubes that throw a strobe effect throughout the room.

Greg shuts down his nostrils and breathes through his mouth. The strobing lights pulse into his eye sockets and crawl back to find a tender spot in his brain to prick at. He closes his eyes, and still the flickering tubes register through his eyelids as a red and gold picture show. Seated on the worn wooden bench and leaning back against the dirty cinderblock wall, Greg slides his pants off. Underneath he is already wearing gym shorts, a tactic Greg adopted early on at the school so as to not have to fully undress and be vulnerable to everything that would entail in a locker room full of cruel boys.

Mr. Corbin finishes with the lights and leaves Greg alone in the room. And just before the bell rings, the rest of the students invade the locker room to change into their gym clothes. Some of the boys use Greg's trick and wear shorts under their pants.

Some quickly doff their pants and underclothes and just as quickly don jocks and shorts and t-shirts, doing as little as possible to draw attention during their brief bouts of naked exposure. In contrast to the other boys, Danny Dolan bursts into the locker room and throws his gym bag against the wall. Danny's physique is that of an athlete, with his bulging arms and muscular chest stretching the fabric of his Lacoste shirt. His hair is not long and not short; it has the appearance of being uncombed but still falls perfectly around his acne-free, chiseled face. Danny drops his pants and underwear to the ground with no reservations about his nudity. He just stands there joking and laughing, oblivious to the uncomfortably averted eyes of his classmates. His enormous dangling hog is like the light of the sun and none of the boys can look directly at it for fear of partial blindness or spotty vision. All eyes in the room look in every direction except toward the appendage on display between Danny's legs.

"Hey guys," says Danny. The boys in the room who look to him make sure that they have constant eye contact. In Danny's eyes they see equal measures of mirth and mischief and malice. "E.T.'s awfully quiet over there. Maybe an underpants storm will perk him up a little." Still naked, Danny balls up his dirty underwear and throws it across the room at Greg.

The underpants land at Greg's feet and he hurriedly kicks them away, as if they were a small, rabid creature getting ready to climb up his leg. And the rest of the boys welcome the diversion from the elephant dong in the room. They all feel relief that Danny's mischief is not visited on them. He puts the other boys in fear of his attention, and then when he singles out one, the others take up his lead because they are glad that they are not in his sights. That is how uber-popular Danny Dolan, varsity basketballer and footballer, manipulates the classmates to turn on Greg.

"Underpants storm!" Danny shouts, calling down a barrage of underpants, jockstraps and balled-up socks on Greg. And the unwashed, sweat-stinking, undergarments bounce off his head and arms and chest, as the rest of the class laughs and jeers. Danny, still entirely pantsless, doubles over in laughter. Everybody laughs along with Danny, but they refuse to look in his direction.

Greg holds his hands out, trying to fend off the disgusting underclothes. And just when Greg thinks his humiliation is over, Stewie Gordon – a heavyweight wrestler and a boy not known for his intellectual prowess or good hygiene – scoots down the bench to get right beside Greg, and places his extra-large, skid marked underpants over Greg's head. Stewie, who genuinely does not recognize the cruelty he is inflicting and believes it all to be in fun, slaps Greg on the back and gives a good-natured laugh, as if the whole event were something other than utterly humiliating.

A deep baritone voice booms out over the laughter, "Awright, you knuckleheads, cut the horseplay." Standing at one end of the locker room, sporting tight blue gym shorts, a white tank top, and a whistle around his neck, is Coach Manlove. His chest thrusts out and his biceps bulge. And the two large bumps above his eyes throb. Todd Chizzum once asked what the bumps were from and Coach Manlove curtly answered, "basketball accident." Greg is glad to see Coach Manlove, and, at the same time, dreads him.

The coach runs his hands over his flattop crew cut and scans the locker room, but none of the students will meet his gaze. Manlove sighs and then says, "So it seems that somebody's mommy has complained that I call you all faggots. Apparently I'm not allowed to use that word anymore because it might hurt somebody's feelings. So no more with the word faggots. Alright.

Now hit the gym, you little fruits. And grab a ball on the way out. We're playing dodge ball today."

Greg waits for every other boy to grab a ball and exit before he stands up. And his erection still throbs, showing no sign of going away. He grabs the last red rubber ball and squeezes. It gives to his grip, but that does not matter to Greg; the underinflated balls hurt worse when Coach Manlove nails you with one. Greg holds the ball in front of his crotch to conceal his tumescence. Filled with dread, he exits the locker room and emerges onto the basketball court.

A whistle cuts through the boys' jabbering and silences them. "Oh good, we have a special guest today. Now that Mr. Samsa has decided to grace us with his presence, I want everybody to place their balls at center court and divide up into two teams."

The entire class mills around and does not head toward either end of the floor.

"Come on, ladies," shouts Coach Manlove, "strap on your cocks and get ready to dodge some balls."

"Uh, Coach," says a meek voice. It's Raymond Daws, an insubstantial, jaundiced boy without any athletic inclination. "I've been exempted from dodge ball. My mom sent a note to the nurse and she said I don't have to play because of my asthma."

"Asthma?" Manlove lasers his intense beady-eyed stare through his large, amber tinted, frameless glasses. He chews at a piece of gum as if trying to destroy it. "Asthma is an excuse, boy. And excuses are like buttholes: everybody has one and they all stink. I don't want to hear anything about some note from the nurse or you're going to run laps while we play. Sac up or pack up, Daws. Now let's get ready for some dodge ball, ladies."

The boys set the balls at center court and run for the ends of the gym, readying themselves for combat. At the screech of the whistle, they scramble for the balls, some grabbing two or three. Greg snatches up a ball and reverts to the corner of the court, holding the ball in front of his incessant erection. He tries to make himself invisible. And the air is a red blur with balls flying in all directions, some hurtling across the room with great velocity, while others are lobbed in high arcs.

Coach Manlove stands opposite Greg's end of the gym, hurling red missiles with all his might. The first ball he throws barely misses Barry Plot's head and slams into the wall so hard that it pops. Stewie Gordon catches a ball that is thrown at him and charges the centerline, giggling like a giddy toddler, his sights set on Coach Manlove. Stewie puts his substantial weight into the throw and whizzes a hard one across the court. Manlove senses the incoming ball and leaps into the air, scissoring his legs out, and the ball passes cleanly under him midair, instead knocking the skinny legs right out from under Harry Merkin. Manlove takes umbrage at Stewie's attack and picks up a ball beside Harry, ignoring the fact that the boy is unable to stand back up. Champing at his gum, Manlove sprints toward Stewie and lets loose with a dodge ball cannon that rifles through the air and pounds Stewie in the gut.

The high-velocity, rubber ball forces an "ooomph," out of Stewie, and then knocks him back against the wall. Stewie, the largest boy in gym class, pulls himself up off of the floor, hands clasped at his belly, an obtuse, confused smile spreading across his face, and stumbles to the bleachers to watch the rest of the dodge ball massacre.

Jerry Norman Unborn sneaks up behind Kirk Hirkle and grabs the unsuspecting boy's arms, twisting them up behind his back. And the scrawny boy struggles to escape from Jerry Norman's hold. But before he can wriggle free, Danny Dolan charges and flings a perfectly aimed ball at Kirk's head. The ball smashes Kirk's face and breaks his glasses right along the bridge. Jerry Norman lets go and Kirk staggers toward the bleachers with his hands holding the broken glasses to his face. Kirk shouts at Danny Dolan, "My dad is gonna sue the crap out you for that. He's a lawyer, ya know?" But Danny doesn't care. He is on a tear, walloping his classmates with the red balls. Glasses and lawsuits be damned, Danny has to inflict as much pain as possible.

Half of the boys still playing run about with looks of absolute glee, slinging balls at each other, laughing, and with a complete lack of malice, inflicting welts and bruises and mild concussions on each other, taking great joy when a ball really whams someone. Still other boys dart around like startled guinea pigs, dodging and cowering and cringing, being picked off one by one by their enthusiastic peers. All the while, Greg remains in the corner, somehow almost blending in with the tan walls of the gym, holding a ball in front of his perpetual boner.

And as the dodge ball losers limp, crawl, and hop toward the bleachers, three players remain on the court – Coach Manlove, Danny Dolan, and Greg with the throbbing rod. Manlove and Dolan high five each other and position themselves just short of center court. Danny gathers up all of the balls on their side of the court and places them at Coach Manlove's feet. Manlove champs at his gum and breathes heavily through flared nostrils, like an angry bull honing in on a toreador.

"Get him," Manlove grunts, and Danny and the coach unleash a relentless fury of a dodge ball blitz on Greg.

Everything slows down for Greg. He plots the trajectories of the rubber balls of death, predicts their paths, and jerks his body about in a seemingly random manner. But the movements are precisely calculated to avoid being hit. As a result of years of dodging hurled objects, Greg's muscle memory and instincts are so honed that he usually ends up being one of the final players on the dodge ball court, and not because he enjoys the game, but more because he profoundly dislikes being struck by high-velocity, flying objects. Greg does not try to throw balls back at Danny and Manlove; he knows that he lacks the athletic ability to throw them out. He instead dodges, jumps, ducks, and hopes that he can avoid injury until the game is called a draw. But Coach Manlove does not like to lose. To him a draw is the same as a loss. And Coach Manlove hates losers. With each ball that Greg sidesteps, Manlove's temper flares closer to an all out meltdown. Manlove notches up his intensity. The balls whiz past Greg within inches, slam into the wall, and bounce back across the gym, where Danny gathers them up and sets them at Coach Manlove's feet.

The clock tells Greg that he has three minutes until the end of the period. He gasps for air, but feels that he can hold out through the rest of the class. He has to hold out because the only other option is to suffer the excruciating pain of being on the receiving end of one of Manlove's enraged balls.

Manlove pauses, gasping for air too, sweat pouring off his forehead and burning his beady eyes. He pulls off his glasses and wipes his face with his t-shirt. Putting the glasses back on, he scorches Greg with an intense glare. His nostrils flare and contract with each breath. Greg looks back to the clock and sees that he has two minutes to go. Sensing Greg's brief hesitation, Manlove resumes his assault and heaves a ball that makes a *whoosh* sound as it just misses Greg's head. And the game is on again, with Manlove throwing with all his might, and Greg dodging for his life. Danny Dolan follows Manlove's lead and joins in the rubber ball-bombardment.

Greg looks to the clock again and sees that he has nearly made it to the end of class. He allows himself to feel relief. He is going to make it. But letting his guard down for just that sliver of a second gives Coach Manlove all the opportunity he needs. Just moments before the bell rings, Manlove hurls a ball that finds its mark right upside Greg's head, blasting the relieved look off of his face and driving him into the wall. And the world tilts and spins faster for Greg, dimming to black and then back to the light again. The rapid squeaking/slapping sound of Danny Dolan's shoes on the gym's wooden floor alerts Greg's defenses and he rolls up like a potato bug, covering his face and head and limiting his exposure, bracing himself for the final insult.

"Suck it, ET!" Danny shouts as he hurls one final ball into Greg's defenseless back, knocking his boner right out of him.

Then the bell rings, thus ending the dodge ball massacre. Boys limp toward the locker room, some holding hands to their heads, some nursing sprains and minor fractures.

"Move it, ladies," shouts Coach Manlove from the locker room door. In a confusing simultaneous effort at encouragement and intimidation, Manlove slaps boys hard on their backs as they pass. "I don't want to hear you all crying about being hurt, girls. No pain, no gain." And the boys cringe and shy away from the encouraging back-pats.

When the gym has mostly cleared, Greg unfurls and rolls over, looking for his glasses. The side of his face stings, and his head throbs at the spot where it slammed into the wall. His back aches and his chest hurts from gasping for air.

"Here you go, Greg." It's Raymond Daws, handing Greg his bent glasses. A grave look of respect crosses Raymond's features. "You did a good job. I thought you were gonna make it. You almost showed those jerks." He takes a pull on his nebulizer and breathes out a high-pitched asthmatic wheeze that corrects itself into regular respiration after several breaths. "I wish somebody would teach them a lesson." He extends a hand to Greg and helps him stand. "I really wish someone would get them."

Greg agrees, "Yeah. It'd be awesome to see somebody put those assholes in their place. But who's gonna do it? You? Harry Merkin, who cowers behind Manlove and still manages to get creamed? Me? I slink quietly in the halls and mostly avoid hassle. And then I still get pelted with dirty underwear. Then I have to run my balls off to get home before Busby and his dipshits can find me. It's a nice thought, Raymond, but I really don't see any of us setting these bastards straight, do you?"

"You have something about you, Greg. And I'm not the only one who sees it. The other kids like us – the dorks and nerds and little pussies that are too afraid to stick up for themselves – I think they all see something in you. You don't let them shake you. You don't give them the pleasure of showing you're scared shitless, even if you are. I mean, yeah, you run home from school every day, but so do the rest of us. But when Wade cornered you, you didn't turn to Jell-O. You at least gave it a shot and tried to kick him in the balls. At least you tried to stick up for yourself. And it is more than what I or anyone else would have tried."

Greg and Raymond slowly make their way to the locker room, hoping to give Danny Dolan enough time to change and get out before they arrive.

"Come on, ladies, move it," Coach Manlove shouts at Greg and Raymond from the doorway. He champs his gum and beams a smile at Greg. Clamping one hand on Greg's shoulder, Manlove uses his other to slap Greg on the ass. "Good job out there, Samsa.

We're going to make a man out of you yet, whether you like it or not. Now go put your bra and panties back on and get to your next class."

For the rest of the day, Greg slinks and creeps between classes, head down and hands clasped in front, on guard for attacks on his person. Between fourth and fifth periods, just before Spanish class, Wade hunts Greg down and shoulder checks him into the wall. A crowd immediately coagulates into a bloodthirsty clot of humanity around Greg and Wade.

But before the bloodlust is slaked, Mr. French arrives. He runs his hand through his hair, straightening his greasy comb-over, and says, "I told you boys yesterday that I don't want you practicing your wrestling moves in the hall. ¿You do remember that, don't you? I don't want to have to do this again. Nunca mas. ¿Entendemos?"

"I'm sorry, Mr. French," Wade says, oozing false remorse. "Greg keeps asking me to show him different holds because he wants to try out for the wrestling team."

"¿Is that right?" Mr. French asks.

Since it's even worse to be a snitch, Greg shrugs his shoulders and says, "Yeah. Wade was just showing me some moves."

"Well I'm glad you're taking an interest in athletics, Greg," Mr. French says. His comb-over slops down against the side of his head. He pulls a comb from his shirt pocket and slicks the sloppy strands back over his exposed scalp. "I've always thought you could use some toughening up. But save it for after school. Maybe I can talk to Coach Manlove about letting you try out for the team."

"Yeah, that'd be great, Samsa," Wade cracks a devious smirk. "I'd love to get you out on the mats."

"I'll talk to the coach after school, boys. But, in the meantime, I want no more horseplay in the halls. Now everybody get to class. Vamanos, vamanos, ahora."

Mr. French swirls his hand in the air as if stirring up mighty winds to disperse the crowd of students. And when he turns to enter his room, Wade blasts a quick punch at Greg's arm, digging his knuckles into the bicep. The pain goes deep, to the bone. Greg loses his vision momentarily and swoons from the shock of it. And then Wade disappears into the crowd, his laughter floating above and finding its way to Greg.

The throb in Greg's arm pulses along with the swelling on the back of his head. He slinks into Mr. French's classroom and flops into his desk. And to his right, Jim Halloway leans back into his seat and smiles at Greg.

"Wow, you're doing a great job of making friends this year," says Jim. "Are you planning on having Wade spend the night at your house any time soon?"

"Cram it up your ass," says Greg, not angry, but actually relieved to see Jim. "I need your help after school." Greg tells Jim about Kelsey and her pigs, and to meet him outside of Mr. Bowderman's classroom after the last period.

After fifth period, Greg, Jim, and Kelsey gather outside of Miss Demerit's room. And they talk under their breath as students and teachers make their way around them. Mr. Bowderman approaches from down the hall in an exaggerated waddle. Before he arrives, Kelsey quickly brings up the pigs, asking Greg, "Did you tell Jim about the...uh...the unmentionables?"

"I did," says Greg just before Mr. Bowderman arrives at Miss Demerit's classroom and beckons her to the door.

Mr. Bowderman frisks Kelsey with his eyes. Ever since his fetal pigs disappeared, he has suspected Kelsey. But he has no witnesses and no way of proving it. So for the time being he takes satisfaction in staring her down and stalking her in the halls with the hopes of discovering where she may have stashed the fetal pigs.

Kelsey flushes at Mr. Bowderman's stare. She turns and hurries down the hall. Mr. Bowderman follows her with the discerning gaze of a veteran detective. Greg's eyes follow her in a full-on fit of schoolboy infatuation.

"Come on, loverboy," says Jim, grabbing Greg by the elbow and dragging him toward class, where they take their seats and make plans for later in the day.

At the end of the day, Greg does not launch from his seat and flee the school grounds as if pursued by rabid, syphilitic werewolves. He does not scurry through back alleys or cower behind dumpsters. Instead, he holes up in a stall of the second floor bathroom, waiting until the halls clear of students, hoping that Wade and Donnie and Chop are already patrolling the streets and looking for him there. Breathing through his mouth and standing on the toilet so his feet do not show beneath the stall, Greg waits silently, listening to the sloppy splashing sounds of Vice Principal Blight forcefully evacuating his bowels in the next stall over. Mr. Blight breathes a sigh of relief, flushes the toilet twice, and exits the bathroom without washing his hands. As the cacophony of the end of the day breaks up and settles, as students hop on their bikes and leave their educations behind for the day, as Wade hunts the streets, eyes wild and nose in the air to catch scent of his prey, Greg emerges from the mephitic miasma of the boys' room and ventures into the halls. Without incident, he descends to the bottom floor of the school, where Kelsey and Jim await him.

"If you're not part of the solution, you're part of the problem. Back when I was your age, we stood up for the things we believed in. We protested. We fought for justice and peace." Mr. Bowderman's deep voice, lecturing the students serving detention, booms out of the classroom and bounces down the hallway. Greg slinks past the science room and sees Kelsey and Jim Halloway waiting for him at Kelsey's locker with gym bags and knapsacks.

Kelsey nervously waves Greg over and whispers to both of the boys, "We need to distract Bowderman. He's laying down one of his 'back in the sixties' raps on the hoods in there right now. But if he comes out, we're busted and in a big pile of stink."

Jim points his thumbs at his chest and says, "This guy's got it." He marches down the hall and into the Mr. Bowderman's classroom. Over the taunting jeers of the kids in detention, Jim says, "Do you have a moment, Mr. Bowderman? I'm sorry to interrupt, but I'm having trouble understanding how osmosis works. I mean, what exactly is a semipermeable membrane and why does it only allow solvent molecules to pass through it?"

Mr. Bowderman's voice takes on a note of excitement. Words like *turgor* and *thermodynamic free energy* and *plasmolyzed* rapidly fly from his mouth and float down the hall before Jim or any of the kids in the classroom can really grasp their meaning. And whether or not they like it, Mr. Bowderman crams scientific theory down their throats, jams it into their ear-holes, and pounds it into any other available and receptive orifices.

With Mr. Bowderman engrossed in the wonders of osmosis, Greg and Kelsey rush to empty her locker of fetal pigs. Greg holds a bag wide open as Kelsey flings the oinkers into it. And they fill the duffle bags and knapsacks with every last piglet. The bags bulge and fight the efforts to zip them shut. But Greg and Kelsey prevail. They throw the overburdened knapsacks on their backs, sling the weighty duffle bags over their shoulders, and speed-walk down the hall, not running, though, because it would draw too much scrutiny if they were to encounter a teacher. When they reach the stairs at the end of the hall, Greg whistles as loud as he can and kicks a locker door several times to alert Jim that he and Kelsey are done. Kelsey grabs Greg's hand and pulls him along behind her as they run up the stairs, hit the landing, and then descend the stairs that lead to the school's back exit near the cafeteria and shop classrooms.

No bananas bounce off of Greg's head as he passes the shop classrooms. The Courtney brothers are not there to laugh like buffoons. Only Mr. Snodgrass, the wood teacher, stands in the doorway, drilling his thumb into his bored-out nostrils as he is known to do compulsively.

"Have a good day, Mr. Snodgrass," says Kelsey as she drags Greg past him and out the door. It is not lost on Kelsey that the teacher's large, upturned, reddish nose looks much like the snouts on the piglets she is liberating. Her mind drifts and she imagines him with a little corkscrew tail hidden away under his saggy, brown pants. And the thought makes her giggle and snort like a pig herself as she exits the school.

Surprised by the students, Mr. Snodgrass yanks his thumb out of his nose and wipes it on his shop apron. He eyes the overloaded knapsacks and duffel bags with suspicion and considers investigating. But, Greg and Kelsey are already out the exit and on their way by the time Snodgrass can mull it over. He watches them through the glass doors, shrugs his suspicions off, and decides he has more important work to do, such as grading the half-assed, poorly cut and finished coat racks and bread boxes slopped together by his students. With Kelsey and Greg gone from sight, the magnetic pull of the nostrils draws Mr. Snodgrass's thumb back and he digs deeply to dislodge some dead, dried skin with the thumbnail.

They duck back beside a detached garage and stash the pigs in a patch of shrubbery alongside the alley. Leaden clouds invade the sky, dimming the daylight, and a brisk wind throws the chill of the oncoming autumn at them. Kelsey shudders involuntarily at the cold breeze and huddles up next to Greg. He breathes in deeply through his nose and smells her. Her aroma, fresh like bath soap and rain, mingles with the pleasant autumnal smells of dead leaves and the dirty ground. And the scent fills him, warms him against the gloomy afternoon.

"I'm sorry we have to hide," says Greg, not feeling entirely bad about having to hide out alone with Kelsey. He closes his eyes and relishes her presence, thinks to himself that it's odd that one can find a moment of bliss sometimes even in the middle of the worst situations. Hating to have to admit it to Kelsey, he continues, "But Wade Busby wants to beat me up.

And I kind of like my face all in one piece. So we have to be careful."

"I don't mind," says Kelsey. "I like your face, too. And I kind of like huddling up together."

"Yeah, me too," says Greg. He breathes in deeply through his nose and smells her again. She puts her head on his shoulder and they wait for Jim Halloway, not feeling the need to talk.

"Alright, asshole-breath, I know you're back there. Now come out of the bushes before I come in and get you." The rough, obtuse voice vaguely approximates the malice and stupidity of Wade Busby's, but doesn't trip Greg's flight reflex.

Greg sighs, regretting the interruption of his alone time with Kelsey, and steps out from his hiding place beside the garage. He grabs Kelsey's hand, pulling her out with him, and says to Jim Halloway, "You're such a douche. You actually thought I'd buy that bad impression of Wade. You're great at some things, but not impersonations."

"I'm pretty great at distracting teachers," Jim says. He claps his hands together and says, "Now what're we doing? I'm supposed to go to Lori's house before her parents get home, and it looks like I'm not going to make it over there today. So if I'm missing out on poontang, this better be important."

Greg cringes at his best friend's crassness and starts to apologize to Kelsey for his behavior.

"Did you actually just say poontang?" Kelsey laughs hard, holding her hands to her gut and bending over. Her laugh, like a sheep bleating and a pig snorting at the same time, swells to hilarity, and she gasps for air in between her snorts. Greg laughs along with her, relieved that she's not offended. And then Kelsey's laughter cuts short. Her face freezes, eyes rolling up into her head. Her joints lock up, and she falls into Greg, her deadweight knocking him to the ground. Her stiff body lands on top of him and then trembles violently for several seconds. And then, just as quickly as the fit set upon her, it subsides.

Greg scrambles out from under Kelsey and helps her sit up, asking, "Are you okay?"

Kelsey sits on the ground beside Greg and waves off her brief seizure. She laughs again, gently this time. "Poontang. That's the grossest thing I've heard today."

"I can get grosser," says Jim Halloway, smirking and trying to make Greg cringe.

"Cut it out," Greg blurts. He stands and helps Kelsey back to her feet. "We've got to get moving before Wade finds me. We've got to get those pigs out of sight." Greg retrieves the pigs from beside the garage, slinging a pack and a duffle bag over his shoulder, and handing two bags to Jim.

"Hey, why doesn't she have to carry anything?" says Jim Halloway. "She's the one who stole the pigs in the first place."

Tossing her head back and holding her nose high in the air, Kelsey takes on an imperious tone and says, "Because I am a proper lady, you scurvy peasant. And I shan't be expected to carry bags of dead pigs like a commoner hefting flesh from the slaughter house." But she cannot keep up the act and she starts snort-laughing again.

Fearing another seizure, Greg puts a hand on Kelsey's arm and one on her back, readying to set her down gently on the ground should she lapse into another fit. Kelsey stifles her laughter and regains her regal tone, "I'm okay. It shan't happen again. Now tell our servant to get moving."

It is decided that the pigs should be stored at Greg's house until they can figure out what to do with them. The threesome totes Kelsey's haul through the alleyways, cuts through yards, climbs fences, and tries to stay out of sight. Out of sight of teachers. Out of sight of the police. And out of sight of Wade Busby. On the way they encounter the usual back-alley denizens. The Big Bopper bounces past, snapping his fingers and moving to the rhythm of his own funky drummer. They see Johnny Close, his face stitched up, his crooked neck straightened with a neck brace, limping through a back yard with the aid of a cane, and peeping into the rear window of a house.

And Wade Busby does not find them. They find him. As they walk down the alley that cuts along the Samsa's back yard, Greg stops and says, "You gotta be kidding me." Jumping behind a patch of shrubbery, he grabs Kelsey's arm and pulls her out of sight with him. Jim Halloway just stands in the middle of the alley, looking toward the spot where Wade, Donnie, and Chop have surrounded Lorenzo Washington, the only black boy in their school.

Lorenzo stands five foot ten, taller than all of the boys picking on him, smiling a bright white smile. And his dark, almost purple body is more fully developed than most kids at school. But he is a big floppy puppy-dog of a boy who just wants to get along with everybody. Lorenzo doesn't see black and white, even when his nose is rubbed hard in it. He sees kind and unkind, with unkind way in the lead in Findlay. His complete lack of a temper makes him an easy target for bullying. Kids walk up to him in the hall and call him porch monkey, nigger lips, shoeshine boy. Lorenzo doesn't get mad or offended. He gets hurt and saddened. But he just wipes his sleeve across the perennial snot bead that hangs from his left nostril and gets on with life. It never crosses Lorenzo's mind that he might have the ability to give any one of his tormentors, including Wade, a solid thumping, that would probably serve as ample warning to the next person to consider mistreating him. The thought of physical violence against another simply doesn't occur to Lorenzo. So he soaks up his punishment and forgets about it as best as he can.

Jim stands in the alley, watching Wade push his foot forward toward Lorenzo. Lorenzo kneels down and starts to tie the shoe. Before he finishes, Chop rushes in and kicks Lorenzo on the shoulder, knocking him to the ground. Wade and Chop and Donnie all laugh and call Lorenzo more names. And Lorenzo, mostly unhurt by the kick, brushes himself off and starts to stand. He laughs along with his tormentors, because to challenge them or to get mad would get him in deeper. Wade pushes his other foot forward and Lorenzo kneels again to tie the shoe.

"This is getting ridiculous," says Jim as he dumps his bags of pigs in the bushes. Sticking his right hand down the back of his pants and fully inserting his pointer finger into his asshole, Jim says, "They're going to get carried away and hurt that boy. I've got to stop this."

"What are you doing?" Greg asks from his hiding spot. "Get out of sight or they're going to start in on us next. What the hell are you gonna to do?"

"I'm gonna to make those jerks smell my asshole," Jim smiles. And then he shouts, "Hey, Wade, get your ass over here." And his voice throws cold water on the back-alley emotional lynching of Lorenzo Washington.

Wade looks down the alley, confusion and anger fighting for control over his gormless face. He jerks his head at Chop and Donnie and they all turn from Lorenzo and look toward Jim. In that brief pause, Lorenzo sees his chance to make a break and dashes down the alley so fast that he stirs up a cloud of dust behind him.

"Come on over this way, I'll give you something you'll really enjoy," Jim calls out.

Like a glittery object, Jim Halloway diverts Wade's short attention span, causing the bully to forget about picking on Lorenzo. A new idea is conceived in Wade's brain, malformed and ugly, and given a premature birth by his words to Chop and Donnie, "Let's kick Halloway's ass instead."

Greg and Kelsey crouch in the bushes and watch with dread as Wade and Chop and Donnie Price approach. Adrenaline courses through Greg's system. His muscles twitch, his skin itches. Sweat drips down his forehead and burns his eyes. He fights the urge to break and run for his house and instead remains in case he can somehow help Jim.

Kelsey wants to run, too. And she starts to jump up and take off, but Greg grabs her by the arm and whispers, "No. I have to stay in case Jim needs help. And if you run, they will probably take the pigs we leave behind and do awful things to them." Kelsey's great concern for the dead piglets prevails over her fear. She kneels down again and watches through the shrubs at the approach of Wade, Donnie, and Chop.

Jim Halloway hears the stirring in the bushes and realizes that he needs to move away. He walks toward Wade and they meet in the alleyway just behind the dilapidated Samsa Mansion.

"Why they hell did you interrupt us?" says Wade. His reptilian features scrunch up into a malignant smile. "We were having fun with Washington and you ruined it. Now we have to pretend that you're Washington, don't we?"

"Yeah," says Chop. "Now we're gonna whip you like a nigger."

And in the bushes, Chop's words sting Kelsey. A yelp of disgust escapes her before she can stop it. Greg leans closer and puts his hand over her mouth to try to stop her from saying something.

"Hey," says Wade, looking directly in Greg and Kelsey's direction, "what's in those bushes?"

Donnie steps toward the bushes, saying, "Yeah, what's going on in the bushes?"

Stricken with fear, Kelsey struggles against Greg to get up and run. But Greg keeps his hand over her mouth and tries to calm her. He whispers to her to settle down and be quiet.

"That's nothing," says Jim quickly. "I saw some cats fucking back there, that's all. Let them have their fun."

"No way," says Donnie. "I gotta see that."

"Yeah," agrees Chop. "I wanna watch the cats fuck, too."

And Wade, Donnie and Chop all step toward the bushes. But before they get close enough to see Greg and Kelsey, Jim Halloway says, "I've got something better than watching cats screw. Unless you guys are a bunch of fags or something."

Jim fights the instinct to flinch as Wade suddenly wheels around and grabs his shirt in both hands. In an instant Chop and Donnie are at Wade's sides, ready to bookend the beating Wade is going to dish out. Wade pulls up on the shirt, lifting Jim to his tiptoes.

"Look," says Jim, "I didn't say you guys were fags. I said I've got something better for you to do if you're not."

Wade leans in close, his saurian features tensed, his lower jaw grinding enamel off of his teeth, his heavy breathing flaring his nostrils wide and closing them like flaps. "You better tell me real quick what you got that's more important than those cats fucking in the bushes." He pushes Jim, propelling him in a backwards stumble. Jim staggers back, flailing arms to steady himself, nearly tripping over his own feet but finally recovering from the stumble.

Jim breathes deeply and exhales. He holds his pointer finger up in the air and says, "It's this."

"Huh?" says Wade, a look of confusion dims the fire in his eyes.

"Is that what I think it is?" asks Donnie, who has a thing for fingers. Donnie is not the smartest or most athletic kid in school. He is certainly not the nicest or the funniest. But he does have that certain something with his feathered, dirty blond hair, and his rough good looks that some girls are drawn to. And Donnie is known for taking girls into hidden spots in the school and fingering them. Finger fucking is only part of the pleasure for Donnie, though. The mere act by itself, while fun, is unsatisfactory unless he can share the experience with others. On any given day, Donnie might be seen standing in the hall between periods, with Wade and Chop and other boys gathered around him, Donnie holding his fingers under the other boys' noses for them to breathe in their first whiffs of vagina.

Jim smiles. "It's what you think it is if you're thinking it's stink-finger."

And the fictitious fucking cats are forgotten. Chop's nostrils home in on Jim's finger and he sniffs and snorts like a bloodhound on a hot trail. Backing off of the finger and adjusting a raging boner in his pants, Chop merely says, "Nice!"

"Cool," says Donnie, nodding his head and beaming an envious smile. "Who'd you finger-blast?"

"I just came from my girlfriend, Lori's house," says Jim.

"Lori Bursitis?" asks Wade.

"Yep."

"I heard she's a lot of guys' girlfriend," says Wade. "They say she's really handy around the high school, if you know what I mean." And he moves in to sample the odor wafting off of Jim's pointer finger. Wade grunts a low, animal sound and huffs at the finger.

Jim grows emboldened by his ruse. He says, "So's you can enjoy it all day," and rubs his shitty finger on Wade's wispy mustache. "You can keep sniffing her poon even after I leave."

"Yeah," interjects Chop. "Rub a little on my lip, too."

Jim gladly obliges Chop, rubbing the finger on his philtrum, giving him a shitty little stink-mustache.

Donnie elbows Chop out of the way. "My turn," he says, grabbing Jim's hand and pulling it toward his face. Donnie, the stink-finger connoisseur, closes his eyes and whiffs at the finger. "Hmmm," he mutters and eyes Jim with a questioning, almost suspicious look. He closes his eyes again and waves his hand above the finger, wafting the aroma toward his nose. Finally Donnie smiles and says, "Now that, my friends, is some Grade A snatch."

"Yeah," agrees Wade. To Jim he says, "Tell your girlfriend that I wanna finger her, too."

"Yeah," says Chop. "Me too."

And they all laugh. Jim laughs with them, trying to act like one of the guys and keep their attention diverted away from the shrubbery.

"No," says Wade, no longer laughing. "I mean it. The next time you see her, tell her I want to finger her, too."

"Seriously?" asks Jim. "Just like that. Tell her that you want to finger her?"

"You better believe I'm serious," says Wade as he steps closer and locks eyes with Jim. "And I want to know what she says."

Physically repulsed by Wade's approach, Jim steps backwards, saying, "Yeah, yeah. I'll let you know what she says."

Wade sneers. He reaches out and pats Jim on the shoulder, "You do that."

"Hey," says Chop. "You haven't seen E.T., have you? We want to have a little talk with him."

"Sure," says Jim Halloway, glad to change the subject from Wade fingering his girlfriend. "He told me he was going to the library after school. He's supposed to be there all afternoon."

"Radical," says Wade. "Let's book on over to the library." He jumps onto his bike, pops a wheelie, and rides it down the alley and away from the shrubbery. Chop and Donnie hop onto their bikes, too, and chase after Wade.

"Later, stink-finger," shouts Donnie just before he pedals out of sight.

And with the danger gone, Jim steps toward the shrubbery and says, "Come on out, you cats, the coast is clear."

The shrubbery shakes and leaves fall from the branches. Kelsey stumbles out of the bushes, hands held to her stomach, doubled over and snort-laughing uncontrollably. Greg follows, hands held together, palm to palm, head bowed down, beaming a huge smile. They look at Jim and he shakes his pointer finger in their direction. Giddy from the adrenaline rush and the passing of the threat, they all explode with laughter. They drop to the ground and sit there howling and snorting and gasping for breath. Every time the laughter subsides they make eye contact and it grips them again.

Finally, Greg stands. He extends a hand and helps Kelsey to her feet. Jim holds out his hand toward Greg, asking for the same assistance that was offered to Kelsey.

Greg says, "I'm not touching that hand, you sick puppy," and brushes gravel and dirt from his pants as Jim helps himself up. "Come on," says Greg. "We need to get those pigs in the house and get out of the way before Wally and his butt-buddies get home."

And they gather up the duffle bags and backpacks and haul them into the rear entrance to Greg's house. Once inside, Greg leads them down the dark steps to the basement. At the bottom of the stairs, Greg pulls a string to light up a single light bulb. The bulb throws a weak glow around some of the dungeon-like room.

"Come on," Greg says, and he leads his friends through a jumble of boxes, antique exercise machines that look more like torture equipment, and miscellaneous bric-a-brac. He finds a dark corner of the basement and sets down his bags of pigs. "Just set them down here."

Once unburdened of the fetal pigs, Greg starts to lead Kelsey and Jim back through the hoarder's maze of junk and toward the steps, up and out of the dungeon. Even with their eyes somewhat adjusted to the dark, Kelsey and Jim are unable to see very well. Kelsey grabs Greg's right hand and allows him to lead her. Jim tries to grab Greg's other hand for guidance, too.

Greg pulls his hand away and says, "I already told you, don't touch me with that nasty hand."

And they ascend the basement stairs, coming out into the enormous kitchen. Li'l Shirl stands at the double sink, hand-washing dishes and scraping crusted leftovers into a steel bucket. Two fat raccoons peek up over the windowsill from outside, eyeing Li'l Shirl and the slop bucket with great intensity.

"Hey, Li'l Shirl," says Greg.

His sister turns to him, a dishrag in one hand and a sponge in the other. "Hi," she says. Her eyes go blank and roll up into her head. Her features slacken as her head strains to process the situation. A little ball of information locks into place in her brain and refuses to budge. Greg's name momentarily escapes Li'l Shirl, but his face triggers something that turns a crank that moves a boot on a pole to kick the ball, and the boot kicks the ball right down a chute, and the ball it rolls and hits a pole, and knocks the ball in the rub-a-dub tub, which hits the man into the pan, and the trap is set, here comes the net, and the net falls down, and the net traps a thought before it escapes. Li'l Shirl's eyes roll back down and a dim look of recognition registers in her gaze. She realizes that the boy is her brother and remembers his name. "Hi, Greg," she says flatly, and then turns to resume her dishwashing.

Greg says, "Li'l Shirl, you're not feeding those coons again, are you?"

Li'l Shirl continues to wash the dishes, not turning to look at Greg. "What coons?" she says.

"The ones sitting at the window right in front of you."

"Oh," says Li'l Shirl, "them's not coons. Them's Captain Jack and Fats Flannigan. They just like to watch me."

"Well don't let them in the house and don't feed them," says Greg. And he reaches around Li'l Shirl to grab the bucket of slop, snatching it and dumping it into the garbage disposal. He runs the faucet, flips a switch beside the sink, and the disposal grinds the leftovers into a sludge that sluices down the pipes.

"Oh," says Li'l Shirl. "Oh no. You shouldn'ta done that." She flips off the disposal and rams her hand into it, trying to salvage the leftovers, but to no avail.

Fats Flannigan and Captain Jack scratch furiously at the window and yowl their disapproval.

"Don't feed those fat bastards," says Greg. And to Jim Halloway and Kelsey, he says, "Come on. Let's go play Space Invaders." He turns away and climbs the narrow stairs to the upper floors of the house, followed by Kelsey and Jim. Behind them they hear the rear door open and slam shut, and Li'l Shirl trying to explain to Fats Flannigan and Captain Jack that it's not her fault that their dinner got thrown away.

5

With each step it's like the Big Bopper tries to push himself up and away from Earth. But the gravitational field is strong wherever he goes and it drags him back to the planet each time he tries to launch himself into the air. The heavy gravity slows the time around him to a crawl, while the pace of things outside of his bubble is frothy and frantic. But the Big Bopper don't care because he just floats in the spacetime, flipping and tripping to the pulsing groove spuming from his headphones. Snapping his fingers and bopping along, a mystic doo-dah man, knowing nothing but soaking everything in.

The Bopper bops for days with no rest, now floating down the late Sunday morning Main Street, past Morey's Books, where men in suits, fresh out of church, lurk side by side in the back of the store, flipping through nudie magazines, avoiding eye contact with each other and sprouting awkward boners in their dress pants as they gaze at two dimensional images of titties and hairy beavers. But the Big Bopper don't pay no attention to the men; they have their priorities and the Bopper has his. The church men need to look at pictures that cause the blood to rush to their genitals. The Bopper needs to keep moving, needs to keep his heart pumping blood evenly to all parts of his body.

And now the Bopper bops past the Bear Flag Restaurant, where an old man with a silver, sparse comb-over and an atrophied frontal lobe awkwardly flirts with his waitress, telling her she doesn't sweat much for a fat girl. In response, the chunky waitress asks the man if his suit used to fit him when it was in style. And they both laugh a good-natured, hardy laugh at each other. The Bopper don't laugh, but he does soak up the energy as he passes, and a smile pulls at the corners of his mouth.

Although time crawls for the Big Bopper as if it is loaded down with bags of cement, it zooms right on by for everyone outside of his bubble. And in the span of his Sunday morning walk, weeks pass by everybody else, because time is all relative and shit, man. In that span of non-Bopper time, Greg and Kelsey become close, and as the Bopper bops past 42 Evergreen Terrace, Greg fumbles ineffectually with bra straps and clasps and eventually just cups his first handful of warm, soft mammary through the bra. And it is wonderful and exciting and intoxicating for him. The Bopper smiles, keeps on boppin', and his pace picks up just a little.

And the Big Bopper struts on through town, through the alleys, and past the detached garage behind the Bursitis house. Jim Halloway performs quick, unsophisticated thrusts into Lori, before blowing his load and leaving the girl wondering what's so great about sex anyway. When it's over, Jim finally asks Lori if she will let Wade Busby finger her. He doesn't want to ask, but he knows that an ass beating is coming down the pike if she doesn't come through for Wade. Lori gets angry and throws him out of the garage. And the Bopper bops by, not even looking at the dejected boy. But the Bopper knows Jim Halloway's sadness. The Bopper soaks up emotional energy and takes it in deeply. A tear streaks the dirt on the Bopper's face.

The torrent of the town's emotional energy is hoovered into the dangling cord of the Big Bopper's headphones. And the headphones pick up the energy of love found and love lost, of lust and laughter, and turn it into a thumping, swerving, funky stew that makes the Bopper move his feet and snap his fingers. And it don't matter where the energy comes from. The Bopper don't care. He just bops, man, because the groove washes him along like an incessant wave, and the beat lays down a far out rhythm for him to slap his feet to.

6

Captain Jack and Fats Flannigan hang from the ladder outside of Greg's lounge and scratch their claws at the windowpane. The furry masked bandits chirp and mew at Greg, begging admittance to his sanctuary. Greg walks to the window, and, in accordance with his *no raccoons* policy, flips the critters the bird and closes the blackout curtains in their pointy little faces. He turns up Little Walter on the stereo to drown out the creatures' sounds, and goes back to sit on the couch with Kelsey.

"My asshole is really starting to get sore," Jim Halloway complains above the music. He stretches out on the red velvet chaise lounge and locks his hands behind his head. "Wade keeps asking to sniff my fingers and he expects something nice. But I don't think I can jam my finger up there anymore. I'm starting to get hemorrhoids. Something's gotta give, and it ain't my o-ring."

Greg and Kelsey sit side by side on their own couch, laughing at Jim and staring at the TV, playing a hotly contested game of Atari basketball.

"Say what?" Kelsey giggles and mashes the red button on her joystick to dump a jump shot through the basket. "Doesn't he know that Lori dumped you?"

"No, and I'm not going to tell him until I figure out how to deal with this. Apparently Lori never thought enough about me to even tell people we were an item. So for all Wade knows, I'm diddling her in between classes and he's smelling her puss."

"God, you're grody," Kelsey says without a trace of disdain. "Greg wouldn't talk about me like that, would you?"

"No," Greg says as his 8-bit baller steals the giant pixilated basketball and breaks down the court for a lay up. "But I would kick your butt at basketball."

Kelsey drops her joystick and punches Greg in the arm. "Have you not a chivalrous bone in your scrawny body, Sir?" she asks as she knocks him over on the couch and leaps on top of him, easily overpowering him, and tickling her fingers into his ribs.

Jim Halloway jumps in, too, probing his fingertips into Greg's soft underarm area and ribs. They roll off of the couch as a big ball of flailing arms and legs, and onto the floor. Greg struggles against the tickle assault, laughing so hard that he starts to cry. A small wet patch begins to dampen his groin area. Finally, Jim and Kelsey let up. And they all fall back on the floor, gasping for air and laughing like lunatics.

And then the horseplay stops in response to a pounding on

the wall. Muffled voices from outside the lounge call out. "Come on you little shit-turds," says Wally from the other side of the wall. "We can hear you in there. Let us in and maybe we won't kick your asses too much."

"Yeah," says Lumpy Rutherford. "Or maybe we will anyway, you little dildos."

And as an echo on the other side of the wall, Eddie says, "Yeah, you little dildos."

"Shut up, Eddie," says Wally, turning on his friend without warning. The *thwack* of palm on face follows. "We want them to come out. And you're acting like a dildo yourself. They ain't coming out if you say shit like that."

The sounds of a muffled scuffle and Eddie's sharp protests carry through the walls. Greg darts over to the record player and lifts the needle to stop the music. The wall shakes as Wally throws Lumpy against it. Instinctively, Kelsey scoots back, a look of concern tightening her face, and asks, "They can't get in here, can they?"

"No," says Greg. "They don't know how. But we better get out of here just in case."

Dashing to the window, Greg pulls back the blackout curtains, and is greeted by the hissing masked duo of Captain Jack and Fats Flannigan. "Shoo," says Greg, waving his hands at the coons to scare them off. But Captain Jack and Fats Flannigan balk, scratching their claws at the window even more frantically, a glint of manic determination in their beady little eyes.

"Great," says Kelsey. "We're trapped in here and I have to be home soon. If I'm late, my dad is gonna kick my ass."

"We're not trapped," says Jim Halloway. He grabs a broom from the corner of the room and walks toward the window. "When I say *now*, you open the window just a little bit. Okay?"

Greg pushes his glasses up on the bridge of his nose and nods at Jim. "Okay."

"I hope you guys aren't going to hurt those cute little fellows out on the ledge," says Kelsey. "I'd rather be late and have my dad take it out on me."

"Nah," says Jim, "we're just gonna talk some sense into them." He winks at Greg, backs away from the window, and does several exaggerated squats. He leaps around the room, swinging the broomstick like a demented custodian. Then, holding the stick out like a lance, Jim charges the window and says, "Now!"

Greg raises the window half a foot and keeps his hands on top of the frame, ready to jam it down on any uninvited pests. Jim thrusts the stick through the open window, and before the raccoons realize what is happening, Jim pokes Captain Jack hard in the belly, knocking him off of the sill, subjecting him to the pull of the earth. And then the broomstick sweeps across the breadth of the open window, swatting Fats Flannigan and sending him down just feet behind his friend. The coons plummet with their bellies open to the skies, their fat little legs thrashing at the air, trying to gain a grip to stop their falls. But their air-swimming does them no good, and Captain Jack smacks flat-backed onto the lawn. Fats Flannigan lands directly on top of him seconds later, smashing the wind, and a string of angry objections, out of Captain Jack, who then jumps to his four feet and shakes off the abrupt collision with the ground. Fats Flannigan sits up, then stands briefly on his back legs, as if saying to his friend, *four legs good, two legs better,* and awkwardly struts in circles, looking up toward Greg's lounge, hissing and complaining.

Jim throws the broom out of the window and it smacks onto the ground right beside Fats Flannigan. And Fats scrambles for safety, knocking over Captain Jack. The coons dive into the shrubbery along the back of the yard and beam their intense eyes toward the open window of Greg's lounge.

First Greg climbs through the window and descends the ladder nailed to the side of the enormous house, followed by Jim and then Kelsey. Greg wonders why Wally has never spotted the various ladders affixed to the sides of the house and figures that it's probably just the way the house works.

Once on the ground, Kelsey pecks Greg on the cheek with a kiss and says, "See you tomorrow. I've gotta get out of here. My dad's seriously gonna whip me if I'm not home for dinner."

Greg pushes up his glasses and smiles. "See ya."

"What about me?" asks Jim. "Don't you have any sugar for me?"

"Not in a million years," laughs Kelsey.

"Alright," says Jim. "See you later, Creepy Kelsey."

She smiles, and without missing a beat, says, "See you later, masturbator."

"Aw, no," says Jim as he and Greg walk past Principal Skinner's office. "No. No. No."

"What?" asks Greg. And then he sees.

Leaned back against a locker, just past Mrs. Miller's classroom, Wade Busby wraps his arms around a skeletal girl with tall bleached blonde bangs that defy gravity and curve up five inches off the front of her head. One arm pulls her in close to his body while his other hand drops down and grips tightly to her Jordache-encased ass cheeks. The girl tilts her head to the side and Wade attaches his lips to her neck like a plecostomus cleaning the side of a fish tank. Her dead eyes look right through Jim. She snaps her gum and looks bored as Wade openly gropes her in a wanton public display of affection.

"Lori," says Jim as his pace slows. And he says to no one in particular, "No, not him."

"Come on," Greg grabs Jim, dragging him past Wade and Lori as quickly as possible.

Wade doesn't see them because he is too busy dry humping Lori and giving her a hickey that will get her grounded for two weeks.

Greg pulls Jim down the hall and around the corner, into the stairway, just before Wade breaks the suction on Lori's neck and starts to scan the halls. Like a predator on the hunt, his eyes narrow, and he lifts his nose to the air, huffing the lingering fumes of Greg's fear. Wade puts his hands on Lori's hips and pushes her back from him. He takes off down the hallway and rounds the corner to the stairwell. And though the hallway reeks of cowardice, Greg and Jim have already ascended the stairs to the third floor and made their way into Mrs. Grenner's room for geometry class.

Every day it's a different path taken to Samsa Mansion. Like rats scurrying through a maze, Greg and Kelsey and Jim Halloway run Findlay's back alleys after school, ducking through back yards, hiding from voices, and dashing for the safety of Greg's lounge. Now Kelsey complicates the after school escape. Not that Greg minds it, but he does not want her to suffer the fallout of his problems with Wade. Earlier, during lunch, Chop cornered Greg and mentioned that Greg and Kelsey seemed to be a real hot item. He also passed along a message that Wade wanted to finger Kelsey.

So Greg worries now not just about himself, but also Kelsey. Wade already took Jim's girlfriend. *He's probably fingering her right now*, thinks Greg. And though Greg tells Kelsey about Wade, she laughs it off.

"Don't worry about me and Wade," says Kelsey. She smiles at Greg and squeezes his hand. "It's just not happening. Could you imagine a proper young lady like me with such a scurvy scurve? As if." And she gives Greg the usual peck on the cheek that makes him smile and blush.

And the three of them stop at the mouth of an alley, scanning the street for Wade and his gang. A commotion arises down the street, causing Greg, Kelsey, and Jim to duck back and hang at the side of a house. Curses, flung wildly into the air, bang off of each other in a cacophonous clatter. Greg pokes his head around the corner to see what is the matter.

A swirling cloud of teens rampages down the street, throwing apples plucked from Old Man Johnson's tree. And the apples bounce off of Crooked Neck's head and shoulders as he scrambles as best he can on his injured leg. His neck brace hangs open around a gnarled, kinked neck, and his head flops wildly, bouncing on his shoulder. He swings his cane behind him, clearing a tiny buffer zone between him and the rowdy teens.

The melee carries on past the alley and down the street until Crooked Neck trips and slams down on the pavement. The crowd of boys converges on him, tenderizing him with fists and feet, bestowing further contusions and fractures and lacerations, until a short stout boy with a puffy red afro and a look of glee on his face leaves a boot print on Johnny's forehead. And when their plaything goes limp and fails to respond to them, they leave the twisted, languid lump facedown in the middle of the street and walk away laughing, recounting their parts in the beating.

"God," says Greg, looking down the street in disgust. "There's something seriously wrong with this town. There's just a big black shit cloud hanging over us. There's something so wrong here." He shakes his head and looks far away from Johnny Close. And he sees not a looming shit storm, but a sky blanketed with grey clouds the color of cadaver skin.

"It's Old Crooked Neck," says Jim. "He deserves whatever happens to him. I heard he molested a baby."

"He's still a person," says Kelsey. "And I don't think that what those boys just did had anything to do with justice or revenge. Greg is right. There's something rotten around here."

"Yeah," says Greg. "It's like this town has a disease. I can feel it as a low hum, deep in my gut, a hum that tells me people want to hurt me. It's a slow, creeping thing that takes hold before people even realize it. And it's not just Wade or the Courtneys. I feel it from my own brother. I feel it from adults, even some of the teachers – like Coach Manlove. Sometimes he seems like he's trying to help me. But when we play dodge ball, he's trying to kill me. No doubt about it. It's like something takes over and he's out of control."

Jim Halloway says, "Well, whatever it is, we should get a move on. Those boys are gone, and we need to get out of here."

As they walk, they talk about the town and the creeping feeling of rot that has blanketed it. Kelsey half-cocks her head and laughs a strange little laugh. Her eyes go blank and her voice flat. To no one in particular, she says, "Who is to blame when a dog bites a child? What is it that makes him bite? Is the dog born bad? Or is it the playful taunts of the toddler himself that drives the dog to snap and lock his jaws on the child's flesh? Is it genetics? Did the gods or the devil make him that way? Or is it because his owner kicks him when he has a bad day? Maybe it's generation after generation of inbreeding to create a perfect dog that actually makes him bad. Or, is it malnutrition? Are the chemicals off in his brain? Did he suffer head trauma or maybe run a fever that fried his wiring? Does he want to be bad? Or has he no control over it? I don't know." She shakes her head and continues, "I don't know. But when a dog becomes too dangerous, nobody ever really worries about why, do they? We just put it down." Kelsey stops talking and just stares off at nothing for just a moment. Then she shakes her head and the light comes back into her eyes. She laughs nervously when she notices that the boys are staring at her and says, "What?"

Greg looks at Kelsey and his lips curl into a gentle smile. A semi-erection pulses in his pants. He stares at Kelsey. She is dressed in too-big overalls with holes worn in the knees and red high-top converse shoes. She wears a Sunday-go-to-meeting red hat with a big plastic purple flower tucked in the band, a hat that matches her hand-me-down red down vest, a hat that she bought for a dollar at a garage sale. The hat pushes down her tangled, curly hair, which is tucked back behind her ears. And to Greg, she is the prettiest girl in his school.

Greg says to Kelsey, "I'm blown away by your mind sometimes. I like the way you talk."

"I like the way you talk, too," says Kelsey.

"What's all this malarkey about dogs?" says Jim Halloway, and he spits through the gap in his front teeth. "I thought we were talking about people being assholes."

They creep the alleys on a meandering, watchful walk until they arrive at Greg's house. On the front porch, at the top of the stairs, stands a towering, mildly retarded boy named Jerry. Jerry stands, vigorously rocking back and forth on his feet. He grips tightly to a broomstick horse with one hand and waves his other hand at cars and people and stray dogs as they pass on the street. His chocolate brown cowboy hat sits tipped back on a head that looks to be the size of a bear's. A tin star that says *Sheriff* is pinned to his suede vest. The spurs on his cowboy boots jingle-jangle as he rocks back and forth, pretending to ride his horse. A loose hand-tooled leather belt hangs at his hip, and the holsters hold two weighty Colt 45 replica starter pistols. And though his given name is Jerry, everybody in town knows him as Hopalong.

Greg sees Hopalong on his porch and immediately leads his friends through the next-door neighbor's yard and around back. Greg actually likes Hopalong and sometimes stops to talk to him when he sees him standing on the corner of Hardin and South Main Street, in front of Wilson's Sandwich Shop. Hopalong is often in front of Wilson's, waving at traffic and talking to anybody who will engage him. He talks about the numbers in the Findlay phone book (which he has memorized in its entirety) and recites, verbatim, the weather forecast from the morning news. Sometimes Greg buys a malt for Hopalong to enjoy as he stands on the corner. But, Greg doesn't want to talk to Hopalong today. It's nothing personal. It's just that Hopalong's little brother, Eddie, is at the other end of the porch, hanging out with Wally and Lumpy.

Wally and Lumpy and Eddie slump and scoff and smoke Blue Llama cigarettes. They blow the smoke through their nostrils, puff out smoke rings, and pass around a bottle of crème de menthe that Lumpy filched from his grandma's liquor cabinet. The cloud of tobacco smoke hangs about their heads like a thick blue fog unmoved by the day's cool breeze. While they joke and smoke and try to look cool, Hopalong looks toward the neighbor's yard and waves to Greg and Jim and Kelsey.

Wally points over at Hopalong and laughs a condescending chuckle. "Look at him. What are you waving at, Jughead? Ain't nothin' over there." And Lumpy and Eddie join Wally in laughing at Hopalong.

"Kids," says Hopalong, smiling an almost beatific smile with a mouth of chipped teeth that look as if they have chewed a good deal of gravel. "I's just wavin' at kids."

At the rear of the house Kelsey jumps back and gasps at finding Li'l Shirl flat on her back in the grass, eyes wide open and not blinking, with not a muscle moving. Captain Jack and Fats Flannigan stand between Li'l Shirl and Kelsey. The coons rear up on their hind legs, hissing and spitting.

"Oh my gawd," says Kelsey, her voice ratcheting up to a panicked pitch. She steps back from the raccoons. "We've gotta do something. Is she even still alive?"

Greg puts his hands on Kelsey's shoulders from behind. He leans in and says calmly, "She's just fine. She lays out in the back yard and stares at clouds. She tries to derive some message from the way they look and move. The coons don't hurt her. It's like they sense that her brain is about the same size as theirs, like she's on their level, or maybe even below. Whatever. They like her."

And the clouds swirl and whip about in a roiling mess of dark condensation above Findlay. They cast a chill over the entire village and hint at snow. Kelsey shivers at the cold. But Li'l Shirl remains completely still, wrapped in a polka dot housedress entirely insufficient for the weather, oblivious to the drop in temperature.

"We should get her inside," says Kelsey. "She'll get sick if we leave her out here."

"She won't come until she's ready," says Greg. "She does this all the time."

"Yeah," agrees Jim. "The only way we'll get her inside right now is if we carry her. And that ain't happening." He kicks a dirt clod at the raccoons and they rear back and hiss at him. Jim hisses back. "Besides, those dirty beasts aren't going to let us close to her."

Kelsey tries to shoo away Captain Jack and Fats Flannigan. She jumps at them and fans her hands, trying to scare them off. The coons stand their ground, not angry or irritated with Kelsey, but not budging either. Kelsey tries to get closer to Li'l Shirl and Captain Jack warns her off with a low, guttural snarl that says *I don't want to hurt you, but I'm quite serious about protecting this tubby girl on the ground.*

Taking several steps back, Kelsey pulls off her down ski vest. She shushes Captain Jack, and he eases off of the warning snarl. Kelsey throws the vest and it flies over the raccoons, landing on Li'l Shirl's substantial midsection. Li'l Shirl does not flinch. She does not look down to the vest on her belly. She merely directs her vacant gaze toward the clouds above. "There," says Kelsey, "at least she has something to keep her warm." And Kelsey turns and walks toward the back door of Greg's house, saying, "I want to go down to the basement and check on my little piggies."

Greg shrugs a *why not* kind of gesture at Jim, who shrugs back, and they turn to follow Kelsey into the back of the house. As they walk away, Fats Flannigan snatches Kelsey's vest from Li'l Shirl's belly and darts into the bushes with it.

Li'l Shirl sits up as Greg, Jim, and Kelsey walk away and enter the house. Li'l Shirl shouts out at them. "Storm's a coming. A big fat storm."

"You guys go on and play your Atari," says Kelsey. "I need to check on my little piggies. Make sure their accommodations are suitable."

"Alright," says Greg as he watches her descend into the basement and blend in with the darkness. "Just be quiet when you're coming upstairs so that you don't run into Wally."

So Greg and Jim climb the stairs from the kitchen. When they reach the second floor, Jim turns toward Greg and says, "I saw the way you were watching ole' Creepy Kelsey. You've got it bad for her, huh?"

Greg shrugs his shoulders. "She's pretty cool."

"Well," says Jim, "have you guys done it yet?"

"No. It's not like that."

"What? You don't wanna?" Jim smiles. "I always knew that we were going to have to deal with this eventually. And it's okay with me that you're into guys. Matter of fact, I think I can set you up with Larry Llamas as a date for the next dance."

Laughing, Greg punches Jim in the arm and says, "Screw you. I like girls. You take Larry Llamas to the dance. He's more your type."

"Well if you're not into guys' balls 'n buttholes, then what's the problem? You're blown away by Kelsey and she's into you. You could nail that easily."

"I'm fourteen and I just started getting pubes," says Greg. "I'm not ready to nail anything. She could get pregnant or something."

"Just use the bathroom at the Bonded gas station and buy some rubbers from the vending machine. That's what I did when I was with Lori."

"I'm not ready. And I don't think Kelsey is either. Thanks for the advice, but we're just fine."

"Well have you at least felt up her titties?"

"What?" Greg says. "Do you have to be such a pig?"

"I'm sorry," says Jim. "I forgot that you're the sensitive type. What I meant to say was have you squeezed her sweater meat?"

A subtle smile cracks Greg's face but he says nothing. He starts to walk down the hall toward the room where he has been staying – a room that he doesn't consider his bedroom, but also one that will do until the house reveals a proper place for him.

Jim follows Greg and says, "I saw that little smile. You did, you masher. How was it?"

"It was nice," says Greg. "But she had a bra on so I just felt them through that."

"My boy, my boy. You have a lot to learn." Jim puts his arm up around Greg's shoulder. "You just slip you hand up under the cup and push it right off of there. Then you've got the direct flesh contact."

"Really?" says Greg.

"Yeah, really. And when you're ready to go farther with her, you let me know and I'll give you all the tips you need. I perfected this stuff on Lori."

"Whatever. Like you're a man of the world or something. I wouldn't ask your advice on girls if...."

Greg stops in front of an open doorway and stares in, his mouth agape. A swarm of raccoons scamper about the room, wrestling with each other and ripping insulation from a hole they chewed in the wall. Several raccoons tear into bags of bread left there by Li'l Shirl earlier in the day. Other coons shred Greg's makeshift bedding. Piles of scat litter the floor. And once again the raccoons act with impunity, expecting no consequences other than the awkward, frustrated cries of the frail, oily haired human standing at the door.

Running into the room, arms flailing above his head, Greg cries out, "Gaaaahhhh!" He tries to kick at the interloping animals. The coons scatter and scramble for the hole they tore in the wall. Greg's feet slip on a pile of scat and his legs fly out from under him. His head and torso jerk backwards, refusing to accompany the legs on their journey. And the wooden floor meets the crown of his head, making a knocking sound like a gavel on a desk. His glasses fly off. A grey film coalesces before his eyes. His awareness collapses in on itself, gaining density and crushing all of Greg's thoughts and emotions and neural impulses into a tiny, dense, black ball that refuses to allow brainwaves or thoughts or light to escape. And the black ball implodes into such a dense pinpoint of energy that it is all that remains in Greg's head. He is aware of nothing but the pulsing compact ball of blackness at the very center of his skull, consuming every thought and sensation.

And then the pinpoint of dark energy contracts to the point where it cannot contain itself and explodes outward with violent intensity, sending potent waves of psychic energy rippling throughout the void of his skull. The explosion expands at an exponential pace and magnitude, until it reaches the contours of the interior of Greg's brain. And the matter from the explosion swirls and burns, and as it cools it coalesces into thoughts and emotions and words. The energy bounces back off of the skull barrier and seeks release, eventually finding it at the point of Greg's eye sockets. His eyelids fly open and he is awake and aware. The throbbing of his head and the sticky sensation of drying blood on the back of his neck reach him.

Just above his face, Greg sees two dewy, slightly out of synch, beautiful brown eyes boring into him. Kelsey's hands cup his face. Her lips kiss his forehead and to Greg it is as if she consumes his pain. He struggles to sit up and Jim steadies him from behind.

"What the hell?" says Greg. He looks around at the disarray of his temporary room. The air seems to flutter briefly and Greg feels the floor rocking as if on a boat. He puts his hands down and locks his elbows to prop himself up. Duffel bags and backpacks full of fetal pigs are piled up just outside the door of his room.

"You slipped on a turd and had a great fall, Humpty," explains Jim. "Knocked your big old egghead pretty good. I hope you didn't crack it."

Greg's vision blacks out briefly, and then everything comes back into view, at first hazy and shimmering, eventually coming back into focus. The pain throbs at the base of his skull, but otherwise his head is okay and his thinking clear. "Damn coons," says Greg, rising to his feet. He looks around again and shakes his head. "Let's go to the lounge. I guess maybe it is going to be my new room."

Jim and Kelsey help to steady Greg as he begins to walk, but he shrugs them off. "I'm okay now," he says. Walking out of the doorway into the hall he steps over the duffel bags and backpacks, and asks, "What's with the pigs?"

Kelsey smiles a lopsided smile. "They were lonely in the basement. That's no place for piggies. They want to stay with you. They love Greggy Weggy." She pulls a bagged pig out, wiggles it in Greg's face, and snort-laughs until a coughing fit snuffs out her porcine lunacy.

"Okay," says Greg. "You're a total lunatic. But, okay. Let's bring 'em along."

In addition to a photographic memory for phone numbers and weather forecasts, Hopalong Haskell has a knack for mashing buttons and getting results. And while Greg lays unconscious amongst scatterings of raccoon feces, Wally, Lumpy, and Eddie bring Hopalong into the house with them. And they all hang about in the room where they previously heard Greg's blues records and the bleeps and bloops of the Atari system seeping through the walls. Wally pulls leather bound antique books from the shelves, dropping them to the ground without a thought about their contents or value. He seeks something within the bookshelf, some sort of switch or handle or lever to access the room on the other side of the wall. Wally also knows that the house hides secret passages and rooms. And he knows that this one must be special if Greg is hiding it from him. Eddie knocks on the walls, not knowing how to interpret the hollow echoes that answer. Lumpy just stares at the ceiling, then the floor, then the ceiling again, trying to work a thought through his mind and finding it more of a challenge than he is up to.

Meanwhile, Hopalong stands beside the bookcase, alternately pushing the on and off buttons of the light switch rapidly while mumbling the weather forecast. "Thank you, Suchee. We have a big early-winter storm heading our way. A powerful system of Arctic air is coming out of the central plains and grabbing moisture from the Gulf of Mexico as it marches toward the east coast. The monster storm is bringing freezing temperatures and lots of snow. Tonight the temperatures will be dropping into the low twenties, with a good chance of snow up to twelve inches. This is going to be a heavy storm and the roads will be icing over. Put the chains on those tires and make sure to bundle up. Now back to you, Suchee Punani."

Wally throws a book at Eddie and says, "Will you shut him the fuck up? I heard the exact same weather forecast on TV this morning. And I've heard Hopalong repeat that shit five hundred fucking times."

Eddie cringes away from Wally and says, "He can't help it, dude. His head's all full of mush."

"Yeah," says Wally, taking a few steps back from Hopalong. "He's a big dumb retard, alright. But he's driving me nucking futs. If he keeps it up, I'm gonna say *the word*."

"Yeah," says Lumpy with a devious grin. "Say the word."

"You shut the hell up," says Eddie. "Do not say the word."

All of the arguing makes Hopalong nervous. He rocks back and forth, his palms on the butts of his starter pistols, and launches into his mantra to calm himself. "Thank you, Suchee. We have a big early-winter storm heading our way...."

"Shut up," yells Wally, and he backs away from Hopalong a few more steps. "I'm gonna say the word."

"...A powerful system of Arctic air is coming out of the central plains and grabbing moisture from the Gulf of Mexico as it marches toward the east coast...."

Eddie steps back from Hopalong, saying, "Don't do it, man."

Lumpy runs toward the room's one door, stands in the threshold, and goads, "Do it, Wally. Say the word."

"...The monster storm is bringing freezing temperatures and lots of snow. Tonight the temperatures will be dropping into the low twenties, with a good chance of snow up to twelve inches...."

"Hopalong," Wally shouts. "Shut the fuck up or I'm gonna say the word."

Sweat beads form on Hopalong's head and fly off of it each time he rocks forward. "Do not say that word!" His eyes flip back and forth, seeking an escape route, and his entire body starts to tremble. "I don't like that word. Do not say that word."

"I'm gonna say it," says Wally as he, too, heads toward the door, ready to knock Lumpy down, jump over him, and flee for his life. "I'm gonna say that word."

"Do not say that word!" Hopalong jumps up and down as he shouts his plea at Wally. "Do not say it."

"Vaaa...."

"Do not say that word." Hopalong begins to pace back and forth.

"...cuuummm...."

"Do not say it," pleads Hopalong. "Do not say that word."

"K-k-k-k-k-leeeeeee...." Wally stretches out the first syllable for what feels like minutes.

Tears streak down Hopalong's face and he involuntarily releases a staccato series of wet, nervous farts. "Do not say that word!"

Wally breaks the word *cleaner* off, mid-word, erupts in laughter and slaps his knees with his hands. Tears flow from his eyes, but not terrified tears like Hopalong's. Wally's are from laughing too hard, from being filled with such enjoyment at Hopalong's expense. "Aw, come on now, Hopalong. You didn't think I was really gonna say the word, did you?"

Hopalong's rocking slows to a calm, steady rhythm and his hands fall from the butts of his starter pistols. "I do not like that word. Do not say that word."

"It's alright, buddy," Wally says. "I wouldn't say the word. I don't want to get you upset or anything."

Eddie steps out of arms' reach of Wally and says, "You're an asshole, you know? You say that word and you know what happens, don't you?"

"Yeah," says Wally. "Full on retard-strength mongoloid-rage."

"Yeah," says Eddie. "But you don't have to put it that way. It's not cool. If you set him off, somebody will get seriously hurt."

"Alright. Alright." Wally laughs again. "I was just playing around. Didn't mean no harm, Hopalong. I was just playing. Are we good, big guy?"

Hopalong nods his head and stutters. "I-I-I-I'm okay." He rocks back and forth slowly. "Just do not say that word."

"Yeah. I won't say it," says Wally. He walks over and pats Hopalong on the shoulder. "Let's just forget about my little joke and keep looking for how to get into that room. I don't know what my brother has in there, but whatever it is, it will be mine."

Hopalong rocks back and forth and returns to his soothing mantra, "Thank you, Suchee. We have a big early-winter storm heading our way. A powerful system of Arctic air...." And the rhythmic recitation of the words calms him. His rocking slows. His fingers return to mashing the light switch buttons on the wall. "...is coming out of the central plains and grabbing moisture from the Gulf of Mexico as it marches toward the east coast...." And as he recites the weather forecast, Hopalong wraps himself in the cozy warmth of the chant. "...The monster storm is bringing freezing temperatures and lots of snow...." His fingers push the on button, then the off, slowly at first. "...Tonight the temperatures will be dropping into the low twenties, with a good chance of snow up to twelve inches...." His fingers clack the buttons faster and faster – on, off, on, off, on, off, on, off, onoffonoffonoffonoff. "...This is going to be a heavy storm and the roads will be icing over. Put the chains on those tires and make sure to bundle up...." Until finally the fingers go so fast that they press the on and off buttons at the same time, and the bookshelf slides back to reveal Greg's lounge. "...Now back to you, Suchee Punani."

The squishy thud of the pig-stuffed backpack smacking onto the floor goes unnoticed by those already in the lounge. Greg stands in the previously-hidden doorway, convulsing with rage, shifting back and forth from foot to foot. Oily hair hangs over his aviator glasses, gently swishing side to side like carwash curtains. He looks on at the chaos raging in his sanctuary. A Howlin' Wolf disc cuts through space and shatters on the wall just to Greg's left. Wally, Eddie, and Lumpy run about the room, cackling like madmen, ducking behind the furniture and flinging Greg's records at each other. A Blind Lemon Chitlin record zings into the side of Lumpy's face so hard that it bursts a taut whitehead and momentarily stuns him. The record player is overturned and smashed into pieces. Willie Dixon collides midair with Memphis Slim, and the brittle discs crack into one hundred black glittering shards that rain down onto the floor, their shattered remains somehow even sadder than the songs that were on the intact records. Clubfoot Jasper Moberly shatters against the wall. The Atari console is ripped from the TV and flung in a corner.

And the TV blares out crackling white-noise static. Cosmic microwave background radiation from the big bang crackles as the black, gray, and white static on the Zenith console television's screen and throws an oddly beautiful glow on the serene, smiling, walleyed face of Hopalong. As the boys in the lounge pelt each other with Greg's favorite things – his blues records and video game cartridges – Hopalong kneels in front of the TV and chants a new mantra, "By the pricking of my thumbs, something wicked this way comes. By the pricking of my thumbs, something wicked this way comes...." And though the records and game cartridges fly about and seem to strike every other surface in the room, they do not land in the small bubble surrounding Hopalong and the television. And as a penitent keeling before an altar, Hopalong is lost in his chanting, lost in the cosmic mysteries flickering before him on the television screen. "By the pricking of my thumbs, something wicked this way comes...."

Before Wally and his friends realize what is happening, Greg screams, "This is my lounge!" He rushes into the room, whanging a bagged fetal pig around in the air and smacks it square into Wally's face. A trickle of blood forms in both of Wally's nostrils and quickly turns into a gushing flow. The pig's plastic bag bursts and formaldehyde rains down on the wooden floor. Wally staggers back, slips on the formaldehyde, and trips over his own feet. The fetal pig slides out of the ripped bag and slops to the floor, right next to Wally. Next, Greg is on Eddie, kicking steel-toed boots at his legs. The surprise of it overwhelms Eddie at first and he runs around the room, swatting back at Greg as if he were an angry hornet dogging him. But Greg's surprise attack is no longer a surprise. Lumpy is ready, and when Greg rushes him, Lumpy ducks, weaves, and slips around Greg, grabbing him from behind and wrestling the much smaller boy to the ground. Eddie regains his feet and runs out of the lounge. He grabs Kelsey and drags her into the room.

Jim Halloway stands far enough out of the room, knowing he cannot overpower the older boys. He shouts names at them in an effort to divert their attention from Greg and Kelsey. Thoughts course through his brain faster than they can find their way out of his mouth, and all that he can say to try to draw the older boys' attention is garbled, vulgar nonsense. He shouts at Lumpy, "Hey, sausage-dick, why don't you come over here and I'll lance those purple boils on your face with a pitchfork."

Lumpy ignores Jim's taunts. He gets up, and from behind he loops his arms through Greg's, pulling them back. Wally gets to his feet and wipes blood and formaldehyde on his pants. He ambles slowly toward Greg and Lumpy, careful not to slip again on the wet floor. Wally's balled up fist thrusts into Greg's gut, dead center and just below his ribs. The air bursts out of Greg and leaves him gasping for its return.

Wally says, "There's a little present for you, ya shit-turd."

All the while, Hopalong sits, rocking back and forth in front of the television static and chanting, "By the pricking of my thumbs, something wicked this way comes...."

And Greg gasps for air, but finds it hard to inhale. The room tilts and his vision tunnels. He looks to his side and sees Kelsey with her arms twisted behind her, too, her big red hat knocked onto the floor. As Wally moseys over toward Kelsey, Greg struggles against Lumpy. But the bigger boy is heavier and stronger and having too much fun dominating Greg. And then, Wally buries his fist into Kelsey's stomach and laughs a hearty guffaw as she crumples to the floor with her hands held to her belly.

"Pick her up," says Wally to Eddie. And with his instinct for inflicting pain on his brother, Wally senses that beating up Kelsey hurts Greg far more than a punch in the gut. "I wanna give her another shot."

Greg struggles against Lumpy and tries to stomp down hard on his feet. But Lumpy does not relent. He holds tight to Greg, waiting for further orders from Wally.

And Eddie stands Kelsey up. She gasps for breath, then spits in Wally's face when she realizes that he is going to hit her again. The spit lands on Wally's forehead and drips down between his eyes. He doesn't even bother to wipe it away. He just laughs at Kelsey, and then socks her again in the gut. The blow knocks the wind out of her and she falls to the ground again with her hands held to her stomach.

Lacking the strength to break away from Lumpy, and knowing that Wally has no compunctions about beating on a girl, Greg does the only thing he can think of. He looks over toward Hopalong and sees him rocking back and forth before the television, chanting his mantra.

"…By the pricking of my thumbs, something wicked this way comes…."

And then Greg does it. He shouts *that* word. **"Vacuum cleaner!!!"**

The words are like a high-voltage, livewire on Hopalong's brain. They light a fire. Synapses explode. Wires cross. Circuits fry. A mad energy begins in his brain and rages throughout his body. Hopalong screams a ragged, cringe-inducing shriek like metal on metal. "Do not say that word!"

And though Greg would normally never want to induce such rage in Hopalong, he sees no other way to stop Wally from hurting Kelsey. He shouts, "Vacuum cleaner! Vacuum cleaner! Vacuum cleaner! Vacuum cleaner! Vacuum cleaner! Vacuum cleaner!"

The television plug does little to anchor the set against Hopalong's senseless fury. He deadlifts the entire console and hurls it across the room. He screams, "Do not say that word."

Wally turns away from Kelsey and stands frozen, eyes wide, feet rooted to the floor, staring at Hopalong. "Oh shit," he says, peeling his feet from the floor and starting for the door. But his sudden movement draws Hopalong's attention, and before Wally makes it to the door, Hopalong lowers his head and charges, driving him hard into the wall. Ribs crack and Wally bends painfully at a right angle. He struggles against Hopalong's hold, but is unable to match the strength of the addled cowboy. Hopalong effortlessly lifts Wally off of the ground and tosses him across the room.

Next, Hopalong charges Lumpy and nearly knocks his head off with a wicked crossface. Lumpy releases Greg and tries to scoot away from the raging maniac. But Hopalong is on him immediately, shouting, "Do not say that word," and battering him with enormous fists.

Amidst the chaos, Greg goes to Kelsey, hands her her hat, and helps her out of the room. All the while Hopalong rails against the use of the words *vacuum cleaner*, and tears apart anything and everything he can get his hands on, including Lumpy and Wally.

In the midst of the raging shit-storm, Eddie slips out and runs from the house, never once looking back to see if he can help his friends. Eddie stands in the front yard, staring at the house and waiting for his brother to wear himself out.

Once out of the room, Greg pushes both light switch buttons on the wall at the same time and the bookcase glides back in front of the doorway, blocking any exit for Wally and Lumpy. Greg and Kelsey find Jim waiting in the hallway. Through the walls, they can hear Hopalong raging, shouting, "Do not say that word!" Muted clangs and clatters and pained yelps ring out from the other side of the bookcase.

Greg tells Jim and Kelsey to follow him. As they scamper through the halls, the sounds of Hopalong's rage recedes to a muted ruckus, and then silence. And the halls and walls all seem to be different and new. Greg feels the floor rumble and shift beneath his feet.

"What was that?" asks Kelsey as she stops and braces herself against the wall. "Was that an earthquake?"

"Nah," says Jim Halloway. "They're probably blasting over at the quarry again. Every time they do, you can feel the ground tremble."

"Nope," says Greg. "The house is shifting. It gives and it takes away. It takes away and it gives. Since it took away my lounge, it's shifting and I'll find a new room for myself. That's the way this place works."

Kelsey laughs and punches Greg in the arm. "You're so weird sometimes."

"Yeah," agrees Jim. "And that's a compliment coming from her."

"Seriously," says Greg. "I've lived here all of my life. And it's like this house has a mind of its own. It will reveal something new to me."

The hallways twist and turn. And the threesome climbs narrow sets of stairs up and down and around, never returning to a spot that they already passed.

"How big is this place?" asks Kelsey. "It's unreal how much we have run around these hallways. It's like one of those cartoons where they go into a tiny tent and the inside is enormous."

"It's big," says Greg. "Really big. Now be quiet and follow me up these stairs. I've got a feeling."

The steep, narrow stairs terminate at the ceiling. On the ceiling is a standard wooden door placed parallel to the floor. They climb the stairs and Jim reaches up, tries to push the door open. But it does not budge. Kelsey twists the doorknob and pushes up, but the door resists her efforts, too.

"Step aside," says Greg, brushing his oily bangs back off of his glasses. He reaches up, raps on the door. A hollow tapping echoes above the ceiling, telling them that it is not one of the many dummy doors in the house, doors that do not open, doors that lead to nowhere. Greg turns the knob and the latch gives. He pushes upward hard, throwing the door open to reveal the mansion's attic. One anemic ray of sunlight, the last of the day, pierces a dormer window and illuminates the swirling dust cloud stirred up by opening the door. The flakes of dust dance and swirl and sprinkle the teenagers on the stairs. And for some reason, those tiny glittering bits give the doorway in the ceiling an almost mystical aura.

Greg climbs the rest of the stairs and steps through the doorway. The dust particles turn gold in the day's waning light and flitter about like tiny aureate fairies. As his eyes adjust to the dim attic, Greg scans the enormous room and sees old sheets thrown over everything. And the sheet-covered piles take up much of the space, leaving narrow pathways much like the crisscrossing tunnels of a rabbit warren. Kelsey and Jim follow right behind, up and into the attic.

"Whoa," says Kelsey. "Can you feel that?"

Jim exhales deeply and says, "Yeah. What the hell?"

"It's my new room," says Greg. His upper lip twitches briefly before settling on a subtle, satisfied smile. "The house is giving me a present. And this is going to stay mine. I can feel it."

The daylight fizzles to nothing outside. Gusts of wind, thick with fat snowflakes, beat against the outside of the mansion. The breeze blows through rotted holes in places on the house, making a low, sad whine that resonates throughout the residence. Kelsey finds an old Tiffany lamp in a corner and flips it on, bathing the room in a muted, kaleidoscopic glow. On the floor, beside the lamp, sits a hatbox. Kelsey lifts the lid and pulls out a battered old top hat. She switches it out with her red hat and tilts it to the side slightly. Greg and Jim shuffle around, pulling sheets off of furniture and opening boxes and crates.

"Look at this," says Jim, pulling the cover off of a large pile of equipment, goods, and gear. He holds a fuzzy green object up and whistles with appreciation. "It's a moss-covered, three-handled, family gredunza."

"And what the heck is this?" asks Kelsey. She holds up a badly taxidermied, green-tinted dog with a crown on its head.

"That's a green manalishi with a two-pronged crown," says Jim with wonder in his voice.

"Whoa," says Greg from across the room. He holds up an old microphone. "And check this out. It's a Telefunken U-47."

"With leather?" asks Jim.

"With leather," says Greg.

"Never mind that stuff," says Kelsey, and she holds a jar up to the Tiffany lamp. "What the heck is this? It's wonderful."

The lamp lights up the fluid in the jar, giving it a bluish tint. Floating there, almost looking like it is swimming, is a tiny, malformed, human fetus. Pea-sized organic bits swirl around it in the fluid. Kelsey puts down her bag of fetal pigs and digs through the box labeled *PIKKLED PUNKS*. Jim grabs a jar and swirls it before his face. A yellowed subject with flappers for arms, fused legs, and an undeniably human face rides the vortex around the edges of the jar, a look of glee on its face as it surfs the swirl.

And there are boxes and boxes of the pikkled punks. Some of the babies float at the top of the preservative fluids, malformed and twisted. Others settle at the bottom, their bodies preserved but warped, looking as if they are melting into fleshy blobs at the bottom of their containers. Kelsey removes a box from the top of a stack and opens the box beneath it to find more pikkled punks. She picks up a jar and the lid is loose. The fluid has evaporated down to the halfway level of the jar. A fat fetus sits cross-legged, with tiny hands on tiny knees. From mid-chest and up the body has shriveled for lack of preservative. The head is shrunken out of proportion to the rest of the body and the face twists up in a mummified look of disdain. Jim and Greg pull other jars out of the boxes and marvel at the variety of deformations and genetic mutations. Many of the jars have evaporated at least partially and some completely, leaving the inhabitants shrunken and contorted, some of them thin and wrinkled and darkened, crumbling like overcooked pieces of bacon.

"I love them," Kelsey squeals. She unloads larger jars containing bigger fetuses. Holding a container in front of her face, she beams at a scrawny, bug-eyed baby and says, "I'm gonna name you Greg, after your daddy."

"Shut the hell up," says Greg, laughing. He swats at her top hat, knocking it off.

"Seriously," says Kelsey, replacing the hat to smash down her tangled mop of hair. "He actually does kind of look like you."

And it is true. With its malnourished body curled up in a defensive pose, wire-thin arms wrapped protectively around tiny legs, and oversized, top-heavy head, the fetus bears a curious resemblance to Greg. Wide-open eyes goggle out and it's as if Greg stares back into a warped carnival mirror that accentuates his alien-like features.

Greg grabs the jar and holds it up. The physical similarities feel like more than just a coincidence. And, despite Kelsey's good-humored ribbing, Greg feels like there is more of a connection with the fetus than just a passing similarity. He feels an affinity with the fetus. He feels a kinship. He walks away, gazing into the jar, and settles down in a corner, staring into the baby's eyes.

"Greg," says Kelsey, "I was just kidding. I didn't mean to hurt your feelings." And she starts toward him.

"Leave him alone," says Jim, grabbing from behind at a strap on Kelsey's overalls. "You didn't do nothing to him. He just needs time when he gets all serious like that."

So while Greg cradles the pikkled punk in his arms and stares into its eyes, Jim and Kelsey unload the rest of the fetuses from their boxes, tightening any loose lids and setting their favorites at the front of the bunch. And when they are done, they turn to go.

"I'll see you later," says Kelsey, hopefully, to Greg.

But Greg does not respond. And he does not say goodbye to Jim as he leads Kelsey through the door and down into the hallways of the mansion. Greg does not hear them. He does not see them. He feels warmth from the jar cradled in his arms. He feels a low, calming thrum emitted from the jar. He closes his eyes and feels himself floating, as if in a jar of warm, soothing liquid himself.

PART TWO

1

Outside is whiteness. Bright, blinding, stunning and numbing whiteness. The snow bleaches the city, leaches its color, obscures objects. Plows shove the packed snow to the sides of the road in an act of futility, clearing the streets briefly, only to make more room for the relentless blizzard onslaught. Drifts pile up to houses' eaves. Wind whips and blows and drowns out the engine roars of snowmobiles and four-by-fours. Not since the blizzard of '78 has such a gnarly winter storm visited the town. And no one braves the storm unless they have to. Even though the electricity is out, the people still have fireplaces to huddle by and most everybody is stocked up on sufficient stores of food. And for the elderly and infirm, the do-gooders are out in their winter vehicles, visiting the needy.

Through the bright, white swirls, a dark dot, barely discernible, bops down Evergreen Terrace. The Big Bopper – clad in oversized moon boots and a blue parka with a tan, fur trim about the edges of the hood – bops through the snow, staying atop the drifts as if wearing snowshoes. The bob-bob-bobbing of his head rhythmically thrusts his pointy face out from the fringed hood. Shaded ski goggles shield his eyes, and puffy red mittens warm his hands. But it is as if the cold gives him no offense. He does not grimace at the snow and wind. He does not shiver or shrink from the storm. The cord from his headphones is frozen stiff to his parka. His grimy hair is frozen to his head.

The Big Bopper don't care about the cold. He don't feel it. He bops on through the winter wonderland and pauses in front of 42 Evergreen Terrace. He stares up toward the attic's dormer windows, but can barely make out the top of the house through the raging snowstorm. He bops his head and snaps his fingers within the mittens. In the attic, Greg sits in the middle of the room, a manic glint in his eyes, opening boxes and crates and trunks. He studies jars filled with powders and potions. He marvels at old canvas freak show banners depicting hideous human malformations and aberrations. He discovers a coffin filled with fine brown dirt. All the while, the pikkled punks float in their jars and look on with their dead, milky eyes. Caressing and studying the relics, Greg feels a strength and a restrained energy, while at the same time peaceful satisfaction fills him. The Bopper feels that pulsing power, and the peacefulness, too. He bops his head and snaps his fingers and then moves on again.

And he bops through the city, past Kelsey's house, as she holds a snowball to her eye where her father socked her one for trying to intervene in the beating he was giving her mother. He stops briefly. A tear leaks from his eye. The Bopper don't care about tears. But he sure don't like the way Kelsey's house makes him feel sad and slow.

The Bopper bops past Wade Busby's house. Inside, the Widow Busby sleeps the drunken slumber of an over-soused wino on the couch. Wade looks at his mother with disgust, and then finishes off her bottle of MD 20/20 strawberry wine. The Bopper don't stop, he just bops. He don't like the feeling around the Busby's home either.

He bops past Jim Halloway's house, where Jim's mother plays a game of Sorry with him in front of the fireplace. Jim stuffs cheese doodles into his mouth and laughs every time he bumps his mother's piece back to the start of the board. "Sorry, Mom," says Jim through a mouthful of masticated cheese doodles, not sounding the least bit remorseful. The Big Bopper pauses, just briefly, and tastes a faint ghost flavor of artificial cheese. And the Bopper feels sadness because he senses danger surrounding Jim Halloway. But the Bopper can't do a thing about it. His place is not to intervene. Even if he did try to explain it, people would blow it off as crazy talk from the dirty walkin' man. So he smiles at the warm pulsing energy blowing off of the house and being picked up by his frozen headphones' cord. The power flowing through the cord thaws it and frees it from the parka. And then the Big Bopper is sparked back into movement by the thudding, looping beat oozing from his headphones. It's not for him to question the beat that drives his feet. He goes with the flow and bops face first into the icy wind, not minding the weather a bit as he checks on the city.

2

And the snow falls and falls and falls on the village. Snowdrifts fifteen feet high block the doors and windows of houses. Power lines accumulate ice until the weight of it snaps the lines and drags them, spewing surges of spark and flame, to the ground. Water pipes burst in houses where the occupants forgot to shut down the supply. Phone lines, dead. School, cancelled. The forgotten elderly expire, scared and lonely in tiny, frigid apartments and trailers, their old bones nestled in afghans and quilts on worn recliners. Businesses, vacant. Roads and interstate highways and turnpikes across the entire state, closed. The heavy white blanket of snow suffocates the state, freezes people in their cars and homes. Sub-zero windchill temperatures assail those heroic enough, stupid enough, or both, to leave shelter and brave the weather.

Greg considers himself neither brave nor heroic. He misses Jim and Kelsey and wishes they could have just stayed at his house to ride the blizzard out. But even without his friends, Greg relishes the opportunity to hide out and discover the mysteries of the attic. For now, things are safe. Wally is downstairs in bed with Big Shirl, nursing his snapped ribs, cracked tailbone, and popped eye. And when Greg does venture down, he heats up bowls of Chunky soup on the gas stove and takes them out to Big Shirl, Li'l Shirl, and even Wally (who calls him a shit-turd and says he'll beat Greg's ass when he recovers). Other than his brief forays into the kitchen and to check on Big Shirl, Greg hides out in the attic, safe in the assumption that Wally will not find his new room for the time being.

And with the water shut off, Greg pisses in mason jars from the attic. At the bottom of each jar is a quarter inch layer of white powder. Greg does not empty the powder before filling the jars. He just lets loose and watches as his urine foams up in reaction to the powder. He caps the jars and sets them in a row on the windowsill. And the white glare from the outside shoots through the amber liquid and focuses into a brilliant ball of light at the center of each jar. Sometimes Greg shakes the jars and watches as the powder floats around in the golden fluid like some strange snow globe, mimicking the snowstorm whipping about outside the window. For whatever reason, the tickle at his bladder becomes more frequent and intense. One corner of the attic is stacked with boxes upon boxes of the mason jars. And as the urge takes over, Greg pisses in the jars every quarter hour and sets them by the window, stacking them in rows until the jars completely block the window and filter the incoming light like a golden stained-glass window.

The storm rages outside for seven days and nights. Time passes and Greg finds himself soundly acclimated to the solitude of his attic lair. And as the piss-jars soak up the glare from outside, the powder flakes grow into minuscule, swimming creatures. Greg sits and stares at the tiny creatures in the jars for hours. He studies their tiny flagellating bodies and thinks of the seriously disappointing sea monkeys kit he purchased through the Johnson Smith catalogue when he was in third grade. With the sea monkeys, Greg expected aquatic humanoids with smiling little faces to build a miniature kingdom within the tiny fishbowl, just as they had on the front of their packaging. But it turned out that sea monkeys were just brine shrimp. They did not build little castles in their bowl. They did not lounge about with the women wearing bows in their hair and holding sea monkey babies. They just kind of swam around and then died after a couple of weeks.

But the creatures in the piss-jars – the non-sea monkeys, the piss-monkeys – are different. They fascinate Greg. And they grow quickly. In one jar, a tadpole-like creature has developed. And it darts about in the urine, swallowing the tinier, flagellating, white creatures. Ravenous tadpoles develop in the other jars and feed upon the piss-monkeys. When he is not filling another jar or venturing onto the first floor of the house, Greg sits in front of the jars, bathed in the golden glow of sunlight through piss, talking to the piss-monkeys. And when he does talk, the quickly growing tadpoles swim to the side of the jars and waggle there in front of Greg, as if taking in his words and seriously considering his opinions.

And then, after seven days of intense, blinding, blizzard conditions, the storm stops. Plows push the snow to the sides of the streets. Trucks dump salt on the roads. Crews work to repair the electric and phone lines. Slowly and surely the city awakens from its forced hibernation, stretches its arms and legs, and trudges back to the daily grind of work and school and life as usual.

"So are they okay, the unmentionables?" Kelsey brings her face in, inches from Greg's. They stand in the middle of the hallway in between classes, and the traffic of students flows around them as a stream around a boulder. "Tell me they're okay."

Greg notices a fading bruise on Kelsey's eye. It pains him, but he knows it's not time to talk about it. He swallows his feelings for the time being and decides to make a joke of things. "I hate to tell you this," says Greg. He watches as Kelsey's face twitches in spasms of profound concern. And he feels bad for baiting her. But she is too cute to Greg, and he lets her squirm for just one moment more so that he can take in and appreciate her full range of facial expressions. "But...."

"But what?" she grabs his Space Invaders shirt, shakes him, and pulls him in closer. "But what?"

Greg starts to laugh, causing Kelsey to shake him harder. He leans in closer and whispers in her ear, "But they're dead They're a bunch of dead pigs. How can it get worse for them?"

Kelsey half-playfully pushes Greg backwards and against a locker, not letting go of his shirt. She moves in close to his face and says, "Tell me they are okay."

"They are as okay as dead pigs can be," says Greg, still taunting a little in the hopes that Kelsey will stay close and chastise him more. "There's a coffin filled with dirt in the attic. I buried them in it so that if Wally does find my room, he at least might not find the pigs. If he opens the coffin, all he'll see is dirt."

Kelsey moves in close, feigning menace, and quickly plants a kiss right on the end of Greg's nose. "You're the best," she says, and then flips around and walks off to class without another word.

His back still to the locker, Greg grins and watches Kelsey walk away. To Greg, she is the prettiest girl in the school. He cannot imagine another girl making a long, purple, polka dot dress, down vest, and clunky snow boots look so good.

And as Greg's vision of beauty flits away down the hall, she is obscured by the alcohol-and-tobacco-stinking, red-eyed, yellow-toothed face of Wade Busby. Wade pokes his finger at Greg's chest and sneers, "I been looking forward to seein' you, E.T." After one week of being cooped up with his incoherently drunk mother, and after drinking a good portion of her fortified wine over the course of the blizzard, Wade is still half-drunk, half hung-over, and fully disagreeable. "I'm tired of looking for you after school. I'm gonna get you here, when no one's looking."

Wade quickly fakes a punch at Greg's face, stopping just before it hits. Greg flinches back and knocks his head against the locker. Coughing up a mean laugh, Wade says, "Keep an eye out. You never know when it's coming."

Just then, Vice Principal Blight walks up on the situation. His mustache twitches. His eyes narrow. "Everything okay here boys? Everybody getting along?"

"Oh yeah, Mr. Blight," says Wade. "We're just playing around, right E.T?"

"Yeah," mumbles Greg. "Just goofing around, Mr. Blight."

"Okey-dokey," says Mr. Blight, and his mustache twitches like a cat that's just been sprinkled with water. "Well, you boys cut the horseplay and get to class." He stands there akimbo and waits for Greg and Wade to get moving. The moment they do, Mr. Blight turns heel and walks to his office with his hands buried deep in his pockets.

Once Mr. Blight is out of sight, Wade shoulder-checks Greg into the lockers, knocking him to the ground. As Greg stands back up, Wade leans in and says, "I'm gonna get you today. Just wait until Blight's not around and I'm gonna pound you."

Greg stands and waits to see if Wade is going to do anything else. But Wade sees several teachers rounding the corner and decides to leave things alone for now. As he turns and heads toward class, Wade says, "And tell your little bitch friend, Halloway, that I'm gonna get him, too."

The last bell of the day chimes, and Greg dashes off to the boys' room on the second floor, just across from the principal's office, to hide out in a stall and wait for Wade to get clear of the school. Greg warned Jim to watch out for Wade. He told Jim and Kelsey to meet him at his house later. And squatting with his feet on the toilet seat to avoid detection, Greg listens to the thinning sounds of students leaving for the day, until he can only hear the occasional student in the hall and the sounds of basketballs bouncing off of the gym floor ricocheting down the halls.

Several adults pass by out in the hall. Greg recognizes the voices of Vice Principal Blight and Miss Fanning, the art teacher. All of the boys in school like Miss Fanning because she is young and pretty and braless, and leaves her shirts unbuttoned just a little too low. Most of the boys – from jocks to stoners to nerds – like to ask for Miss Fanning's input on their work so that she will move in close and bend down to study their drawings, and in the process bestow a vision of the pendulous wonders lurking just beneath the surface of her shirt. And even Greg, though ever respectful of girls and women, sometimes finds his own eyes irresistibly drawn to that small gap of space where the curtains of Miss Fanning's shirt pull back just a little to reveal that brief and wonderful view. Greg realizes that Miss Fanning has the same effect on Mr. Blight. She laughs at a joke, and in her spacey, soft tone, says, "Oh, Kevin, that's too, too, funny." And though he cannot hear Vice Principal Blight's response clearly, the inflection of his voice has the same prurient ring as that of an eighth grade, puberty-stricken boy attempting to get Miss Fanning to lean in closer. And then the sounds of Vice Principal Blight and Miss Fanning get softer and softer until they are well down the hall, out of Greg's hearing.

Strangely enough, Greg feels a sense of security and calm there, squatting on the toilet, hiding out in a stall. He lets his mind drift, pictures hanging out with Kelsey when he gets home. The thought makes him happy. His eyes go unfocused and a smile pulls up the sides of his mouth.

And without warning, Greg is rudely ripped from his reverie. The stall door bursts open from the kick of a heavy hiking boot. And standing there in the doorway is Wade Busby, red-eyed and high, shaking from an adrenaline rush. Behind him, Chop and Donnie Price nearly salivate from the anticipation of imminent violence.

"This is gonna be cool," says Chop, and he punches a clenched fist into his other hand. "Get 'im, Wade."

"Yeah, yeah," agrees Donnie, cackling a stoned and stupid laugh. "Get that little butt-munch."

Greg snaps to attention and tries to jump off of the toilet. His left foot slips, lands in the toilet, and wedges into the bowl's drainage hole, getting stuck there. He struggles unsuccessfully to extricate his foot, in the process flushing the toilet. The water overflows and cascades onto the tile floor. And Greg's foot remains stuck.

Like an animal in a trap, Greg struggles to free himself. Unlike the trapped beast, though, Greg is not willing to chew his leg off to escape. Instead, he covers up as well as he can and absorbs Wade's punches. The blows hit from all angles. Punches fueled by a deep anger that has nothing to do with Greg. Punches powered by a dysfunctional home and an absent father and insecurity and self-loathing. Wade grunts and growls and even starts to cry as he wails away on Greg. Donnie and Chop crowd the door to the stall, laughing, and occasionally sneaking in around Wade to throw a kick or punch, too.

In the midst of the beating, something breaks inside of Greg. It is not a bone or organ or tendon. It is not something tangible. The thing that snaps is that warm spot that lets things go, that forgives, that looks for the best in people. And once injured, that softness bleeds a blackness that stains his core. Greg drops his guard and stops trying to block the punches. He goes numb. For just a moment he feels like he floats above the stall and looks down upon Wade's frenzy. At the bathroom's entrance he sees Mr. Blight enter and try to break things up. Donnie and Chop step back with the looks of scared children on their faces. But Wade pulls himself away from Greg and steps toward Mr. Blight.

And the bloody-fisted, feral, juvenile delinquent scares the bejesus out of the vice principal. Wade says, "Get out of here, or you're next."

Mr. Blight acts not as a grown man, but more like a nerdy seventh grader on his first day at school. He clears his throat and straightens his tie. "Now look here, young man," he says, without authority. But he says no more because Wade runs at him. And instead of being a man, instead of standing up to the boy, Vice Principal Blight forgets that he is supposed to be in control. He reverts to the nerdy teenager that he once was in junior high school and panics. Mr. Blight sprints down the hall to his office and locks the door. He drops into his chair, his heart bumping and thumping to break out of his chest, and hyperventilates. He does nothing to help Greg and instead hides until he thinks Wade is gone from the building.

Wade's anger calms to a low boil. He walks back to the stall and punches Greg one last time. "Tell your butt-buddy, Halloway, that I'm coming for him next." And then Wade walks out of the bathroom and out of the school, with Chop and Donnie trailing at his sides like remora attached to a shark.

Only after Wade is gone from the school does Mr. Blight return to the bathroom. Even then, he is of no help. Instead, he calls on Mr. Corbin to help extract Greg's foot from the toilet. Though pins and needles prick at Greg's leg, his foot and leg are relatively undamaged. And the bumps and bruises from Wade, though painful, are no more of a bother than the injuries that Wally randomly inflicts.

Behind the custodian, Mr. Blight watches on, not making eye contact with Greg. And Greg asks, "Why didn't you help me?"

"He was going to hurt me," says Mr. Blight. "I didn't want to get hurt."

"Hmmphh," Mr. Corbin grumbles.

"Excuse me," says Mr. Blight to Mr. Corbin. "But do you have something to say?"

"Just that you are a sorry excuse for a man," says Mr. Corbin. He wipes his wet hands on the legs of his slate grey coveralls and then removes his horn-rimmed glasses so that he can make direct eye contact with Mr. Blight. The judgment in his glare shrivels the vice principal. "Just that you are a lily livered, yellow bellied, chicken-hearted, jellyfish."

"You should watch yourself," says Mr. Blight, straightening out his tie and trying to deflect his shame. "You should remember whom you are talking to."

"I do remember," says Mr. Corbin, the deep imposing bass of his voice echoing off of the bathroom's tile walls. "I remember that you are the same sniveling little crybaby that you were when I watched you come through this school as a boy. I remember very well *whom* I am speaking with. It is you who does not remember. You forgot that you are a man. You forgot that it was your job to keep this boy safe. You ran out on him while those hoodlums beat him. I ought to give you the same treatment. Maybe stick your foot in the toilet and Gregory and I can take turns dotting you with punches and kicks." Mr. Corbin puts his glasses back on and steps toward Mr. Blight, as if to follow through with the threat.

And the shame and fear and humiliation of it are too much.

Mr. Blight cowers, backs away from the bespectacled, old custodian, and trips over his own feet, falling to the bathroom floor. As Mr. Corbin slowly advances, Vice Principal Blight crabwalks backwards on the bathroom floor, right into the wall.

"Get away from me," Mr. Blight squawks, his voice trilling at an awkwardly high register. He uses the wall to help himself stand, then turns and runs from the bathroom. On the way out he shouts, "You better remember your place, James Corbin."

Mr. Corbin leads Greg to his office – a large closet with a cot, a small table with a hotplate, and a wall full of tools. In the corner is an empty spackle bucket that smells of urine. A shotgun and several antique handguns hang on the wall with the other tools. The heat of the room makes Greg tired.

Greg asks, "Do you live in here?"

"I do, Gregory. This is home sweet home." Mr. Corbin sits down and opens a warm can of Old Dutch beer. He holds it out, offering it, and Greg shakes his head. "I don't need much of anything since Missus Corbin left us. The house seemed empty. This is just fine for me."

And it doesn't seem sad to Greg. The room is comfortable and lived in. It makes sense that it is all that Mr. Corbin needs. Greg stares at the floor and says, "Well thank you for helping me." Mr. Corbin doesn't answer, so Greg continues. "Those boys have been picking on me for a while now and I knew that something like this would happen. That's pretty much the way things go for me. But I would have thought that Mr. Blight would have at least stopped it. Maybe you're right. Maybe it would be nice to see somebody do something like that to him. I don't mean hurt him. Maybe if he just found himself with a part of his body stuck in a toilet with nobody to help him. Yeah, that's what I wish."

But Mr. Corbin does not answer. He does not reprimand Greg for talking like that about an adult. He does not agree. He says nothing.

Greg looks up and sees Mr. Corbin sprawled out on an office chair, his arms crossed and chin on his chest, sleeping soundly. And with each gentle snore, thick nose hairs wave from his nostrils like a flag in a breeze. And then Mr. Corbin snorts and snores and half wakes. "What's that?" says Mr. Corbin. "What did you say, Gregory?"

"Nothing, Mr. Corbin. Nothing really. I was just saying that I thought it would be good if somebody did the same thing to Mr. Blight."

"Yes, I suppose," says Mr. Corbin. His chin drops back to his chest and his eyelids droop. As he drifts off, he mumbles, "It's fun to think about that. But be careful what you wish for."

And then Mr. Corbin's snores come hard and loud. Greg looks at him and feels a warmth for the janitor. Before this, he always saw Mr. Corbin as a gruff, grumpy, doddering old man with Brillo pad hair. It seemed that all the old man cared about was griping at kids for gum stuck under tables and black shoe marks left on the floors. Greg didn't know that the old man had the balls to stick up for him with Mr. Blight. He didn't realize that the janitor could have a soft spot for one of the kids that he regularly growled at in the halls. Greg certainly never thought of him as anything other than the janitor. But now Mr. Corbin becomes more of a hero and a protector. And still, he is an old man, falling asleep after the excitement of the day. Greg takes a coarse blanket from the cot, puts it over Mr. Corbin, and thinks, *So this is what it's like to have a grandfather.* He leaves Mr. Corbin's office. Leaves the school. Goes home.

Upon returning home, Greg finds Jim Halloway and Kelsey waiting for him on the porch. Kelsey gasps when she sees him.

Jim says, "Holy balls."

"What happened?" Kelsey asks. "Are you okay?"

The swelling distorts Greg's face into a gory Picasso. On the left side, where Wade landed most of the shots, Greg's face bulges and the white of his eye is ruby red. A distended hematoma pulses on the side of his forehead, like some squirming, tumid tumor, looking ready to pop. His fattened lip pushes out from his mouth, trying to escape the horror of the rest of his face. Blood stains his gums and the spaces between his teeth.

Greg gasps and each breath stabs at his side, where several ribs are cracked. "I don't want to talk about it. I want to be alone." And he pushes past them into the house, leaving his very concerned friends on the porch to wonder what happened to him.

And on his way to the attic, on the landing at the second floor, Wally pins Greg to the wall. "What happened to you, shit-turd? You're even uglier than usual."

And none of it matters to Greg. There is no fear left in him. With his one eye blackened and one unscathed, he locks a stare on Wally, "Screw you. You're the shit-turd, Wally."

Wally holds him against the wall and slams his fist into the unmarked eye. "There," he laughs. "Now, they'll match." And he turns away and walks down the hall, no longer interested in Greg.

With all of the strength that Greg has left, he climbs stairs and follows darkened halls, backtracks to make sure that Wally is not following him, climbs more stairs, goes through doors and more halls, until he reaches the staircase that takes him to the attic. Once in the attic, he throws himself on the floor and leans his back against the coffin in the middle of the room. Greg grabs a notebook and opens it to an empty page. At the top of the page he writes *Shit List.* And then he begins to write. His writing is all-encompassing. He notices nothing else. He does not notice that the piss-monkeys have grown to the point where they look uncomfortable and angry in their jars. He does not notice the scratching noises coming from the coffin. He does not notice that Jim and Kelsey have let themselves into the house and are knocking (gently so as not to draw Wally's attention) on the door that is closed and locked at the entrance to the attic. He notices nothing but the scratching of his pencil on paper.

3

The Big Bopper lopes southerly down Main Street, a strong steady wind blowing at his back and pushing him along his path. His feet never stop moving, legs never stop strutting as he walks lightly atop the frozen crust of snow without falling through. Captain Jack and Fats Flannigan bounce along behind him to the same beat, drawn along in his funky wake. And the Bopper don't notice the coons because he has his own built in blinders that keep him looking ahead, moving forward. But they notice him. And as he travels, more coons join the entourage, all of them tuning in to the Bopper's frequency and strutting along behind him.

Turning right, the Big Bopper bops into the town's tangle of alleyways. His groove wriggles out in invisible rays, a trippy pied piper dragging a gaggle of raccoons behind him. And in the morning hours, he passes Greg Samsa in a backstreet near Donnell Junior High. The Bopper don't notice Greg. The Bopper is on his own plane. He keeps bopping. But the raccoons stop and sit up on their haunches. They clasp their front paws together and look up to Greg's face. With his two black eyes, he looks like them. The coons chitter in greeting. Greg looks away and keeps moving, heading to school. And with the eye contact broken, the coons lose their interest in the battered boy. The Bopper's net sweeps them up and they are dragged along behind again, scrambling to catch up and follow the Big Bopper on his morning rounds through the town.

4

Mr. Corbin stands stone-faced at the front doors of the school, nods at Greg, and pulls him aside. "Gregory, you need to be very careful. Those boys came back to school today. And Mr. Blight has taken sick leave – the little pansy. You be careful."

And though no inflection clouds his voice, and his face betrays no emotion, the concern of Mr. Corbin touches Greg, makes him feel a little safer.

"I'll be careful, Mr. Corbin. Thanks."

"You do that, Gregory." Mr. Corbin turns and walks down the hall, shoving scraps of paper, dust balls, and candy wrappers with his large, wooden push broom. And the kids clear a path as the grumbling, gray-haired, flatulent custodian swipes clear a swath of the hallway and leaves a cloud of methane trailing behind.

Waiting at Greg's locker, Jim Halloway smiles and says, "Damn, Sam, I didn't think you were gonna come in today."

"I don't have much choice, do I?" says Greg, stuffing his bulky winter jacket into his locker. "I can't really hide anywhere because those dirt-bags find me wherever I go, don't they? And anyway, I needed to warn you."

Jim's smile falters just briefly, and then he says, "Warn me about what?"

But before Greg can explain, Wade Busby appears out of nowhere, it seems, and punches at Jim's ribs. Jim falls back and his elbow dents the locker door. He struggles to get back the breath that Wade knocked out of him, finding it to be quite the challenge.

"He wanted to warn you about me," says Wade. And he throws another punch, this one hitting Jim right in the solar plexus and knocking any remaining breath from him. Wade steps back for a second and breathes deeply through flared nostrils.

Jim gasps for breath and dry retches, tries to cover up to block the next shot.

Wade laughs and steps forward. He leans in too close to Jim's face and says, "You know Lori's my girl now, don't you?"

"Yeah," says Jim. "Whatever. You can have her."

"There's still a problem," says Wade. And his features wrinkle up into something even uglier than normal. A face of misdirected anger and ignorance. A face like an unwiped asshole.

"You had me smelling your finger and you told me it was Lori. But I've been with Lori. And she don't smell like that. The more I think about it, the more I wonder what I was smelling."

"Izzat so?" says Jim, and he stands straight again, locking eyes with Wade.

"It is," says Wade. "See, I ain't as dumb as I look, am I?"

And before he can help himself, Jim says, "I should hope not. I don't think anybody's that dumb." He tried to stop himself. He tried to lock his lips and throw away the key. But he already knew he was going to catch a beating. And the opportunity was too perfect to pass up. Now that he is committed to his own destruction, he decides to go all in. Jim is a clown and he wants to entertain the crowd gathering around them. If he is going to catch an ass-beating, he is going to make it worth his while. So he jams his hand down the back of his pants and pokes his finger into his asshole. He brings his stinkfist out and holds it toward Wade's face. "Here, take another sniff of Lori."

And instead of backing away from the finger or smacking Jim's hand out of his face, Wade becomes a feral animal. Like a dog sniffing another dog's asshole, Wade leans in to get his nose right up on the finger and inhales. And he breathes deeply. His eyes bulge and veins pop on his forehead and neck. The rage brews up to the brim and nearly boils over. Wade says, "Smells like fear to me," and draws back a fist, readying himself to inflict serious injury. He leans in slowly, fuming with menace. But before Wade touches Jim, the wide end of a push broom smacks him in the chest and pushes him back, pinning the bully back against the lockers. Greg and Jim step away from Wade. Mr. Corbin stands in front of the boys with his push broom pressing hard enough on Wade's chest that he cannot free himself, pinning him like a bug to the wall, hard enough that Wade has trouble breathing. And Wade shakes and froths and tries to free himself. The muscles on Mr. Corbin's arms strain, and his jaw tenses and loosens, tenses and loosens. He no longer looks like a doddering octogenarian. The threat of violence transforms Mr. Corbin into a protective, menacing figure. The burn of his stare through thick-lensed glasses wilts Wade.

"Leave these boys alone," says Mr. Corbin, his words accentuated by a burst of unexpected flatulence. "I don't like bullies. And unlike your vice principal, I'm not afraid of a little boy like you. You will have to answer to me if these boys have any further trouble with you, Mr. Busby. Do you understand?"

And when the broom is pulled away from his chest, Wade does not have a sarcastic reply or a threat. He has nothing but an unexpected fear of the elderly custodian. Wade never noticed how strong Mr. Corbin's arms looked. He never paid attention to the old man in the grey jumpsuit who cleaned up puke and piss and mud and blood around the school. Knowing that he cannot intimidate Mr. Corbin the way that he did Mr. Blight, Wade turns tail and walks a safe enough distance before spinning around and waving both middle fingers in the air. Wade dredges up sputum from his lungs and spits it on the floor. He says, "Fuck you, old man," and then hurries down the hall.

"Hmmph," Mr. Corbin grunts. He turns and pushes the gum wrappers, stray hairs, and dust balls down the hall with his pushbroom.

And for the rest of the day Greg notices Mr. Corbin in the background – sweeping floors, polishing handrails on the stairs, fixing hinges on a broken door, throwing sawdust on vomit – almost always present, never hovering, but keeping tabs on Greg. And when the final bell rings, Greg, Jim, and Kelsey find each other. They scan the outside of the school for Wade and Donnie and Chop. But the coast looks clear, so Greg and his friends duck out and into the alleyways, skittering nervously through the winter weather, left and right, north and south, circling around and backtracking to throw off anybody trying to follow their footprints in the snow, behind houses and through yards, until they arrive at the gate of the wrought iron fence at Greg's house.

And the fence gate is designed like a spider web with the number 4 caught in the web of the left gate, and the number 2 caught in the web of the right. Black iron bats perch atop the gateposts as sentinels on each side, spreading their bat wings and bat legs lasciviously, hissing at all intruders. At regular intervals of ten feet, winged, three-headed iron gargoyles sneer and writhe atop thick black fence posts. Pointed spontoon finials cap all of the other six-foot high fence spires.

Greg pushes through the gates with Jim and Kelsey trailing him. They bound up the porch steps, careful to avoid the rotten spots. The front door squeaks a rusty protest upon being opened. Phil Donahue's contentious voice carries to the front of the house, and Big Shirl calls out from the TV room, greeting the threesome. "Come on back here, baby. I've haven't even set eyes on you for days now."

And Greg and his friends stand at the foot of the grand stairs, Greg looking up toward the landing. He says, "awww crap," and starts to climb the stairs.

"Greg," says Kelsey, and she grabs him by the elbow. "That's your mother. Go talk to her."

Greg, Kelsey, and Jim enter the TV room. Big Shirl sits propped up in her bed with a peach wine cooler wedged tightly between her thighs. A Pizza Brother's box with a half-eaten gyro foldover balances on her belly. She drags her forearm across her face to wipe away shredded lettuce and tzatziki sauce, and beams at Greg. Pulling the strap of her housedress up on her shoulder, Big Shirl opens her arms, inviting Greg for a big, soft, sweaty embrace. "Come give mama a hug," she says.

Greg stands still, cringing, embarrassed. He loves Big Shirl, but he doesn't feel like being smothered by her in front of his girlfriend. Kelsey nudges him with her elbow. So Greg leans in and is embraced in his mother's warm, moist, gyro-scented love.

"I've missed you, baby," Big Shirl says. "You never come down. Just lock yourself away somewhere in this house and never show your handsome face." She brushes hair back from his glasses and looks at him. "Oh," she gasps, taking in his blackened eyes. She gently touches the hematoma on his forehead. "What happened to you?"

"Nothing, Ma," says Greg. "I took a ball to the face in dodgeball. It's no big deal. I'm fine." And he shakes his hair back down over his glasses.

"Well, even beat up, you are still gorgeous," Big Shirl says, and she hugs Greg even tighter. "He's such a handsome boy," she says, smiling at Kelsey.

Kelsey sticks her hand out to shake Big Shirl's. "Hi. I'm Kelsey."

Big Shirl releases Greg and latches on to Kelsey's hand. But instead of shaking it, she drags Kelsey in for a hug and wraps her arms around the surprised girl.

Greg backs up and looks away in embarrassment, stares at the TV and sees Phil Donahue standing in front of his audience, one foot up on the edge of the stage, and leaning in on the propped up knee with one elbow, shaking his microphone at a teenaged girl done up in punk rock clothes. The punker's mother sits beside her with a look of shame on her face, her hands pressed between her knees. And Greg knows the woman's shame and embarrassment. He feels the same about his mother's behavior.

Big Shirl releases Kelsey and looks at Greg, "She's cute. Is she your girlfriend?"

Greg flushes in embarrassment. He stammers and starts to say, "Nnnn…"

"Yes," says Kelsey. "I am."

"Oh, my baby," Big Shirl starts to tear up. "My baby. My baby."

Greg wishes for his heart to explode. He wishes for the ceiling to collapse on him. He wishes for Wally to come home and beat him into a coma. But none of that happens. Instead, Greg tries to melt back into the walls, away from the whole scene.

Sensing Greg's extreme discomfort, Jim Halloway steps up toward Big Shirl and says, "Hey Big Mama, why's everybody else getting hugs and Old Jimmy here is standing around all lonely?"

And Big Shirl lets loose with a blast of a laugh that sends a shockwave through the room. She grabs at Jim and practically drags him right on top of her. She pulls him in close, smashing Jim against her bosom, and plants a sloppy wet kiss on his cheek. "You always get a hug, Jimmy," she laughs. "You're like another son to me. And I see you just about as much as I do Greg, which is almost never."

Greg backs toward the door and says, "Mom, we've gotta go do homework." He turns and scrambles for the grand stairway at the front of the house.

Kelsey says, "Nice to meet you, ma'am," and then turns to follow Greg.

Jim winks at Big Shirl and says, "I'll see you around, doll," provoking another hearty laugh from her.

And as they leave, Big Shirl picks up the Pizza Brothers box and tears into the rest of the foldover. She plucks the wine cooler from between her thighs and turns up the sound on the TV to hear what Phil Donahue has to say to the kids that do their hair funny and dress in strange clothes.

Jim catches up to Greg on the stairs and elbows him. "Dude, I've got a semi. Your mom hugged me a little too close, and now I've got some mixed feelings and a half-chub."

"Shut up," says Greg. "Don't start right now."

"I'm serious," says Jim. "I think I have some feelings for your mom, dude."

"Shut up," says Greg again. "Just shut up."

"I mean, it felt like she feels the same way. It's conceivable that I could end up being your stepfather. If so, will you call me Daddy?"

"Shut up," say Greg and Kelsey at the same time. And Kelsey emphasizes the order by swinging her backpack and smacking Jim in the back. The blow, although playful, is hard enough to knock Jim to the floor on the second story landing. And then Greg and Kelsey are upon him, pinning Jim down, tickling him, laughing. And the three of them tussle and roll around on the floor, giggling and inflicting minor pain on each other.

Below, the front door swings open. Wally's voice calls out,

"Hey, shit-turds, I need to have a little talk with you."

Eddie's voice follows, "Yeah, you little shit-turds." And he cackles a nervous laugh.

Greg, Kelsey, and Jim all stop their wrestling match. Greg looks at the bottom of the stairs to see Wally, Eddy, and Lumpy. He says, "Run. Follow me."

And they take off in a sprint down the hall, leaving behind them the sound of drunken, stumbling footsteps coming up the stairs. Greg, Kelsey, and Jim dash around corners and up stairs, into rooms with windows overlooking other rooms, through doors and into new hallways, up another flight of narrow stairs and down two more, until Jim and Kelsey have no idea where they are in the mansion. And the floors shift under their feet. The house shudders. The halls shuffle.

"Do you know where the hell we are?" asks Jim Halloway. "I've never seen this part of the house. And after climbing all of those stairs it feels like we should be on the fifteenth floor. But I know that can't be so."

"Yeah," agrees Kelsey. "But to me it seems like we should be in the basement by now."

"We're fine," says Greg. "Things can get confusing in here if you try to think them through too much. Just follow me and everything will be just fine." He ducks around corners and into rooms, runs down more halls and sprints up and down and around narrow stairways.

The sounds of Wally, Eddy, and Lumpy shouting and tripping over each other in their bumbling pursuit fade away. And though Jim Halloway and Kelsey have lost their bearings, Greg knows where they are. He leads them to a stained-glass window, opens it, and climbs on another ladder made of two by fours affixed to the side of the house. Jim and Kelsey follow him through the window and they scale the ladder to another spider-web patterned stained glass window that opens to another room. And Greg leads his friends through laundry chutes and up and down more narrow spiraling stairs until they find themselves standing before the staircase that terminates at the door in the ceiling.

Greg throws open the attic door and steps into his room. Jim and Kelsey follow him through and look around in surprise. The room is organized. The sheets that previously covered everything were actually side show banners advertising old timey freak shows – banners for the Lobster Boy, the Two-Headed Baby, the Chupacabra, Strange Girls, the Dust Witch, and the World's Strongest Dwarf. And during his blizzard hibernation, Greg hung the banners on the walls around the attic. The late afternoon light shines through the stacked wall of piss jars blocking the windows, casting a golden glow over the room. Fat pollywogs wiggle in the jars, swimming toward the top as if trying to escape. Taxidermied monkeys and cats and dogs pose about the room, flashing various looks of surprise and anger and fear. Jars of pikkled punks sit scattered about the great room, their occupants floating lazily, some of them rolled up in fetal position, some with arms and legs spread and reaching out.

"What the hell are these?" Jim asks, eyeing the rows upon rows of piss-monkeys in jars.

Kelsey finds the Tiffany lamp and switches it on. "Never mind that, I need to see the babies," she says. "Where are they?"

Greg grins. Even though he understands the question, he innocently says, "Whom?"

"You know whom," she says, punching Greg in the arm playfully. "The unmentionables. My little babies."

"They're over here," says Greg and he steps over several jars of pikkled punks to get to the ornately carved coffin sitting in front of one of the piss jar-obscured windows.

Kelsey steps up to the ebony coffin and runs her fingers over the intricate carvings along the edges. The lid is expertly chiseled into a grotesque, hellish spectacle. Chimeric creatures with fish heads and goat legs heft axes and cleave the distended bellies of prostrate men who hold their hands up in futile acts of defense. Couples furiously copulate and scream out in agony. Birdmen sit on chairs and pass judgment on the lowly creatures within the carving. Wild boar creatures bound about the ebony landscape, tearing into men and women with their oversized tusks. Reptilian globsters slink throughout the writhing and suffering men. Kelsey runs her fingers along the carvings, marveling at the intricacy of the work. She momentarily loses herself in the convoluted scene, imagining herself in the setting and practically feeling the flames of damnation licking at her face and arms, forgetting that it is merely wood cut and chiseled for visual effect. Then a scratching beneath the lid brings her back to reality.

"What the...?" she starts, and then lays both hands atop the lid to feel the vibrations within the coffin. The scratching becomes louder, more insistent.

"Oh crap, the raccoons," Greg says, thinking that Captain Jack and Fats Flannigan have pillaged the bagged piglets in the coffin. "Open it."

Kelsey throws the heavy coffin lid up and does not discover raccoons. The fetal pigs, still swimming in formaldehyde and encased in plastic bags, half buried in the coffin dirt, writhe and wriggle and try to escape their enclosures. And Kelsey sees a luminescent green cloud wafting off of the bagged pigs.

"The aura, what a strange aura," is all that Kelsey says. Her body goes stiff and a goofy smirk breaks over her face. Blank eyes stare out of her head. No longer studying the pigs, her balance leaves her to the will of gravity. Her rigid body falls backwards into Jim's arms.

Jim eases Kelsey down to the floor just as neurons misfire in her brain and waves of seizures grip her. As the convulsions wrack her body, Greg and Jim hold her down and keep her head from slamming onto the floor. Greg swipes hair out of her now-sweaty face and gently rubs at her forehead to try to coax her out of the seizure. Jim holds her hands to keep them from smacking and scratching at her own face. And as fast one can say *tonic clonic*, the grand mal seizure stops. Kelsey's eyes pop open and she sees Greg just above her, staring into her eyes.

"Great googly moogly," she says, smiling, reaching out to caress Greg's face. "Did I just see what I think I did?"

Neither Greg nor Jim Halloway answer. They help her up and they all gaze into the open coffin, Jim and Kelsey with jaws gaping and incredulous. Greg looks on, nonplussed, and pulls one of the bagged pigs from the coffin dirt. He takes the pig to a desk and grabs a knife from the top drawer. Greg slits the bag open, draining the fluid into a puddle on the floor. The wriggling pig slops out of the bag, splashing in the puddle of formaldehyde, in a strange sort of birth ritual that it was previously denied. The pig struggles to its feet and wobbles there on unsure legs. It wheezes and sprays a mist of fluid from its little snout.

Greg bends down and strokes the pig's back. It turns toward him and bunts its head against his leg, rubs its snout on his hand like an affectionate cat. In the process a small tusk tears at the skin on Greg's hand. He pulls back in surprise, almost angry at first, and then realizes that the piglet meant him no harm.

"Oh my god," says Kelsey, and she scoops the baby pig up into her arms. She holds it like a human baby, stares into its eyes, coos at it. "He is adorable. I'm going to name him Napoleon." And she is lost in the moment. The mystery of how a dead pig has been reanimated doesn't concern her.

"The rest of these things are wiggling around, too," says Jim Halloway as he digs another bagged pig out of the coffin dirt.

Greg returns to the coffin, extracting piglets and slitting the bags open, allowing the contents to slide out at his feet. The formaldehyde and coffin-dirt mix into a sludgy, muddy mess on the floor and the piglets roll about in it, climbing over each other, knocking one another down, and wallowing in the muddy puddle as pigs will do. Greg and Jim and Kelsey all flop down onto the floor and play with the pigs and hold them and pet them. Kelsey gives out all of the great pig names she can think of: Porky, Petunia, Plopper, Old Major, Snowball and Squealer, Sir Oinksalot, Wendel, Hamilton, Piggy, Bluto, Wilbur, Arnold. And when Kelsey finally runs out of creative names, she dubs the remaining piglets the Three Little Bops.

The pigs frolic and chase each other. Kelsey, more than the others, relishes it. She lies on her belly in the muddy mess on the floor and plays with the babies. She scratches their chins and picks them up and cuddles them. But one by one they settle and plop onto their hindquarters in front of Greg, staring up into his eyes and looking like they are awaiting some sort of command. And when Greg stands and walks to the window to look outside, a single file line of little piggies trails him. He squats down to study them. Their corkscrew tails wiggle and wag, but their faces project blankness.

Greg leans in closer to one pig and stares into its eyes. "It's weird," he says. "Something's missing. In their eyes there's something lacking." He claps his hands and tries to wave the piggies away, but they just cast a blank gaze and wait for him to move again. Their vacant stares unsettle Greg and he tells the pigs, "Go now. Go back to your little mud puddle." Immediately, the piglets turn away and return to the muddy mess in front of the coffin.

"Whoa," says Jim, "that's freakin' weird. Tell them to come back to you."

Greg laughs gently, spreads his arms wide, and says, "Come to me, my children."

The pigs leap up from their mud puddle and run to Greg. They plop their hindquarters on the floor again, tails wiggling away, and goggle Greg with their dead eyes.

"Now get out of my sight," commands Greg. And the porcine babies scramble away and hide behind chairs and desks and boxes. They peek out from behind stacked jars of pikkled punks. Dead eyes peer out from hiding places all over the room, watching and waiting for further orders.

Kelsey steps around the back of the coffin and picks up Napoleon. She cradles the baby pig in her arms and coos at it like a mother with a newborn. She tells Greg, "Aw, look at the rest of them, hiding because of you. Tell them to come out again."

"No," says Greg. "There's some weird crap going on here and we need to figure it out. I mean, those pigs were dead. They were completely dead. And we cut them out of their bags and just start playing with them like they're puppies at the pet shop. Nope, nothing wrong here. Just playing with reanimated fetal pigs."

"Yeah," says Jim. "What the hell? I mean, how? When? What?"

He looks around at the piglets cowering in corners and behind furniture.

"I don't know," says Greg. "It doesn't make sense. But it's gotta have something to do with all of my grandpa's weird crap. There's something really freaky about this attic. I spent almost the entire blizzard up here going through the stuff. And this place ain't normal. I can tell you that. There's an energy. I don't think it's bad energy, but it's weird. And sometimes, when it's real quiet, I think that I can hear circus music coming from somewhere in the room."

"Yeah," says Kelsey, "there's something going on here – like the aura I saw above the pigs."

"And those jars," says Greg. "Look at those things in the jars. I call them piss-monkeys. But I don't really know what they are. I peed in the empty jars during the blizzard and those things started growing in them. There was a little bit of powder in the jars, but I didn't give it much thought. I just needed something to pee in because the water was off. But, yeah, there's something odd here. It's like there's some weird life force, something that creates life, or brings things back to life, or something. And I feel crazy even saying that. But then I look at the pigs and the piss-monkeys and I know you guys are seeing them, too. And, though it seems crazy, I know it's for real."

Kelsey walks to a window, still cradling Napoleon, and stares at the piss-monkeys. The pig strains to get near Kelsey's face and licks at her chin. She laughs and taps the pig on the nose, making him start a little. "I don't know what's going on," says Kelsey, "but I know I like these little piggies. And the pee-monkeys are interesting too. It's weird and creepy and kind of scary, but I don't feel totally creeped out."

"I don't know," says Jim Halloway. He walks to the same window as Kelsey and puts his finger near one of the pee jars. The piss-monkey pollywog opens its mouth to reveal a beastly set of sharp, jagged teeth, and then rams into the side of the jar in an attempt to attack Jim's finger. The little teeth make a muted clinking sound as they hit the glass, and the jar wobbles just a little. Jim jerks his hand back and shakes it, almost as if the piss-monkey actually did nip him. He laughs nervously and continues, "I don't know. These piss-monkeys freak me out. And these pigs, they were dead and now they're not. That ain't right, my friends."

"I agree with Kelsey," says Greg. "I don't know what to make of all of this, but it all goes along perfectly with this house. It has something to do with my grandpa. I mean, the carnival stuff, the pikkled punks, that creepy coffin, the circus music. It's all weird, but I'm not like…you know…like, creeped out by it or anything."

And they talk and play with the pigs and dig through boxes and crates and chests in the attic. They discover antique apothecary sets, surgical tools such as forceps and scalpels and irrigation syringes. They find books with foreign letters and hieroglyphics and strange diagrams of men in robes, fire, orgies, and scenes not unlike the carvings on the top of the ebony coffin. Some of the books show hand-drawn diagrams of exotic fruits morphing into reptiles and then into humans twisted in impossible poses. They try to decipher the obscure and cryptic messages in the books to no avail. They gather up the empty jars and consolidate the remaining white powder into one jar. Eventually Kelsey and Jim have to go home, leaving Greg alone in the big attic with the pigs and piss-monkeys and his own thoughts.

Alone now, Greg curls up on a sheetless mattress in the corner and falls into a deep sleep as the earth spins and hurtles through space in its orbit. Before he knows it, he wakes in the morning to a litter of cold-skinned fetal pigs nuzzling his belly –

their tusks poking his skin and unintentionally drawing blood – treating him like a lactating sow, and looking for fat leaky nipples to nurse upon.

5

It's not the snow that chills the Big Bopper. It's something else. A darkness has fallen on the town. A cold, damp, darkness. And the polar blast blows especially hard off of Donnell Junior High. The Bopper bops by and a shivering fit grips him, shakes his bones, clatters his teeth, nearly frostbites his skin. He only stops briefly to question the building about its frigid bearing. In a window on the second floor, he sees a man with a cheesy mustache peek around the curtains and gaze out at him nervously. Then a barrage of snowballs slams into the Bopper's back. One knocks his headphones off, and a shrill tone bores into his ears, spikes straight into the base of his brain. The Bopper falls to his knees, nearly paralyzed by the screech, and fumbles for his headphones, placing them properly back over his ears. And a soothing warm jam, a supersensual unguent, layers a sonic balm down over the psychic gashes.

The Bopper stays on his knees and lets the headphones filter the noises whipping about outside his head. He lets the consonance flow through him. From the warm cocoon of his headphones' groove, he watches three boys run past him, laughing and scrambling for the front doors of the school. Black and red trails, rotten and festering, stream from the tops of their heads and then dissipate in the cold wind blowing down from the roof of the school. The face in the window with the cheesy mustache tenses and ducks back behind the curtains like a frightened squirrel. The Bopper sees the steamy stench of cowardice fuming in the void where the face was.

And the Bopper senses the corruption, the dark energy dripping from those boys. He feels the sickness, the same sickness that he sees fuming from the sewer drains and the hole in the ground out in the woods at the south edge of town. The Bopper clears his throat, coughs out the blackness he took in from the boys, and gets to his feet. The headphones' jam restores him and he moves along, away from the school, grooving on to other space-time that comforts him more.

6

Slush-covered boots and shoes track in drippy, melting snow, smearing black marks on the floor. Kids pull off their gloves and hats and try to shake off the cold. The aroma of coffee and tobacco smoke wafts from the teachers' lounge and into the halls. Hormones and pheromones flow. Teachers patrol the hall, breaking up overzealous public displays of affection. And amidst the morning scramble for lockers and homeroom, Greg and Kelsey find each other and talk in hushed voices about the piglets and piss-monkeys, about the unmentionables.

"Well," says Kelsey. "Did they do anything else? Did they eat? Are they all okay?"

"Yeah," says Greg. "They mostly just followed me around. It was kind of weird at first but then I started to get used to it."

Down the hall, Mr. Corbin pushes a mop, swabbing muddy puddles. The overwhelmed mop mostly just moves the water to different places on the floor and does little to actually clean it. The custodian pretends to focus on his duties, breathing heavily through his nose, sending nostril hairs flagging like banners in the wind, but he keeps watch on Greg and Kelsey.

And as Greg and Kelsey talk about the pigs, Wade Busby and his lackeys accost them. Wade's jaw and fists clench in a synchronized demonstration of barely restrained hostility. He moves in, encroaching on Greg's personal space and backing him up against the lockers.

"Stop being such a penis-wrinkle, Wade," says Kelsey, trying to distract the bully. She takes off her bulky winter gloves and smacks them at Wade's head in an effort to back him down.

But Wade just laughs at the feeble attempt to defend Greg. He rips the gloves from Kelsey's hand in one quick movement and throws them to the ground. With animal quickness he turns to Kelsey and pulls back his fist as if to wallop her. Kelsey stands her ground, unflinching, and laughs. "Go ahead," she says, "hit a girl and show everybody how tough you are."

"I wouldn't hit you," says Wade. He unclenches his fist and rubs the back of his hand on Kelsey's cheek. "I'm gonna make you my next girlfriend."

From the other end of the hall, Mr. Corbin moves with the agility of someone sixty years his junior, quickly closing the gap between him and Wade.

Wade senses the incoming janitor and steps back from Greg and Kelsey. He says, "Hey Greg, where's your little faggot friend Jim? I still need to have a long talk with him."

Before Mr. Corbin gets to them, Wade and Chop and Donnie scramble down the hall and up the stairs. Mr. Corbin stops his charge and resumes mopping. He nods at Greg and says, "Gregory," and then moves down the hall, ineffectually swabbing the puddles on the floor.

Greg slinks from class to class, head down, hands clasped, blending in and hiding in plain sight. He catches glimpses of Mr. Corbin throughout the day. The custodian never looks Greg's way or interacts with him, but Greg senses him watching and feels safer under Mr. Corbin's gaze. And though he does his best to protect Greg, Mr. Corbin does not follow him into gym class.

In the locker room, Greg once again tries to dress for class without drawing attention. But, as usual, Danny Dolan, strutting around half naked, pecker swinging like a weighted pendulum, singles out Greg.

"Hey everybody," shouts Danny, "check out E.T." And he charges Greg and flips him around. Before Greg can push Danny away or scuttle for safety, Danny jams his hand down the back of Greg's gym shorts and locks a grip on the elastic waistband of his tighty whiteys. Danny shouts, "Atomic wedgie!" and yanks on Greg's underpants, lifting him inches off of the ground.

Greg struggles and kicks out at Danny to no avail. Danny hangs him in the air for a good ten seconds before Coach Manlove enters the locker room.

Manlove struts into the room wearing only a tight, blue and white singlet and wrestling shoes. The bumps above his eyes throb with intensity. With his thick arms pulled back and chest thrust out, Manlove yells, "All right, you knuckleheads. Cut it with the shenanigans. We're wrestling today. Get out on the mat and get ready for some grappling."

Danny Dolan releases Greg, letting him drop to the ground. Stewie Gordon rushes over, slaps Greg on the back, and says, "That was hilarious, Samsa. You always crack me up." And he flashes a good-natured, stupid smile at Greg.

The class exits the locker room and gathers in a circle on the wrestling mat. Coach Manlove struts about the center of the circle, eyeballing the boys, saying nothing. He takes off his glasses and hands them to Harry Merkin. Manlove runs his fingers over his crew cut and exhales heavy breaths through flared nostrils. Finally, he says, "This is going to be round robin. I'm in the middle and I will take on all comers, one at a time. You ladies need to try to beat me. Whoever pins me takes the center of the circle and defends it."

Without hesitation, Stewie Gordon bursts out laughing and charges Manlove. The coach grabs Stewie's left arm, drops to one knee, and throws his other arm up between Stewie's legs, lifting the heavy boy with ease, throwing him over his shoulders and to the ground. "Fireman's carry," shouts Manlove as he tosses Stewie. The boy hits the mat hard and a gasp of air shoots from his mouth. With the wind knocked out of him, Stewie lies supine on the mat, struggling for air and trying to laugh at the same time, the effort causing his face to redden like a ripe apple.

"Roll this sorry excuse for a human off of my mat," Manlove barks. Danny Dolan and Jerry Norman Unborn rush to the task and roll Stewie, still huffing for air, out of the center of the circle.

"Who's next for the pain train?" says Coach Manlove, licking his index finger and smoothing down his eyebrows. Manlove latches on to Kirk Hirkle, who still wears the taped glasses, pulling the scrawny boy into the circle. And Manlove clamps a massive arm around Kirk's head and shoulder and tosses the helpless boy to the ground. "Hip toss," Manlove shouts.

And as Manlove lands on Kirk, the boy yelps a high-pitched, inarticulate complaint. Manlove stands and brushes his hands off. Kirk curls up on the ground defensively to protect himself from any further abuse, his taped-up glasses once again broken into pieces and scattered on the mat beside his head. "Do not pass go, do not collect two hundred dollars," Manlove says. "Now get this squid off of my mat." Danny Dolan and Jerry Norman Unborn leap into the circle and drag Kirk Hirkle to safety at the edge of the mat.

Like an angry gorilla, Coach Manlove stomps about inside the circle, plucking boys and twisting them into painful, contorted knots. He bends arms and legs in manners unsuitable for the human body. Danny Dolan and Jerry Norman Unborn drag the bent and broken students to the side of the mat, where they recover and watch the massacre of their classmates. Manlove grabs Raymond Daws by the wrist with one hand and the elbow with the other, he drops and pulls the boy's arm toward the ground, driving Raymond's face hard into the mat. A cracking sound echoes in the gym and the boy goes limp, facedown on the mat. Manlove froths and sprays a mist of spittle as he shouts, "Arm drag! Goodnight Irene!"

Harry Merkin tries to hide behind another student, but Manlove tracks him down, drags him to the center of the circle, and pushes the boy to the ground. Manlove drops heavily on top of the boy and snakes his arm up under Harry's and around the back of his neck. Manlove pushes with his feet and cranks with his arm, twisting Harry in circles on the floor until he flips onto his back and Manlove pins him to the mat with his massive chest. Slapping his hand on the mat three times, Manlove yells, "match over," and springs to his feet again. The crotch bulge, already accentuated by the tight singlet, appears to have plumped up somewhat. Manlove tugs here and there on the singlet in an effort to readjust the stretchy fabric while Harry crawls away to the edge of the mat.

Having regained his breath, Stewie Gordon charges Manlove again, laughing, and drops down to wrap his arms around one of Manlove's massive legs in an effort at a single leg takedown. Manlove moves as much as a stump would, sprawls, and throws a crossface that nearly takes Stewie's head off. The concussive force briefly knocks Stewie out and he falls limp. Manlove momentarily looks concerned as he gazes down at his victim. But Stewie Gordon comes to and begins giggling. He rolls toward the side of the mat and sits with a dopey smile on his face as the coach manhandles his helpless classmates.

The slow moving hands of the gymnasium clock never leave Greg's sight. He does his best to blend in, to avoid Coach Manlove's attention. And the minutes tick down to the point where Greg hopes he might be able to make it through class without being brutalized. Littered on the mat all around him are Greg's broken and bruised, concussed and contused classmates. But with only minutes left in the class, as Greg allows his mind to drift just briefly, Coach Manlove jumps on top of Greg and drags him to the middle of the mat. Greg goes limp and does not even try to resist. Manlove forces Greg's head, face down, between two massive thighs and clamps them onto the boy's head. Holding Greg's arms so that he does not just wilt to the mat, Manlove begins jumping up and down, rattling Greg's brain within his skull, and then drops the dazed boy to the mat. Manlove claps his hands together hard and says, "Oh yeah! That one's called the milkshake."

Manlove struts off of the mat, toward the locker room, leaving a broken bevy of boys to crawl and limp and stagger to the locker room and get dressed for their next classes. Tears pour down Mickey Mooney's cheeks as he holds his swollen wrist out in front of himself. Kirk Hirkle tries to unravel tape from his glasses and piece them back together as he mumbles about how his dad is going to sue Coach Manlove for everything he has. Greg stands, fighting the vertigo and tunnel vision, shaking his head to clear his thoughts. And Stewie Gordon limps to the locker room, laughing and smacking other kids on the back and saying, "That was great. Just great."

And when the bell rings at the end of the day, Greg and Kelsey meet Jim at his locker. Greg says, "Wade is really pissed off. We need to get out of here and get to my house as fast as possible. If he catches us today, something bad is gonna happen."

Down the hall, Mr. Corbin jimmies open a stuck locker door for a student and glances toward Greg.

Jim slams his locker shut and spins the dial. He smiles and moves leisurely down the hall. "Wade can fold it over twice and jam it up his poop-shoot sideways. I called my mom and she's picking us up today. No worries about running into those ballsacks on the way home."

Kelsey jabs Jim with her elbow and says, "You are the grossest person I know. If anybody else said the things you do, I'd want to puke. But you kind of make them funny."

And the threesome goes to Greg's locker, then Kelsey's, putting on winter jackets and hats and gloves. Around every corner,

Mr. Corbin is fixing something, or polishing rails, or sweeping floors, always watching Greg peripherally. Mr. Corbin's ever-present, looming figure seems to ward off the evils seeking Greg and his friends in the school.

Greg, Kelsey, and Jim exit the school through the front glass doors and down the steps, past all of the kids loading onto buses. An orange VW pop-top van waits at the curb behind the line of buses. The van's horn bleats out a nasal *meep meep*, and Jim's mom waves to her son.

"Sweet," says Jim. "Mama's here with safe passage home." And they load up in the van, with Greg in the front passenger seat and Kelsey and Jim on the rear bench seat.

Mary Waldon sits crying in the back seat of the bus just in front of Mrs. Halloway's van, zipping up her coat to cover her Def Leppard t-shirt. Robbie Beuler shouts out, "Hey, Mary, cool Def Leppard shirt. Where'd you get it, K-Mart? Hey Mary, Def Leppard's soooo cool. And you are now too because you have a Def Leppard shirt. It don't matter that you're tubby 'cause you got a Def Leppard shirt. Would you be my girlfriend, Mary?" But Robbie doesn't like Def Leppard. And he doesn't like Mary. He is mean and mocking and condescending and he makes Mary feel stupid and ashamed of her shirt. Since it's too cold out for Mary to walk home, she has to take the bus. And she has to take the emotional beating from Robbie because Earl, the bus driver, is hard of hearing and would do nothing about the teasing even if he did notice. Earl did the same thing when he was a kid, picking on others to make himself feel big. So Mary absorbs the abuse.

And when she gets home, she will take a pair of sewing shears and shred the t-shirt that was bought at K-Mart. She never even liked Def Leppard. Her mom bought her the shirt so that she could fit in better, maybe not get picked on so much. But it only made things worse. So Mary just sits at the back of the bus, crying and staring out the back window. And, briefly, her sad eyes lock with Greg's, and then she averts her gaze.

Mary's eyes tell Greg everything he needs to know about what is happening in the bus. He cannot hear Robbie taunting her, but Greg has heard it so many times already. If there is a kid in school who gets picked on more than Greg, it's Mary. And in that moment, Greg burns with hate for the Robbies and the Wades of the world. His stomach twists and his head aches from the pain of it all. He wishes that all of the Robbies and the Wades would just die. He prays to whichever gods might be listening for slow, torturous deaths for such people.

As Greg daydreams about harm to the bullies, he is brought back to the moment by the snowball that smacks into the side of the van. Standing on the front lawn of the school, Wade, Chop, and Donnie laugh and hurl more snowballs at the van.

"Well," says Mrs. Halloway, "I'm going to get out and give those little brats a piece of my mind."

But Greg grabs onto Mrs. Halloway's arm and says, "No."

Jim chimes in, "No, Mom. Don't do it. That will just make things worse. Please, the buses are pulling out. Just drive."

"Please," says Kelsey.

Mrs. Halloway reluctantly relaxes and eases back into her seat as several more snowballs slam the side of her van. Her face twitches each time a snowball hits. "Okay," she says. "Those boys are lucky you are here to control me. I was going to give them what for."

As the orange van pulls away, something comes over Greg, he beams his biggest smile and holds both hands up in middle finger salutes to Wade.

"Gregory!" Mrs. Halloway says in mock surprise. "How rude."

Jim and Kelsey laugh and follow Greg's lead, both flipping the bird at Wade. Even Mrs. Halloway starts laughing. She stops the van, turns around in her seat, and flips Wade off, too, making everybody laugh even harder. And then she turns, grabs the wheel and pulls away before Wade, Donnie and Chop can get off another round of snowballs at the van.

Unbeknownst to Mrs. Halloway, during her brief stoppage to waggle her middle finger at Wade, Tim and Jim Courtney snuck up behind the van, squatted low, and latched onto the bumper. The Courtneys hold tight to the van and bumper-hop down the slick street, their tattered boots gliding over the sheet of ice on the road, and hope not to be noticed.

Mrs. Halloway stops the car at the intersection of Baldwin Avenue and Main Street. Something doesn't feel right. She puts the van in park, gets out, and walks around to the rear bumper, where she finds Tim and Jim Courtney covered in slushy road sludge, squatting down and hoping not to be caught.

"Tim, Jim," says Mrs. Halloway. "Would you boys like a ride? Hop in the back of the van and I'll take you home." Mrs. Halloway knows about Tim and Jim. She went to school with their father, and he was just like them – dirty and dumb, strange and sad. With their upbringing, she was not surprised that Tim and Jim were feral little urchins. Not much else could be expected. But, just as Mrs. Halloway was wont to take in sick birds and stray cats, she felt an obligation to help the Courtney boys. And even if they did mess her van up a little bit with their sludge covered clothes, she didn't mind, especially if maybe just showing a little kindness might help the boys. "Come on," she says, "come along."

Tim and Jim say nothing. They just stand and walk to the sliding door on the side of the van. Mrs. Halloway opens the door and says, "Scoot over kiddos. Make room. We're going to give Tim and Jim a ride."

Jim Halloway groans. Kelsey leaps for the lone, square-seated stool placed just behind the driver's seat. Tim and Jim scramble into the van, dragging with them a cold whiff of body odor and bad breath. And they sandwich Jim Halloway on the bench seat of the van.

Happy to be separated from the dirty twins, Kelsey smiles and says, "Hey, we have two Jims in the car. I wonder what else you Jims have in common besides your names." Jim Halloway merely glares. Jim Courtney sits slack jawed and vacant eyed, exhaling puffs of rotten breath that nauseate Jim Halloway.

The VW's weakly heater provides enough warmth to energize the stink molecules hovering around the Courtney boys and their odor assumes a weighty presence in the van. Greg cracks his window and Kelsey throws the sliding window on her side wide open. Frigid air fills the VW but at least the funk is sucked out the windows.

Mrs. Halloway turns right here, left there, right again and so on, perhaps driving a bit faster than she should on the icy roads, in an effort to get Tim and Jim Courtney to their home and out of her car. And on the outskirts of the village, the van takes a left off of Olive Street and down a neglected private drive. Off to the right, just along the edges of Eagle Creek, sits a dilapidated doublewide trailer under the remaining metal roof of an abandoned industrial building. The Courtneys live in the trailer with their habitually drunk and dysfunctional father.

Mrs. Halloway stops the car and says, "Here you go boys. I'm glad I could give you a ride so that you didn't freeze yourselves on the way home."

Tim and Jim say nothing. Jim Courtney opens the sliding door and climbs out without looking back or acknowledging Mrs. Halloway's kindness. Tim follows, climbing past Jim Halloway and intentionally jostling him on the way out. And then, without a word of thanks, Tim and Jim Courtney disappear into the overgrown area surrounding the metal roof.

Mrs. Halloway says, "Hmmm? Those boys could stand to learn some manners."

Greg says, "You are putting it nicely. Those boys are buttholes."

"Now, Greg," explains Mrs. Halloway, "you need to keep in mind that they come from a broken home and that their dad is an alcoholic. They can't really help themselves. They, more than anybody else, need the kindness of others if they are ever going to rise above what they are facing."

"He's right, Mom," says Jim Halloway. "Those kids are buttholes."

"Jim," says Mrs. Halloway sternly. "That's not nice. Try to put yourself in their shoes." She puts the VW into gear, maneuvers the van in a three-point turn and heads back out to Olive Street. As the van pulls away, a barrage of snowballs flies from the bushes. Mrs. Halloway stops the car and watches Tim and Jim scurry through the vegetation toward their trailer.

"Okay," Mrs. Halloway says, "those boys are buttholes."

Hopalong stands on the front porch of Samsa Mansion with his hobbyhorse tucked between his legs and hands on the starter pistols hanging from his belt. He takes one hand off of a gun and tips his cowboy hat at Mrs. Halloway as she pulls up in the street.

"Oh dear," says Mrs. Halloway, startled. "That big retarded boy is on your porch. Should I pull around to the back of the house?"

Greg laughs. "He's okay, Mrs. H. That's just Hopalong. He's not dangerous or anything."

"Yeah," agrees Kelsey. "He's really nice."

"And he always knows the weather forecast," says Jim.

"Well," says Mrs. Halloway, "then why is he standing outside in the freezing cold without a winter jacket or gloves? That poor boy must be freezing to death out there. I want you all to take him inside and give him some hot chocolate."

"Will do, Mrs. H," says Greg, opening the van door. "Thanks for the ride."

Greg, Kelsey, and Jim exit the van and say goodbye to Mrs. Halloway. On the front porch Greg greets Hopalong, saying, "What are you doing out here in the cold, Hopalong? Come on inside and warm up. We'll get you some hot chocolate."

And they all enter the front door. But when Greg tries to lead Hopalong to the kitchen, Hopalong stops and says, "No. I do not want hot chocolate. You should follow me. I have something important for you to see."

And even though Greg and Kelsey and Jim insist that Hopalong follow them to the kitchen, he does not budge. "No," he says. "This is important. You need to follow me."

Greg shrugs at his friends and then says, "Okay big guy, you win. Lead the way and we'll follow."

Hopalong climbs the stairs to the second story and leads the group through a series of twists and turns, up stairs and down, through hidden doors, and up and up and up, until he stops at the flight of stairs that lead to the attic. The attic door in the ceiling is open. The sounds of little cloven feet scampering around above float down to them and then stop as piglets lean over and look through the open doorway. The little pigs grunt and oink in greeting to Greg and his friends.

"Ughh," Greg groans. The open door can only mean that Wally has once again found his private room and will ruin things for him. All he can say is, "Not again."

"Go ahead," says Hopalong, gently putting a hand on Greg's shoulder and nudging him forward. "It is safe."

Greg slowly climbs the stairs to the attic, followed by Kelsey, then Jim, and finally Hopalong. Dread and the certainty that he is about to be assaulted fill him. But nothing bad happens when he steps through the ceiling and into the attic. He is not jumped upon or punched or kicked or knocked to the ground. Nobody grabs Kelsey and holds her for Wally to use as a punching bag. Instead, the pigs greet him, rubbing against his calves like friendly cats who missed their owner. But Greg pays no attention to the piglets. He merely groans and says, "Not again."

Kneeling and hunched over on the floor, circled around a mirror lying flat, are Wally, Eddie, and Lumpy. The Mason jar that Greg used to consolidate the remaining piss-monkey powder is on its side with most of the contents spilled onto the mirror. Long lines of the substance are arranged like the walls of a maze. A rolled up dollar bill sits beside the mirror. Wally's nose and upper lip are covered with the fine talc-like dust. The rest of his face is pale, white as the snowdrifts outside. Bloody trails dribble from his eyes and nostrils. His swollen, cracked lips open and close and he chews on his tongue involuntarily, juicing blood out of it each time his jaw clamps down. And Eddie and Lumpy look much the same, with their powdered-donut faces, vacant stares, and bleeding eyes and noses.

But the sight of Wally and his friends in the attic doesn't scare Greg. It doesn't trigger his flight reflex. His body is not flooded with adrenaline, and he senses no danger. Greg's body has a finely tuned alarm system that alerts him to any threats to his wellbeing and it is not sounding the sirens. Something about the situation strikes him as strange. Wally doesn't say anything. He doesn't even look up at Greg and his friends, and neither do Eddie and Lumpy.

"No way," says Jim Halloway. "Those idiots snorted the piss-monkey powder."

"They did," says Hopalong. He shakes his head back and forth in disapproval. "I told them that drugs are bad. But they did not listen."

Greg waves his hand in front of Wally's face, but his big brother does not do so much as blink. Bloody drool dribbles from the side of his mouth and runs down his face and neck. Wally chews at his tongue, and his vacant eyes stare straight ahead. Greg taps on Wally's shoulder but receives no response.

"This is crazy," says Greg. "They can't even move. They've finally gone and done it. They fried their brains."

Kelsey steps forward and bends down to look into Eddie's eyes. But he looks straight through her. She gently slaps his pale cheeks and says, "This is freaky-deaky. There ain't nobody home. How long have they been like this?"

"Since twelve-o-five p.m.," says Hopalong. He stands straighter while his brain gears up to dispense information. A tic twitches the right side of his face several times and then his eyes light up. "At that time the temperature was 24 degrees Fahrenheit, the sky was overcast, and there were mild snow flurries."

Greg asks, "Have they moved? Have they done anything? Or have they been like this the whole time?"

"They took the drugs," says Hopalong. "I told them they were bad. But they would not listen. And they have not moved since. The temperature has remained in the mid twenties while they have been up here. And heavier snow is forecast for this evening, with the temperatures dropping into the teens."

Squatting down, his face at Wally's level, Greg says, "Look at me, Wally." And Wally slowly turns his head, his eyes looking at and through Greg. "Can you talk?"

It starts with a slight movement of the cracked, powder-dusted lips, and then develops into a sad, labored struggle to open and close his mouth. Bloody slobber cascades out of both sides of Wally's mouth as he begins to make a clicking noise in the back of his throat.

"What is it?" asks Greg. He leans in, puts a supportive hand on Wally's shoulder, and says, "What?"

The drool pools in Wally's mouth and sprays out when he finally manages to dislodge a word from somewhere deep within him. Wally bears down hard and pushes out one shaky, breathless, hyphenated word: "Shit-turd."

And it is as if time stops in the attic. The waning daylight casts a golden beam through the piss-monkey jars and directly onto the spot where Wally and his pals sit in oblivion. The piss-monkeys, now much larger and filling nearly half of the volume of their jars, wriggle around uncomfortably in their insufficient space, their shadows dancing clumsily on the ground and over Wally, Lumpy, and Eddie. Greg sits and stares at the awkward dancing shadows on his brother, mesmerized as if watching melted balls of wax rising and dropping in a lava lamp. And he says nothing. Kelsey says nothing. Jim Halloway lets out a long sigh and merely says, "Wow."

Jim leans in close to study Lumpy's face. Lumpy stares straight ahead. His eyes, they see nothing. Somewhere outside, just above the sound of the heavy winds, the strains of a slightly out of tune calliope warble and visit a barely discernible, winter carol upon the mansion. And even more softly than the calliope's tune, Lumpy hums along in a rough and gurgly, two-toned throat song.

"Great googly moogly," says Jim Halloway, leaning in closer. "That boy was fugly before. But look at his mug now."

Jim is right. Lumpy looks worse than ever. His purple acne throbs and bubbles. Taut whiteheads, like broken egg yolks, split and ooze a foul yellowish custard. His unblinking, bloodshot eyes gaze at nothing. Lumpy does not try to grab Jim. He does not lunge or jump or even start. He sits and his head bobs. His powdered face twitches. Sickly, soft mews escape his slack and drooling mouth. They all stare at Lumpy with morbid fascination because he looks worse than death. Time stretches out and hangs lazily. And the light that passes through the piss-monkey jars fades and gives way to night.

Only the scratching of raccoon paws at one of the attic windows startles Greg, Kelsey, and Jim from their daze. Outside, in the light of a bone white moon, with wind whipping flurries of snowflakes about, Captain Jack and Fats Flannigan scratch at the window, pleading to be let in from the cold. But their distressed faces have little effect on Greg.

"I hope those giant rats freeze out there," says Greg.

Kelsey gasps. "Gregory. That is so rude. I know you don't like them, but you can't mean what you just said. I know you don't wish them any harm."

"You're right," agrees Greg. "I don't want them to freeze. I want somebody to just exterminate them as soon as possible. That's what I really wish for. And they could leave them at my doorstep, like trophies – like cats do for their owners."

Kelsey slaps at Greg's arm, hard but not violently and says, "You're bad." But she smiles at him, too. And Greg flashes a shy grin back.

Suddenly, without warning, Lumpy stands and shuffles slowly away with his arms out in front of him and his head slung low. He says nothing and only makes a gentle wheezing sound with each step he takes. He goes through the attic entrance and descends the stairs.

"What the…?" says Jim to Lumpy. "Hey, where do you think you're going you big, dumb, lunkhead?"

But Lumpy does not stop. He does not come back in response to the provocation. He does not retaliate. He just walks away with some clearly apparent but unknown purpose. His jaw shifts back and forth, the grinding of his teeth making sounds that draw cringes from Kelsey.

Greg looks at his brother, the person who inflicts so much misery, the person who he fears the most, and feels sadness at seeing Wally in such a state. And a strong intuition tells Greg that Wally has gone out too far to ever come back. Whatever was in Montag Samsa's powders and potions had powers beyond what Greg or anybody else could understand, power to revive the dead. But now the question is, what does it do to the living? Greg just knows, looking at his brother, that Wally will never be the same again. The seeming impossibility of the situation doesn't cause Greg to question reality. Greg knows what he sees, and what he has seen happen in the attic. There's no question that Montag Samsa's property has powers. And Greg sees that Wally is reduced to a breathing, drooling, glob of sweaty, pale flesh that serves no purpose beyond producing carbon dioxide for the trees and plants. Despite Wally's mean and senseless mistreatment of his little brother, Greg feels a sense of loss at what has happened to him. Despite all of the times Greg has wished his brother dead or disabled, there is no satisfaction in seeing Wally like this. Because even more than wishing harm on Wally, Greg really wished to have a big brother who would like him, who would include him sometimes. Maybe even give him advice about girls or dealing with bullies. Or maybe even just someone to play video games and laugh with. Ultimately that was all that Greg really wanted out of his brother. And in some little place in his heart, Greg had always reserved a spot for such a big brother in case something would somehow change.

Tears well up in Greg's eyes and he shudders, shaking off the emotions. He says, "I don't even know what to do here. We can't let any of these guys leave the house. They'll just end up in juvie, or more likely, the psych ward. I've hated these buttholes for so long and I've wished them ill. And now that it's happened, I don't like it one bit. Nobody can see them until we figure out what to do with them." He wipes at his eyes. A nervous laugh escapes him as Kelsey puts a hand on his arm. He says, "I need a snack. I need something to eat and I need to sit and process all of this."

And just as Lumpy did before, Wally and Eddie both stand up and walk away, past the coffin, through the playful pigs on the floor, down and out the attic door. Greg just stands there, helpless, watching his brother shuffle out of the room.

"I will follow Eddie," says Hopalong, moving toward the stairs. "He is my brother and he is not thinking straight. The temperatures will be dipping into the teens and we may get as much as four inches of snow. I do not want him wandering around outside." Hopalong lopes after his brother and leaves Greg, Jim Halloway, and Kelsey alone in the attic.

Kelsey walks about, flipping on lamps and lighting candles, never quite able to adequately illuminate the attic. The strangely tinted lamps and candles cast a reddish light on everything in the room. Pikkled punks appear to float in blood. The abominations on the freak show banners dance in the flicker of the candle flames. Rosy hues color Greg's face. He drops to the floor and crosses his legs Indian style, while piglets form a circle about him and sit, too. The now-alive fetal pigs gently grunt at Greg, as if requesting further instructions. They sit and stare with their dead eyes, wriggling their corkscrew tails happily at him.

Waving his hands at the pigs, Greg says, "Be gone, swine. Go. Go away and stay out of my sight." Without hesitation, the piglets scramble and hide behind chairs and desks and freak show banners. Every single pig quickly vanishes from sight, their presence only noticeable because they continue to gently squeak and squeal from their hiding places, as if crying out to show Greg they obeyed.

"I don't know what to do about all of this," says Greg. His hand plows the remaining powder into a pile in the center of the mirror. He picks up a playing card from the mirror and stares at it – the King of Hearts. The hearts in the corners of the card are human hearts, and the flicker of the candles makes them appear to throb. The King, wild-haired and bearded, emotionlessly thrusts a dagger into the side of his head. Connected at the torso of the King, and mirroring his actions on the bottom of the card, is a man with slicked-back, black hair, and a priest collar. He, too, stoically thrusts a dagger into the side of his head. Greg uses the card to scoop the powder from the mirror and return it to its place in the Mason jar. He says, "I just don't know what to do."

Kelsey and Jim sit down with Greg. They just sit. There is no talk. No effort to make sense of the unbelievable things in the attic. They just sit, and sit, and sit. And the night grows darker, the snow falls harder. As the candles burn low, and as both Jim and Kelsey begin to recognize the need to return to their own homes, footsteps and dry, raspy croaks come up the stairs.

Wally steps into the attic, bags of Ballreich's marcelled potato chips clutched in his arms. He croaks and drops the bags on the floor in front of Greg. Eddie follows Wally into the attic and sets glass bottles of Orange Crush on the floor for Greg and his friends. Eddie and Wally stand in front of Greg, swaying and staring forward with vacant eyes and empty heads.

"Um," says Greg, "thanks for the chips."

But Wally and Eddie do not answer. They do not look down. They do not move.

"They want you to tell them what to do," says Hopalong as he steps through the attic door. "You asked for a snack and they got you one. Now they want you to tell them to do something else."

Greg stands and stares up at his brother's pale face and sunken eyes. He sees nothing there – no anger, no recognition, no thought. Greg points to a corner of the attic and says, "Go sit in the corner."

Like an obedient dog, Wally immediately turns, shuffles toward the corner, and sits. Eddie remains standing in the same spot until Greg says, "You too. Go sit." And Eddie goes along with Wally. They sit and await further orders.

"Wow," says Greg.

"Yeah," agree Kelsey and Jim.

It is all too weird. And they talk about how unreal everything seems. About reanimated pigs and piss-monkeys. About the calliope music thrumming through the walls. About the white powder and subservient, drugged up zombie teens. They talk about Greg's grandfather. They wonder where Lumpy went. And though it seems like a fever dream, they all agree that it is happening and it is real. Before they realize it, the night has moved quickly on them.

Kelsey looks at her oversized Texas Instruments digital watch and gasps. "Oh my god, it's ten o'clock. Stanley's gonna murder me. I've got to go."

Jim Halloway laughs. "Stanley. Who the hell is that?"

"He's my dumb, drunk dad. He's a stupid Stanley." She quickly throws on her down vest and brightly-colored knit cap with oversized tassels. Tossing her backpack over one shoulder, she bolts out the door, yelling "see you later, masturbators."

"I've gotta go, too," says Jim. "I'm gonna call my mom and have her pick me up. I don't feel like running home in the snow. I wish I could stick around and help you figure all this mess out. But my mom will take my Atari away if I don't call her soon. I'll catch you at school tomorrow."

And then Greg is alone with Wally and Eddie. He paces around the attic and mumbles to himself. He picks up the old top hat that Kelsey found and holds it, studies it. The band on the inside of the hat is discolored from sweat and body oils, but the monogram on the band – M.S. – is still visible. The battered old hat fits Greg perfectly. He tilts it to one side and likes the feel of the fit. And while Greg paces about and fiddles with his new lid, the older boys just sit. Greg tells them to stand and they do. He tells them to do jumping jacks and they perform sloppy, uncoordinated jumps and flop their arms about. He tells Wally to bow down and kiss his bare foot, and Wally plants a kiss right on his big toe. Greg tells Wally and Eddie to sit again, and they do. As if they were dogs, Greg tells the boys to roll over. Eddie and Wally roll about on the floor, steamrolling each other and then rolling away again until Greg tells them to stop. Greg stares at the boys and tries to get a grip on the situation. He sits in front of them and watches for what seems like hours, until he falls asleep, sitting with his arms wrapped around his knees. The top hat slides forward and covers his eyes. Like guardians of sleep, the piglets emerge and form a semi-circle around Greg's back. The pigs sit and eye the strangely-still teenagers. And as Greg sleeps, the piss-monkeys go wild, slamming against the jars, their muted thuds providing a soothing background noise.

The breaking dawn flings bolts of sunlight through the attic windows, through the piss-monkey jars, and onto the lids of Greg's eyes, creating a stroboscopic eyelid picture show that gradually stirs him from his sleep. He still sits cross-legged on the floor in front of Wally and Eddie. Greg sees that at some point during the night, Lumpy has returned and settled on the floor with his friends. And the three lunkheads sit side by side, looking like drugged monkeys – Wally holding his hands over his eyes, Eddie with hands over his ears, and Lumpy holding a hand across his mouth. Somewhere deep in Lumpy's gaze Greg sees a look of pride or satisfaction.

Greg stands and stretches and pisses into an empty mason jar. He laughs at himself for the bad habit that he finds hard to break. Twisting the lid back onto the jar, he puts it in one of the windows to soak up the sun. Outside, the Big Bopper shuffles past Samsa Mansion and gazes up at the attic window where Greg stands. And the two briefly look at each other. Greg waves, wishing the strange little homeless man luck against the elements. The Big Bopper breaks the staring contest first, turns, and continues his funky strut down the street.

A rumble starts softly in Greg's belly and slowly develops into a ravenous growl. He turns away from the window, and away from his brother, to head downstairs for some breakfast before school. Laid out and waiting for Greg at the bottom of the attic stairs are two fat, dead raccoons – Captain Jack and Fats Flannigan. Greg's hunger subsides and a queasy feeling replaces it. He did say he wanted somebody to kill the coons. Lumpy apparently filled that order. But being irritated by the coons didn't equal Greg wanting them dead. And that queasy feeling turns to bubbling guilt. Greg said he wanted the coons dead and Lumpy granted his wishes. It is Greg's fault and he knows it.

So, one at a time, Greg hefts the dead animals and carries them into the attic. He scoops out indentations in the dirt of the coffin and lays the coons out. And though he despised them when they lived, Greg sprinkles dirt over their corpses and wishes for their return.

Big Shirl shouts out from somewhere in the house. Her voice carries through the rooms and hallways like an electrical signal on a wire. Greg hears his mother calling for him and Wally to wake up and get ready for school. He turns and looks at Wally,

Eddie, and Lumpy, at the pigs and at the piss-monkeys, and now at the raccoons. "Behave," he says to all. "Stay here and behave. Don't leave the attic. Don't hurt each other. Don't make a mess. This is my room. I'll be back after school and we'll think some more about what we're going to do." And Greg walks out, leaving the unmentionables to the semidarkness of the mystical attic. He scurries and scampers through the tight hallways and stairs and hidden passages until he reaches the first floor to find Big Shirl and Li'l Shirl in the TV room, watching the Today Show and sharing a box of Frankenberry.

Greg sits beside his mother on her bed and fills an oversized bowl with the sugary cereal. Li'l Shirl glares at him as if she knows what he has done. She does not avert her gaze until Greg looks down and away from her accusing eyes. He spoons cereal into his mouth just to do something to not look guilty. And the Frankenberry is good, good enough to twist a soft grin onto Greg's face. Greg doesn't know what to do about Wally and the others in the attic. He doesn't know who to tell or whether he even should. He does know that the cereal is delicious, and that Li'l Shirl is still staring at him, and that despite the heat of the guilt he feels under Li'l Shirl's stare, he will have another bowl of cereal before he goes to school.

"Baby," says Big Shirl to Greg. And she begins a laborious process of twisting and turning and readjusting her bra straps and waistband and housedress. The bed shakes and creaks under the shifting, weighty mass. The floorboards groan. "Where is your brother? He needs to get ready for school, too. Have you seen him?"

"No, Mom," says Greg, "I don't know where stupid Wally is. Maybe he wanted to get to school early so he could get help from his teachers. More likely, though, he's out somewhere smoking dope or breaking out streetlights or something wonderful like that. Wherever he is, I'm sure he is fine."

With his teeth tinted pink from the Frankenberry, Greg summons up the courage to face Li'l Shirl's accusing glare and smiles at her. Suddenly the ice in her eyes is gone. Her face relaxes. She sends back a big, dumb, soft smile at her brother, as if forgiving him or something. Relieved of his guilt, and knowing that the coons will be okay, Greg kisses Big Shirl on the cheek and runs out of the house. He runs through back alleys. The winter chill chaps his face and lips. But he does not run into Wade or the Courtneys or any of his other infinitely cruel schoolmates. Greg makes it to school and to his locker, to find Kelsey waiting for him with a weighty concern pulling down the corners of her mouth.

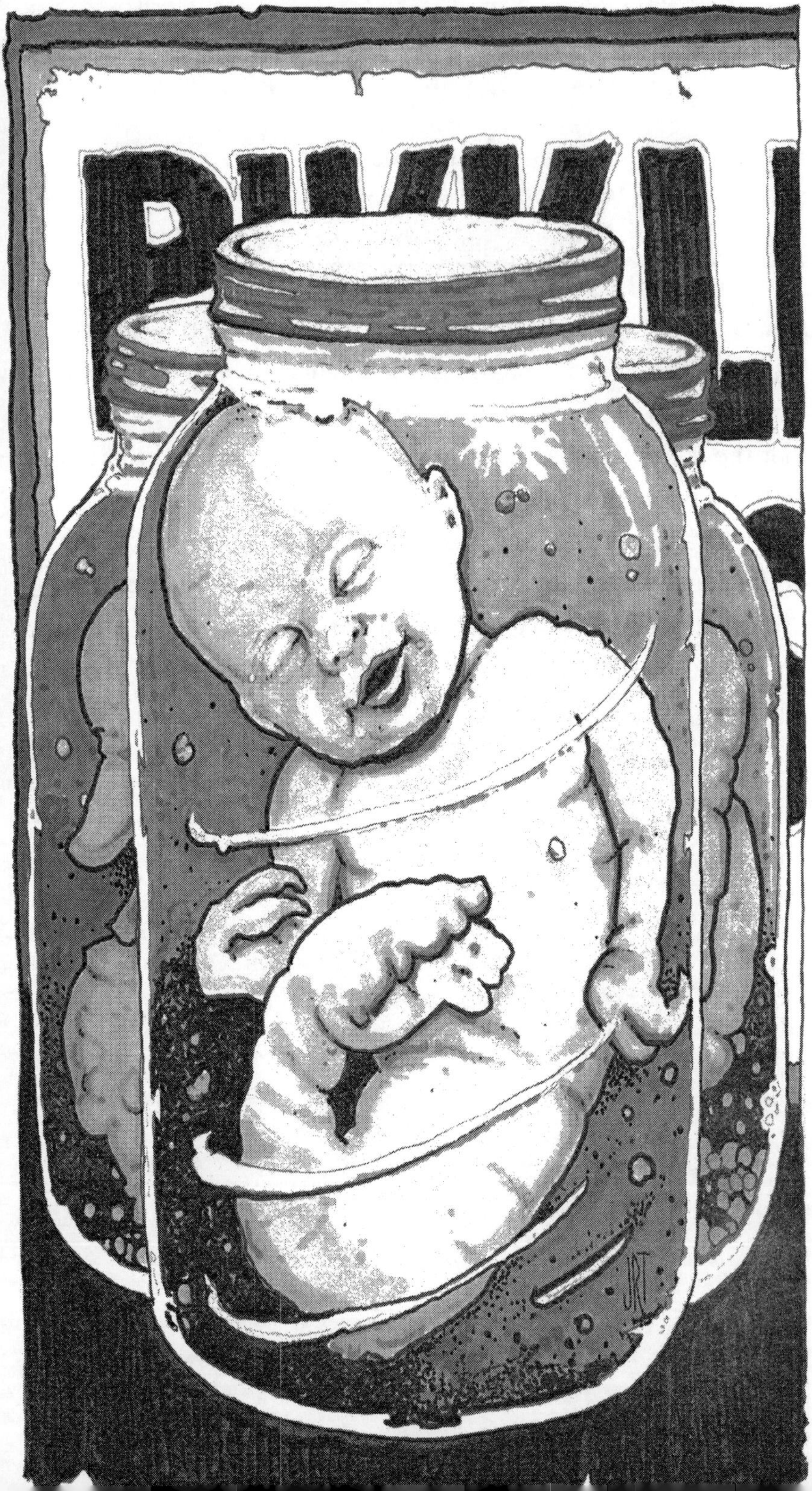

7

With a fur-lined hood pulled over his head and his moonboots leaving a trail of waffled footprints over the snow, the Big Bopper bops away the night and struts into the breaking dawn. His headphones pump a pulsating jam that slithers along his auditory canals, thumps a smooth groove on his eardrums that turns into a fluid message rippling through his cochlea, washing over the hair cells and sending the tune through auditory nerves to the brain. And the signals caress and massage the Big Bopper's primary auditory cortex, spreading warmth and serenity throughout the entire brain. The serene brainwaves spread and bathe the Big Bopper's entire body in a soothing, peaceful warmth. An almost imperceptible golden glow envelops the Bopper. He bounces along as if on spring-loaded legs. And the golden warmth drifts off of his body, flagging behind in steamy saffron tendrils.

The Bopper bops through alleys and soaks up energy from the early morning sun beaming down on him. As he turns the corner into an alley near Donnell Junior High, the blare of harsh static fills his headphones and crams itself painfully into the Bopper's ears. Along with the static, a red spot in the snow fills his vision. An excruciating jolt shoots down the Bopper's spine and drops him to his knees. He sees the bloody splotch in the snow. The haematic blotch blares and pulsates before his eyes. The pain of the person who leaked all over the ground slams the Bopper. Though nobody is there to strike him, the Bopper feels blows crushing into his head and neck and ribs. The sensation of hiking boots stomping on his arms and legs draws an injured yowl from the Bopper. Then the pain subsides, and the gray static in his head dissipates and wisps away in the morning breeze. The Bopper stands and shakes off the unseen assault. A tear leaks from his eye for the boy who took a beating, for the boy whose blood stained the ground like a gory snow cone.

Readjusting his headphones, the Big Bopper recovers from the jolt that dropped him to his knees. The acid-jazz smoothness of the universal groove pumps through the headphones again and applies a psychic balm to the Bopper. He brushes snow from his legs and struts quickly away from the alley. Away from the scene. Away to somewhere safer.

8

"Have you seen Jim this morning?" says Kelsey with surprising abruptness. The curls of her dirty blond hair are smashed down by a ratty, fur lined, red flannel bomber hat. The hat's sides hang over her ears and her curly locks dangle over her eyes. But, through the curls, the concern burns in her eyes.

The urgency of Kelsey's tone surprises Greg. "No," he says. "What's wrong?"

"I don't know." She twists nervously at one ringlet of hair, wrapping it tightly around her pointer finger. "I'm just worried. Wade came up to me when I got here this morning and said he had a nice visit with Jim before school. And I haven't seen him around. It worries me."

Greg sweeps his thin, oily bangs away from his glasses and says, "I know. Wade's been trying to get him. And he's really pissed off about Jim tricking him into smelling his butthole." And even with the concern that they both feel, the thought of Wade sniffing Jim's finger makes both Greg and Kelsey involuntarily smile, at least slightly. "Let's go look around for him. Maybe he just got here late or something."

But Greg doesn't really think that Jim is okay. The churning in his gut tells him that everything is very not-okay. Jim is not at his locker. He is not in his homeroom. He is not lurking at the far end of the second floor, near Lori Bursitis's locker. He is not asking Ms. Fanning for extra help with his art project. He is not in the lunchroom, flirting with the lunch ladies to get free biscuits. He is not at school. Not at all.

And as Greg and Kelsey scurry through the hallways, poking their heads into classrooms, Mr. Corbin lags behind them, always scrubbing or polishing or buffing, but always there in the background, always watching.

Jim does not show up. He's not in class. After fourth period, Kelsey catches Greg at his locker. The curly hair that hung in her eyes before now sticks to her sweaty, nervous forehead and cheeks. She tugs at the earflaps of her bomber hat and chews at the insides of her cheeks. "Something is very, very wrong," she says. "I can feel it. Jim isn't okay. They did something to him."

"I know," agrees Greg. "I told Mr. Blight that I thought Wade has done something to Jim. I told him I'm worried and asked him to look into it."

"Mr. Blight? He's the worst. He won't help."

"I know," says Greg. "I asked him to call Wade to his office and question him. When I did that, Blight got all shaky and weird. Said he had to take care of something immediately. He hustled me out of his office and wouldn't listen anymore."

"Yeah. I saw him heading for the parking lot just a little while ago."

"Oh my god!" says Greg. "He's afraid of Wade and he's actually taken off so he doesn't have to confront him. He's a total freakin' coward."

"That's exactly what he is," agrees a deep, resonant rumble of a voice. As if materializing from out of nowhere, Mr. Corbin is suddenly behind Greg. He digs a key in his ear and wiggles it around before withdrawing it and wiping it on his coveralls. "Always has been a coward. Always will be."

"Mr. Corbin," says Greg. "Have you seen Jim Halloway today? We think that Wade did something to him, hurt him or something."

"I haven't seen Mr. Halloway today," says Mr. Corbin. "And I have been keeping a watch on him as well as you two lately. He's absent today."

"Well we gotta find out what happened," says Kelsey. "I think he's hurt or something."

"You both need to get to class," says Mr. Corbin. "I'll investigate the situation. Maybe give Mr. Halloway's mother a call. I'll get to the bottom of things and let you know what I find. But get along right now. Get to class."

Greg and Kelsey reluctantly go to their classes. And their concern weighs down the day, turns time into a sickly, sluggish sloth. In the next break between periods, Mr. Corbin tells them that he spoke with Jim's mother and that she said he left the house and walked to school that morning.

And at the end of the school day, a crush of loud, laughing and shouting students gathers in the hall to watch the elderly custodian pinning a panicked Wade Busby to the wall of lockers with a push broom. At the back of the crowd, Greg jumps into the air to try to see what is going on. Over heads and shoulders, in brief snippets, he catches glimpses of Wade wriggling and trying to get away from Mr. Corbin, looking like a beetle pinned to a Styrofoam bug collection board and trying to escape. Glimpses of Mr. Corbin leaning in and mumbling something to Wade. Glimpses of the fear flashing in Wade's eyes. And with each jump, Greg glimpses bits and pieces, enough to know that Wade has good reason to be concerned. And the kids in the crowd cheer and jeer and relish the sight of Wade Busby, the school's top tormentor, frightened and vulnerable. Someone shouts, "Mess him up, Mr. Corbin," and others chime in with like sentiments.

Mr. Corbin leans in toward Wade and grumbles. But before he can say something, he is blindsided. Donnie Price springs from the crowd and runs into Mr. Corbin, knocking him down. Chop follows suit, knocking the broomstick from Mr. Corbin's gnarled, arthritic hands. Before the custodian can regain his feet, Wade, Donnie, and Chop are running through the crowd, knocking curious bystanders out of the way. They run right past Greg (who sticks his foot out to trip Wade). But Wade jumps right over the extended leg and sprints down the hall, around the corner, and out of sight.

The crowd disperses and only Greg and Kelsey go to Mr.

Corbin's aid. They grab his arms and pull him to his feet. Kelsey brushes off Mr. Corbin's back and Greg picks up the push broom.

"Are you all right?" asks Greg, handing the broom to Mr. Corbin.

The old man takes the broom and leans on it. "I'll be okay, Gregory. I'm more worried about you two and Mr. Halloway. Be very careful, because those boys are dangerous right now. They are out of control and nobody in this school seems to have the stomach to do anything about it."

Dread slams Greg in the gut and follows up with a right hook to his head, momentarily staggering him. Greg realizes that Mr. Corbin is right. Wade is becoming more brazen at school while the authorities cower and flee from their obligations to keep students safe. The only adult at school willing to stand up to Wade is the elderly custodian. And now Jim is missing, and Greg and Kelsey have to try to get home safely.

So the teens thank Mr. Corbin and leave the school, trying to avoid Wade and his cronies. They cut through back yards and hop chain link fences. They run down alleys and constantly scan all around them for any threats. When they reach Jim's house, nobody answers. Mrs. Halloway's orange VW is gone and all of the lights are off in the house. Greg tries the front door, but it's locked, as are the doors at the sides and back of the house. The empty house inspires panic in both Greg and Kelsey. It is very clear to them that something is not right. Greg grabs Kelsey's hand and drags her through backstreets. They hide behind bushes and sprint around corners, always watching for Wade.

The backstreets are clear and luck seems to be on their side. As they near the Samsa Mansion, walking the alleys that border the back yard, Greg allows himself a sigh of relief. He gives a gentle squeeze on Kelsey's hand and smiles just a little at her. And though still worried about Jim, she smiles back. But the smile flatlines into a tight, lipless slit at the sound behind them.

"Thought we'd find you here," Wade Busby says.

"Yeah, E.T.," says Chop. "We've been waiting for you."

Greg and Kelsey stand, not turning to look, knowing that Donnie Price is with them, too.

Greg grips onto Kelsey's hand and whispers, "Shit." He looks to the back of his house and considers making a break for it. He knows that he can beat the bullies in a foot race to the house but isn't so sure about Kelsey. So he decides to make a stand and try to give her a chance to escape. He whispers to himself, "Shit, shit, shit, shit, shit," then releases Kelsey's hand and turns toward Wade.

Greg straightens his posture and pulls back his shoulders, lifts his head high and stares straight into Wade's eyes. "What did you do to Jim Halloway?" Fighting every instinct he has, he steps toward Wade. "What did you do to him?"

Momentarily taken aback by Greg's brazenness, and even feeling a little unsure of himself, Wade says nothing. But he feels Chop's and Donnie Price's eyes on him and knows he cannot show weakness. "We beat the ever-loving snot out of Halloway," says Wade, laughing. Donnie and Chop join in with their obtuse chortles.

"Yeah," agrees Chop, "the ever-loving snot." He shuffles his feet and shadow boxes, punching body blows into a pretend Jim Halloway.

"Where is he?" asks Greg, maintaining a surprising coolness to his voice, stepping slowly and deliberately toward Wade, hoping that Kelsey takes the opportunity to break for the house. "What did you do to him?"

Wade's lips sneer and reveal a rotten, tobacco stained smile. He nods at Greg and says to Donnie and Chop, "Let's show him what we did to Halloway."

In an instant, Donnie locks onto one of Greg's arms and Chop grabs the other. And before Greg can struggle or run, Wade is crushing his fists into Greg's gut and ribs, knocking the wind out of him, cracking ribs, bruising internal organs. Wade's fists piston into Greg's liver and spleen and solar plexus, leaving Greg in agony and gasping for air. Kelsey jumps onto Wade's back and claws at his face, screaming at him to stop. But Wade shakes her off with ease. Wade steps back, looks at his work, laughs. Donnie and Chop laugh along, still holding Greg by the arms to keep him standing.

Greg straightens up and chokes in air. He stares, unflinching and unblinking, into Wade's eyes, and something about the look spooks the bully. It sends chills down Wade's back and makes his fine hairs stand on end. Wade says, "I'm gonna knock that look off your face and then I'm gonna finger pop your girl." He backs up and then runs at Greg, his arm cocked back and then looping wide. The punch lands square on Greg's jaw, just below the ear, and the force of the blow is like an explosion sending shock waves throughout his skull. Greg's vision blanks, and a burning pain pulses throughout his head. He crumples to the ground with his arms and legs numb and twisted up beneath him. For the moment he is paralyzed and can only feel the cold of the snow on his face.

Greg's vision blinks in and out. From his sideways view on the ground, he sees Wade, looking like a caveman with a freshly clubbed female, dragging Kelsey by one leg toward the bushes. Kelsey kicks out with her free leg and claws at the frozen ground.

Through his strobing blackouts, Greg sees Donnie and Chop converge on Kelsey and hold her arms down. Greg tells his body to move, but it does not respond. Through it all, Kelsey yells "fire" instead of rape, because a teacher once told her that was more likely to bring help. Wade bends down toward Kelsey and catches an upkick right on the chin from the partially-restrained girl. The kick stuns him but he shakes it off and throws Kelsey's legs to the side. And then he fumbles with the snap on her pants. But he is interrupted by Chop.

"What the fuck?" says Chop. He lets go of Kelsey's arm, stands, and steps back.

"Holy shit," says Donnie Price as he stands and backs away from Kelsey, too.

Wade stops trying to unbutton Kelsey's pants and looks up. Frothy foam erupts from her mouth. Her body seizes and flails back and forth. And Wade realizes that Kelsey is not fending off his attack, but instead is going into major seizures.

"That's messed up," says Chop. "Creepy Kelsey's freakin' dying or something."

"I ain't getting involved with that shit," says Donnie Price as he backs away from the quaking body on the ground.

"Yeah," says Wade, "let's beat it. I don't even want to finger some foamed-up, crippled spaz like that."

Wade takes off down the alley with Donnie and Chop trailing

him, leaving Greg and Kelsey injured and lain out on the snow. And then feeling returns to Greg's extremities and he pushes himself up to his knees. With great effort he struggles to stand, his arms and legs shaky and unsure, like a baby doe taking its first steps. He stumbles over to Kelsey and drops to the ground. She still flails, but Greg cradles her sweaty head in his arms and strokes her hair out of her face. He coos and talks to her and says, "Come on girl. Snap out of it. Come on."

The shaking and quaking subsides. Kelsey's eyes go wide and then she shakes her head, throwing off the remnants of the seizure. Greg holds her head and still strokes gently at her face, looking down into her eyes and seeing clarity return. She half smiles and says, "You're very nice to me, Greg Samsa."

And he helps Kelsey up, but they are both unsteady on their feet. Arms around one another for support, they stumble to the back of the mansion and into the house.

Greg and Kelsey help each other into the back of the house. As they stumble up the rear stairs, Big Shirl calls out for Greg.

"Aw, crap," says Greg. "I can't let her see me right now. She'll freak."

And this time Kelsey does not lay a guilt trip about Greg's mother wanting to see him. They struggle up the stairs, stopping at the first floor landing, where Li'l Shirl blocks their way.

Greg says, "Get out of the way, Li'l Shirl. I'm not in the mood."

But Li'l Shirl looms in front of them, swaying back and forth gently, her mouth agape and her mind clearly trying to conjure a thought. A streamlet of drool dribbles down her chin and drips onto her substantial bosom. Greg momentarily thinks that Li'l Shirl has somehow gotten into the piss-monkey powder. Following that thought, he wonders how he would be able to tell the difference. And then something clicks, Li'l Shirl's eyes shed their bovine quality, and she says, "Momma needs to talk to you about Jim Halloway."

Big Shirl lounges on her oversized bed in the front parlor, staring at the big screen TV. She scoops a handful of cheese-stuffed pretzels out of a bag and pops them in her mouth one at a time. On the TV, a pretty blond girl gets hit in the face with a football, covers her face with her hands, and yells, "Ow, my nose."

Greg and Kelsey walk into the room. Dried blood covers Greg's face and shirt and he winces as he walks. Kelsey's complete lack of color and pained expression make her look like a ghost.

Big Shirl gasps and mutes the TV. She wiggles into a sitting position on the bed and cries out, "Oh my lord. What happened to you?"

Greg shrugs his shoulders, which pains him and makes him wince again. "Nothing, Ma. I just fell down some stairs at school and...."

"Come here, Baby," says Big Shirl and she struggles to maneuver her massive body to make room for Greg.

Greg does not argue or reject Big Shirl. He sits at the edge of the bed and feels the warmth of the mattress. He allows himself to be enveloped in his mother's flabby arms. And the embrace is good, and warm, and comforting. He nearly allows himself to cry into her bosom, but he chokes it back and merely takes comfort in the fact that his mother loves him. And that consoles him, but it does not heal the mental wound that has been reopened. That something inside of him that allowed forgiveness, that expected things to somehow get better, is gone. It is replaced with a need for retribution. Greg hugs his mother, then pushes back and stands at the edge of the bed.

"Li'l Shirl said you needed to tell me something about Jim Halloway," Greg says. "What's up?"

Big Shirl adjusts her housedress and brushes crumbs off of her stomach. She sees the pained looks on both Greg's and Kelsey's faces, and hesitates briefly. Greg pushes for an answer, "What's up with Jim, Mom?"

Big Shirl just blurts it out, not knowing how to put it gently. "Jim Halloway is in intensive care at Blanchard Valley Hospital right now. He's been beaten badly. Been drifting in and out of consciousness. He hasn't been able to tell anybody what happened. But, his mother suggested that you might be able to help them figure it out. Do you two have any idea who could have done such an awful thing?"

Kelsey's eyes tear up. Greg stumbles backwards, then grabs Kelsey by the elbow and steadies himself. His vision tunnels and the room begins to spin. But then the vertigo leaves him.

Kelsey begins to answer Big Shirl, "I know what happened...."

But Greg interrupts. "We don't know nothing, Mom. We've been looking all day for Jim. I've gotta go and see him."

"You can't, baby," says Big Shirl. "He's got head trauma and the doctors won't let anybody but family see him. And they've got him in a secure area of the hospital because they don't know if whoever did this will come back for him."

Greg stumbles out of the room, stunned and confused. He

puts an arm over Kelsey's shoulder and they lean on one another, staggering through the halls and stairways until they find themselves in the attic.

Wally stands guard at the bottom of the attic stairs like a lobotomized doorman. His head hangs forward and frothy slobber slops from the side of his mouth. When he sees Greg his eyelids lift slightly, his posture straightens. He groans, "Shitturd," as Greg walks by.

Greg and Kelsey pass by Wally, barely looking at him. They climb the stairs into the attic and Wally follows. Eddie and Lumpy wait for Greg's arrival at the top of the stairs.

Greg says, "Move the hell out of the way," and Eddie and Lumpy each step back, clearing a path.

Greg paces the attic. He grabs the top hat off of the coffin and puts it on. The hat tilts to the left and makes Greg look slightly mad. Or maybe it is the look in his eyes that makes him seem mad. Or maybe the agitated manner in which he paces about and wrings his hands. It certainly is not his words that make him appear crazed, because he says nothing.

Walking past stacks of piss-monkey jars, Greg does not notice that the creatures have grown to fill the entirety of the jars. If Greg were to look, he would see greenish-brown lumps with bulging eyes and claws and folded wings, crammed and squirming uncomfortably inside of the jars. He would see them gnashing their teeth. But he doesn't notice the piss-monkeys.

Greg doesn't notice that the feral pigs have taken on a greenish tint and have nearly doubled their size. He doesn't notice the sounder of swine shadowing him. He doesn't notice that the skin on Wally, Lumpy, and Eddie doesn't hang on them right and looks more like loose, ill-fitting clothing draped over their bones. He doesn't notice the swollen and seeping purple pustules barnacling on Lumpy's face.

Greg doesn't notice Kelsey following him about the room, trying to rub his shoulders to calm him down. He doesn't notice the panicked look in her eyes, or the fear she feels as she tries to help him settle. Greg notices nothing. He grabs a piece of paper from the desk and reads it quietly to himself again and again as he paces about.

Kelsey tries to swipe the paper from Greg's hand, but he moves it out of the way and keeps pacing, mouthing the words on the paper to himself, until finally Kelsey corners him. Grabbing Greg's elbows, Kelsey shakes him and says, "Snap out of it Greg. I know things are bad, but you're kind of starting to creep me out."

And he lifts his head and looks into Kelsey's eyes. Her presence shakes something loose and Greg regains his composure. He says, "I'm sorry. I kind of lost it there. I've been knocked in the head so much lately that I'm not sure I'm altogether right up here." He gently slaps his forehead and laughs humorlessly. "And then there's what they did to you. And to Jim. And the way everybody in this town is so damn mean. I mean, hell, even your dad punches you. I think it's all starting to make me a little crazy."

Kelsey flinches at Greg's words. The situation with her dad was always left off limits. She shakes it off and says, "Well, what's on that paper that you keep reading? Let me see it."

Greg folds the paper over and holds it to his side. A wild look flickers in his eyes, like that of a cornered animal.

"Don't worry," says Kelsey. "You don't have to show me if you don't want to. I guess that I'd just like to see it, though." She puts on a little pout, obviously fake, but cute enough to win Greg over.

"Okay," he says. "But don't go thinking I'm a psycho or something. I just wrote this after a really bad day. It made me feel better. It's not like I mean it or anything." He hands her the paper. "And don't go laughing. I know my poetry is some seriously cheesy, teen angst crap."

Kelsey laughs a little, stands straight, and waves her hand around theatrically as she reads the paper in a melodramatic tone:

For all of those who've treated me bad
Who've beaten and taunted and made me feel sad
Look into my eyes, look into my head
The thing that I need is to see you all dead

For you Mr. Blight, the thing that I wish
Is to see you face down in a watery dish
As for Wade Busby, the thing that I'd like
Is to see your head mounted, on a long pointy spike
And as for your monkeys, Chop and Donnie Price
I have some thoughts that are not very nice
A smash in the faces
A slash in the guts
And then mounted beside Wade
On spikes rammed through your butts

As for the others still waiting on deck
who've harmed,
and hit,
and heckled,
and hurt me
Who've long put me down
and treated me shitty

For the Courtneys and Beulers
and crooked of neck
For the bigger and stronger
who won't take it back
You too will pay,
and regret your trespasses
When I strike out with vengeance
And smite all of your asses

Greg grabs the paper, crumples it up, and throws it over his shoulder. The pigs playfully chase after it, picking it up and trying to keep it from each other, until it breaks down to a slobbery, shredded, mess of masticated paper.

"See," says Greg, feeling embarrassed and worried about what Kelsey thinks. "It's stupid and it makes me look like a psycho. Feel free to stay as far away from as you can. Otherwise I might just creep you out even worse."

But Kelsey doesn't back away from him. She closes in and puts her arms around Greg. She holds him tight, pulls off his hat and glasses, and stares directly into his bulging eyes. And they both start to cry, but there is nothing uncomfortable about it. They know things suck. They know that they deserve a good cry.

They know that there is little hope of things getting better.

"I'm sorry you had to read that," says Greg, pulling back from Kelsey just a little.

"Nothing to be sorry about, you freakin' psycho," she laughs.

And everything feels just a little bit better. The pigs gather around them in a circle and stare up with dead black eyes. Wally, Eddie, and Lumpy pull in close around the circle and stare at them, too. Wally groans, "shit-turd," with a dopey smile on his face.

Greg laughs, "Yeah, Wally, you're a shit-turd, too." And they have a moment. Greg feels a connection with his big brother. All he ever really wanted was for his big brother to like him. Greg always told himself that he hated Wally and wanted to see him gone. But that wasn't really true. Wally is his big brother. And Greg wanted him to protect him, to give him advice, sometimes just to hang out and talk. But they never had that relationship. And now Greg feels something from Wally, maybe closeness or protectiveness or some other big-brotherly stuff. But he feels it, and that's really all he had ever wanted from Wally.

Wally and Greg look at each other again and, at the same time, say to each other, "Shit-turd."

The moon glides across the sky and Kelsey has to leave. She kisses Greg on the mouth, harder and a little bit longer than usual. When she pulls back, she looks into his eyes and says, "I know that poem was just a release for you. Let the writing of it be what heals you. But don't become that person. Promise me you won't try to hurt anybody. I don't know what the answer is, but that's not it."

Greg half grins, still feeling a little funny from Kelsey's long kiss, and says, "I promise I won't lay a finger on anybody."

Kelsey pecks him with several more quick kisses and then is

gone. And the good feeling that her kisses brought float right out of the attic behind her. With Kelsey gone, the physical pain returns with a ferocity. Greg's head hurts. His ears ring with a constant high-pitched hum. He clasps his hands together and paces the room, mumbling the poem that is etched into his brain. His words block the squeal in his head, so he says them louder. As he stomps about, picking up momentum, the words fly from his mouth, clearly and loudly, until he is shouting and dashing about the room. Gasping for air and feeling like he is getting stabbed in the side with each breath, Greg finally drops to the floor in exhaustion. He did not notice the parade of unmentionables – Wally, Eddie, and Lumpy, and a sounder of greenish, walking dead swine – trailing his mad dash about the attic and paying attention to his words. The throbbing of his many different bumps and contusions pulses throughout his body, from head to feet. And when he can take it no more, his eyes close. Peaceful nothingness swirls around him, tossing off flecks of gold and strands of cool blue. And the ten thousand things flee and leave in their place a cozy void.

PART THREE

1

The harsh winter weather relents. Spiky crystal stalactites dangle and drip from gutters until they disconnect and crash to the ground. Snowdrifts melt, turning yards soggy. The fifty-degree weather has school kids ditching their winter gear and walking to school in t-shirts without jackets.

In the light of the early morning, the Big Bopper bounces along, *sans* moonboots and winter jacket, bopping to a spaced out, fuzz-tone bass groove, snapping his fingers and bobbing his head. Funked out guitar be-deep-deedle-dee-dees over the bass, and syncopated drum beats kick the groove along. And the Bopper feels it, he really feels it, man.

At the south end of town, the Bopper bops along Olive Street and into the country. He leaves the road and bops along the railroad tracks that border Hancor Industries. The Bopper happens upon three deer, sending the startled ruminants into alarmed, bouncing flights, boinging along on the ground and disappearing into the forest. The Bopper bops over the rail bridge that spans Eagle Creek and continues to head south. A velvet eared goofus of a basset hound follows along behind, bouncing to the same beat, as though he too can feel the groove from the Bopper's headphones. And trailing the hound, trying to keep up, a shabby three-legged dog stumbles along, panting and looking ready to drop.

The smell hound stops, sniffs the ground, and catches the scent of wild critters. He tears away from the Big Bopper's far out groove and lopes along, droopy ears flopping behind him, following the scent trail, howling and yowling, barking and baying, disappearing into the woods. The three-legged mongrel looks at the Big Bopper and then in the direction of his friend. He reluctantly tears himself away from the Bopper's trail and takes off into the woods.

But the Bopper don't worry about smell hounds and three legged mongrels. He just keeps bopping. Shortly after he crosses the rail bridge, the Bopper passes a gash in the ground that blows dark smoke into the sky. The smoke billows and a moderate wind wafts a continuous streamer of it toward Findlay. But the Bopper don't worry about the fuming gash in the earth. He don't worry about nothing. He just keeps bopping to the groove in his headphones, strutting along the tracks and snapping his fingers to the beat.

2

The morning commences with a harsh, high-pitched squeal, which turns into the warbling strains of the calliope ringing in Greg's head. Golden beams of light shine through the piss jars and focus an amber glow on him. He opens his eyes and refocuses his consciousness, for he was not really sleeping. Instead he sat all night and let his mental and physical wounds fester and bubble and boil, becoming one and the same, and turning him into something he never wanted. A sickness burns in his head and body, a sickness that seeks retribution. Greg does not know what he wants to do, but he knows he isn't going to take it anymore. He's not going to let people hurt him or his friends. He's not going to be put down and made to hide and run and cower.

He shakes off the dull ache in his brain and brushes his hair away from his glasses. Lifting the top hat from the floor, Greg places it back atop his head. He finds Captain Jack and Fats Flannigan curled up in front of him, and gently passes his hands over the fat coons' fur, brushing the coffin dirt off of them. The animals sit up at attention before Greg, rubbing their little front paws together anxiously.

"Scoot," says Greg, and the coons move out of his way. He looks around the attic, but does not see Wally, Eddie, and Lumpy. And the coons and piglets gather about his feet, looking to him for guidance.

Greg realizes that he has never fed the pigs, and wonders if they will eat. He goes downstairs and fixes himself a bowl of E.T. Cereal. And he knows how much the kids at school would love to know that he actually eats E.T. Cereal. He knows that would be a real hoot for them. But it doesn't bother him because he really just likes it. And it doesn't concern him what anybody would say or if they would call him E.T. Something has changed, and the silly concerns and insecurities that plagued Greg in the past don't matter because he has changed.

After eating, Greg finds a case of canned dog food that Li'l Shirl keeps in the cupboards for the sole purpose of feeding raccoons. Greg empties four cans of the food into a mixing bowl. The smell, like rotten meat, dirt, and feces all cooked together, makes Greg grimace. He breathes through his mouth as he carries the food up to the attic. And when he sets the bowl down, the pigs and raccoons just sit in front of it, showing no interest whatsoever in the meal.

Top hat tilted slightly atop his head, Greg leisurely strolls to school. He does not scurry or jump or hide at sudden sounds. He does not scan the streets for peril. Something tells him that he is now the dangerous one. Behind him, Captain Jack and Fats Flannigan scramble to keep up.

And because he woke early, Greg decides to take the long way to school, walking along the streets instead of scampering through the alleys. He turns onto Lima Avenue and strolls along the sidewalk. At Karcher's carryout he turns right onto South West Street. Lost in his thoughts about Jim Halloway, Greg walks right into something – something that grabs onto his arms. He looks up to see the twisted face of Johnny Close tilted sideways on a crooked neck and smiling a malevolent rictus at him. Greg jerks back and his hat falls to the ground.

"Hey there, buddy," says Johnny, his face close enough for Greg to smell the sour beer and cigarette breath. Johnny wobbles a little and grips harder onto Greg's arms to regain his balance. A nervous tic makes Crooked Neck scrunch up his face involuntarily. He clenches his teeth and fights off the minor spasm. "I haven't seen you around for a while. It seems to me that we never finished our last conversation."

Johnny lets go of an arm and tugs his sweatpants down enough to expose himself to Greg. Instead of flinching of fighting or fleeing, Greg just sighs, as if bored and disappointed. And something about his demeanor throws Johnny off. Crooked neck gets off on domination and scaring his victims. He lives for the fear in their eyes and the disgust on their faces. But Greg's response perplexes Johnny.

"What?" says Johnny, cocking his crooked neck a little more toward his shoulder and squinting his eyes in a question at Greg. "What's that little sigh mean? Am I boring you?" He lets go of Greg's other arm, confident his prey will not run, and backs up several steps.

"You are boring me," says Greg. "You are a twisted old fruit that gets off on scaring kids. Well, I'm not scared of you. You can't do anything else to hurt me because it's already all been done. So screw off."

The words knock Johnny back a step. And Greg's defiance, though confusing, arouses Johnny. In the heat of the moment, Johnny forgets that he is not in a back alley, but actually on a residential street with cars driving by, people looking out of their front windows. He leaps at Greg like a broken spring toy that seizes up just as it gets moving. His hand slaps Greg and turns the boy's face to the side, knocks the top hat to the ground.

Before the open hand is off of his face, as his head turns, Greg laughs and says, "Screw you, Crooked Neck." The slap knocks Greg to the cold ground, but does not hurt him.

Johnny Close puts his hands to his head and twists his crooked neck. The crackling creptitations pop and grind like a foot crunching ice on the ground. Crooked Neck laughs and grabs at his erection. He leans in toward Greg, ready to grab him and drag the boy into the alley.

Slowly, calmly, Greg laughs a gentle chuckle that again confuses Johnny and stops his approach. Greg says, "Captain Jack, Fats Flannigan, get him."

Johnny's eyes cloud with confusion and all he manages to say is, "Huh?" before the raccoons are on him.

Captain Jack locks his claws onto Johnny's head and chomps his sharp little teeth right onto the tip of Johnny's nose. Staggering backwards, Johnny flails his arms at the masked animal on his face. As he falls, Fats Flannigan leaps at Johnny's crotch and tears at his genitals with a mouth like a tiny wood chipper.

Eyes peek through front windows and heads poke out of front doors in response to Johnny's agonized screams. The residents of South West Street watch on in horror as Crooked Neck writhes on the ground, flailing his arms and trying to dislodge the raccoons. Yet none of the villagers come out of their houses or shout for the situation stop. Not one calls the police. Not one takes the first step toward helping Old Crooked Neck.

Greg dons his top hat and stands over Johnny, doing nothing to stop the attack, saying nothing. He watches and knows that he has the power to end it, but does nothing. And then he feels the eyes of the neighborhood focused on him. He knows that it is time to stop. He claps his hands and clicks his tongue at the coons. And as suddenly as they began, the coons stop and dismount a bloody and weeping Johnny Close. Captain Jack kicks slushy snow at Johnny with his back feet before once again taking up his position with Fats Flannigan behind Greg.

Seeing that it is done and that Johnny offers no further threat, Greg turns and bends down, patting the coons on their backs, rubbing their coarse fur. And the animals put their ears back and gaze up at him with dead eyes, awaiting further orders. But Greg is done with Johnny and can feel the people staring out from their houses. As if nothing happened, Greg walks away from Johnny, down the street toward Donnell Junior High, ready for Wade or the Courtneys or anybody else who wants to give him a hard time.

Red lights swirl and flash on the front of the school. A cloud-trail of black smoke blows northerly in the sky, blotting out the morning sun. Black and white police cruisers block off Baldwin Avenue while rotund, mustachioed officers stand about on the landing at the front of the school, drinking coffee and talking into their radios. As Greg approaches, teachers mill around on the sidewalk and smoke. Ms. Fanning's face is puffy from crying. Mrs. Grenner flicks an ash off of a long, thin cigarette, looking more annoyed than anything else. An officer stops school buses as they approach and boards them briefly. The buses back up and turn right to take the road that circles the football stadium and Donnell Pond, and then head off to take the students back to their bus stops because school is cancelled for the day. In the distance, the warbling of an ambulance siren dopplers toward them with a subtle undertone reminiscent of a calliope.

With his joints swollen and achy as they always are in the morning, Mr. Corbin slowly steps off of the sidewalk and crosses Baldwin Avenue, intercepting Greg. The janitor pushes his glasses up on his nose and looks at the raccoons behind Greg with a note of curiosity. The coons' shadows waver on the ground as heat ripples. Mr. Corbin's shadow mimics his every move. But by some trick of the light, Greg casts no umbra. Mr.

Corbin grunts an interrogatory in the direction of the raccoons and, receiving no explanation from Greg, he says, "They found Mr. Blight face down in a toilet, drowned."

"He's dead?" asks Greg, not shocked, not sad, not happy.

"As can be," says Mr. Corbin, matter-of-factly.

"And I wished that," says Greg. "Did I cause it?"

"I don't know, Gregory," says Mr. Corbin, taking off his glasses and wiping them with a dirty handkerchief. "Like I said before, be careful what you wish for. Desperate wishes from injured souls just might have enough strength to come true. And perhaps they can veer wildly out of control, beyond whatever can be expected, sometimes in frightening ways."

"But I didn't do this," says Greg defensively. "I mean, I wished for it, but I didn't really mean it."

"I know, Gregory. I know." Mr. Corbin puts his thick glasses back on and looks toward the paramedics exiting the school. "There'll be no school today."

"Cool," says Greg, completely ignoring the gurney being wheeled out of the school with a sheet-covered lump on it. Mr. Corbin flashes a look of disapproval at the nonchalance, and Greg says, "What? I'm sorry. It's not like I did that. I didn't wish him dead...well, yeah, I mean, I did and all, but that was because he turned away when Wade was beating the crap out of me. He had nothing to offer me. Now I've got nothing for him. I've got nothing left inside to feel. Even if I did, I wouldn't waste it feeling bad about him."

Greg gives back a look that defies Mr. Corbin's judgment. And the almost imperceptible strains of the calliope warble from somewhere on another street. A black flow of smoke courses overhead as a river in the sky, moving faster than the other clouds, and bisecting the heavens above Findlay.

Finally, Mr. Corbin clears his throat and pensively digs a finger in his ear. He harrumphs at Greg. "I cannot tell you what to do, Gregory. But I do believe that you still have something good inside of you. Please do not tarnish that. If you lose the goodness, you lose yourself. Be good, be safe, and be well. Whatever it is that's starting to go on around here makes my hair buzz. I don't like it and I don't like the path you seem to be taking. Don't let this town, this school, bring you down to their level. Be the better man."

Greg nods at the old man and steps backwards. He tips his top hat, turns on his heels, and walks westerly on Baldwin Avenue. Captain Jack and Fats Flannigan sit back on their hindquarters and tip their heads at Mr. Corbin, as if also nodding at him. And as Mr. Corbin looks at the animals in perplexity, they turn and scramble down the street after Greg.

A look of pure disgust twists up the wrinkled face on the middle-aged man staring out through the screen door. He shows no shame or embarrassment about the fact that he is wearing only black dress socks and a yellowed tank top t-shirt tucked into his sagging Fruit of the Looms. He cares not about Greg seeing his sunken chest and potbelly, his piss-stained underpants. Running a hand over his thinning strands of blond hair, the man rearranges his comb-over into another placement that still fails to conceal his male pattern baldness. Smoke pours off of the cheap cigar clenched between his teeth and clings to the sides of his face as it rises, forming a wreath of smoke around his head.

Through the smoke, and behind the wrinkles and bags under the man's eyes, Greg sees a flash of a look. And in the man's tired, hungover, angry face, there is a brief glint of Kelsey – a resemblance that cannot be denied. Greg sees where Kelsey got the eyes that go all wonky when she starts to squinting and giggling. But the man does not giggle. He does not squint. His eyes do not go wonky in the cutest little way. No, instead, the man looks like a bitter sewer-dwelling troll, while Kelsey is sweet and cute and quirky.

The family resemblance throws Greg for just a moment as he stands at Kelsey's front door, flanked by Captain Jack and Fats Flannigan. His mouth opens and then just gapes, he leaves it that way hoping that some words will fall out.

"What?" says Kelsey's dad. "What the hell do you want, kid?"

"Uhh, um," says Greg. He takes off his top hat and asks, "Is Kelsey home?"

And the wrinkles and scars and bags under eyes twist and strain and scrunch into a scowl on the man's face. "Goddammit," he growls and turns and walks away, slamming the door behind him. The muffled curses of the man find their way through the door and Greg hears himself referred to as *some weird four-eyed kid*.

The front door opens a crack and a wide-eyed Kelsey peeks her head out. "You have to get out of here," she says, panicked. "Stanley is drunk and mean and extremely pissed off that you woke him up. He has to be to work at the factory in a couple of hours and he's gonna take it out on me if he doesn't get his sleep."

"And tell that little shithead to get those filthy animals off of our porch or I'll call animal control," Kelsey's dad shouts from somewhere in the house.

Kelsey steps through the screen door and gently pushes Greg backwards. "Go," she says, her eyes conveying her strong conviction that he leave and not cause any trouble with her dad.

"That boy and his pets better be off our porch and running down the road or I'm gonna get up and…."

"He's going, Dad," shouts Kelsey back into the house. "He's going now." She looks at Greg again and says, "Go. Please just go. Come back later, when he's gone."

And Kelsey gently puts her hand on Greg's chest. She leans in, plants a warm, wet kiss on his cheek, and then gently pushes him backwards. "Go. I'll see you later."

Greg immediately sprouts a rod and turns down the sidewalk, followed by his raccoons. He looks back to see Kelsey wave one last time before shutting the door. He wanted Kelsey to go to the hospital with him to see Jim. But bringing her along right now would just cause domestic distress. So Greg walks away, adjusting his tumescence. Alone with only his raging boner and two creepy raccoons to keep him company, Greg stomps his way to Blanchard Valley Hospital.

The emergency room doors slide open and welcome Greg into the building. Captain Jack and Fats Flannigan stop and wait outside like sentinels at the entrance. Nobody stops Greg or asks where he is going. Nobody questions kids walking around in the hospital. Greg and Jim have gone into the cafeteria many times and bought Scooter Crunch bars from the ice cream vending machines. They've walked the halls and looked into rooms. And never has anybody said a cross word to them.

So Greg walks the hallways, just trying to locate Jim's room. He smells the antiseptic disinfectants and cleaning fluids, hears the hospital's nonstop medley of moans and beeps and buzzes coming out of rooms. A pretty nurse at the visitor's desk has no answers for him. She curtly says that she is not allowed to give out patient information and then her eyes snap back to her romance novel. But, Greg's efforts to find Jim are not fruitless. Finally and fortuitously, he nearly runs right into Mrs. Halloway coming around a corner.

Mrs. Halloway dabs at her eyes with a tissue and then gives Greg a tight hug, smashing him with her bosom in a way that gives him mixed feelings of arousal and shame and embarrassment at feeling that way about his best friend's mother. Mrs. Halloway says, "Oh, Greg. I'm so glad you are here. Jimmy is waking up and he has been asking about you. I'll take you to see him. He'll feel so much better now that you're here."

Not making eye contact with Mrs. Halloway, and feeling the onset of another raging erection, Greg awkwardly follows her to Jim's room. And it hurts Greg to see his best friend hooked up to tubes and wires, having bags of fluid hanging beside the bed and draining into his arm. It kicks his heart in the balls. Jim's face is beaten and crusted with scabs. His exposed skin is black and blue. Jim looks like Greg feels inside, and that hurts Greg even more deeply. He steps to the bedside and grips onto Jim's hand, saying, "Hey, jackass, it's me. Wake up."

Jim's eyelids slowly lift, and through the haze of morphine he recognizes his best friend. His eyes focus and his mind momentarily clears. He opens his swollen, split lips and smiles a gummy smile at Greg. The footprint on his face and the missing teeth tell Greg that that he was kicked while down. Jim laughs a hoarse laugh and mumbles, "I made those fudge-packers smell my asshole."

"It was Wade who did this, wasn't it?" Greg asks, and coldness washes over him.

"Yep," Jim gurgles through a mouthful of drool. "The old asshole sniffer."

A curtain divides the room and a gentle, pained moan comes across from behind it. A voice that sounds one hundred years old, crusty and crumbly and dry as dust, complains, saying, "I need a nurse. I pooped 'em."

Greg looks toward the room divider and says, "Uhh, maybe I should get him some help."

But Jim Halloway grips onto Greg's hand, not letting go. He groans, "Worst roommate ever. He does this all day. Don't worry about him."

And just as suddenly as lucidity visited Jim, it flitters off, leaving the thick fog of pain medications to take over. Jim's eyes roll back into his head and he falls deep into oblivion again. And though he is unconscious, Jim Halloway squeezes hard on Greg's hand, refusing to let go.

The burbling snore that escapes Jim Halloway seems to synchronize with the beeps of his cardiac monitor. The low, moist, almost rhythmic rumble of the roommate's flatulence joins in on the hospital music from behind the curtain. And Greg sits with his unconscious friend, staring at his injuries, hurting inside to have to see his best friend in such a sorry state. Looking at what Wade Busby did to Jim Halloway, Greg's heart shrank three sizes that day.

On the way out of the hospital, Greg sees Johnny Close sitting in the emergency room, bleeding all over the seats and gently weeping to himself. But Greg pays no attention to Crooked Neck. He walks right by, not even giving Johnny a glance. And the emergency room's automatic doors slide open and spit Greg out into the fresh air again. As he walks away from the hospital, Captain Jack and Fats Flannigan fall in behind him.

The Lime and Stone Quarry Company hacked a gaping hole on the surface of the city. Earth blown out by dynamite and hauled away with heavy equipment left a massive pit from which limestone is removed. A strip of land at the edge of the pit borders the quarry and is fenced off from the medical complex behind Blanchard Valley Hospital. But the tiny fence, seeming more like a gentle suggestion than a prohibition, does nothing to deter Greg from hopping it and walking along the thin path worn into the strip of land by teens who use the route as a shortcut from school to their houses at the south end of town. Since there is no school today, Greg guesses that he will encounter no other kids along the path. He guesses wrong.

The stanky, cloying smoke of Swisher Sweets cigarillos wafts down the trail and worms its way into Greg's nostrils. The smell is that of teenage boys who don't like cigarettes but still want to look cool smoking something they don't have to inhale. Usually the cigarillo boys wear button up shirts and corduroy pants, and are the type who splash on half a bottle of Brut in an effort to kick the blossoming teen girls' libido into overdrive. But Greg smells no Brut. The reek of the cheap cologne would be welcome. Instead, Greg smells sour, sweaty body odor. And he recognizes the aroma. The distinctively pungent odor can only mean Tim and Jim Courtney.

Normally the Courtneys' presence would make Greg detour to avoid conflict. Normally, Greg wouldn't be walking the path alongside the quarry. But nothing is normal for Greg anymore. The raccoons trailing at his heels, ready to do his bidding, provide ample evidence of the current abnormality of his life.

Just ahead Tim and Jim sit on a downed tree, smoking their cigarillos. The ground around them is littered with empty Old Dutch cans. And the Courtneys see Greg and stand up to greet him. They sway drunkenly back and forth and watch in surprise as Greg continues in their direction. Tim crushes an empty can and chucks it at Greg. The crumpled can bounces off of Greg's chest and falls over the edge, down into the quarry. Greg brushes at the wet spot on his shirt where the can hit, and continues along the path.

Side by side on the path, Tim and Jim refuse to move when Greg reaches them. Greg stops, clasps his hands together, and looks toward the ground. He rocks forward and back, breathes deeply, and raises his gaze to the Courtneys. "Let me through," he says softly, confidently.

But the path does not clear for Greg. Instead, Jim laughs and says, "Shut up, E.T." He reaches out and pushes hard on Greg's chest, easily knocking him to the ground.

Greg gets back to his feet and brushes his hands against his pants. He sets his top hat right, straightens his Atari shirt, and steps up to face the Courtneys again. When he gets within inches of the brothers, Greg breathes in their beer-and-tobacco-and-body-odor-stench, and says, "I will say it one more time: let me through."

Tim and Jim are so fascinated by Greg's demeanor that they fail to notice the two fat and fidgety raccoons standing behind him. And, this time Jim swings his arm wide and high, knocking the top hat off of Greg's head. Tim and Jim high five each other and laugh. Jim pops the top off of an Old Dutch and chugs the entire can of beer-like swill. Tim does the same. Greg picks up the top hat again and sets it on his head. He clasps his hands in front of his chest. And, once again, the Courtneys advance on him. Greg does not move. He does not flinch. He averts his eyes to the ground and waits for Tim and Jim to try to push him again. When they get close enough, Greg merely says in a soft, calm voice, "Get them."

Instantaneously, Captain Jacks and Fats Flannigan attack Jim's legs, biting and tearing at him through his threadbare jeans. The growling and howling from the animals sounds like feral dogs fighting over food, not anything like what one would expect from raccoons. Greg remains rocking forward and back in his stance, hands clasped and eyes to the ground, as if in a trance, while the coons gnash and gash at Jim's legs. As the animals take bloody, mouth-sized chunks from calves and thighs, Tim stands back, slack-jawed and entirely gobsmacked by the turn of events.

Tim looks to Greg but receives no feedback from the scrawny boy, who almost looks to be praying, as the animals attack. So Tim resorts to the only solution he has ever really known, mindless cruelty and violence. He picks up a thick stick from the ground and brings it down hard on Fats Flannigan's back. The stick breaks and draws an outraged yowl from the coon. And Fats Flannigan, his snout dripping with Jim's blood, looks up from his feast of flesh, his demented eyes locking with Tim's. Tim swings the stick back and realizes it is completely broken and useless. He reads the coon's intent. "Oh shit," is all that Tim utters before he turns and sprints down the trail.

But intoxication slows Tim and trips up his feet. He stumbles over a root and knocks his face and forehead against the limestone the edge of the quarry. Fats Flannigan and Captain Jacks pull back from Jim and chitter at each other as if discussing a game plan.

"Go," says Greg, and the raccoons scurry down the trail after Tim.

Jim holds his hands to the gashes on his legs, trying to stanch the bleeding, and watches as the raccoons take off after his brother. Greg, with hands still clasped, approaches and stands over Jim, saying nothing. Now gripped with terror, Jim crab walks backwards away from Greg, whimpering, "Leave me alone. Just leave me alone."

With a tip of his top hat to Jim, Greg turns and leisurely walks away. He stops in front of Tim, who thrashes about on the trail, trying to shake Captain Jack from his head and Fats Flannigan from his chest. But the coons grip on with their claws and tear at the frantic boy with their teeth. Tim rolls to the edge of the quarry and his legs slip over the edge. His fingers claw at the ground as the raccoons dismount, leaving him flailing for something to grasp onto to stop from sliding over the edge and down the twenty-foot drop to a steep slope of loose gravel below.

On the trail, just feet from Tim, Greg stands with his head bowed and his hands clasped. He makes eye contact with Tim as the boy fitfully grasps for something to keep him from slipping over the edge. And with just his shoulders, arms and head above the rim of the quarry, Tim manages to lock his hands onto a tree root. Greg stands before him, flanked by the furry bandits, and continues to stare into Tim's tearful eyes. With his hands still clasped in front of his chest, Greg gives a slight nod to Tim, as if to say, *Good day, Sir.*

Without a word from Greg, Captain Jack and Fats Flannigan pounce on Tim's hands and bite at his fingers. The boy holds the root as long as he can, desperately clinging to his anchor. But his bloody fingers makes the root slippery and impossible to grip. He slowly slips over the edge, and then gravity takes control of the situation, slamming Tim to the gravelly slope below, breaking bones and knocking the air out of him.

Before Tim passes out from shock, he gazes up to the rim of the quarry. Just above the edge of the trail, Tim sees a trail of black smoke whipping by in the sky. Standing at the edge of the cliff, with a raccoon on each side, Greg looks down at Tim and tips his hat. As Tim loses consciousness, he sees Greg turn and walk away with the raccoons waddling after him.

Something stiffens Greg's spine, straightens his posture. And wearing the top hat, Greg seems to have grown two feet. Maybe it's the improvement in his posture, maybe the top hat, maybe that he looks large in comparison to the coons that trail him. Whatever it is, he gives off an aura of danger. He walks home with determination and confidence, and a slight smirk on his face. The kids he encounters do not shout E.T. at him. They do not molest him. They cross the street to avoid him as they would one afflicted with weeping, leprous sores.

And as Greg approaches his house, he sees Hopalong on the front porch, puffs of hot breath issuing from his mouth like a train's smokestack, galloping in circles on his hobbyhorse, gripping it by the head and holding its broomstick tightly between his thighs. The large awkward cowboy slaps his hand on his own ass and shouts "giddy up," as he clomps about, bending and bowing the decrepit porch boards beneath his substantial heft. When Hopalong sees Greg, he stops riding his stick horse and strikes his best cowboy pose. He says, "Howdy, pardner," and tips his Stetson at Greg.

    Greg tips his top hat right back and says, "Howdy." As he walks in the front door, Hopalong gallops behind on his horse. Greg pays no mind to Hopalong as he walks through the house, and through the TV room. He passes Big Shirl with merely a tip of his hat and an unfocused, "Love you too, Mom." The smirk on his face send chills down the fat rolls on Big Shirl's back. But before she can inquire, Greg is out of the room and into the kitchen. Big Shirl barely notices the large, slow cowboy and the two raccoons trailing her darling boy.

    In the kitchen, Li'l Shirl sweats down the front of her baggy housedress and scoops cans of wet dog food into multiple bowls. She turns her back to Greg when he enters and tries to hide the fact that she is getting ready to feed raccoons. "I hain't doin' nothin'," she offers up, unsolicited and overly defensive. "Certainly hain't feeding no coons." She hunches over the bowls of dog food to hide them from Greg.

    "It's all right, Li'l Shirl," says Greg. He puts a hand on her shoulder and eases her to one side, exposing the stinking bowls of meaty muck. "It's all good. I'm not going to stop you from feeding them. In fact, I've got some vitamins to make them strong and healthy."

    Li'l Shirl scrunches up her face in surprise as Greg pulls a Ziploc baggie of white powder from his pants pocket. He sprinkles the powder over the glistening mounds of stinking meat and gravy. "It's good for them," says Greg, smiling encouragement at Li'l Shirl. "It'll make 'em strong like bull. Look at Captain Jacks and Fats Flannigan, here."

    The coons sit up and fiddle with their front paws, as if confused about where they should hold them. A darkness stains their claws and snouts, but they do not lick at it or pick at it. They just sit on their haunches, front paws fiddling, and smiling raccoon smiles that do not match the vacancy in their eyes.

A laugh escapes Li'l Shirl's dumb *O* of a mouth. "Strong like bull," she says as she grabs as many bowls as she can to take them out of the kitchen. "I like that."

Entering the kitchen, Hopalong steps in front of Li'l Shirl, and joins the conversation, "Adult bulls weigh between 1,100 and 2,200 pounds. They can be very aggressive and account for twenty-five percent of all animal-related injuries on farms. The world's largest bull is six feet five inches tall and weighs three thousand five hundred pounds. Forty-five percent of bulls…."

"Strong like bull," says Li'l Shirl again, cutting off Hopalong's flow of bull-related statistics.

"Strong like bull," agrees Hopalong with a half-formed idiot grin. He and Li'l Shirl lock eyes and stare for an uncomfortable interval, the both of them just grinning and staring. A trickle of saliva begins to dribble from the side of Li'l Shirl's mouth.

"Yes, you two," says Greg, breaking the staring contest, "strong like bull. Now let's get them their vitamins. Set those bowls all over the house. I want to make sure those cute little critters are good and healthy."

Grabbing up the dog food bowls, Hopalong and Li'l Shirl leave Greg alone and set about their chore of feeding all of the raccoons. They exit the kitchen in a hurry, side by side, both sporting happy, vacuous smirks. As they leave Greg behind, he hears Hopalong explaining to Li'l Shirl that bulls have thirty-two teeth and 207 bones in their bodies. Just before they are out of Greg's hearing, Hopalong says, "strong like bull," and both he and Li'l Shirl laugh like it's the funniest thing they've ever heard.

Grunts and heavy breathing. Glass breaking. Liquid splashing. Wet tearing and crunching noises. These are the sounds that greet Greg from the bottom of the attic stairs. Sensing a problem, Greg rushes up and into the attic. He blinks his eyes and shakes his head to adjust to the low light and make sure he is seeing things right. But there is no trick of the light. Greg sees a horror show.

Gathered together in a corner of the attic and kneeling in puddles of some fuming solution, Wally, Eddie, and Lumpy crouch over a mess of grey flesh and bones and hair on the floor. Tiny hands and legs and malformed faces stick out from the great, gloppy, puddly pile before them. Wally leans down and broken glass crackles, pierces his palms. He plants his face into the pile of defiled pikkled punks and comes up with a tiny conjoined twin fetus dangling from his mouth. Like a dog with a toy, he shakes his head and the coupled fetus flops back and forth against his chest. And the shared shoulder between the twins' heads suffers the crunch of Wally's teeth as he rips at the grey, dead flesh and slurps it like linguine into his mouth. Lumpy and Eddie lean down and bob for babies, too, smashing their faces into the pile, coming up with their own stillborn prizes. Lumpy chomps onto an arm of a large-headed abortion and pulls it off as if eating chicken wings. Eddie digs his teeth into the cheek of a monkey-faced fetus, like biting into an apple. And the threesome feasts on the rancid pile of death, animals consuming animals.

Before they can do any more damage to the pikkled punks, Greg shouts, "Bad!" He snatches a Mad magazine from the floor and rolls it up. Slapping the magazine hard against the palm of his hand, he runs toward the mess, shouting, "Bad! Bad! Bad! Bad! Bad!" Wally, Eddie, and Lumpy scatter on all fours as Greg whacks at them with the magazine and continues to chastise them. In the fracas, Greg steps on a pikkled punk and slips, falling splat in the middle of the gloppy pile of fetus parts. He jumps back up, still thwacking at Wally, Lumpy, and Eddie with the magazine, scattering them to other parts of the room.

With the threesome dispersed, Greg's fury subsides. He approaches Wally, who cowers on hands and knees beside the coffin and averts his eyes to the floor. Gripping onto the collar of Wally's Quiet Riot shirt, he drags his big brother over to the pikkled punk mess and shoves Wally's head toward the floor. "Look at what you did," orders Greg, pushing harder on Wally's head. "What did you do? What did you do?"

And Wally keeps his eyes cast downward. He cowers on hands and knees before the mess. Meanwhile, Lumpy and Eddie crouch in other safe spots of the room, flinching as if stricken at every word that leaves Greg's mouth, cringing as Greg turns their way.

"Come," orders Greg. Lumpy and Eddie hesitate, and then emerge from the couches and crates they hide behind.

Greg points at the floor and says, "This is very, very bad! No more. No jars. No. No. No. No. Now clean up this mess. I don't want to be able to see that it ever happened." And he paces around the attic, checking on the remaining pikkled punk jars. They are more than curiosities to him. He cares for them in some strange way that he does not fully understand. And he continues to take stock of the remaining jars until he finds the one he is looking for. Against a wall, just under a window obscured by piss-monkeys, Greg finds the jar on its side but unbroken. He holds it up and stares at the pikkled punk that Kelsey named Greg. The baby sits cross-legged, with head bowed and hands pressed together as if praying. A bug-eyed stare from the bigheaded baby seems to tell Greg that it is unharmed. He looks at the baby and notes once again that its features are remarkably like his own. The pikkled punk makes Greg think of himself as a fetus, lounging in the warm, watery, ample accommodations of his mother's womb.

While Wally, Eddie, and Lumpy clean up their mess, Greg sits cross-legged on the floor, cradling Pikkled- Greg in his arms. Whatever it is about the strange dead baby, Greg feels a connection. The thought crosses his mind that he could sprinkle some powder in the jar and give the little fellow a second chance. But a moan from the other side of the attic derails Greg's train of thought.

On his hands and knees in the middle of a pile of dismantled pikkled punks, Lumpy grabs great glopping handfuls and slops them into a garbage bag. Large, taut, purple boils throb on his face and neck, some of them seeping yellow pus. Clumps of hair fall from his head and reveal a purple, splotchy scalp. Lumpy moans, not in pain or distress, he just moans because that's how air escapes him now. His respirations ebb and flow in a constant rhythm of groaning inhalations and grunting exhalations. Accompanying the moans and groans, a stream of spittle leaks from the side of his mouth and adds to the puddle already all around him on the floor. And Greg looks to Lumpy and then to the pikkled punk resting in his lap. No, the pikkled punks will not be powdered and reanimated. Although Greg feels as if he may have lost his mind, he still recognizes the cruelty of such an act.

What good would powdering pikkled punks do? *None*, Greg thinks to himself. He recognizes that they would probably never grow or mature intellectually. They would be tiny, brainless idiots like miniature versions of Wally, Lumpy, and Eddie. Little monsters. And, with whatever suffering those babies already endured, to bring them back now would just add insult to injury. Greg stands and takes the jar over to set it down beside his mattress on the floor. He sits on the mattress and gazes at the jar, now oblivious to the cleanup job transpiring on the other side of the attic. He doesn't notice Wally, or Eddie, or Lumpy. He doesn't notice the pigs that gather around him, wiggling their corkscrew tails and staring at him with their dead fish-eyes. He doesn't notice the strains of the calliope that fill the attic. He doesn't notice Hopalong.

"It is now 3:30 p.m.," announces Hopalong, knocking Greg out of his daze. "And it's a beautiful day out there, with the temperature currently at a balmy fifty degrees Fahrenheit. Later tonight temperatures will drop to a low of forty degrees."

Standing at the attic entrance, holding a bowl of dog food in each hand, Hopalong smiles and waits for Greg to acknowledge the weather report. And Greg nods a hello. "Thanks, Hopalong. I was wondering about the temperature."

And Hopalong's moon-face lights up at Greg's appreciation of the weather report. He stands and grins, staring at Greg.

"Just set those bowls over there," Greg says. He waves his hands in the direction of Wally, Eddie, and Lumpy cleaning up their pikkled punk mess, and then goes back to staring at his own little pikkled punk.

"Okay, Greg," says Hopalong, still beaming. He lumbers across the room and sets the bowls on the ground. Hopalong receives no further input from Greg, so he repeats his weather forecast to soothe himself, to fill the room with sound. "It is now 3:31 p.m. And it's a beautiful day out there, with the temperature currently at a balmy fifty degrees Fahrenheit. Later tonight temperatures will drop to a low of forty degrees."

The smell of formaldehyde and ancient fetuses wafts off of Greg's shirt and pants. He changes into a new pair of boot cut jeans and throws on his t-shirt with Mr. T. Saying *I PITY THE FOOL*. And the draw of his pikkled punk is strong. Greg sits on the bed again and holds the jar in his arms like a mother nursing a baby. The repetitious weather report drones on in the background like white noise, drowning out the snarling and yipping noises of Wally, Eddie, and Lumpy fighting like dogs over the bowls of dog food that Hopalong set out for them.

But the fight over the food becomes too much. Lumpy pins Eddie to the floor and bites him on the neck. Eddie yelps in pain and pounds on the ground. And the fracas once again brings Greg above the surface of consciousness. Greg sets the jar on his mattress and stands. Picking up the Mad magazine he rolls it up and slaps it against his palm. "Bad," he shouts at Lumpy. "Bad. Bad. Bad." And Wally, Eddie, and Lumpy all stop and cower as if about to be swatted.

And a thought occurs to Greg. It's strange to him that Eddie and Lumpy have been at the house and nobody has come looking for them. "Hopalong," says Greg, cutting off the repetitive flow of the weather report.

"Yes, Greg."

"Has anybody asked you where your brother is? Aren't your parents worried about him?"

Hopalong scrunches up his face, squeezing hard to force a thought out of his head, and then smiles as it all comes together for him. "No sir, Greg," says Hopalong. "Ma and Pa don't notice nothing. Sometimes Eddie gets gone for weeks. They don't fuss and fiddle about when Eddie's gone 'cause he always comes home at some point."

The realization dawns on Greg that Eddie and Lumpy are throwaway kids whose parents don't care if or when they come home. Nobody will even worry about them missing. They've stayed at Greg's house for weeks on end. If anybody ever does raise any questions about their whereabouts, it won't be for quite some time. With his battered top hat tilted back on his head, Greg puts his fingers to his mouth and whistles, drawing the attention of Wally, Eddie, and Lumpy. "Come on, boys," says Greg, "we're going to Kelsey's."

Wally, Eddie, and Lumpy shuffle about at the curb, pale and slumping and sickly looking in the day's waning sunlight. Greg says, "Stay. Do you understand me?"

A vague smile turns up Wally's lips and he merely says, "Shit-turd." And the name no longer sounds hateful in his mouth. Instead it carries a warmth, an affection, and Greg finds that he actually likes it as a term of endearment.

"You're a shit-turd, too," he says playfully as he turns and walks to the front door of Kelsey's house. Rapping his knuckles sharply on the door, Greg tilts his hat slightly on his head and fixes a big smile on his face to bestow a pleasant greeting on his girl. But his smile evaporates into angry fumes, leaving his mouth dry and downturned and clenched when Kelsey opens the door.

Kelsey's swollen eye and the hematoma on her forehead tell Greg that her father took his anger out on her. She sniffles, wipes tears from her eyes. "You have to go," she says urgently.

Seeing Kelsey in such a state nearly knocks Greg on his ass. He shakes his head and gasps, "I'm not going anywhere without you. I'm not going to let your dad hurt you any more than he already has." Grabbing at her hand, Greg tugs at Kelsey, gently coaxing her out of the house.

"Greg, no," says Kelsey in a loud whisper. She resists his pull and steps backward into the house half a step.

Without warning, the front door flies all the way back and Stanley Stevens appears behind Kelsey, sneering and clenching a lit cigar in his teeth. Grabbing at his daughter's other arm, he yanks her back into the house. The smoke and stench of gin fumes off of Stanley Stevens and burns at Greg's eyes.

Greg wipes at his tears and calmly warns Kelsey's dad, "Get your hands off of her, Stanley. I'm asking nicely and I won't be so polite next time."

Stanley Stevens' face frosts over. Then, with just a hint of a smirk, he lets go of Kelsey's arm, letting Greg and Kelsey tumble out of the front door onto the sidewalk. Stanley steps through the door, advances on Greg, and begins bellowing, "Did you just call me Stanley, you little punk? You call me Mr. Stevens. You call me sir. You do not call me by my first name."

Scrambling to his feet, Greg steps in front of Kelsey to shield her from her father. Stanley Stevens pokes a finger into Greg's chest and continues to shout. "You do not come to my house and tell me what to do. You do not disrespect me. I am Stanley Stevens and you are nothing, little boy."

The ruckus draws an audience as neighbors peer through windows and out of front doors to see Stanley Stevens screaming and poking Greg in the chest. Greg, realizing that he now has many witnesses, decides to egg Kelsey's father on, saying in a calm, soft tone, "I'm sorry, STANLEY. I didn't mean to disrespect you, STANLEY. STANLEY. STANLEY. STANLEY. STANLEY. STANLEY."

With each reiteration of his name, Stanley Stevens pokes Greg in the chest harder and harder, pushing him all of the way out to the road. And once Greg finds his feet on the public street, under a streetlight that just turned on for the approaching night, and he is sure that Kelsey is out of Stanley's reach, Greg says, "You are a pathetic man, Stanley. You are a sad, sick, pathetic little man." Greg stands with arms to his sides, back slumped to appear even smaller and more vulnerable, looking up at Stanley Stevens.

And Stanley Stevens' face grows as dark as the stream of smoke billowing over the city. Daylight winks out and the streetlight throws a spotlight on the conflict, highlighting Stanley's rage for all of the neighbors who peer out from their homes.

Unable to take any more, Stanley Stevens cocks his fist back and punches Greg square in the face, popping the top hat off like a cork and sending the much smaller boy to the ground. Stanley Stevens wobbles on his drunken legs and looks down at Greg struggling to stand back up. And Stanley winds up again, readying to land another shot. But before he can, a balled-up fist lands squarely in the back of his neck, right at the base of his skull. The world tilts and lists for Stanley Stevens. Then two more punches land. Boom, boom, out go the lights. Stanley drops to his knees, then falls, face flat on the ground. Wally shakes his fist, trying to straighten out the bones he just broke. He drops down to the ground and with his unbroken hand starts hitting Stanley's ribs and arms and face with a metronomic precision, *bop, bop, bop, bop.* Eddie catches on to the rhythm and tunes up Stanley's legs with syncopated kicks to the thighs and knees. Lumpy digs the groove and beats out a bones-on-meat bongo accompaniment, thudding fists into Stanley's back. Regaining consciousness, Stanley cries out. His pained yelps and grunts ring out in time with the crushing blows, accentuating the rhythms of the brutal drum circle. His calls for help draw more and more neighbors from their homes, like meerkats popping their heads from dens. And while many of the neighbors come out to watch, nobody intervenes.

Greg puts his top hat back on, tilting it to one side, and stands just outside the melee. When he puts a hand on his brother's shoulder, the fire in Wally's eyes goes out. He pulls back off of Stanley Stevens and reverts to dead-eyed, empty Wally. And Greg walks around and puts a hand on Lumpy, who stops pounding fists into Stanley's back. Lumpy rises and stands next to Wally with a vagueness in his eyes. Finally, Greg puts a hand on Eddie and gently says, "Stop." Eddie does. He rises and sidles over to Wally and Lumpy, and they stand, empty-headed and slack-jawed, awaiting further instructions. Aware of the entire neighborhood's eyes on him, Greg shouts so everybody can hear, "Leave this man alone. He's done nothing to you. Go home. Go away from here."

Wally smiles a half-smile at Greg and says, "Shit- turd."

"You're the shit-turd," says Greg, "Now get out of here. Go home."

As Wally leads his two pals back to Samsa Mansion, some of the neighbors watch the creepy threesome lumber and lurch down the street, their gaits not quite human but not exactly inhuman either. Others in the neighborhood watch on as Greg sits down cross-legged in the light of the streetlamp, just in front of Stanley Stevens' head. In a smooth, serene tone, Greg leans in and says, "You are a bully. You bully your daughter. You probably bully your wife. You just bullied me. I don't like bullies. I'm giving you an opportunity to change your ways. I've sent those awful boys on their way. I'd like to think there's no reason for them to ever come back this way again. What do you think?"

Stanley Stevens shakes his head in an emphatic *NO*.

"Good," says Greg. "Kelsey's going to come with me until you get your act together and can be nice to her. Got it?"

Stanley coughs and a bubble of blood inflates from his nostril and then bursts into a spray. He gags on the blood draining down the back of his throat and then nods his head to indicate that he will be nice to his daughter.

"All right, then," says Greg. He pats Stanley on the head and stands up, backing away. Turning to Kelsey, he holds out his arm for her to loop her hand through the crook of his elbow. And the two amble down the street, fading into the darkness and then reappearing in the light of the next streetlamp, arm in arm and ignoring the stares of the neighbors. As they walk, one raccoon joins in behind them. From one streetlamp to the next, Greg and Kelsey appear with more coons following them. They walk without talking. And by the time they near Greg's house, an entire army of raccoons trails them.

Standing sentry on the lighted front porch, hobbyhorse between his legs, Hopalong tips his hat to Greg and Kelsey, and says in a passable John Wayne imitation, "Howdy, pardners."

"Howdy," say Greg and Kelsey at the same time, uttering words for the first time since Kelsey's house. Greg tips his hat at Hopalong.

"Them's a lot of varmints, eighty-three by my count," says Hopalong, nodding out toward the gaggle of raccoons on the front lawn. Their eyes reflect the porch light like floating green globes on the front lawn.

"Sure is," agrees Greg. "They just seem to follow me around."

Hopalong fidgets with his guns, straightens his tin star, and readjusts the Stetson on his head. "It's a very nice night out," he says, eying Greg and Kelsey with a pleading look.

Greg takes the bait. "It is a nice night. Do you know anything about the weather forecast?"

Teeth flash, eyes light up, posture straightens. "Sure do," says Hopalong. He drops the hobbyhorse on the porch and follows Greg and Kelsey through the front door, saying, "Tonight is going to remain warm, at around fifty degrees, and we should see some melting of the remaining snow on the ground. Tomorrow will be unseasonably warm, with possibilities of temperatures in the low sixties. With warm southerly air flowing over the snow that is still on the ground, there should be plenty of fog in the a.m. You'll want to check the radio in the morning for school delays."

And they find themselves in the front hall with the front door open. Just past the threshold, on the rotting porch outside, what looks like hundreds of green glowing eyes stare in at the house, waiting.

Hopalong kicks the front door closed with his foot and latches the lock. He turns and repeats his weather report. "Tonight is going to remain warm, at around fifty degrees, and we should see some melting of the remaining snow on the ground. Tomorrow will be unseasonably warm, with possibilities of temperatures in the low sixties. With warm southerly air flowing over the snow that is still on the ground, there should be plenty of fog in the a.m. You'll want to check the radio in the morning for school delays."

Big Shirl's labored snores build in intensity and carry

throughout the house. Then they stop for five, ten, fifteen seconds, before Shirl gasps and grasps for air in surprised-sounding, high-pitched sucking noises. Unaccustomed to the sound of Big Shirl's sleep apnea, Hopalong jumps every time he hears the gasps for air. He turns in the direction of the sounds and sees Li'l Shirl peeking her head around the corner of a doorway. And when Li'l Shirl sees Hopalong, her eyes saucer and she involuntarily gasps, sounding just like her mother sucking for air. Li'l Shirl quickly disappears around the corner, knocking things from a shelf in a clattering, battering manner. Without a word of warning, Hopalong changes tack and bolts for the door through which Li'l Shirl fled. And his weather report can be heard trailing off as he pursues Li'l Shirl through the house.

Guttural and drunken grunts and gurgles crawl all over a greasy blues track and ooze down the stairs to greet Greg and Kelsey as they arrive at the attic. The yowls and howls of Screaming Jay Hawkins drift about on air currents, riding wild bucking musical notes and casting spells. Greg looks at Kelsey, still not really talking, and nods his head toward the attic, urging her to go on up.

Wally stands sentry at the attic entry, shuffling from foot to foot, his eyes unfocused. As Greg steps into the attic, Wally says, "Shit-turd," in an expectant tone.

An empty chuckle falls from Lumpy's mouth and he echoes Wally, "Shit-turd."

Eddie, standing by a window stacked with amber jars, joins in, too, "Shit-turd."

And beside Eddie, on an elaborately carved antique end table, a hand cranked Victor phonograph spins the Screaming Jay Hawkins record, picking up on the nasty, crackling grooves and exhaling them hard out of the flared brass speaker-horn. A stack of old 79 rpm blues records leans against one leg of the end table. Screaming Jay Hawkins ends his song. Eddie lifts the needle and sets it to the side of the record. Loading another disk onto the turntable, Eddie cranks the handle and puts the needle down again. The crackles introduce Charlie Patton signing in a coarse voice about high water everywhere.

Across the room, Lumpy turns on an Atari system hooked up to a TV, both of which are new to the attic. A simple, squared-off orange man with no neck runs through a maze on the screen, blasting dashes of light at one-eyed, armed robots, exploding them. The pixilated man runs from maze to maze, transitioning through exits at the edges of the television screen. He stays diagonal from the robots because they can only shoot horizontally and vertically, sometimes tricking the robots to walk into the maze walls and electrocute themselves. When the man hesitates too long in one maze, a bouncing, evil smiley face chases him away, forcing the man to run through one of the maze exits to avoid execution.

Greg stands before the TV, holding Kelsey's hand and watching the Berserk demo repeat itself on the screen. Another blues record blows in cool from the corner of the room. And the things that usually soothe Greg – the blues and video games – just leave him flat. Berserk is one of his favorite games. And there is something nice about the crackly phonograph and old records. But Greg is empty. The blues and the video game barely register with him. Only Kelsey's touch reaches past the numbed out crust of Greg's exterior and touches the kernel of his former self.

They don't talk about Kelsey's dad. They don't talk about Jim Halloway. They don't talk about anything. Greg and Kelsey sit down in front of the TV and Kelsey runs the Berserk fugitive through the mazes, blasting robots. Wally remains at the attic entry, Lumpy stays near the TV, and Eddie replaces records and cranks the phonograph to keep the blues filling the emptiness of the room. Piglets emerge from behind boxes and chairs, and form a circle around Greg and Kelsey. Eventually weariness wins and Greg and Kelsey fall asleep on the floor, their bodies spooned closely together.

3

The warbled strains of the calliope, twisted and tangled into the groove of a funky circus song, pump from the headphones and directly into the Big Bopper's brain. His bop is nearly a skip as he boogies up Main Street, floating along through the thick fog that has befallen the village. The moist, warmish air blows over and around the Bopper, making him regret his thick jacket and scarves. So he doffs the jacket and hat and scarves, stripping down his upper half to a tattered and stained white undershirt. And taking exception to the undershirt too, the Bopper tears that off and ties it around his head, flying a tattered freak flag in the morning fog.

The gaunt man weaves through the fog, cutting it and trailing streamers of moisture in the air behind him. He heaves and breathes as he bops, drawing in deep inhalations that accentuate the rawboned ribs, and exhaling as if releasing all tensions.

Bounding along after the Big Bopper, looking as if he is swimming in the thick condensation, the droopy basset hound follows closely. Shortly thereafter, the three-legged, rumpled mutt chases along, trying to keep up.

On the corner of Baldwin and Locust Streets, Hopalong and Li'l Shirl stand hand in hand, idiot grins plastered on their vacant faces. And they wave at the Big Bopper as he bounces by them. The basset hound bays a happy hello at the couple as he is washed along in the Big Bopper's wake. The howls blend in with the calliope tune and draw a grin from the Bopper.

And the Bopper keeps on bopping, 'cause that's what he does. The dogs run behind, and Hopalong and Li'l Shirl continue to wave at him as he vanishes into the fog. They even wave in his direction after he has disappeared from their view. And the Bopper twists and swirls in the nebulous morning brume, smirking as the ten thousand things fall into the irrelevance of the past.

As he bops easterly on Lima Avenue he passes Greg in his top hat, walking hand in hand with Kelsey on the opposite side of the street. The Bopper uncharacteristically waves at the couple. Kelsey waves back and shouts, "Keep on truckin' Mr. Bopper."

Behind Greg and Kelsey, a procession of vacant-eyed raccoons trails for thirty feet. And the coons hiss and spit at the dogs trailing the Big Bopper. The basset hound and the three-legged mongrel stop to howl across the street, but the Big Bopper doesn't wait for his canine friends (who eventually feel the pull of the Bopper's groove and run to catch up with him). Greg and Kelsey pay no attention to the animals' petty bickering and continue walking to school. And the Big Bopper likewise bops along to his own beat.

4

Greg and Kelsey turn onto South West Street with the gaggle of raccoons following them. Before they get close to school, Kelsey stops walking and keeps a grip on Greg's hand. And Greg is lost in the fog of his own head. He jerks to a stop, too, as Kelsey abruptly halts his stride.

"You need to talk to me, you big weirdo," she says to Greg in a half-joking tone, but meaning it.

"What?" says Greg, looking down at the fog that nearly obscures his feet.

Frustrated, Kelsey laughs and says, "What?"

"What?" says Greg again.

"You need to talk to me. You come over to my house and have Wally and those goony goons beat up my dad, and pretty bad, too. And then you haven't said a word to me since. It's weird, Greg. You're acting weird. And I know weird, I'm Creepy Kelsey. Talk to me. Tell me what's going on."

"Nothing's going on," says Greg defensively. "Your dad hit you. He attacked me, and my big brother stood up for me. He had it coming."

"And what about Mr. Blight?" asks Kelsey.

"He was a jerk-ass."

"That may be so, but he didn't deserve to die, did he?"

"I don't know," says Greg. "But I didn't have anything to do with it." He holds his hands clasped together and stares at the ground, slowly rocking from his toes to his heels and back again.

The raccoons gather in a circle around the couple and sit back on their haunches, wringing their paws just like Greg, looking on curiously.

And then Greg offers up more information. "I also didn't try to hurt the Johnny Close or the Courtneys yesterday."

Kelsey cringes and says, "Oh god. What happened with Crooked Neck and the Courtneys?"

"Crooked Neck hassled me and the coons stopped him, tore him up a little. And the Courtneys, they started in on me on my way back from seeing Jim Halloway. I didn't do nothing to them. But they got rough with me and the raccoons stepped in to protect me. Jim got a little chewed up and Tim fell over the edge of a little cliff."

"Over a cliff? Are you freakin' serious? What happened to them then? Did they go to the hospital?"

"Don't know," says Greg. "Don't care. I went home, like I was trying to do in the first place, before they attacked me."

"You need to stop, Greg. People are getting hurt and you're going to get in trouble."

"I haven't done anything," says Greg as he rocks back and forth on his heels, eyes cast downward, clasping his hands together. "I can't get in trouble. I haven't touched one person."

"Promise me you won't hurt anybody else," begs Kelsey. "That's not you. You're not mean."

"I will not lay a hand on anybody."

"That's not what I mean and you know it. You don't have to touch people. They still get hurt. You need to stop."

"I will not start any problems with anybody," says Greg.

And the argument continues, with Greg dodging responsibility, and Kelsey pressing for better behavior. The raccoons watch quietly, mimicking Greg's nervous hand wringing and rocking back and forth.

A car horn interrupts the discussion, scaring raccoons out of the street and giving Greg a convenient stopping point for the conversation.

Greg starts walking toward school again and says, "I'll behave. I won't start any problems with anyone."

Kelsey groans in frustration and starts after Greg, grabbing his hand and holding it as they walk toward the school, not talking any further.

Up, up, up, the backpack flies into the air, over Mary Waldon's head and outstretched, grasping hands. Tony Grulo catches it and blurts a cruel laugh before throwing it in the air to Mark Masey. And Mark tosses it to Robbie Beuler. All the while, just across the street from school, the boys chant, "Mary, Mary, fat and hairy," over and over, as they play keep away with her backpack.

Scrambling about and wheezing for air in the middle of the group of cruel boys, Mary cries and shouts, "Gimme my stuff, you dirty assholes. Give me my stuff."

But Mary's desperation only fuels the boys' brutish behavior, making them laugh harder. They even trip her as she runs between them, trying to regain her possessions.

"Leave her alone," says Greg, stepping into the middle of the fracas. He grabs the bag from Tony's hand.

And Tony is too surprised to do anything but stand there and try to process the fact that scrawny Greg Samsa just terminated his fun. Process the fact that scores of raccoons have surrounded Greg and Mary and the mean boys. Tony takes it all in and then looks back to Greg. Mark Masey and Robbie Beuler are likewise perplexed by the situation.

Tony reaches out for the backpack and says, "Hand it over, E.T., or we'll start throwing you around too." But Greg stands firm as Tony tries to take the pack away. And before he can wrench the backpack from Greg's hands, the raccoons rear up on their hind legs and begin to hiss and growl until Tony backs off.

Greg does not give the backpack to Tony. He hands it to Mary instead and tells her, "Go across the street. Go to school. These boys won't bother you anymore." Almost before he is done with his words, Mary scrambles across the street for the school.

Tony, Robbie, and Mark just stand, surrounding Greg. And not one of them makes a move to touch him because they fear the sharp teeth that the many, many, raccoons are baring at them. Robbie says, "Fuck you, E.T. Fuck you and Creepy Kelsey." He pushes Kelsey to the ground and turns his back, running through the mass of coons, away from Greg and to the school. Once across the street, Robbie turns and flips the middle finger at Greg, shouting, "Fuck you, E.T."

And the raccoons rage and swirl about around Greg and Kelsey, Mark and Robbie. The critters' eyes flash at Greg, then at the bullies, and then back to Greg, as if asking what they should do. And some of the coons latch on to the pant-legs of Mark and Robbie. One coon scales Robbie's leg until it is knocked off. And the animals still look at Greg as if asking permission to attack.

Greg speaks softly and calmly amidst the chaos and says, "Stop. Let them go." And the coons sit and rub their front claws, staring at Robbie and Mark. Greg shakes his head in disgust and says, "Just go. Go away."

Like parting the Red Sea, a path clears between the mass of raccoons and opens an escape route for the boys. Mark takes off first, dashing across the street and running up the front stairs to the school, with Robbie following right behind him. They both stop at the top of the stairs, turn toward Greg, and waggle their middle fingers in Greg's direction before entering the school.

They sit atop cars and on roofs, still and tensed, like sinister lawn ornaments covering yards and driveways. With their intense, beady eyes fixed on the front of the school, the raccoons patiently await Greg's return. And the residents try to chase the coons off, stomping about on their porches and through yards, shaking brooms and shouting to no avail, clearing empty pathways that only close again behind them.

Inside the school, Greg's top hat moves through the throngs of teenagers in the halls. Under the hat, Greg's eyes burn. He walks through the crowd, casting no shadow, hands held together as if in prayer, face tilted slightly toward the ground. An invisible energy sparks and crackles off of Greg and kids move out of his path.

Tim and Jim Courtney stand together, leaning against their lockers. Tim props himself up on crutches, patches of blood-soaked gauze cover his arms and legs. A neck brace holds his greasy, unwashed head uncomfortably in place. The brothers push back against their lockers as if trying to crawl inside them. But Greg pays no attention to the boys as he passes, other than to step to the side of Kelsey as a buffer against their smell and general offensiveness.

And in his first class, Greg sits next to an empty chair where Jim Halloway should be. Greg sets his top hat on Jim's desk and stares straight ahead, ignoring the other kids. Whispers and pointed fingers and sideways glances bounce off of Greg and shatter into a million inconsequential fragments. He ignores it all, his disinterest setting the other students ill at ease. But he does not care. He cares about Jim. He cares about Kelsey. It matters not to Greg that the others are scared of him. It matters not that he is not harassed or tripped or called E.T. Greg's anger and resentment elevates him above it all.

In the locker room, Danny Dolan, standing naked and proud, tries to rile his classmates into holding Greg so he can administer a wedgie. But the other boys cast their eyes down and dress quickly, pretending that they do not hear Danny. Still, Danny stands in front of Greg and tells him to stand up and take his wedgie like a man. Setting his top hat beside him, Greg rises and lifts his gaze to meet Danny's. And something inside of Danny shakes and shrieks and shrinks. The naked teen backs off, mumbling, "Sorry. Sorry, dude." And as Greg exits the locker room for the gym, Coach Manlove slaps him on the back, leaving a stinging handprint of approval.

From class to class, Greg's presence repels the other students like reverse magnetism. Boys and girls step back the hallways. The desks around Greg remain empty in his classes. The only person who nears him is Kelsey.

During the school day Greg comes into contact with the Courtney brothers and Danny Dolan and nearly all of his other tormentors. But, he notices curiously that Wade Busby, Chop, and Donnie are absent from school.

And just before the last period of the day, Greg is summonsed to Principal Holden's office. Mrs. Beasley nods her head toward the principal's door and tells Greg to go in. As he knocks, the partially open door swings and reveals Principal Holden at his desk, and two portly, identical, mustachioed police officers seated and waiting.

"Have a seat, Greg," says Mr. Holden. He motions toward a chair positioned between the two officers. "And please take off your hat. These gentleman need to talk to you."

Taking off his hat, Greg sits. And though he knows not the officers' intentions, his heart nearly pounds right out of his chest.

The badge on the officer to Greg's left reads *X. Snively*. Officer X asks, "Why so nervous Mr. Samsa? Have you done something wrong?"

"No," says Greg, clasping his hands and bowing his head. "I'm not nervous."

The officer to the right, identified by his badge as *Y. Snively*, takes a big swig from a stained coffee mug and then sets his drink on Mr. Holden's desk. He smiles at Greg, wipes beads of coffee from his mustache, and says, "It looks like you're nervous to me. I can see your heart beating right through your shirt."

Greg looks down and sees it is true. His heart throbs so much that it presents a telltale thump-thump that visibly moves the fabric of his t-shirt. The sound of his blood pumping through his body thrums in his ears and resonates in his head, so much so that it feels like everybody in the room can hear his heart beating.

Shuffling in his seat, Greg shakes his head. "I'm not nervous. What's this about?"

Officer X shifts his substantial body, leans in, and says, "You've had some problems with Wade Busby, haven't you?"

"No more than anybody else," says Greg, rocking slightly in his chair and clasping his hands together. "Why?"

"You let us ask the questions," says Y.

"Yeah," agrees X. "We'll be asking the questions."

"Well, I didn't do anything," says Greg. "And don't I have the right to speak with a lawyer? Aren't you supposed to read me my rights? And don't you have to get my Mom's permission to question me?"

The officers lock eyes and then shake their heads.

Mr. Holden clears his throat, taps a pen on his desk, and says, "I believe he's right, gentlemen. He is a minor and you should get his mother's permission if you plan on questioning him any further."

Officer X sighs and says, "Okay, Gregory. Let's go and talk to your mother."

All along the front of Greg's house, yellow police lines block off the sidewalk. A newspaper photographer from the Courier kneels down in front of the fence, his camera rapidly popping off flashes like a strobe light. A police officer steps in and pushes vultures off of the fence with a rake, chasing the birds away. And the turkey vultures hiss and spit and spray vomit, but they do back off and fly awkwardly to the upper parts of Samsa Manor. Their greedy eyes fix on the fence spikes as they await a good opportunity to drop back down.

And then Greg sees Wade Busby's face staring at him (sort of). Actually, one of Wade's eyes partially hangs out of the socket because a vulture had been working on pulling it free. The other socket is empty and gaping right at Greg. The decapitated head is pushed down so hard on the fence post that the tip of the spike pokes right through the top of his skull and looks like a tiny, vicious church spire. Chop's and Donnie Price's heads also stare out at Greg. But their bodies do not run at Greg to intimidate him. They do not even walk slowly and menacingly at Greg. That is because their bodies sit impaled on fence spikes that go straight through their assholes and pop out through their backs. With Donnie's legs dangling uselessly, and Chop's legs tangled in the fence posts, their bodies slump as if deflated and empty. Donnie's head lolls over, tilting to the left. His mouth hangs open and drips bubbly red foam. Chop's head looks worse, with the edges of his mouth torn wide open, letting his chin hang down to his neck. His head waggles in the wind and the cheek tears more, little by little, leaving his face to look like a broken puppet with the jaw hanging open.

The black and white police car sits in front of Greg's house. A wave of raccoons skitters down the street, around the cruiser, and overtakes the sidewalk and front yard. Captain Jack and Fats Flannigan run about in front of the fence, tearing at the yellow police lines and rolling around with them like kittens toying with a ball of yarn.

Greg pays no attention to the raccoons, but instead looks from Chop to Wade to Donnie Price. He is not overjoyed to see his tormentors slaughtered in his front yard. He is not sad, nor scared, nor disgusted. He feels no more about viewing the scene than he does looking at the butcher's cooler at Food Town. He stares at the heads for a good while as he waits to be taken into his house. And the most he can muster emotionally is relief that he will not be harassed by Wade anymore.

"What the shit?" says Officer X. He uses the cruiser's public address system to direct the officer with the rake to clear the area of the raccoons.

And the rake swings in wide arcs, clearing a circle around the officer, backing off the hissing, chittering raccoons. Officer X jumps from the car and opens the back door. "Come on," he says, grabbing Greg's arm and pulling him from the car. Officer Y grabs Greg's other arm and they all run for the front door, the officers dragging the boy by the arms and kicking their legs out at the raccoons as they dash for the house. A clear path opens up as the creatures back off enough to allow Greg and the officers through.

The officers fumble with the front door's knob, struggling to get it open. Greg turns to look at the scene. Already, two cops push at Chop's body, easing his corpse off of the fence. The officers then work on Donnie Price, and with a little more effort, he pops off of the fence and crashes to the sidewalk. Wade's head, as with everything else about him, is stubborn and disagreeable. One officer pushes hard at it with the rake. The yard tool slips and gashes the dead, grey flesh of Wade's face. Trying another tack, the rake swings at Wade's head, and a metal-on-bone gong rings out. And then again the rake pushes at the bottom of the head until, finally, the pent up energy overtakes Wade's resistance and launches the head from the spike and onto the lawn. Raccoons dive over the fence and vultures fall from the sky, all converging on the head, ripping out Wade's remaining eye, tearing off his reptilian lips, and devouring his face.

"Holy crap," says Greg as a panicked Officer X finally throws open the front door and drags him into the house.

Big Shirl struggles and sits up in her bed, back against the wall. Beside her on one of the dining table chairs is a very much overweight lump of a man, with an oversized, twitchy mustache that droops to obscure the mouth underneath it. Such a mustache can only be worn seriously by a cop, and a very high level one, at that.

"Hello, Gregory. I'm Detective Snively," says the oversized man with the oversized mustache. Unlike the deputies (who look very much like younger versions of him), Snively wears cheap dress slacks, a button up shirt, and a too-small tie that loses most of its length around his thick, flabulous neck. The bottom of the tie sits high on his padded chest and looks like a kid's clip on. Snively adjusts his tie and clears his throat. He shifts his weight, making the chair legs bow and creak. Snively looks to Officers X and Y and says, "That'll do, Boys. That'll do. Go help out front."

"Okay, Dad," says Officer X. He and Y exit the room, leaving Greg to face the detective.

"I trust you saw the horror show out front," says Snively, turning to Greg with a disgusted grimace.

Greg nods slowly but says nothing.

"Have a seat, Gregory." Snively motions to a wooden chair opposite him. He dips his hand into a bowl on the edge of Big Shirl's bed and pops several potato chips into his mouth. Still chewing, he says, "I'd like to talk to you about what's going on if you don't mind. And if it's okay with your mother, of course."

Big Shirl shakes her head in agreement. Her eyes are dewy and Greg can see that she's been crying. She starts to talk, then just nods her head again. And though Greg's heart has hardened to most of humanity, it still pains him to see his mother upset.

Still wearing his top hat, Greg sits and places his folded hands in his lap.

"Greg," says Big Shirl. "Take your hat off and show Detective Snively some respect."

Taking his hat off and setting it on the floor, Greg says, "I'm sorry to show you my lack of respect. What can I tell you about that business, sir? I don't know anything. I was in school."

"That you were," says Snively, and he frowns as he belatedly catches Greg's wording (*my lack of respect*). A few chewed up bits of chips fly out of his mouth along with his words. "That you were. But there have been some strange things going on around town and when I look into them, your name keeps popping up." Snively fixes his best version of an intense stare on Greg.

Greg stares straight into Snively's prying eyes. Flatly, he says, "How so, sir? I'm afraid I don't get your meaning. Are you accusing me of something?"

And Greg's calm, measured demeanor grates at Snively. The detective loses his cool momentarily and snaps, "I think you do know what I'm talking about, Mr. Samsa. How about Johnny Close? Huh? How about that?"

"What about him?"

"You attacked him on the street just yesterday."

"Says who?" Greg locks eyes with Snively. "Do you have witnesses?"

"We do. People watched the incident from their houses."

"Good," says Greg. "Then they saw Crooked Neck grab me by the arm and try to drag me into the alley. He's a pervert, you know? I'm sure your witnesses saw him expose himself to me right there on the street. You do know that he does that, don't you? You've probably arrested him for it before. And I'm sure that your witnesses saw him knock me to the ground. And since you have witnesses, I'd like to press charges. Johnny needs to be stopped before he hurts someone."

Snively's mouth twists up. He shakes his head and says, "I don't know what he did, but it doesn't excuse what you did to him."

"What did I do?"

"You know what you did," says Snively. "Johnny tells us that you sicced your raccoons on him? And the neighbors saw it."

"Sicced my raccoons on him?" Greg laughs. "The neighbors saw the raccoons attack Johnny. But they didn't see me do anything, did they? I was on the ground after he hit me. How do I make wild raccoons attack somebody?"

"Well," says Snively, perplexed, "what about the Courtney brothers?"

"What about them?" asks Greg, and he leans in to grab a handful of the chips from beside Big Shirl. "They're jerks. So what?"

"So you don't like them, huh?" Snively points an accusatory finger at Greg. "Just as I thought."

"No, I don't like them. They are dirty and smelly and mean. Nobody likes them. So what?"

"So you sicced your raccoons on them, too, didn't you?"

"I did see them get attacked by raccoons, but I didn't have any control over it." Greg nibbles at a chip and then pops the whole thing in his mouth. "If you ask me, it seems like we have a huge vermin problem in this city. I'm just lucky I wasn't attacked by those animals, too."

"You made the coons attack those boys, didn't you?"

"Are you listening to yourself?" asks Greg. "How do I make wild animals attack somebody? Do you think I have some kind of mind control? Am I an evil Dr. Doolittle? Seriously, you are sounding kind of cuckoo for Cocoa Puffs, Sonny."

"Greg," snaps Big Shirl. "I don't like these accusations either.

But, be respectful of Detective Snively. He's a guest in our house."

Leaning in to grab more potato chips, Greg shrugs his shoulders and says, "Sorry about my lack of respect for you."

And the dig jabs at a soft spot in one of Snively's many soft areas. He bursts out, "What about those boys in front of your house? What about that? It's sick. And once again, it comes right back to you. Right in your front yard."

Greg remains calm and nibbles at another chip. Says nothing. Just stares at Snively.

"You didn't like those boys, either. They picked on you, didn't they?"

"I didn't like them one bit," agrees Greg. "They were mean and stupid. They picked on everybody. Not just me. Everybody was afraid of them. And if you check at school, you will find that I was there all day. I couldn't have made that mess in the front yard. So I don't know what you are getting your panties in a wad for."

"Greg," blurts Big Shirl. She sits up suddenly to chastise her son and her body jiggles all over. Something about it distracts Detective Snively and he momentarily looks at her as if she were a bowl of tasty potato chips. "Respect, please."

And Snively feels whatever advantage he had turning greasy and slipping out of his fat little hands. He taps his foot on the floor nervously and says, "You have all the answers don't you smart guy?"

"I'm sure I don't know what you mean," Greg says, staring innocently at Snively.

Snively blurts out, "What about Mr. Blight? What about him? Huh?"

"He's dead," says Greg, his calm contrasting sharply to the barely restrained anger of Snively. "I don't know nothin' about nothin'. Do you have any evidence or witnesses that somehow link me to the murder of a full grown man twice my size?"

"And what about Stanley Stevens?" Snively's mouth forms into a triumphant smile. "We gotcha there, don't we? We have witnesses, you know."

"Good, then they saw Stanley attack me. Did you ask them about that? He punched me and knocked me down. I'm a kid and he's a grown man. I'd like to press charges."

"Oh, really," Snively leans in toward Greg, his mustache twitching wildly. "Your brother and his friends beat the daylights out of Mr. Stevens. What do you say about that?"

"Oh, you mean when they came to my defense against the grown man who punched me. Talk to your witnesses, 'cuz that's what they're gonna tell you."

"We will, Mr. Samsa," says Snively. He wriggles around uncomfortably on his wooden seat and adjusts his tie. "We will."

Greg stands up from his seat and puts his top hat back on, cocking it just a little to one side. He starts to pace, looks to Big Shirl, and says, "Mom, do I have to sit here and be accused of stuff that I couldn't have done? I mean really, do I somehow have mind control over raccoons? And the mess in the front yard, I was in school, how could I do that? And tell me when I've ever been able to control anything Wally has done. Seriously, can I go to my room, Ma?"

And just as Snively reaches for more chips, Big Shirl grabs the bowl and sets it on her other side, well out of the detective's reach. With a sharp edge to her voice, Big Shirl says, "You know what, detective? My boy is right. He has answered your questions and after hearing his answers, I don't understand why you suspect him of any of this."

"Because he's our top suspect," says Snively. "I don't know

what's going on, but I know he's behind all of this."

The wood floor creaks as Big Shirl struggles and wiggles and wriggles on the bed, negotiating her body into sitting position. She sweats and breathes heavily, panting as she pushes up off of the bed and stands on elephantine legs before Detective Snively. She raises her enormous arm and the flabby flesh wiggles as she shakes a finger toward the front of the house. Her face reddens like a ripe tomato from her effort and anger. "I will ask you to leave now, sir. You do not have my permission to speak with my son any further."

Snively stands, too, his face now flushed with frustration. "Think what you'd like, ma'am. I know that something funny is going on here and I'm going to find out. I'm going to search this house."

"I think you need a warrant for that," says Greg as he walks away.

"Hold it right there, young man." Snively reaches out and grabs Greg by the arm.

Snatching his arm away from the detective, Greg jumps back, saying, "Am I under arrest? If so, then go ahead and cuff me. Otherwise, I don't think I have to stand here and be accused of things I didn't do."

"He's right," says Big Shirl, stepping in between Greg and Snively. "You go get yourself a warrant if you can. Otherwise, leave this house now." And she leans in toward Snively, her sheer immensity intimidating the detective.

Hoisting his pants up and straightening his too-small tie, Snively grimaces and says, "Oh, I'll leave. And I promise you this: I will be back with a warrant and a small army of police. And we'll tear this house apart. I will figure out what's going on."

Detective Snively slams the front door as he exits the

mansion, knocking drippy icicles from the porch's gutters. He stamps about on the front porch like an enraged rhino until one foot breaks through a rotten board and sends him sprawling. His sons, X and Y, help him to his feet and brush him off. Snively pushes the officers away and says, "Get me out of here. I need to see Judge Hargus immediately."

Grasping a search warrant tightly in his plump, sweaty hand, Detective Snively stomps through Greg's front yard, making his way around the many raccoons gathered there. Ten Findlay police officers march behind him in a single file line. And as the police proceed up the front walk, animal control workers scurry about the lawn, unsuccessfully trying to capture and cage the raccoons. One animal control officer rolls around on the ground with a coon latched onto his leg. Another man beats at the animal with a wooden club, but the raccoon does not relent until his masked face is smashed to a pulpy mess. Then more coons set upon the workers until the men flee from the front yard for the safety of their dogcatcher wagon. Snively ignores the ruckus, strutting unscathed through the swirling raccoon riot with his head held high and his paunch thrust haughtily forward.

Before Snively can knock, Big Shirl opens the front door to see his smug, grinning face. Big Shirl stands there, gasping for air and leaning heavily on the doorframe. A sheen of sweat glistens on her rotund face. "I guess you got your search warrant, then?" she says through labored breaths.

Crumpling up a piece of paper and throwing it on the floor, Snively puts a hand on Big Shirl's shoulder, pushing her out of the way as he barges into the house. He laughs, hikes up his pants, and says, "There's your warrant, lady."

Before Big Shirl can object, Snively and his crew invade the house. The officers dig right in, tearing apart the front hall, making more of a mess than the raccoons ever did. And they move from room to room like a whirlwind, tearing rugs from the floor, knocking pictures off of walls, overturning tables, pulling out drawers and dumping the contents.

Meanwhile, Snively stomps about the mansion, calling out for Greg. His voice carries through the home, up stairs and around corners, through doorways, until it finally reaches Greg's ears. Sensing trouble below and not wanting to leave Big Shirl to deal with it on her own, Greg descends a set of servant stairs and enters the kitchen to face Snively. From somewhere above, the strains of a calliope roll down the stairs behind Greg.

And the triumphant grin on Snively's face says it all. The detective is enjoying things far too much for it to merely be a job for him. Snively is a cruel man that hides behind his badge to bully people. He enjoys that his men are completely ruining the interior of the home. Greg and his mother dared to defy him, and now they are paying the price. Snively reaches for the handcuffs on his belt and steps toward Greg. Thinking that the boy is going to try to flee, Snively jumps on him, knocking off the top hat, and pins him to the floor, first twisting one arm up behind Greg's back to slap a cuff on it, and then doing the same with the other arm.

Snively forces Greg to sit and cuffs the boy's restrained arms to the chair. The detective leans in close, top lip turned up in a subtle sneer, a vengeful glint in his eye, and stares at Greg with a practiced intensity. "You are in custody now, boy. Remain where you are until we are done so we'll have no trouble."

The calliope song picks up in volume, still floating down from somewhere above. Greg shakes his hair from his eyes and looks up at Snively. "I'll not do a thing to hurt your men. Nor will I do anything to help them." Greg returns Snively's steely stare, his response conveying a gravitas that plants a fertile seed of doubt into Snively's crapulous belly.

The detective scoffs and turns to go check on his men. He stomps off to where he thinks he hears them, and though the sound of their destructive force calls out to him, he fails to locate the men. And as he rushes about through the mansion, the laughter of his men seems to come at him from above and below and all around, making it difficult to determine their whereabouts. While the sounds of glass crunching and feet stomping and furniture breaking grows ever more distant, the strains of the calliope ramp up in volume, finally drowning out the distant sounds of the other officers. Just before the men's voices fade out, the sound changes from a gleeful ransacking party to shouts for help.

And Snively finally finds himself lost and alone in the maze of Samsa Mansion's twisting halls and narrow stairways, panting heavily and wondering how a house can be so large and confusing, how it can feel like he has climbed forty stories, how the rooms and halls seem to shift on him. His breathing quickens. Sweat beads form on his forehead and cheeks. Runs of sweat dribble from his armpits, faintly tickling at his sides, soaking his shirt. The electricity has been turned off or blown out in this part of the house. The halls and rooms become darker and darker, and the calliope music screams out at him. From above and below and behind the walls come snorts, squeals, and the *clip clop* of cloven hooves. Footsteps sound out behind Snively, but it is too dark and when he turns to look, it is hard to tell if he sees movement or not. Along with the footsteps, he hears heavy breathing and the low, repeated whisper of a voice that merely says one measly, hyphenated word: *shit-turd.*

An almost irrational panic grips Snively and wrings a rank, nervous fart from his gut. He tries to tell himself that the sounds are not somebody following in the dark, that his mind is just playing tricks on him. Still, his head reels with hyperventilation dizziness. Scratching noises from behind the walls shoot shivers down his back and legs. A sudden fear that he will not find his way out of the house smothers every rational thought that he tries to summon.

Just behind Snively, the soggy, mush-mouthed words are louder, "Shit-turd. Shit-turd. Shit-turd." Something brushes his back. And all reason vacates the portly detective's mind. Without consulting his brain, Snively's feet take off in an all-out, stumbling and bumbling run through the dark hallways. He blindly crashes into walls and trips over himself, struggling to get back to his feet and run. He does not know where he's running. He cannot see where he's going. But running is better than facing whatever it is that follows him. Somewhere, farther behind now, he still hears feet shuffling. And the whispers resume, sounding like they're coming from several people, just loud enough for Snively to hear over the strains of the calliope: "Shit-turd. Shit-turd. Shit-turd."

In his panicked scramble for safety, Snively's foot seeks out floor to step on but finds empty space instead. His body tumbles, rolling end over end, slamming arms and shoulders, legs and head, elbows and knees against steps and walls as the staircase drags him downward. It feels to Snively as if each and every part of his body manages to strike something hard on the way down. He blindly gropes for a handrail or something to stop his fall. But reaching out only makes it so that he bangs his hands and arms even worse, until his limbs become numb and unwilling to respond to any commands that his brain sends them. And it seems that he falls for an eternity. But then the kitchen floor abruptly stops his descent.

Snively rolls into the kitchen and lands at Greg's feet. He struggles to sit, fumbling at Greg's legs for something to pull himself up with. Snively sees that Greg is still handcuffed to the chair, but somehow is wearing his top hat again. Greg looks down at him with bored eyes.

"Help me," croaks Snively as he struggles to stand. Once on his feet, he wobbles and then loses his balance, plopping back down onto his well-padded backside with a pained "oomph."

"You're the policeman," says Greg flatly. "You're supposed to help me. Get me out of these stupid cuffs and I'll see what I can do."

Snively does not uncuff Greg. He does not release him. Instead he slumps over and goes slack on the floor. And Greg can only nudge at the detective with his feet. But the nudging does not rouse Snively. So Greg sits, cuffed to the chair, unable to go anywhere, and eventually drifts off to sleep. All the while, voices call from within the house for help; some cry out, some shout, and some scream in panic. As a backdrop to the other house-noises, a calliope tune lilts in a springy, buoyant movement, booming out, then ramping down to a soft sing-song, and then blaring again in a happy, bouncy melody.

And then Greg is roused by Hopalong and Li'l Shirl shaking him awake.

"It's 10:30 and the temperature outside is unseasonably warm at 60 degrees. We should be in for pleasant weather all night. Open those windows and let the fresh air in for good sleeping conditions."

"Oh, hey Hopalong," says Greg with half-opened, sleepy eyes. "Hey Li'l Shirl."

Li'l Shirl gapes at Greg with vacant eyes and a ringent mouth, then looks down at the man on the floor. Although her lips move as if to say something, her jaw just hangs, waiting for the words to dislodge from her brain and find their way out of her mouth. But the words take a wrong turn on the way, getting lost, and the only thing that comes out of her mouth is a soft grunt and a string of drool.

"Uh, yeah, that," says Greg, looking down at Snively. "He fell down the stairs and I think he's hurt pretty bad. He's got me handcuffed here. I saw him put the keys in his front pocket. See if you can get them so that I can get up."

Hopalong drops to his knees and rolls the detective over to get into his pocket. A gurgle of saliva bubbles in Snively's throat and effervesces from his mouth. Hopalong fishes in the pants' pocket, finds the keys, and begins to retrieve them. And like a switch being flicked, Snively snaps back to the moment and latches onto Hopalong's wrist.

"Hold it right there," says Snively, holding tightly to Hopalong, who helps him sit up. Scooting on his butt, Snively wriggles several feet across the floor and props himself up against the wall. He looks at Hopalong with his idiot grin, then decides to look elsewhere for further help. Li'l Shirl stands next to the big cowboy, slack-jawed and swaying on her feet as if being moved by a gentle ocean current. Then Snively looks again to the boy he handcuffed. Greg stares back with icy eyes.

Snively's battered legs give out on him when he tries to stand. Yet he knows he needs to do something to help his men.

Frightened yelps and cries for help still call out from within the house, almost in time with the calliope song. Yet Snively is helpless to do anything. With great effort and pains, he fishes the handcuff keys from his pocket and holds them out toward Greg, saying, "Now help me, please."

Greg looks down from his chair and says, "I told you before that I will do nothing to help you or your men. I won't do anything to hurt you. But, I won't help. You've treated me and my mom horribly, and now you want something from me. You need to think about how you treat people, because if you treat them crappy, they may just return the favor when they can. Don't bother uncuffing me if you're doing it to get help."

Snively croaks again. A gurgling cough escapes his throat as he reaches out. But Greg does not move, nor does he say anything further. He averts his eyes from the detective's pleading looks. So Snively is forced to rely on the large retarded man-child dressed as a sheriff or the sluggard dolt known as Li'l Shirl. Perhaps it's because of the slightly demented but still alert glint in his eyes, or maybe the tin badge and holstered guns lend something of an air of authority, but Hopalong presents as the more capable of the two simpletons. Snively holds out his hand to the big, grinning cowboy, and says, "Please bring me the phone."

Always happy to help, Hopalong salutes Snively and retrieves the handset from the wall phone across the room, stretching its long, curled cord out to bring the phone to Snively. And though he cannot move or do anything else to help his men, Snively has Hopalong dial the station for reinforcements.

By the time reinforcements arrive, Snively is once again unconscious at the feet of a still-handcuffed Greg. The paramedics rouse the detective and lift him onto a gurney. Snively rolls to his side and throws his keys in Greg's lap before passing out again. The paramedics breathe sighs of relief as they wheel the detective out of the creepy house and into a waiting ambulance.

Several officers surround Greg, crossing arms, flexing mustaches, and leveling accusatory, non-blinking indictments in his direction. They remove his top hat and set it on the counter, yet every time they return to Greg, the hat is once again tilted slightly atop his head. And Greg just sits there, straight and sure and casting no shadow, with his hands cuffed, saying, "I don't know nothin' about nothin'. I don't even get why you guys are here."

Despite what they say and what they do and what they promise, Greg refuses to help. They offer to take his handcuffs off, but Snively's keys are missing. When they suggest a hacksaw to remove the cuffs, Greg says, "No, don't worry about me. You have important business. You obviously feel that something very bad has gone on here. You even have your precious search warrant. You have the run of the house. If there's anything important here, you're sure to find it. That is, you're sure to find it if your men can stop tripping over their own balls and getting lost in this little old house."

First one officer comes tumbling down the grand stairway at the front of the house. Then another bounces down a set of servants' stairs. Then another from the stairs leading down into the kitchen. And the sounds of men grunting as they roll down steps and slam off of walls fills the house, thumping out a strange rhythm in time with the strains of the calliope song oozing from the walls. Men in torn blue uniforms tumble down to the first floor from previously unseen stairways, like steel Plinko balls bouncing ever downward in a Chinese pinball machine. And when it is all done, the first floor of the house is littered with injured patrolmen dressed in blue and covered in red. The men drag themselves toward the front of the house and call out for help. The late-coming officers – those who did not get lost within the house – run from cop to cop, tending to injuries. And all ambulances in the city are summoned. Red and blue flashers atop police cruisers bathe the front of Samsa Mansion with swirling lights as paramedics rush in to haul out the injured.

Once all of the casualties are carted off, the remaining officers vacate the house, unsure of how to handle the situation for lack of anyone in charge. They leave the place torn up and tossed about. They leave Big Shirl reclined in her bed, watching the Morton Downey Jr. Show as she sips at a can of Tab with a straw and shovels Funyuns into her mouth, fully ignoring the hubbub. They leave Greg cuffed to his chair. And when the house spits out the last of the police, Greg calls out for help.

Hopalong appears and tips his hat at Greg. "Howdy, pardner. That's a right sorry fix you're in there."

"Hey, Hopalong," says Greg. "There're some keys there on the floor behind me. Would you mind uncuffing me?"

Hopalong rounds Greg and finds the keys. He quickly removes the cuffs. "I'm sorry if they hurt you," says Hopalong, and Greg is unsure if he is talking about the cops or the cuffs.

"It's alright," says Greg. "Just a bunch of bullies bullying like bullies do. Nothing new, huh?"

"I reckon not," Hopalong nods his head, because he knows about bullies and being bullied. He knows about mean and he knows about ugly. "I reckon not."

Greg rubs at his wrists and walks around the house, shaking his head in disbelief at the mess. The mayhem wreaked on the house far outdoes anything that Captain Jacks, Fats Flannigan, and the rest of the raccoons ever did. Greg stops in the TV room and crawls onto the bed. He hugs Big Shirl and says, "I'm sorry, Mom."

Big Shirl plants a loud kiss on Greg's forehead, leaving a bright red lipstick smudge. "You don't need to be sorry, baby. I know you haven't done anything. There's just a foul wind blowing over this place. I've seen it before. It's in the air. You can feel it. You can see it in the eyes of our neighbors. You can smell it. It's there. And it makes people crazy. I've seen it before. This town turns mean against us for some reason. We all need to stick together. This is about family. This is about our place here. We need to stay close and watch out for each other, because believe me, people in town are going to have something to say about us."

So Greg does stick close to family. He rounds up Li'l Shirl and Hopalong, and they gather up dog food bowls. Li'l Shirl scoops wet, lumpy, brown mush into the bowls, and Greg dusts the food with powders from the attic. The three of them stick close as they carry the bowls outside and set them all around the front and back yards. But Greg is tired and he doesn't have the energy to watch the animals feed. He walks inside, leaving Li'l

Shirl and Hopalong to hang out in the cool night, under a full moon, watching coons and cats, dogs and skunks, and buzzards and bluebirds converge on the food and devour it.

Tired and ready for rest, Greg navigates the halls of the house, stumbling from exhaustion. On his way to the attic, he passes Li'l Shirl and Hopalong sitting on a loveseat at the end of a long hall. Greg knows he just left them outside, but he also knows that time works strangely in the mansion. It could be two minutes later, or it could be two hours. Regardless, the couple holds hands and sits motionless, staring straight ahead, looking doltish and stupid and happy, not saying a word. Seeing their moronic grins reminds Greg of how he feels when Kelsey is close.

Suddenly, Greg feels the need to talk to Kelsey. And he notices that a phone he has never seen before is on the wall, just to his left. He picks up the receiver and dials. Kelsey's dad answers and refuses to let Greg talk to her. The thought of taking Wally, Eddie, and Lumpy over to Kelsey's house crosses his mind, but Greg thinks better of it. He knows not to show up on the street, unless he wants to draw the heat. If he leaves the house with the lumbering threesome in tow, he is sure to attract the attention of the cops. It's just not safe to leave the house. So Greg is left to deal with his rapid-fire thoughts of frustration, anger, and retribution without the calming influence of Kelsey.

Upon entering the attic, Greg is greeted by Wally, Eddie, and Lumpy. Wally wears a patrolman's hat on his head and a badge pinned to the grayish skin of his bare chest. Lumpy and Eddie sport similar attire. Lumpy wears the blue shirt of the patrolman's uniform. Eddie has a hat similar to Wally's, as well as a pair of mirrored sunglasses. All three of the boys have gun belts. Wally's belt still has a service revolver in the holster. All three of the belts have expandable billy clubs attached.

The Victor phonograph bellows the sounds of Blind Melon Chitlin stomping his foot, honking on a harmonica, and crooning about going downtown, seeing his girl and singing her a song. The strains of the calliope blow in from somewhere in the house as a warbling accompaniment to the blues harp. And for just long enough, the music draws Greg's mind away from the chaos of the day, and exhaustion takes over, dragging him down into sleep.

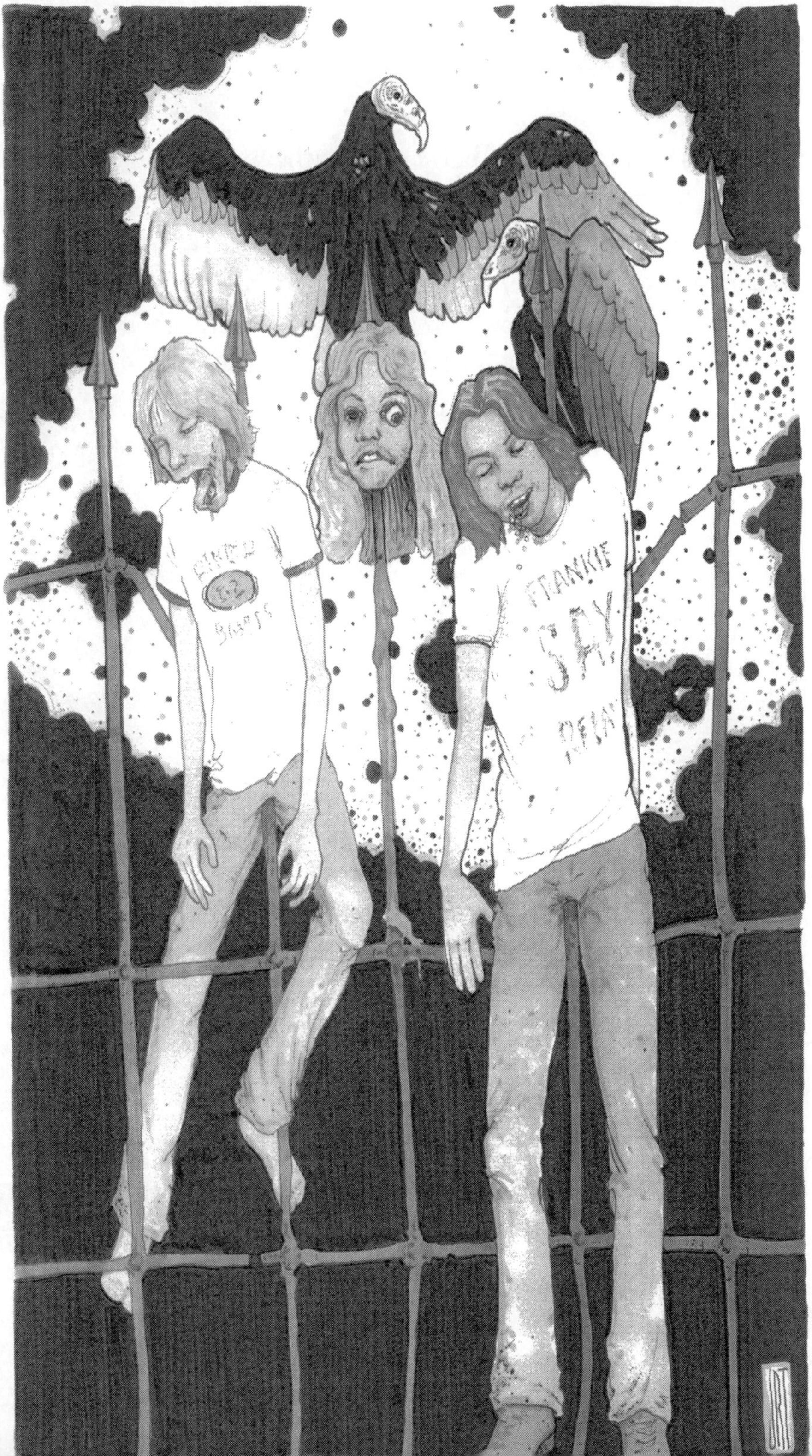
FRANKIE
SAY

5

The Big Bopper snaps his fingers and bounces like a rubber ball down the street, his legs churning and his feet seeming to never quite touch the ground. A sinister, driving bass line flows from his headphones in repetitive loops and drives his boots to keep pumping. And the music drops in volume and pace as Samsa Mansion looms over him. The Bopper stops and snaps and claps as he turns his droopy eyes skyward.

A kettle of turkey buzzards swirls and swoops in funky loops in time with the Bopper's private groove. And the birds' drunken circular formation wreathes the full, greenish moon, before they dive down and form a line atop the mansion's highest points.

In front of the mansion the lawn is blanketed in a writhing mass of raccoons and groundhogs, possums and rats, stray dogs and cats, all feeding on the feast in the silvery bowls that gleam in the reflected green light of the moon. Hopalong and Li'l Shirl sit on the front steps, surrounded by bowls and the critters feeding from them. With a beatific look on her face, Li'l Shirl holds a fat raccoon in her lap and lets it eat from food in one cupped hand as her other hand lovingly scratches the coon's head.

And the vibe from the street is overwhelming to the Bopper. There's good and bad, innocent and evil, all twisted up together in misty trails of reds and blacks and greens, and swirling in a many-armed vortex around the property. The intensity of the groove increases in his headphones and before he knows it, the

Bopper is madly clapping his hands and stomping his feet. And then his basset hound friend howls and yowls at the green moon. The hound's baying shakes the Bopper from the grip of the pumping groove just enough to get him bopping again. The Bopper smiles at Hopalong and Li'l Shirl before his feet bounce him down the street and on his way.

6

If anybody would have asked Hopalong that morning, he would have told them that Flip Dixon, the always grinning Channel 8 weatherman out of Toledo, said the following about the weather: "Go ahead and put those winter jackets and snowboots in the closet. Mild air from the Pacific Ocean and Gulf of Mexico are becoming the dominant influences on temperatures nationwide. For those of us in Northwest Ohio, that means premature spring-like weather. It will be an unseasonably warm and sunny day with highs in the mid-sixties. So go ahead, put on those shorts and flip-flops and enjoy this weather while it lasts."

But nobody asked Hopalong about the weather, so he didn't tell them about Flip Dixon's forecast. And anyway, Flip Dixon didn't know about the hole in the ground just south of Findlay that gushes toxic smoke from the bowels of the earth. He certainly didn't know that the cloud was so thick that it sat in place over the entire city, turning the sky black and blocking out the sun. So Flip Dixon's forecast had nothing to do with Findlay's weather.

And nobody asked Hopalong about the rest of the news either. Everybody in Findlay knew the big news anyway. They knew that Wade, Donnie, and Chop had been brutally murdered and spiked on the fence at Samsa Mansion. They knew that there was something weird about that Samsa house in the first place. And now they knew that members of the police force were attacked and unable to even defend themselves inside the house. They knew there was always something wrong with that house and the people in it. They knew it was high time for something to be done about it.

The darkness that fell upon the town set the villagers to muttering and murmuring and gossiping. In Wilsons and the Bear Flag Restaurant the people talked over burgers and malts and steaming cups of coffee. Doctors and teachers and workers from the tire factory, housewives and waitresses and salesmen, they all talked. They talked about Greg Samsa and his troubled big brother, and don't forget that elephant of a mother and the just-as-big retard of a sister. They said that something ain't right with that family, never has been. And now, they said, they've taken up with the cowboy hat wearing retard that stands out on the street with his broomstick hobbyhorse and waves at everybody. Nobody's safe, they said, with weirdoes like that in town. And they questioned why they ever tolerated the Samsas in their village.

Greg can read the mood of the town in the smothering smoke that fell over the city. He knows better than to go to school or even leave the house. Wearing sweatpants, a baggy bathrobe, and his top hat, he sits on the front porch, surrounded by raccoons and stray dogs and cats and sundry four-legged friends. Turkey buzzards line the edges of the roof, and Greg hears the *scratch-scratch* of their heavy bodies shuffling around overhead. And the animals on the lawn stare up at him, as if awaiting orders. But Greg ignores the animals and gazes out at the street. Black and white police cruisers circle the block and slow, almost to a stop, in front of the house, constantly reminding Greg that bad things could happen if he leaves his property. And yet the officers patrolling the area do not get out of their cars, and they certainly do not set foot on the Samsa lawn. None of the patrolmen approach the front door of the mansion. Greg realizes that it is a Mexican standoff. He can't leave and they won't come after him.

So stay at home it is. Greg doesn't want to go to school anyway. He tries to phone Kelsey, but when her dad answers Greg just hangs up. He knows Stanley Stevens is not going to let him speak with his daughter. Instead, Greg calls the hospital and rings up Jim Halloway's room.

"Hello," says Jim's mother into the phone.

"Mrs. Halloway, it's Greg. How's Jim doing?"

"Oh Greg," says Mrs. Halloway, her voice heavy with concern. "He's in and out of it. Right now he's sleeping. The doctors say he's starting to turn a corner, so that's good."

"Good," says Greg. "I've been worried about him."

"Well I've been worried about you. Your house has been all over the news. And I've heard people talking about you and your family. And the things they're saying aren't very nice. You need to be careful, kiddo."

"I know. I'm staying home."

"Good. Don't go out. There's too much ugliness today."

"Mrs. Halloway," says Greg, "can I talk to Jim?"

"He's unconscious, Greg. He's not going to be much of a conversationalist."

"That's okay, I think it might do him some good to hear my voice."

Greg can hear Mrs. Halloway sniffling snot, and when she speaks again her voice wavers with emotion. "You know what, Greg? I think you might be right. I'm going to put the phone right up where he can hear you, and you go ahead and talk his ear off."

In the earpiece, Greg hears the beep-beep-beeping of the heart monitor and labored respiration. Hearing those noises, it's almost as if Greg can also see nurses schlepping patients down the halls in wheelchairs and smell the solvents used to clean the hospital rooms. And it's almost as if Greg can see Mrs. Halloway sitting right beside Jim, tears rolling down her cheeks as she holds the phone up to her son's ear.

Greg says, "Jim? You there?" And then he pauses. The noises coming through the earpiece are just the same as before, but they carry a different tone. Greg can tell that Jim is there and listening. And it is a relief to at least have one of his two friends to talk to.

Greg spits out his words in a rapid, nervous patter, "I'm missing you right now, you big dumb-ass. Things have gotten crazy and I've got nobody to talk to about it. You're in the hospital, and Kelsey's dad is trying to keep her away from me. There are dead people in Findlay. A lot of dead people. Mr. Blight. Wade. Chop. Donnie Price. All dead. And the cops think I did it. But I didn't."

On the other end of the line, Jim Halloway replies with a gurgly, burbly respiration and the steady beeping of his heart monitor.

"Yeah," continues Greg, "I know. Crazy, right? But you don't even know the half of it. Blight was found face down in a toilet. And Wade, Chop, and Donnie Price were spiked on the fence in front of my house. It was pretty freakin' gruesome. The cops handcuffed me and tore up the house looking for evidence."

Gurgle, burble, beep-beep-beep.

"Yep," says Greg. "No crap. And the cops questioned me about Crooked Neck and the Courtneys. They all say that I made raccoons attack them. Can't prove a thing though. Who's gonna believe that I have powers over animals, right?"

Gurgle, burble, beep-beep-beep.

"Exactly. They can't pin nothin' on me. But I know I gotta be careful. It seems like almost everybody is mad at me. Well, you know what? I'm done putting up with it. I'm not gonna take it anymore. I don't want trouble. But if people want to mess with me, I'm gonna mess back. Anyway, I know you need to rest up so you can get better. When you do, I'll kick your ass at Space Invaders. So hurry up, ass-face, get better and get back home."

Gurgle, burble, beep-beep-beep.

"Same to you, buddy. I'll come see you tomorrow."

And as if she knows the conversation is over, Mrs. Halloway takes the phone away from Jim's ear and says into the mouthpiece, "Thank you, Greg. You're a good boy. All this stuff people are saying is not true. You're a good boy, better than the other people in this town. You be careful and don't let them get you down." She sniffles again, and then there is silence on the phone.

"Thanks, Mrs. Halloway."

Greg hangs up and tries to call Kelsey again. "Hello," says the nasal voice that can only be Stanley Stevens. Greg hangs up.

Howlin' Wolf yowls that he ain't superstitious (but a black cat just crossed his path). Lumpy doesn't know anything about a black cat, he just knows about cranking the phonograph so that the music plays. Greg doesn't know about a black cat either, but he does know about raccoons. Captain Jack and Fats Flannigan sit up in front of the record player, chittering at Greg as he enters the attic. The farrow of pigs gathers at his feet, oinking at him. And Wally calls out in greeting, "Shit-turd."

Eddie and Lumpy echo the greeting, saying in unison, "Shit-turd."

"Hey, shit-turds," says Greg, without enthusiasm. He looks around and sees that the attic has changed. The piss-monkey jars have moved from their window to the floor. And the window is gone. In its place, two glass doors open onto a balcony. Greg wanders over to the balcony, trailed by pigs who have grown significantly larger since being reanimated. Emerging on the balcony, Greg looks skyward. Dark clouds hang over the city while a river of black smoke rapidly winds through them.

And the new balcony opens out to a view of the front yard. Greg stands at the rail, looking over his neighborhood, seeing it from a different angle than ever before.

A police cruiser rolls past the house so slowly that old Mrs. Murphy, out on her morning walk, passes up the car and leaves it well behind. Through mirrored sunglasses, the officers stare up at the balcony. Greg waves at them but receives no response. As the police car inches down the street, a pair of turkey vultures alights on the balcony and flanks Greg.

Lumpy changes up the record on the Victor and cranks the handle. *Bad Luck Blues* blares from the phonograph's brass horn. And from somewhere in the house, a calliope joins in on the melody. Nearly mesmerized by the bluesy calliope music, Greg and the turkey vultures remain on the balcony, staring out at nothing, gently swaying back and forth like weeds in the cool breeze that blows up from below.

Greg does not move from the balcony for the most part of the day, but instead stays in place, soaking up the scratchy blues music oozing from the phonograph. He watches the street as more people than usual walk slowly past the mansion and point upward at him. At first it is just one or two people. Then larger groups pass, sometimes stopping, sometimes shouting names at Greg. Some of the people carry axe handles and pitchforks. Some have baseball bats. They look toward the balcony and see Greg and the turkey buzzards standing stock still, Greg in his top hat, and the buzzards with their heads slung low and staring back with blank, beady eyes.

By the time dusk rolls around, a full moon squeezes its light through the smoggy cover, the smoke making the moon appear green behind the clouds. Greg watches the street below as more and more people walk past his house. And the grumbling of the people floats up as an indecipherable, angry grouse that burbles just below the sounds of calliope music and Howlin' Wolf's *Killing Floor*.

Greg can see teens gathering down the street in Mr. Goodman's front yard, laughing and jostling each other. He hears their beer bottles smashing on the road and smells their cigarette and marijuana smoke. A boom box plays fuzzy heavy metal music through a blown speaker. And the music disagrees with Greg's ears. It hits them wrong and hurts them. But more than that, it seeps into his head and pricks at him deep down, reminding him of the Wade Busbys and Danny Dolans and Courtney brothers of the city. It reminds him of being picked on. It puts him on guard. And though he has started to stick up for himself, to fight back, it makes him feel small again, as if somebody is going to slam him into a locker or mock the way he looks or talks or smells. It makes him feel as if Wally is going to pound him. It makes him feel as if the responsible adults of the city are going to turn their heads and look the other way while Greg takes a beating.

And from the balcony, Greg watches the events down the street. He looks on with interest as Mr. Goodman bursts out of his house, charging the youths on his lawn, shouting at them to get out of his yard. One skinny boy stands his ground and refuses to leave. Mr. Goodman smashes a fist into the boy's face. The teen's head snaps backward from the force of the punch and he drops to the ground. Two of his friends dash into the yard and drag their friend away while Mr. Goodman yells at them, warning them never to set foot on his property again.

The teens help their skinny friend get his legs again. They walk down the street laughing and shouting back at Mr. Goodman. Greg's fists clench, his teeth grind. The teens and their music set him on edge, so Greg removes himself from the balcony, leaving two hunched-over turkey vultures there to stand sentry. And the turkey vultures shit their chalky white feces down their legs and caw out into the night, telling the youths below to keep their distance.

Greg stumbles into the attic and knocks a piss-monkey jar to the ground, shattering it on impact. But, hardly any urine spills out. Instead, the piss-monkey slowly rolls about on the broken glass, struggling to unfurl its limbs, struggling to stand. A rank wave of urine-stench wafts up to tickle at Greg's nose. The piss-monkey makes a gurgling, squishing sound as it struggles to gain control of its body. And as the creature unrolls itself, it seems to inflate, doubling in size. It stretches out and stands on eight wobbly legs. One leg buckles and then hangs limply. A tail, like that of a large rat, wags frantically. Pointy spikes poke through the entire visible ridge of the beast's spine. Wings spread out to a four-foot span. Its head, dog-like but with the hooked beak of a bird, scans its surroundings. The beak slowly opens to release a raspy squeak. The beast's body is coal black and slathered in an oily slime. The piss-monkey (hardly a monkey at all) gazes up at Greg and squeaks again, as if asking a question.

Greg does not answer the piss-monkey. He does not look on in wonder. He's seen too much lately and the outrageous has become commonplace to him. He merely points a finger toward the pigs gathered in a corner and then walks to his mattress and flops down. The piss-monkey runs and jumps on a pig and rips its hooked beak into the swine's back. The pig squeals and flails, trying to shake the piss-monkey.

"No," Greg shouts, and the piss-monkey unhooks itself from the pig's back, averting its eyes to the floor, avoiding Greg's angry stare. "No, no, no."

With the piss-monkey under control, Greg lies on his back, staring at the ceiling. And the world goes on. People gather on the streets. The earth exhales blackness from the hole at the south end of town, and the smoke inundates the city, becoming a roiling vortex above the village. Lightning high in the sky illuminates the thick, smoky cloud cover, like a bulb lighting up a lampshade. Thunder booms above the city and shakes windows, scares children.

Now and then Greg's room is filled with the popping sound of piss-monkey jars shattering from the outward-pushing pressure of the quick-growing beasts. But Greg takes no notice. He only looks at the ceiling, ignoring the bursting jars and the gradually growing thrum of the villagers gathering on the street. He ignores the crackling lightning show above the city and the thunderclaps that vibrate his roof. He ignores the squeals of pigs and growing chorus of turkey vulture cries outside his balcony. He allows his mind to go slack and briefly forgets about his loneliness and the friends he cannot reach.

For just a moment an opening appears in the black cloud hanging over the city, revealing a full green moon looming large in the sky. The moon's reflection illuminates the attic in an emerald glow that tints Greg a sickly green. And Greg is elbowed from his blank numbness by one questioning, hyphenated word: "Shit-turd?"

Wally stands before Greg, swaying back and forth, chewing at his tongue and drooling a bloody froth. His eyes squint and look almost like the Xs on the faces of dead cartoon characters. Behind him, Lumpy cranks the Victor up and slaps down a new record, Son House's *Death Letter Blues*. After the jangly slide guitar kicks in, Lumpy goes slack, with his head hung low and shoulders slumped, a deflated husk of his former self. And he remains that way, waiting for the record to end so that he can throw another one on the turntable for Greg.

Greg does not acknowledge his brother standing directly in front of him. So Wally sways back and forth, awaiting an answer. But with no response forthcoming, Wally tries again, "Shit-turd?"

Both Lumpy and Eddie echo the question, "Shit-turd?" And it's like the persistent cluck, cluck, clucking of a brood of hens calling out for food.

"Shit-turd?"

"Shit-turd?"

"Shit-turd?" *Ba-kaw, ba-kaw, Bak-bak-bak-bak-bak-ba-kaw.* "Shit-turd?"

Finally, Greg snaps out of his daze and looks up to see Wally, Eddie, and Lumpy rocking back and forth in front of him and chanting their *shit-turd mantra*. He stands, head bowed, and clasps his hands as if in prayer. He rocks side to side in time with Wally, Eddie, and Lumpy. And the threesome hopefully questions Greg once more, "Shit-turd?"

Greg looks up and gives a weak reply of, "Hey, shit-turds." He goes to an ancient wooden trunk and lifts the top. In the trunk is a perfectly preserved, perfectly pressed, perfectly sized black tuxedo for Greg. And he dons the formal vest and suit jacket, wearing no shirt underneath. He puts on the matching pants and shoes so black that they swallow any light that dares to fall on them. Slicking his oily hair back, Greg picks up the beat-up top hat and sets it at an angle on his head. "Shit-turd," he says and chuckles to himself.

And the rumble from the street grows into a cacophony, with foul words sometimes distinguishing themselves and sometimes blending in with other noises to make a sound entirely worse. The din floats up to Greg on the balcony. In the dim green moonlight, Greg sees a river of humanity streaming down his street and pooling in front of his house. The people carry flashlights and torches, shovels and axe handles. They carry bricks and sticks, rocks and blocks. They carry the sick and sad baggage of the village in their hearts. In the crowd Greg sees the Courtney brothers hobbling along, still recovering from their injuries. And there's old Crooked Neck, thrusting a cane in the air toward Greg. And all the others: Danny Dolan, Robbie Beuler, Tony Grulo, Mark Masey, and scores of other black-hearted souls just like them. The whites of their eyes reflect fear and misdirected anger and madness. The stench of the mob's rot fumes off of them and wafts up to Greg, making him wrinkle his nose at the offense. He briefly removes his top hat to brush his hair from his face, and then replaces the hat to its proper resting place, tilted slightly on his head.

The piss-monkeys on the balcony hiss and spit toward the noisy crowd below. They gnash their beaks at the air and angrily flap their wings. They stretch their multiple legs to work out cramps and kinks. And when the first few try to fly, they merely jump from the balcony and slam into the ground, smashing exoskeletons asunder and splotching the yard, like tarantulas dropped from too high. Their shattered parts wriggle on the ground as if trying to piece themselves back together. Other piss-monkeys flex their wings on the balcony and look down at the mess of piss-monkey parts on the ground. And the creatures stare down and hiss. They flap their wings, learning how they feel.

On the front porch, Hopalong and Li'l Shirl stand, hand in hand and gape-jawed, watching the growing congregation form before the mansion. Watching the flaming torches as they sway back and forth with the crowd. Li'l Shirl says flatly, "It's a living thing out there, that. And a bad one, I says."

Hopalong drops both of his hands to the starter pistols slung on his hips. He straightens his hat and rubs a sleeve over the badge on his vest to ensure that it's shiny as can be. "It is alive," he agrees. "You go inside with your mama and I'll stand guard out here."

Standing on her tiptoes, and somehow managing not to break her tiny feet bones under the tremendous mass, Li'l Shirl puts her hands on Hopalong's head and pulls it toward her. She plants a sloppy kiss on his cheek and says, "I's gonna make us some vittles." She turns and walks away, her ample bulk bowing the porch boards. As the slobber dries on his cheek, Hopalong stands with a giant goofy grin on his face and hands on his starter pistols, staring out on the growing mob and trying to count the bodies (the hundreds of bodies), becoming nearly mesmerized by the flickering flames of the torches.

The crowd thickens just outside of Samsa Mansion's gates. And Li'l Shirl was right, it wasn't merely a gathering of people. Instead, the throng of humanity becomes a single living, throbbing, angry being. Its many gargoyled faces blur into one outraged expression of disgust. It undulates and exhales a foul stench. Hate flows from the beast's many mouths. Bad mojo courses through the crowd like electricity, jumping from one person to the next and robbing the townsfolk of the ability to think rationally. The mob, the singular entity, screams its cacophony and gnashes the teeth of its many mouths, and the shouts and screams and howls come together as one enormous, angry voice. People bang shovels on the ground and heave axe handles in the air, pointing them at the house as a damning indictment of not just Greg, but the entire Samsa family.

And while the house usually appears to shrug, collapsing under the weight of its decrepitude, it now straightens up and stands tall and defiant in the face of the crowd. The gutters do not sag, and the weeds in them bloom with full, brightly colored flowers. The windows do not look like dead, grey eyes, but instead sparkle and throb with a low but intense light from within the house. And for anyone looking on who is not in the grip of the mob's mania (and there are those bystanders in the shadows who watch on only out of concern or curiosity) they can see that the house itself appears to expand and contract in deep respirations. Those still on a speaking basis with sanity can see, despite what they know cannot be, that the house is a living and breathing thing that does not take kindly to the gathering before it.

As if in answer to the dark energy flowing throughout the mob, a jolt of lightning booms and strikes an electrical transformer down the street. And the transformer erupts in a spray of white, crackling flames. The power pole catches fire and cants toward the ground, only still held up by the taut, stretched power lines. Another bolt splits the thick trunk of an ancient oak and sets the majestic tree to burning. Thunderclaps shake windows and rattle walls. The swirling vortex of clouds and sulfuric black smoke descends on the village, smothering everything in maleficent black smog. And as if in response to the percussive thunder, the ground heaves and rumbles. Were the villagers to explain the shaking of the earth, they would say that the rumbles and grumbles are the result of blasting at the limestone quarry. But they would be wrong. And they do not try to understand the tremors anyway, because their group-mind is singularly focused on the Samsa household and wiping its taint from the face of their supposedly perfect little town.

Time is lost on Greg and the growing crowd in front of the mansion. But it is late. Greg knows that. When Lumpy cranks the handle on the Victor phonograph and drops the needle on Howlin' Wolf's *Moaning at Midnight*, the witching hour seems to be the most appropriate approximation of time. Even the phonograph itself is temporally challenged, though, and no matter how much Lumpy cranks the motor or fiddles with the speed regulator, the record plays slower than normal, making the song ooze out, thick, slow, and ominous, like clotting blood from a partially healed wound. From somewhere in the house, the strains of a calliope trudge along at the same creeping pace.

A man on the street begins to drag an axe handle across the wrought iron fence, making a rapid metallic *clack-clack-clack*. Another man, wearing a John Deere hat and checkered flannel shirt joins in, raking a two-by-four over the fence's pickets. From somewhere in the middle of the crowd a woman bangs a shovel on the street. The people smack their clubs and baseball bats, their pitchforks and other implements of destruction, on the ground like a manic, demented percussion section.

With a blazing torch gripped in one hand, a flabby old man points up at Greg on the balcony. A look of purest hate twists up his face as he shouts, "There he is. The murderer."

And the crowd echoes that one wavering word, "murderer."

In the middle of the street, a young man with a proper business haircut – trimmed short and parted far on the side – holds a glass soda bottle over his head. A flicker of a flame dances at the end of the fabric wick stuffed into the bottle. Cocking his hand back, the man throws the Molotov cocktail over the wrought iron fence. The bottle arcs through the air, trailing a small tail of flames behind it. When it hits the front porch the firebomb smashes and immediately explodes.

And the flames spread over the porch, stopping just short of Hopalong, who looks on, bug-eyed and panicked, out of his mind with fear. Fire licks at the porch rails. It dances across the floorboards. The oversized cowboy flails around on the porch, trying to avoid the fire but finding it in his face every which way he turns. His knees lock up and he lumbers about, stiff-legged, flapping his arms, looking as if he is waving the crowd away. And without thought of what he is doing, without concern for consequences, without any conscious decision, Hopalong leaps over the flaming porch rails and sprints away from the house, away from the heat. The light of the moon tints the man-child's face a sickly green, making him look like a mad scientist's monster. He lowers his massive shoulder and crashes through the front gate, plowing into the middle of the angry mob. Those gathered directly in front of the gate find themselves smashed beneath it as Hopalong runs straight over them and into the street. He swings his arms about wildly, knocking people in the heads and shoulders. And those around him begin to strike out at Hopalong. Because he comes from the house, he is evil to them.

From the balcony, Greg watches Hopalong go berserk on the street. He sees the villagers attacking the big, sweet, gentle man, and Greg nearly explodes from the fury that fills him. All of the feelings of anger and spite toward bullies and abusers overwhelm him. And in that moment, Greg feels the mad insanity of murderous rage. The people in the crowd are one big gathering of malevolent tormentors. Greg shouts out, "Lumpy, Eddie, to the streets. Bring Hopalong inside before they kill him."

Before Greg can say more, Lumpy abandons the phonograph and follows Eddie to the balcony. Lumpy and Eddie still wear the police caps and carry their recently acquired billy clubs. They still sport their police badges pinned to the flesh of their chests. Beside the balcony, a ladder made of two-by-fours is attached to the house. And though Greg didn't nail the ladder to the house, it doesn't surprise him that it is there any more than he was surprised to see a balcony appear out of the attic. This is what the house does. It provides in times of need. Lumpy and Eddie slide down the ladder as quickly as if they had just jumped off of the balcony and let gravity take over.

Meanwhile, Greg slaps a piss-monkey on the ass, kicking the baby from the nest. The horrid beast falls from the balcony rail, awkwardly flapping its wings in an effort to catch the air and ride it to the ground. Then, with wings outstretched and ugly head held high, the thing stops spinning and rides up on a gust of foul air. It flies. It flaps its leathery wings and flutters drunkenly like a giant confused moth, challenging the laws of aerodynamics with its seemingly unairworthy body and wings. Greg pushes more piss-monkeys from the balcony, sending them hurtling toward the earth. And some nearly manage to attain mastery of their wings, but splatter and break on the ground before they are able, while others catch blasts of wind and hover clumsily above the mob.

As a swarm of piss-monkeys flits just above the crowd, Hopalong flails and knocks attackers to the ground. And the mob encircles Hopalong, thrusting torches and pitchforks at him, fueling his panicked spasms. The big cowboy draws his starter pistols and blasts them into the air, shouting, "Fire bad! Fire bad!"

Greg shouts to Wally, "Stay here. Throw those jars into the crowd," and he points to the large stack of piss-monkey jars.

Wally slowly nods and says, "Shit-turd."

But before Wally's words have even made it out of his mouth, Greg is over the balcony rail and climbing down the side of the house. His feet hit the ground, he sprints toward the crowd. The front door flies open and a wave of raccoons and pigs bursts from the house, charging through the flames on the porch. Dogs and cats and possums and skunks round the side of the house and join in the charge. The smell of burnt hair fills the air as the animals follow Greg toward the angry mob.

A hail of rocks and bottles pelt Greg and his army as they charge the crowd. A brick strikes the top of Greg's top hat and knocks it from his head. Following that, a half-full Genesee bottle collides with Greg's forehead, the bottom of the bottle leaving a bloodied, ridged, circular pattern tattooed on his skin. The bottle bonks off of his head, unbroken, and shatters on the sidewalk at his feet. A rock hits his forehead just after the bottle, gouging out a deep gash. Greg stops running and bends down to pick up his top hat and put it back atop his head. His vision blurs and then tunnels to a pinpoint. The ground tilts and Greg braces himself against the feeling that he is going to faint. Then his body runs on autopilot, sending him hurtling into the crowd, his mind not thinking, not processing, but his legs pumping and pushing him forward. And all that he knows is rage and the color red. And then he knows not even that.

Up above, the Victor phonograph needle skips, making Howlin' Wolf stutter a pained yowl over and over and over. The calliope song echoes the skipping record, blowing the repeating yowl out of the attic and into the night. And from the balcony, Wally jaculates piss-monkey jars into the maddened mob. Jar after jar shatters on people in the angry crowd. One jar smashes over a heavyset woman's head, but does not knock her down; instead, she stands there, stunned and stupid, as a piss-monkey digs its claws into the her face and head, gashing at her eyes with its hooked beak. The woman realizes what is happening and takes off running through the crowd, beating at the monster, as the piss-monkey flaps its leathery wings and continues to tear at her.

In the center of the mob, in the middle of the street, Lumpy and Eddie join Hopalong in fending off attackers. They swing their billy clubs, cracking skulls, breaking bones. All above and around them, piss-monkeys fly in circles. One at a time the creatures drop clumsily from the air and latch onto people in the crowd. And the piss-monkeys claw out eyes and tear off ears. All the while, Wally continues to launch jars onto the crowd from above.

In the midst of it all, Greg walks through the crowd untouched, strutting as if walking atop a wave, snapping his fingers and pointing at individuals. And though Greg does not recognize all of the faces in the crowd, there are many that are familiar. Danny Dolan stomps about and screams obscenities at the house. Danny laughs when he sees Greg and runs toward the smallish boy. But before Danny reaches him, Greg snaps his fingers and points. Instantly, Danny's legs are knocked out from under him by a gang of fetal pigs. Before he can regain his feet, coons and pigs and cats and dogs (even one or two skunks) converge on Danny, biting and tearing at him, ignoring his screams for help. Others in the crowd follow Danny's lead and charge at Greg. Some are felled by piss-monkey jars from above, and others are taken down by the pigs and raccoons and nearly torn to shreds by the multiplicity of animals.

And later – days, weeks and months later – some of those who are in the crowd will tell people that as Greg walked among them, sparks and smoke flew from his fingers when he snapped and pointed. Some will say that tattoos danced on Greg's arms, hands, and neck as he moved through the crowd, even though everybody knows that is not true. Others will say that he had long black hair flowing under his top hat and a long beard, although everybody knows that was not really true either. But it was true. And it wasn't.

Black smog swirls overhead, as if the piss-monkeys stirred up a giant whirlpool in the air above the crowd. The piss-monkeys fall upon and attack the people, then take to the air again. All the while, Wally continues to throw jars from the attic. The crowd returns fire at the house with flaming Molotov cocktails. As the bottles smash against the house, the kerosene and gasoline explodes into flames that nearly cover the entire front of the mansion. Wally remains on the balcony, standing just behind the flaming handrail, and answers the attack with more piss-monkey jars. Fire blazes all around him, chaps his skin, but he does not retreat into the attic. And the flames creep toward the roof and blow out more black smoke to mix with the already smoggy air.

And still, Hopalong, Eddie, and Lumpy kick and punch out in an effort to fend off attackers. Pigs and possums and raccoons and cats help, tripping up the people and jumping on them when they go down. Greg continues to walk through the crowd, a vacant look in his eyes and sparks shooting from his fingers as he points at people. He walks right past Johnny Close, pointing at Old Crooked Neck without missing a step. And for the second time in days, Johnny Close is on the ground, flailing limbs and screaming, doing his pathetic best to fend off raccoons. But Greg doesn't stop there, he glides through the throng, pointing his fingers, throwing sparks. As he nears the melee at the center of the crowd, Greg cuts through the people like a shark through water. He stops just short of stepping into the circle with Hopalong and Eddie and Lumpy. And as the coons and pigs tear into those indicated by Greg, as skunks spray their eye-watering stench, as piss-monkeys drop from the sky and rip at peoples' faces, Greg stands nearly motionless. His face goes slack. His eyes are deep, dead, black pools, showing no emotion or thought. He sways in that one spot, looking ready to topple over. Someone knocks Greg's glasses and top hat off. His longish hair sticks to the bloody gash on his forehead.

This time Greg does not bend down for his hat. He does not think about it because the blow to his head gave him a major concussion. It makes him dizzy and disconnected from thought. And now he swoons and puts his arms out for balance, looking like a demented surfer catching a wave. Before he can steady himself, an axe handle smashes down on the back of his head. The third blow peels away the scalp with a gruesome ripping sound and drops Greg to the ground. His entire body goes limp and remains motionless.

Stanley Stevens stands over Greg's prone body, poking at him with the axe handle. A sneer turns up Stanley's lip as he looks down at his victim. He brings the axe handle above his head, readying to bring it down on the defenseless boy. But before he can, a well-aimed piss-monkey jar falls from the sky and smashes on his shoulder. The piss-monkey immediately latches on to the side of Stanley's head and tears at his face. The creature buries its curved beak into an eye socket and claims Stanley's eye as a delicious treat. Stanley breaks into a swinging, spinning, circling dance, trying to throw the piss-monkey off of him, but trips over a pig and crashes to the ground. Somewhere, someone shouting *shit-turd* over and over again vaguely registers in Stanley Stevens' head as he squirms and flails, trying to pry the piss-monkey from his face. But before he can remove the creature, a sharp talon drags across his neck, gashing the jugular vein. And with each beat of his heart, the wound spouts Stanley's blood into a growing puddle, until the fluid barely oozes from his neck, and his remaining eye closes for good.

The mob closes in on Greg's motionless body. A foot flies out from the crowd and buries itself into Greg's defenseless stomach. Then another into his groin. In response, piss-monkey jars rain down from above. Raccoons and pigs rip through the mob and encircle Greg, cats hiss and dogs snarl and snip at those not deterred by Wally's blitzkrieg. And when legs strike out to kick Greg, they pull back covered with snarling black and grey balls of fur, teeth, and claws. But the mob still presses in, kicking at Greg, poking at him with clubs and shovels and implements of destruction.

Hopalong stands in the middle of his own swarm of attackers with Eddie and Lumpy. And the tall simpleton sees another ruckus going on across the street. Something in his simple brain sounds an alarm. Something is wrong. And it has to do with Greg. Panic grips Hopalong. His head buzzes and his chest tightens with anxiety. His heart pumps so fast it feels ready to explode. Without a thought, Hopalong barrels into the crowd, bowling them over and leaving a corridor of trampled villagers in his wake. Bodies are launched into short flights as the big cowboy collides with those in his path. Those who avoid the collisions strike out at him as he passes, but the ineffectual blows register with Hopalong little more than drops of rain would. His mind is singularly focused on getting to Greg.

And when the big cowboy bursts through the opening where Greg is situated, the pigs and raccoons make way for him. The dogs and cats all pull back. Hopalong stands, wild-eyed and huffing for air, shaking violently from the adrenaline coursing through his system. He goggles the crowd with bugged-out, maniacal eyes. Unconsciously clenching his hands into enormous fists, he dares anyone to try striking out at him. And the villagers back away, just out of Hopalong's reach, not retreating, but not ready to challenge the sweaty, bloody, gigantic, quaking simpleton.

Hopalong looks down on a slight, battered body. He sees Greg in a puddle of blood, top hat on the ground beside him. Tears blur the big man's vision. As he bends down, a short, round, pug-faced woman charges, swinging a shovel back and preparing to lay the tool upside his head. And Hopalong instinctively stands up, bringing a massive fist all of the way up from the ground. When the walloping uppercut makes contact with the woman's fleshy jaw, the shovel immediately drops from her hand. And the punch follows through with such power that it lifts the heavy woman's feet off the ground. Her eyes roll back in her head as she is launched into the air. The force of the blow disconnects her from consciousness before her body can reacquaint itself with the Earth. Hopalong leaps outward, throwing haymakers at the crowd, laying those he connects with level with the ground. And when he stops, when his attack is done, piles of unconscious villagers encircle him and Greg. Raccoons and pigs stand atop Hopalong's victims, snarling at the rest of the crowd. Cats arch their backs and hiss, dogs bark and growl, all daring the villagers to try to get to Greg. But, none dare approach, even with their superior numbers and weapons.

Hopalong kneels down and looks upon Greg's battered face. He peels back the eyelids and tries to look into Greg's eyes. The asymmetrically dilated pupils stare back blankly, registering nothing, acknowledging nothing. A panic, worse than the one brought on by the fire, nearly paralyzes Hopalong. Tears gush from his eyes. His lungs pull deep breaths. Acting on pure instinct, Hopalong lifts Greg from the ground. The boy's head lolls over and Hopalong shifts him in his arms, holding Greg like a baby, supporting his head. And then he runs from the crowd, through the front yard, through the flames on the front porch, and into the burning house.

The villagers do not chase Hopalong. Instead, they converge on Eddie and Lumpy to tear them down. A plank of wood with a nail poking out of the end smacks Eddie, the nail tearing the police badge from his chest. A man in a priest's collar swings a shovel and buckles Lumpy's leg backward, making him fall to the ground. And the villagers bring down their weapons on the boy. Although seriously injured, Lumpy continues to swing out at his attackers with a billy club. He grabs the priest's leg and bites the calf, locking his jaws and refusing to let go. He does not release the leg until a baseball bat unlocks his jaws for him. And then Lumpy crumples up into a helpless ball of nothing on the street.

Eddie continues to fight, despite having his chest torn open by the nail-spiked wooden plank. As he swings at those assailing him, Eddie screams out a slurred "shit-turd." And his screams tear the lining from his throat, making him spray a mist of blood. Wally continues to throw jars from the balcony, his aim improving with every throw, hitting whatever targets he chooses. But the well-aimed jars do nothing to stop the mob. Each attacker that Wally takes out is replaced by three more equally malicious people who overwhelm Eddie and pummel him into unconsciousness.

When Eddie and Lumpy can fight no more, when their bodies refuse to move and their brains go blank from blunt force trauma, and when it appears that the spark of life has already left them, the crowd ties ropes around them and drags their battered bodies down the street behind a rusty El Camino with a seemingly out of place (but not uncommon in the village) confederate flag flying from a pole anchored in its bed.

And dragging the boys behind the El Camino gives the mob's angry group-brain an idea. An awful idea. The mob gets a wonderful, awful idea. And the old tales, whispered by children in basements and attics and hidden places, they were all true. The tale of James Lytle and how he murdered his family comes back to them. And the way that James was treated by the villagers is brought up. And it is an awful, wonderful idea. So the villagers drag Eddie's and Lumpy's unconscious bodies through the streets of Findlay. And when they arrive at the bridge over the Blanchard River, the men, women, and even children, unchain the boys from the car.

The purple-black smog swirls around the mob and clings to the bridge. A few remaining piss-monkeys drop down in a surprise attack on a sneering, mean-faced girl. The men around her beat the creatures until they fall from the girl's head. And when the piss-monkeys drop to the ground, injured, the men stomp them into puddles of strangely steaming jelly.

With the remaining piss-monkeys eliminated, the crowd turns back to Eddie and Lumpy. They tie ropes around their necks. First they throw Eddie over the side of the bridge, and his body jerks and dances at the end of the rope until the dance slows to a stop and the spark of life is finally gone. Then they throw Lumpy from the bridge. His body is heavy, the drop is far, and the rope used on him is inelastic. So when he hits the end of his rope, his head pops off like a champagne cork. First the body splashes down in the river, followed by the head seconds later. And the head sinks to the muddy riverbed, with eyes wide open but not seeing the massive, pale catfish that converge and peck on its rotten flesh. Meanwhile, the body washes along with the current, not to be seen again for weeks when the bloated, headless corpse is discovered by a very surprised gang of boys fishing along the banks of the river, just outside of Ottawa.

And then the people of the city hoist Eddie's limp body back onto the bridge and gather around in a circle, looking down on their work. Still their group-rage boils. They drag Eddie through the streets once again and stop in the police station parking lot. There they find a perfect telephone pole from which to hang him again. A short, rotund policeman exits the station and walks toward the crowd. And the villagers turn toward the officer and move in his direction. The policeman quickly turns heel and runs back into the station, locking the front doors behind him. With impunity, the crowd strings the rope on the telephone pole and hoists up what remains of Eddie to let him dangle ten feet above the ground by his neck. But even this is not enough for the mob. Several older men retrieve rifles from their cars and trucks and commence target practice on Eddie, punching holes in his corpse to show that they really mean business.

When the crowd decides it is done, pitchforks and shovels and axes drop to the ground. People in the mob turn away from Eddie's body and the crowd disperses. Nobody says a word. They all shuffle off in different directions and disappear into the night.

Back at Samsa Mansion, flames lick at the outside of the house and light up the street. Despite the massive blaze, no fire trucks come to put out the fire. No police come to help the people inside. No neighbors turn hoses on the house. All of the villagers are gone from the area, thoughts of Greg and the Samsa Mansion completely vanished from their minds.

Inside the mansion, the residents do not choke on the smoke of a house fire. They do not flee into the night in fear for their lives. The inferno outside does not enter the house. Smoke does not fill the rooms. It does not affect anything besides perhaps raising the inside temperature a degree or two. The Samsas carry on in the face of adversity as they always have. Big Shirl lies on her oversized bed, cradling Greg's battered body on her ample lap, just as she did when he was a baby. She holds her boy's head in the warm, fleshy crook of one arm and smoothes his hair back as she stares at her muted television.

On the TV, Morton Downey Jr. stamps about on the stage, wearing camouflage, chain smoking and breathing smoke out past snarling, enormous, white dentures, like an angry wrinkled dragon with a bad dental plan. Members of his audience line up, frothing at the mouths, ready to lay into the show's guest.

Shirl does not take her eyes from the TV. But she does hug and caress her boy. She rubs at his face and whispers and coos to him, telling Greg he is going to be okay.

Greg coughs a cruffulous cough that rattles around in his chest and gurgles in his throat. He stirs in Big Shirl's arms. And then his eyes open to see his mom smiling warmly down at him, her eyes moist with tears. She plants a kiss on his forehead and smoothes his hair back.

Big Shirl whispers, "Thank goodness, you're awake now."

Hopalong and Li'l Shirl stand at the edge of the bed, holding hands and looking down at Greg. Li'l Shirl's eyes are vacant as ever, but Hopalong's gush tears of concern. The big cowboy's lip quivers and a sad smile barely reveals itself.

"I'm okay," says Greg, as he tries to sit up. A sharp pain stabs at his side, alerting him to broken ribs or perhaps a collapsed lung. He gasps and sits up a little more. Mustering all of his strength, Greg pushes away from Big Shirl and throws his legs over the side of the bed. Aches and pains ring in from all over his body as he tries to stand. The room tilts as Greg's vision begins to fade.

"Or maybe I'm not okay," says Greg as he collapses back on the bed, lying as still as possible, trying to calm the aching throb that punishes his entire body. "But I've got to get to the attic." And then the pain is too much. His head thubs rhythmically, feeling as if the top is going to blow right off and spew blood and brains on the ceiling.

"Take him," says Big Shirl to Hopalong. "Take him to the attic."

Taking Greg into his arms once again, Hopalong lifts the boy and cradles him like a baby. He walks gently, making not a sound and barely jostling Greg. Li'l Shirl follows as Hopalong steps out of the room and makes his way up the front stairway. And they disappear into the labyrinth of halls. It doesn't matter that the corridors have shifted. It doesn't matter that Hopalong does not know the way to the attic anymore. He follows his instincts, that little tickle at the base of his brain, taking the hallways and stairways that his intuition tells him are correct.

Greg's breathing grows shallow, his eyes close. Panic floods Hopalong's thick head as he realizes that things are not right with the boy. And he sprints down the hallways and around corners, up stairways, until he finally reaches the top of the house.

Like heavy, creeping smoke, mournful calliope music cascades down the stairs from the attic and washes over Hopalong,

Greg, and Li'l Shirl as they ascend the steps. Wally awaits Greg and takes his brother into his arms when Hopalong bursts into the attic.

"Shit-turd?" says Wally, confused. His blank eyes betray no feelings as he looks on his brother, but something in his words rings of emotion still buried somewhere deep within his apparently still-human heart. "Shit-turd?"

Greg half-opens his eyes. His dilated pupils (one so big that it makes his entire eye look black) strain to focus on Wally's face. And though his lips move, no sound comes out. Finally, with all of his remaining energy, Greg manages to grunt one word: "Coffin."

Without losing a beat, Hopalong lifts the coffin lid, and Wally is there beside him, gently laying Greg's body atop the dirt. Li'l Shirl stands at the coffin, too, looking down on her little brother. She stares with dull, bovine curiosity, and a trickle of drool dribbling from the side of her mouth. Beside Li'l Shirl, Wally looks down at Greg with a nearly identical, dimwitted stare.

Looking first at Wally, then Li'l Shirl, and working things over in his head, Hopalong realizes an uncommon occurrence: he is currently the smartest person in the room. And that prods the big cowboy into action. He crosses Greg's arms over his chest and tries to arrange him in a comfortable position. Next Hopalong snatches the Lobster Boy sideshow banner from the wall and uses it as a shroud to wrap Greg.

The rasping sound of Greg's labored breaths ramps down to a soft, occasional snuffle. His chest barely moves with his respirations.

"I thinks he's dyin'," says Li'l Shirl, without any hint that she grasps the gravity of her statement.

"Shit-turd?" says Wally, looking down on his little brother.

Putting his hand on Greg's chest, Hopalong is thrown into despair. He feels no heartbeat. He is not the brightest bulb, but he knows that no heartbeat means death. A gasp of a cry escapes the big cowboy's mouth. But Hopalong keeps his hand on Greg's chest, and then he does feel one weak beat of the heart. He keeps his hand there for what feels like minutes. And just when Hopalong is ready to once again conclude that Greg has given up the ghost, the boy's heart thumps again.

And all through the night, Hopalong, Wally, and Li'l Shirl stand beside the coffin, looking down on the pale, waxy, dead-looking boy. Hopalong keeps one hand on Greg's chest, waiting in absolute misery in between the infrequent respirations and heartbeats. And each stretch between perceptible vital signs is a personal hell for Hopalong, because each time he has to wait, he is sure that Greg has passed on. And each infrequent heartbeat brings back hope. And so it goes throughout the night. As the hours pass, raccoons and pigs and piss-monkeys gather and encircle the coffin, until there is an enormous vigil of vermin and swine and halfwits in the attic, watching Greg lay motionless.

The dreams come to Greg in the coffin while the flames outside cover the house and fill the attic with wispy, crispy, dry heat. And it is as if Greg has gone into hibernation, closing himself off from the external stimuli, slowing his vital functions, keeping an ember burning deep in his core. He turns his eyes inward and at first sees himself as a moist, meaty, wriggling, blind thing.

As he squirms about in the blackness, an exoskeleton forms

over his entire body. He senses the rigid casing that holds him and restricts his movement. He wriggles and fights against his enclosure. And the light bursts in his eyes as he molts the old shell and begins once again to form larger, stronger armor.

And as if watching on from above, Greg sees that his body is metamorphosizing from human to cockroach. Extra legs form on his sides and antennae sprout from his forehead. Then Greg is back in his body. He looks through the thousands of lenses of his new eyes and perceives colors he never knew existed. The new swirls of color shoot through his eyes and scorch his insides, making everything within him squirm in pain. Then he is molting again, shedding the old shell and feeling new chitinous armor forming and constricting him.

The colors, the new, wonderful, painful hues, burst before Greg with increasing intensity. Faintly, a calliope sings a slow and mournful dirge that intermeshes with the squishing sound that Greg's new body makes as it molts and reforms. And he smells the colors with his mouth and chews them into a mash that burns his throat and numbs him throughout. In his dream he crawls between thin cracks and through tight, dank tunnels, emitting a chemical trail of shimmering colors and scents as he wriggles along on his many new legs. His sensitive antennae grope about, touching lightly on the path before him, making up for the confusing input from his multifaceted eyes, feeling the way to go. As the tunnels grow smaller and the cracks become tighter, the exoskeleton is again painfully shucked from Greg, and with the restriction temporarily gone, his body expands and once again covers itself with a slime that hardens into new and stronger armor.

And then Greg knows he has completed his transformation. He no longer looks on at himself from above. He knows that he has become a cockroach. It is not horror that fills him at the thought. Instead, he feels invincible. With newfound vigor, he pulls himself through the last and smallest opening, dragging himself onto the ground and into daylight. And the morning sun blasts him with a prismatic rainbow assault. The glare overloads Greg's compound eyes and sends a cold jolt of pain straight to his brain. The cockroach-boy shades his eyes and looks downward.

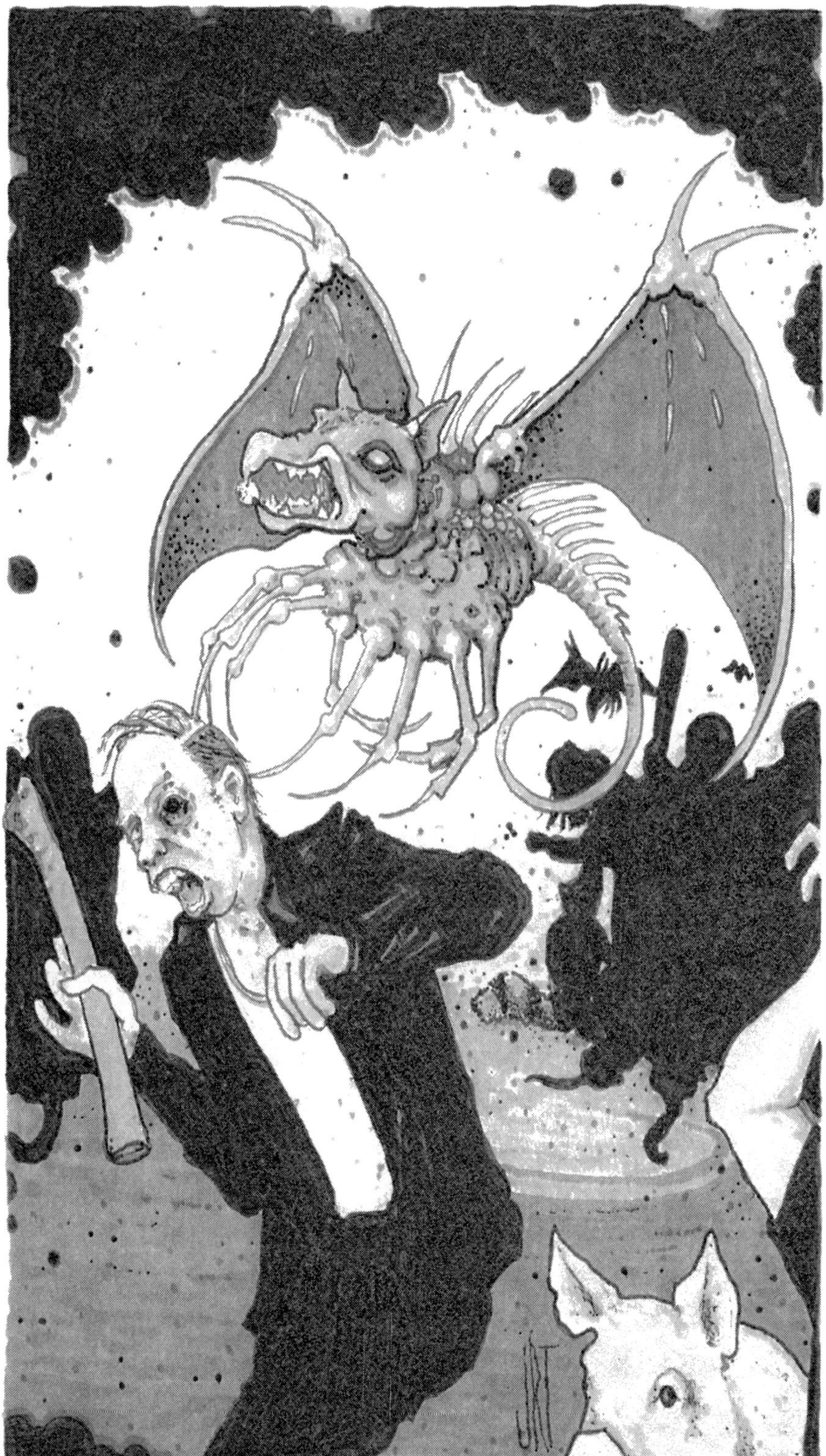

7

The fat and fiery center of the solar system peaks over the horizon and throws orange radiance at Evergreen Terrace, casting brilliant lemony beams of light on Samsa Mansion. The Big Bopper struts barefoot down the street, stepping over broken glass, over pick axes and shovels, over dead raccoons and smashed pigs. He stares straight into the sun because he can. It ain't nothing but scorched retinas. And he don't see things the way everyone else does, anyway. His eyes still see the auras, the streaks that dissipate like warm breaths on a cold morning, the iridescent shimmers, and the outlines of forms. He still sees the colors. And that's all that matters to him.

The Bopper stops and looks up at Samsa Mansion with his damaged eyes. And he feels the shape and shadows and shimmers of the house. It radiates healthy pinks and greens and golds like oil in a rain puddle, its emanations surging off of the house in wild looping streamers that break free and float up to opaline clouds. Were his eyes not temporarily damaged, he would see that the mansion looks as good as it ever did. He would see that the house took on the fire, withstood the flames, and came through looking cleansed and renewed, like a phoenix emerging from the ashes. Weeds grow in the gutters no more. Siding falls from the walls no more. The porch is on the point of collapse no more.

Also, were the Big Bopper able to see clearly, he would notice an enormous cowboy standing on the front porch, a broomstick hobbyhorse held between his legs, shyly tipping his cowboy hat in a warm *howdy-do* of a greeting. And he would see Greg standing naked on his balcony with the sun's rays reflecting off of the house and encircling him in a golden halo. The Bopper does not see Hopalong or Greg, but he senses them. And he stops his bopping just in front of the broken front gates, bobs his head to his own beat, and snaps his fingers in time. Hopalong smiles awkwardly and gives a tentative wave.

The Big Bopper don't wave back. He don't see Hopalong. Instead he stares toward the attic, past the turkey buzzards flanking the open balcony doors. He looks to the spectral trails wafting off of Greg, and the trails break up into multi-colored glitter as they float down to the lawn on a gentle draft.

8

Then Greg is awake, standing naked and shivering on his balcony. He feels good, not as if he were on the brink of death just hours before. He feels healthy and strong. And he remembers his dream. He runs his hands over his forehead and finds it to be smooth. No antennae jut out, but there is a warm tingle where they would be. No extra legs protrude from his sides, but yet again, the warm tingle. No stiff exoskeleton encases him, but he does feel harder, bigger, stronger. He is not a cockroach, but just a teenage boy.

And the morning sun is bright and warm on Greg's skin. It casts gleaming rays at him and throws his shadow on the floor behind him. Greg stretches and his shadow does the same. He rubs at his face, wiping away the crusted eye cheese, realizing that he is not wearing his glasses. But his vision is clear. He doesn't need the spectacles anymore. Greg looks out from the balcony and sees that the sky is a beautiful cerulean blue. The noxious black smoke no longer billows over the city from the south.

Buzzards rest on the balcony rail, staring out at nothing with uninterested, unfocused gazes. Down on the ground, more turkey vultures land and tear strings of meat from the remains of dead raccoons and piglets and some large, unidentifiable form. And the Big Bopper bops down the street, stepping around the buzzards' carrion feast, over broken bottles and rakes and abandoned implements of destruction, surveying the scene and bopping on by.

Greg returns to the attic and plops a Little Walter record down on the turntable. He cranks the phonograph and the scratchy recorded sounds of a lively harmonica fill the attic. The phantom strains of the calliope join in with Little Walter as he starts to sing, "My babe, she don't stand no cheating, my babe...." Greg actually smiles and bops his head to the beat as he puts on his Atari shirt and a clean pair of bootcut jeans. He brushes dirt and gravel from his battered top hat and sets it on his head, giving it a slight tilt.

A scratching, clamorous sound comes to Greg from the balcony. The turkey vulture-sentries spit and hiss and screech as Captain Jack and Fats Flannigan scramble over the handrail. And the buzzards take to the air and circle Samsa Mansion in their awkward, drunken flight, still making a racket about the raccoons' intrusion. The look on Captain Jack's face almost seems to say to the buzzards, *hey, don't get all offended, all animals are equal, some are just more equal than others.* The coons pay no attention to the turkey vultures' grievances. Fats Flannigan waddles into the attic on his hind legs with an entitled, smug look on his face.

Wally appears behind Greg and says, "Shit-turds," toward the raccoons.

"Yeah," says Greg, "they're shit-turds. But they're our shit-turds." He smiles as the coons stare up at him and rub their front paws together as if washing them. Greg sets a half-eaten box of Chicken-n-Biscuit crackers on the floor for the animals.

And, once again, Greg is surprised by how good he feels. Energy buzzes through his body. Warmth enfolds him. He feels a sense of well-being. It doesn't bother him that he and his family and house were attacked. It doesn't bother him that he was knocked unconscious and badly injured. He knows that nobody he loves was hurt. He doesn't worry that townspeople were hurt. That wasn't his fault – they started it. He just doesn't worry about it. And he wonders how anybody could worry about anything when Little Walter is honking on his harmonica like that.

It is a school day, so there's no reason Greg shouldn't go to school. He has a hunch that the business with the police is over. He has a hunch that business with the villagers is over. The thick smog over the city has blown away to the four corners of Hancock County. For whatever reason, Greg knows things are okay.

Before leaving for school, though, Greg sits in the TV room with his entire family and eats breakfast. The Shirls ladle breakfast into their mouths from large salad bowls filled with entire boxes of their favorite cereals – Quisp for Big Shirl and King Vitamin for Li'l Shirl. Wally grunts and gnaws the meat off of a hambone that Hopalong gave him. Hopalong thrusts his giant hand into a box of Mr. T cereal and scoops it up to his mouth, burying his face into his palm and munching at it like a horse with a feedbag. And Greg sits beside Big Shirl's bed with a bowl of Booberry.

They all stare at the television as the tubby, toupee-topped morning show weatherman flashes a gap toothed smile and sends out birthday wishes to centenarians who are "one hundred years young." It's as if the chaos of the day and night before never occurred. A picture of a wrinkled, dusty-looking old woman flashes on TV and Wally says, "Shit-turd."

Giving Big Shirl a kiss on the cheek, Greg says, "Love you, Ma." She grabs his arm and pulls him onto the bed, smothering him with a warm, sweaty hug, and spilling cereal all over her comforter. Greg struggles against his mother's embrace, laughing and trying to pry Big Shirl's arms from him. But Big Shirl's embrace is too tight, there is no escaping.

Big Shirl laughs, too, and tells Greg she never wants to let him go. When she does release her grip on the boy, tears moisten her eyes. "You be careful," she says, and plants a sloppy kiss on his cheek.

"Ugh," says Greg, wiping the kiss away. "Mom, please. I'll be okay. And here's something you can keep by you when I'm not around, so you don't miss me too much. He kind of looks like me."

Greg hands Big Shirl the pikkled punk that looks like a mini-Greg. His mother takes the jar and swirls it. The fetus spins in the water and ends up with its face against the glass, fluid still gently swirling around it. And the fetus looks as if it winks at Big

Shirl, but it is probably just the pikkled punk's head settling against the glass.

Greg smiles and says, "And if you feel like slopping your kisses all over me, you can just do it to him instead. He won't mind."

"I'll kiss you if I want to, you little turd," says Big Shirl, laughing once again. But then she kisses the jar and hugs it tightly to her bosom.

"Shit-turd," says Wally.

Li'l Shirl gobbles her cereal and stares blankly at the TV. Hopalong sits beside her, grinning and looking smitten. The big cowboy tells Greg, "Once again we can expect unseasonably warm weather, with clear skies and sunshine all day. Highs will be in the low seventies, with the temperature dropping down to sixty tonight. So ditch your snow boots and winter jackets and swap them out for shorts and flip-flops. And remember to check us for traffic and weather at the start of each hour."

Greg looks at his family and laughs at their absurdity. He laughs in wonder and he laughs out of love. Fat ladies fit for the circus. A brain-dead brother who barely manages to spit out his one hyphenated shit-turd of a word. And despite all of Wally's prior misdeeds and meanness, Greg now feels love for his brother. With his brain now dead and dumb, Wally is a better brother than he ever was before. And, Hopalong, now family just as much as the others, sits stupidly dressed up like a cheesy movie sheriff, spouting off a weather forecast while flashing an idiot grin and fitting in perfectly with the rest of the mansion's misfits.

Greg feels loved. He feels right. As he walks out the front door, Captain Jack and Fats Flannigan fall in behind and trail him down the street. Calliope music pumps from the attic balcony, blasting the neighborhood with the sounds of Samsa Mansion, daring the neighbors to call the police about the racket.

Greg's shadow stretches out, tall and confident. He looks down and notices the long, dark silhouette on the ground mimicking his movements. He beams a calm, satisfied smile. He smiles because things are okay.

When Greg arrives at school, Captain Jack and Fats Flannigan stop on the sidewalk across the street and chitter excitedly as he leaves them behind. Tears form in his eyes as he turns to look at the coons. And the coons' eyes, although glazed and beady, appear to mist up, too.

Greg is momentarily touched. Then he shakes it off, and without looking back, says, "It's fine, you guys. Everything's fine."

He climbs the steps up to the school and enters the front doors. And when he steps into the hallway, the laughter and the general bustle of kids and teachers goes silent. A path the length of the hallway clears in the crowd as Greg makes his way to his locker. He casts a long, top hat-capped shadow as he passes his schoolmates.

Mr. Corbin pushes a dust mop along the floor at the end of the hall. As Greg approaches, the elderly janitor raises his head and grunts an inarticulate greeting. The old man says nothing more, because his grunt says it all. It says, *good to see you back.*

"Hey, Mr. Corbin," says Greg, happy to see him, but knowing that nothing more needs to be said for now.

And then Greg turns and bounds up the steps two at a time. He doesn't worry about getting tripped or punches flying at him from out of nowhere. The kids shrink back toward the walls, crushing those behind them, in order to give Greg sufficient space to make it through.

When he finally arrives at his locker, there she is. Kelsey waits for him, dressed in an orange jumpsuit and combat boots. Her hair is pulled back through her Cleveland Browns baseball cap. She wears tube socks with holes cut out for her fingers over her hands. The fresh purple bruising from her father's fist the night before darkens her swollen left eye. She is bizarre. And to Greg she is the prettiest girl in the school.

Kelsey throws her arms around Greg and squeezes him. She says, "I was worried about you. I tried to get over to see you last night but my dad locked me in my room. I couldn't get out until this morning when my mom got home from her shift at the factory." She wrinkles up her nose and smiles a silly, strange smile. "My dad hasn't come back yet. I don't know where he is. But I hope he never comes back. There's something wrong with him." She wrinkles up her face again and shrugs her shoulders. "People are talking about last night. Saying all kinds of crazy things. Is any of it true?"

Greg hugs Kelsey again, relishing the feel of her thin body against his, inhaling her scent. He nuzzles her neck and his top hat falls off. "I don't really want to talk about that," he says. "At least not right now."

Kelsey picks up the top hat and swaps it out with her cap. To Greg she looks even better. She slaps the Cleveland Browns cap on Greg's head, and it sits there askew, making him look just a little bit goofy. But he doesn't mind. Nobody is going to make fun of him. And they don't need to talk. They just walk down the hall together, hand in hand, their shadows stretching out behind them. The other kids clear out of the way, letting the couple pass unmolested. And as Greg drops Kelsey off at her homeroom, their shadows kiss in a prohibited display of public affection.

And nobody dares say anything to Greg at school. The rumors of the night before buzz in the mouths of the students. They talk in hushed tones about bodies being hung and shot and thrown from bridges. About strange creatures attacking people from above. About Greg's house being set to flames. They speak of pigs and raccoons and a melee in the streets. But nobody is really sure who had supposedly been killed or what actually happened to them. And the rumors grow to be more incredible than the very strange reality. Even the teachers keep their distance and only look quickly at Greg with sideways glances. Greg hears all of the scandalous whispers but acknowledges nothing. Nobody says a word about it to him, though. Nobody says a word about anything to him. And he likes it that way, because nobody is being cruel.

As Greg and Kelsey walk out of the school, hand in hand, they need not scamper through the alleys and cower for fear of being attacked by cruel teens. They walk leisurely down the middle of the street, heads held high, shadows stretching out behind them, trailed by Fats Flannigan, Captain Jack, and a parade of coons and cats and dogs. Greg looks at Kelsey and thinks she looks prettier than ever. He smiles and she smiles back. He takes in a deep breath through his nose, smelling the outdoors, smelling Kelsey's clean aroma, and he momentarily goes lightheaded with joy. Tripping over his own feet, Greg stumbles and his top hat pops up from his head, then lands there again, slightly askew.

Kelsey snorts out a laugh and punches Greg in the arm. She says, "Watch where you're going, Goofus," and snorts again.

Greg smiles at Kelsey. And the strains of a calliope blow along on the wind and escort them and their animal entourage to Blanchard Valley Hospital. Greg has a feeling that Jim Halloway is much improved. He has a feeling that things are going to be okay.

Mrs. Halloway has hooked up an Atari system to the hospital room TV. And Jim Halloway is awake, alert, and furiously cranking on the joystick to move his Pac-Man around the maze and gobble up as many dots as possible. But the ghosts on the screen converge and pin him in a corner before destroying him. Jim beams a broken smile at his friends and hands the joystick over to Greg. Jim heard about the night before. The hospital buzzed with tales of what happened to the unusually high number of emergency room patients. Jim knows what is true and what is not. And what is true is his friendship with Greg and Kelsey.

Mrs. Halloway opens the curtains and golden sunshine lights up the room. Greg and Kelsey sit at Jim's bedside. They all know that Jim's recovery has a long way to go. They know that they are the outcasts in town. They know that they have each other. And for now, it's nice to sit and play Atari. Greg's Pac-Man gobbles up a power pellet and turns on the ghosts, catching and consuming them as they flee in terror. Outside, on the windowsill, Captain Jack and Fats Flannigan scratch at the glass, begging entry into the room. Kelsey snort-laughs at the ridiculous coons and punches Greg on the shoulder. And the sound effects of the video game ring out strangely like a calliope.

9

The sun tints the town's air with a clear golden cast. The murky smog blanket has lifted from the city. The only smoke in the air comes from a Marlboro Red clamped in the Big Bopper's grinning teeth as he bops through town, billowing puffs like a funky locomotive balling that jack. It's a wild, weird 23 skidoo out of town.

The unplugged headphones pick up on a funky bass line intertwined with warbling calliope music. And it all sounds good to the Bopper. It makes him move and groove and pump his skinny legs.

The basset hound and his three-legged friend peek their heads around the side of a particularly tasty, tipped-over garbage can, slop glopping from their floppy dog lips. And the dogs howl and fall in behind the Bopper as he struts past Blanchard Valley Hospital. He bops past the old, three-story houses on Main Street, past the First Presbyterian Church, past Great Scot's supermarket, and takes a left on Olive Street. And when the railroad tracks intersect his course, the Bopper turns south and bops out of town. He bounces over the railroad bridge, his head bobbin' the whole time and his eyes straight ahead, as if focused on something that only he can see.

The Bopper don't even look to his side to check on the open gash in the ground. He don't notice that the hole that loosed the cloud of madness over the city has calmed and barely fumes now. He don't care, because he knows it ain't nothing to him. His work is done here. Ain't nothing for him to do but what he does. So he bops on out of town, digging' on the funky groove in his headphones. The basset and the three-legged dog stop briefly to bay at the barely-fuming hole in the ground, and then turn to run after the Bopper.

ALL APOLOGIES

The Unmentionables is a story based in my hometown. It is inspired in large part by people I knew and grew up with in Findlay. A lot of the characters in my book are assholes. That's because I knew a lot of assholes in my town. But that doesn't mean that the city is composed entirely of mean and hateful people. In fact, I still have friends and family living in Findlay. The fact that I set my story in my hometown is largely just a function of *write what you know*. I know Findlay. I grew up there. I knew the characters in my book in one way or another. So it was fun to set the story in a place where I was familiar with all of the settings. If anybody from Findlay reads this and sees themselves in any of the characters, disregard yours suspicions, the assholes were not based upon you but rather those other guys, you know, those assholes. So if I have offended anybody by making fun of your city, I'm sorry. It's my city, too. I love Findlay and still return for visits occasionally.

Another apology is in order. Once again, the mean kids in the story were loosely based upon people I knew. I knew bullies. Sometimes I was bullied. Sometimes I bullied. Sometimes both occurred within the same day. It's a shitty thing that kids seem to like to do to each other, and I cannot claim to have been a perfect angel. To anybody who I was a dick to, I'm sorry. I've grown up and done my best to become a better person. I encourage my kids to be nicer to others than I was. In a funny kind of way I guess that this book is sort of my apology for a part of my teen years.

ACKNOWLEDGEMENTS, AND GRATITUDE

Firstly, I want to thank my kids for being the inspiration for this story. You all are incredible. I am a better person because of you. And I hope that you are better people because of me. I can't be there to fight all of your battles for you. So, the best advice I can give you is when life gets tough, build a raccoon army and fight back.

Also, thanks are due to several people who have helped this book to develop. Firstly, a huge thank you is due to Joe Tomlinson for the incredible cover art and illustrations. I sought you out and you exceeded my hopes. I totally dig your work and am honored to be able to include it in my book.

Thank you to Lori Hettler for helping to edit *The Unmentionables*. In addition to helping promote my work in the past through The Next Best Book Club, you did a full-on editing job on *The Unmentionables*. You did more than I asked for and I really appreciate it. In return, I have named one of the popular cheerleaders in my book after you.

Thank you to Garrett Cook for helping to edit my story. I appreciate your advice, some of which I took, much of which I didn't because I'm stubborn. Your input helped to shape the story. Thanks.

Thanks to my high school English teacher, Todd Gratz, wherever you are. You made me realize that I could write. You encouraged creative writing. You taught me how to write clearly and persuasively. I wrote my first short story as an assignment in your class. In a large way you are to blame for my books. Thanks for setting me on the right course.

Finally, thank you to my readers. I try to write books that I would want to read. It seems that I have found enough people who also appreciate my stories. Hearing from readers who have enjoyed my books is a huge part of what makes all of the effort worth it. If you keep reading them, I'll keep writing.

ABOUT THE AUTHOR

The Dr. Reverend Lance Carbuncle was born sometime during the last millennium and he's been getting bigger, older and uglier ever since. Carbuncle is an ordained minister with the Church of Spiritual Humanism. Carbuncle doesn't eat deviled eggs, and he doesn't drink cheap beer. Carbuncle doesn't wear sock garters. Carbuncle does tell stories. His stories are channeled through a pathetic little man who has to work a respectable job during the days in order to feed the infestation of children in his house. Carbuncle is the author of: *Smashed, Squashed, Splattered, Chewed, Chunked and Spewed*; *Grundish and Askew*; *Sloughing Off the Rot*; and *The Unmentionables*. Carbuncle likes to hear what his readers think. You can let him know how you feel about his books, or just send him strange questions and/or pictures, at bonesbarbuncle@lancecarbuncle.com.

ABOUT THE
COVER ARTIST/ILLUSTRATOR

Joseph Tomlinson is a partially self-trained artist who resides in the Pacific Northwest. His work is normally a bit too dark for his wife, Suk, to understand or appreciate. Working with pens and different pigments are his weapons of choice, but there are times when he makes ceramic sculptures that Suk refers to as monsters. His work can be found online at Instagram under the name of jorotom.

ALSO BY LANCE CARBUNCLE

GRUNDISH AND ASKEW – Strap on your athletic cup and grab a barf bag. The Dr. Reverend Lance Carbuncle is going to kick you square in the balls and send you on a wild ride that may or may not answer the following questions: what happens when two white trash, trailer park-dwelling, platonic life partners go on a moronic and misdirected crime spree?; can their manly love for each other endure when one of them suffers a psychological bitch-slap that renders him a homicidal maniac?; will a snaggletoothed teenage prostitute tear them apart?; what is the best way to use a dead illegal alien to your advantage in a hostage situation?; what's that smell?; and, what the hell is Alf the Sacred Burro coughing up? *Grundish and Askew* ponders these troubling questions and more. So sit down, put on some protective goggles, and get ready for Carbuncle to blast you in the face with a warm load of fictitious sickness.

SMASHED, SQUASHED, SPLATTERED, CHEWED, CHUNKED, AND SPEWED – Idjit Galoot has a problem. He escaped from his master's house for a brief romp around town, seeking out easy targets such as bitches in heat, fresh roadkill and unguarded garbage cans. When he returns to his house, the aged basset hound discovers that his master has packed up their belongings and moved to Florida without him. *Smashed, Squashed, Splattered, Chewed, Chunked and Spewed* is the story of Idjit Galoot's ne'er do well owner and his efforts to work his way back to the dog that he loves. Along the way, Idjit's owner encounters Christian terrorists, swamp-dwelling taxidermists, carnies, a b-list poopie-groupie, bluesmen on the run from a trickster deity, and the Florida Skunk Ape.

SLOUGHING OFF THE ROT – John the Revelator awakens in a cave with no memory of his prior life. Guided along El Camino de la Muerte by a demented madman and a philosophical giant, John sets out on a quest to fill in his blank slate and slough off the rot of his soul. Part dark comedy road trip, part spiritual quest, and part horror story, *Sloughing Off the Rot* is literary alchemy about John's transformation from repugnant wretch to reluctant hero.

CPSIA information can be obtained
at www.ICGtesting.com
Printed in the USA
LVOW10s0415270417
532376LV00006B/62/P